SABOTAGE

SABOTAGE

MATT COOK

A TOM DOHERTY ASSOCIATES BOOK · NEW YORK

SABOTAGE

Copyright © 2009, 2014 by Matt Cook

A Forge Book
Published by Tom Doherty Associates, LLC
175 Fifth Avenue
New York, NY 10010

www.tor-forge.com

Forge® is a registered trademark of Tom Doherty Associates, LLC.

The Library of Congress Cataloging-in-Publication Data is available upon request.

ISBN 978-0-7653-3811-2 (hardcover)
ISBN 978-1-4668-3787-4 (e-book)

Forge books may be purchased for educational, business, or promotional use. For information on bulk purchases, please contact Macmillan Corporate and Premium Sales Department at 1-800-221-7945, extension 5442, or write specialmarkets@macmillan.com.

First Edition: September 2014

Printed in the United States of America

0 9 8 7 6 5 4 3 2

To my mother and father

ACKNOWLEDGMENTS

Patient souls accompanied me on this writing adventure. I am grateful to all of you for enriching my life.

Victoria Skurnick, my trusted agent, you blend intuition and creative vision with abundant wisdom. I am a better writer for your guidance. Our collaboration has been a joy.

Tim Wojcik, Beth Fisher, and Lindsay Edgecomb, you are the A-Team at Levine Greenberg. Your support along the way has lifted my spirits.

A writer could not hope to work with a more passionate editor and risk-taker than Bob Gleason of Tor/Forge. Thank you, Bob, for betting on *Sabotage*.

Nature's most skilled aerial acrobat is a hummingbird. The publishing world knows her as Kelly Quinn. Thank you, Kelly, for your superb piloting, speed, and agility.

I owe a special debt of gratitude to retired U.S. Navy Chief Petty Officer and novelist Jeff Edwards, whose expert counsel in technical matters enhanced the story's plausibility. Jeff, you have a gift for fielding questions through the lens of a storyteller.

Howard Wolf, you believed in *Sabotage* after a short ride home from the airport. Stanford loyalty lives large. When it comes to the Tree, you are not afraid to go out on a limb. Thank you for your introduction to Scott, an early advocate, now my attorney and friend.

The stars were aligned when Dirk Cussler and Jack du Brul graciously took the time to critique my manuscript. Many thanks to both of you for sharing your valuable insights and feedback. I am also grateful to you, Karl Monger and Evan Storms, for your help in polishing an early draft.

Much credit goes to Frank (Tha-An) Lin for his inventive puzzle in the Stanford "Game," the principle of which now underlies the secret radio transmission in this book. I loved your challenges, Frank—especially that one. Great fun. Big thanks.

My early writing exercises yielded articles concerning the military as well as a motivational book for youth. Maria Edwards offered to champion those works. Your respect, referrals, and support validated my efforts, Maria. Thank you. I admire your generous spirit.

Victoria Normington, Terry Andrews, George Ramos, and Cotter Donnell, you showed me how language is as much a medium for inventing art as it is a means of transferring thought. I am grateful to you for making English one of my favorite classes.

Travis Cohoon, Fidel Hernandez, Erica Morgan, Nick Niemann, and Jon Zhang, we go back a long way, dear friends. I continue to learn by your example. It is your character, integrity, and appetite for challenge that inspired my good guys.

Some imagine adventure. Others create it. Few live it. Thank you, Louise, for sharing the journey. Your laughter is the best antidote for writer's block. Our story grows richer as time goes by.

Mom and Dad, I forgive you for sometimes shading the truth. In fact, your assurances that *Tovar's Enchantment* was a masterpiece in the making convinced an eight-year-old boy that a published novel was within his reach. I hope you are proud of what you accomplished.

Finally, I am grateful to the critic who first spotted promise in this project, and who has helped me navigate the publishing industry with unwavering support. Thank you, Scott Schwimer, for your guidance as my entertainment attorney. I treasure your friendship. You truly can leap tall buildings.

SABOTAGE

Arctic winds drove needles of ice into the trespasser's skin. As the prickling sensation faded to numbness, he pulled a black ski mask over his head and fought to bring his pulse below a hundred beats.

He crouched low, donning a pair of leather gloves. Warm fingers meant nimble fingers. Tonight he needed both.

The runway followed a paved line to a small network of taxiways. He spotted hangars at the far end of the tarmac. Zeroing in on one of the buildings, he sprinted toward the compound.

A chain-link fence blocked access. Finding easy footholds, he scaled the barrier and snipped off a section of barbed wire before pocketing his pliers and climbing over the edge.

Losing his grip, he landed with a loud thud—too loud, as he could hear his fall over the rhythmic drumming in his ears. Sweat plastered his hair to his scalp. He scanned the area for signs of danger and took several moments to recover.

The compound appeared empty. After five minutes of absolute stillness, he began to crawl, adhering to the shadowy perimeter and following the fence to a cluster of buildings.

He arrived at a recessed portal that pushed open with ease. He softened his stride as he entered the hangar, where a metallic bird nested in the center of the room. A sleek burgundy fuselage, flamed underbelly, hot-red propeller, and matching elevator suggested a free and defiant nature. The biplane's double wings stretched wide, angling skyward. Even in the dark she found a way to glisten.

The man paced beside the taildragger undercarriage and ran a glove along the body. He wasted no time. Checking his watch, he hoisted himself into the cockpit and inspected the helm and controls. Producing a small box of tools from his coat pocket, his delicate fingers inserted a skinny rod near the yoke and loosened four screws. He worked with the skill of a locksmith.

For all his paraphernalia, he was no expert infiltrator. He'd failed to notice any movement behind him. Soon after he'd climbed the fence, an automobile had cut its engine and parked outside the airfield, not two hundred yards from the trespasser's vehicle.

The car's passenger stole into the hangar and concealed himself behind a stack of storage crates, his gaze never leaving the intruder. As the man in the ski mask groped around the cockpit, the newcomer reached into his rucksack, pulled out a camera, and trained its high optical zoom on the prowler's busywork. Two dozen snapshots later, he packed away his device and continued to observe.

*   *   *

Sleet-filled, overcast skies mirrored an icy wasteland. Guards lounged in their seats and stared at screens from four towers around the colony. Their entertainment was the news channel, the sole connection to the outside world. The attraction had grown dull with time. Armed sentries patrolled the surrounding stone ramparts, assault rifles slung over their shoulders.

Only the hardest criminals suffered Siberia, and only the toughest survived. Ragnar leaned against the stone walls of the prison yard, cupping a hand over his mouth to light a cigarette.

Flicking his lighter a few times, he created a flame that quivered in the subzero extreme. He inhaled slowly, then breathed out, his lungful of mingling steam and smoke whisked away in a violent blitz of gales. He turned down the flaps of his fur *shapka-ushanka,* protecting his ears from the onslaught.

Ragnar gazed at his fellow inmates. A hulking mountain of a man with wide, protruding cheekbones and a jutting chin, he dwarfed most of the other prisoners. Jasper hair burned down his shoulder blades. His arms, flecked with scars, had clear definition, though his muscles more resembled knotty burls than pleasing curves. His left bicep bore a simple tattoo, a single word inscribed in plain cursive: *Firecat.* A horned helmet rested beneath it, superimposed over a double-sided ax.

His mind drifted to the territory beyond the walls. Outside were vast stretches of desolate land. With more than a hundred miles to the nearest village, the frozen tundra blocked any escape.

Ragnar took one last drag and tossed his cigarette to the ground, watching the embers die before he could squelch them. From a recess in the wall, he observed other captives hewing wood and stacking timber for shipment. A few clustered around a makeshift chessboard, where two rivals faced off in concentration. Nearby, a pair of bald men locked wrists in an arm wrestle, as betting spectators rooted for their champion. The wrestlers suffered mutely in the numbing cold, their fingers soon to be black as soot and ravaged by frostbite without protection.

Ragnar rarely said a word to the other inmates. An observer of human nature, he kept to himself, content with his estrangement. No one went near him anymore; they'd seen what happened to the hostile few who had tried to bait him into scuffles. His past was a mystery into which no one probed.

But today was different. A man approached. Ragnar recognized the smooth, oil-on-glass voice.

"Hello, Captain."

The newcomer strode into Ragnar's corner. He spoke with the air of a sophisticate in convict's attire, his clean grooming and lack of stubble suggesting he was a recent transplant from the outside world. His thick brows might have been prominent without scrupulous trimming. Unlike the other inmates, he had no signs of wear and tear; his hands looked manicured, his skin unsullied by grime or perspiration. His nose and chin were defined by acute angles, combining with a head of charcoal hair in an attractive mix of Russian and Romanian gypsy. The combing emphasized a sharp widow's peak.

A few other inmates looked in their direction as if intrigued by the unusual interaction involving Ragnar. He glanced back at them, and they turned away.

"Just finished my shift in the machine shop," said the man. He was holding a sack. "Look inside."

Ragnar opened the sack to find a bottle of vodka, a towel, and a can of degreaser. He uncorked the bottle and emptied the vodka onto the ground, then filled it to the brim with degreaser.

"Where'd you get this?" he asked as he took hold of the towel, ripped off a rag-sized portion, and stuffed the fabric into the bottleneck like a plug.

"Guards' locker room. Same as the bottle."

Ragnar nodded. "And fuel from the machine shop," he said. He paused a moment. "When does he come?"

"He's already here."

Ragnar arched a suspicious brow. Then he heard it: a faint thrumming in the distance. Even as the percussive rhythm grew steadily louder, the guards failed to notice anything amiss over the battering hail. To Ragnar and his accomplice, the sound of freedom was crystal.

"Distract them," the newcomer instructed.

With a firm grip on the bottle, Ragnar ambled toward the closest of the four guard towers. He drew his lighter and ignited the cloth soaked in degreaser, then lobbed the bottle at the tower.

The cocktail soared in a wide arc before shattering a glass window panel. Flames exploded inside the tower room. Frenzied guards dashed out, shouting for help.

Ragnar looked on as chaos erupted throughout the colony. Sentries opened fire and cried for reinforcements. Streams of bullets lay siege to the yard, kicking up snow and ice as guards searched for the culprit. The other inmates scattered, screaming in confusion and crazed jubilation, sprinting toward the sidelines to escape the barrage and bloodshed.

The peaceful compound had descended into bedlam. Black curls of smoke coalesced into pillars, rising from the tower and sweeping away with the cold Siberian wind. Guards cast buckets of water over the spreading flames and unleashed extinguishers while the blaze raged out of control. Workers in chains flung chunks of timber at the tower to feed the conflagration. Pistols raised, guards poured into the yard at ground level to contain the anarchy.

Ragnar jogged to his corner and joined his abettor. At first the din of machine-gun fire masked the sound for which they'd so keenly listened. Then they felt the pulsations. A black apparition climbed over the tower opposite the fire, its blades kicking up gray swirls of dust and debris. The helicopter hovered over the colony for several seconds before descending into the center of the yard. The chopper's skids scarcely tapped the ground. Prisoners fled at the sight of the aircraft, and guards ceased fire, surprised their reinforcements had arrived so promptly. The Kamov helo was a civilian craft closely modeled after a Russian Air Force helicopter intended for reconnaissance, anti-tank, radio-electronic jamming, and distant hauling of air-assault forces. Designed to fly with stealth and maneuverability worthy of special ops, the Kamov demonstrated its true colors by hovering inches above the snow with no sign of powering down.

Ragnar and his conspirator made for the chopper, which lingered in place as they climbed inside and slammed the door behind them.

Guards and inmates gawked in disbelief as the two men disappeared behind the helicopter's reflective windows. The rotor blades began to revolve faster, lifting their attached machinery skyward.

The aircraft veered in a one-eighty. Sparks flew as a volley of rounds grazed the hull, all sentries now training their aim on the chopper as it soared. For all their relentless shelling, the guards were too late. Riding an easterly wind, the Kamov climbed to a safe distance and became a dot in the clouds, leaving in its wake a glowing inferno amid stretches of ice.

PART I
THE PEARL ENCHANTRESS

White froth rolled shoreward and dissipated. A tall, slender form unfurled from the water and stood in defiance of a stiff wind. The body turned to the sea and dove against an oncoming wave, then surfaced as the wave passed.

His eyes were two black opals panning the seascape. An insatiable desire to see, to feel, to experience, could be seen in their crystalline intensity. Bronzed only slightly by the sun, the face held a look of wayward independence under thick waves of dark brown hair. He was twenty-four.

The noon sun blazed overhead, easing the chill of the ocean air. Visibility was perfect, the sky cloudless and clear, rare in Northern California's Half Moon Bay. This beach was always empty when he came. He thought of it as his beach.

A crest loomed, capped with white. The young man's arms plunged into the water with force, and his legs kicked up to a horizontal, carrying him against the tide until he reached the base of the mounting arc. An engine hummed in the distance; he ignored it. He took in a sharp breath and flipped around, holding his body in the shape of the curved wall as he timed his launch, and thrust his torso forward.

The wave engulfed and propelled him. A surge of cold streamed through the layer of water caught inside his full-length wetsuit, flushing across the skin of his chest and back. He laughed under the surface, his mind filled with the awareness of his own body; he could feel the vibrations of his laughter in a mix with the tumult. Soon the wave became a gentle hand stroking the sandbank.

He stood again, a six-foot-three silhouette of slim musculature. Then he dove back, arms churning to catch another.

The sound of the engine grew louder. When he surfaced, he realized the source was practically riding on top of him. A deluge of saltwater splashed over his face, and the humming diminished.

A female voice spoke.

"Looking lean and mean in neoprene, Austin Hardy."

Blond curls fluttering behind her as she jockeyed the water scooter head-on into the crosswind, Rachel Mason was grinning. The passenger behind her was not. Sitting on the pad and still clinging to her waist, a young Japanese man had wedged his feet inside the Jet Ski for safety, his expression laced with queasiness and regret. The life vest hugged so tightly around his waist and aloha shirt that his cheeks were flushing red.

His name was Ichiro Yamada, and his face had pulled taut. "Austin, hurry! Save me from this madwoman!" he shouted.

Rachel tossed her passenger a pitiless glance, her dimples caving with amusement and condescension. "You haven't lost any limbs. That's good enough for me."

Austin smiled back at them.

"Hello, Rachel, Itchy. How are you two enjoying your romp around the Bay?"

"You've told us about this place for too long," Rachel said. "We had to see the swimmer in his element."

"You make a grand entrance."

She tossed her hair, and a cascade fell over a strap of her light green bikini. "We rented the Jet Ski for the hour. Unfortunately, Itchy here may be too scrawny to last."

"Don't call me that," Ichiro said irritably, removing a pair of goggles.

Austin asked, "How has my brave roommate fared?"

"Your brave roommate loves his life and wishes to keep it," Ichiro said. "Which means it's time for him to disembark."

Ichiro pinched his nose and jumped into the water. He came up shivering.

"Cold?" said Rachel.

"Torturous, but better than riding with you."

Austin took two strokes and came up alongside the scooter. He kicked his legs to impel himself upward, then hoisted himself aloft. The Jet Ski wobbled until he gained his balance. In one motion he swiped the lanyard from Rachel's wrist and placed it around his own. She yelped as he lifted her onto the passenger seat behind him.

"What are you doing?" she asked.

With a hand on the controls, he gunned the motor and twisted the throttle clockwise. The craft pitched and kicked up a misty spray.

"Riding off to an undisclosed location, where I can take advantage of you under the hot sun."

"And then what?"

"I'll drop you as far out as I can to hide the evidence. But I'd better get busy. Class starts soon."

They were gone before she could protest.

Ichiro watched them shrink in the distance as they glided over the surface like a rock skipping a lake.

"Nice to see you, roomie," he said. "I do hope you'll come back for me."

Virtually airborne, the racer banked and twisted, skimming the wave crests. After staking off a mile-wide loop of ocean, the duo traversed a self-styled slalom, chasing gulls in figure eights.

"So this is where you come to bodysurf?" Rachel asked, shouting to be heard over the wind.

"Once a week," Austin said.

"Pretty luxurious, having a beach to yourself."

He had grown up in Malibu, spending many a high school sunset bodysurfing at Zuma Beach. After moving to Northern California, he had claimed this spot off Highway 1, a sanctuary for mulling over puzzles and projects.

"Helps me think," he said.

He slowed the Jet Ski and cut the engine.

"Is this where you take advantage of me?" she asked, wringing out her hair.

"Of course not. We go way out to sea for that. If I tried anything here, you could just swim ashore and get away. That's what the last one did."

She cocked her head. "Oh? There was another?"

"Actually, you're number fifty-five, but I like you better than the others. They put up a fight." Rachel leaned down to the water and splashed a handful in his mouth. He coughed, adding, "I didn't deserve that, and you better remember I retaliate."

She flailed as he picked her up and tossed her into the water. She made a small splash and rose to the surface struggling to control her laughter through chattering teeth. He dove in after her.

"Too bad Ichiro jumped ship," he said, smiling at her with affection, as he would a sister. "He's missing out."

"We should go get him."

"Good idea. I'd rather not hear news of a human-shaped ice cube washing ashore." He paused. "What's the matter?"

She looked beyond him. "I thought you said this beach was private."

"Not officially, though I've never seen anyone else. Why?"

She pointed. Treading water, he turned around to follow her finger.

"Looks like a small daytime campfire," he said, though he wasn't sure if he believed his own words.

"Look harder."

A head of blazing red hair had tricked his eye. A man was standing at the edge of the water. The red color bled down to his shoulders and moved with the breeze, giving the appearance of a flame dancing on a candle. The man's arms were crossed, hands tucked and hidden. Wearing a knee-length woolen coat, he stood with solemn stillness. His legs bore into the sand like monoliths, giving Austin the impression that it would take more than rough tides to remove this man's physical connection with the earth; he could have kicked any wave back into the sea.

"You've never seen him before?"

"Never," Austin said.

He noted the man's vehicle, a black sedan parked behind a cluster of trees.

"Is he staring at us?"

"Don't think so."

"You sure? We can't see his eyes."

"He looks like someone who loves the sea, and came to meditate."

Not buying Austin's tranquility, Rachel felt a sharp frisson and said, "Yeah, and I wonder how long he's been there."

"I'd say the cold is giving you the willies. Let's head back." He checked his watch as he helped her climb onto the Jet Ski. "And we better go fast. I'm already running late, and now I'm thinking about the winding roads back to school. I'll have to drive like a maniac."

"Ichiro and I just got here!"

"Come earlier next time."

She began to pout. "You can miss one class. Just one class."

He found it difficult to refuse. "Not this one."

Austin had graduated two years before with a bachelor's in mechanical engineering. He had spent one year traveling and completed one year of aerospace research, studying turbulence mechanics with a professor in Bologna, before returning to Stanford to begin the doctoral program in aeronautics and astronautics.

"Don't you want to stay?"

"And skim the wave tops with a fiendishly attractive creature clad in scanty swimwear? Desperately. But it's important I attend this lecture. I haven't missed one all quarter. If you knew the professor, you'd understand."

She sighed. "You live the life of three people. Which class is it?"

"Aircraft and Rocket Propulsion."

The motor groaned under his directive. Austin veered toward the beach and teased the break line, then spun the Jet Ski around to face the open water. They found Ichiro bobbing a half-mile down, and he and Austin traded places.

Austin gave Rachel a playful bite on the neck before swimming ashore and changing out of his wetsuit. She watched as he slipped into his car and drove off into the forest. For a few minutes, she stayed on the scooter, staring wistfully at the beach.

TWO

You have probably heard the urban legend of the space-pen. As the story goes, during the heat of the space race of the 1960s, NASA scientists were determined to develop a pen that could write in zero gravity. They tried everything from pressurized capsules to ballpoints with new ink formulas. Finally, after months of research and millions invested, they succeeded. Meanwhile, the Russians used a pencil."

He didn't speak his words; he liberated them in his distinguished London accent. They carried an understated rubato, an artful bending and shaping of tempo. He'd enter a sotto voce now and again for emphasis. The soft tones would build and build until they reached an exultant fortissimo—and then they would stop, and he'd let an expressive silence linger.

The man was in his early sixties, commanding the stage with the vibrancy and gusto of a man one-third his age. His gestures and animation induced a hypnotic yet enlivening effect on his audience. Slight and bony-limbed, he looked not the least bit fragile; rather, a vigorous persona made his delicate physique seem uncannily robust. His focused squint captured the intensity of a jockey certain of a solid standing only seconds from the finish line. Owlish behind thick spectacles, he faced his listeners with unwavering concentration. A jolly ruddiness speckled his cheeks above the white of his sideburns. Hearing him speak was like listening to a novel on tape, the prose polished, the tenor styled to captivate.

"While the anecdote provides an example in creative thinking, the facts teach a different lesson," he said. "In reality, Americans did use graphite pencils on all Mercury and Gemini space flights prior to 1968, as did the Russians—but not without problems. Bits of wood and graphite broke off, creating floating debris hazardous to the eyes and nose. Due to electron delocalization within its carbon layers, graphite conducts electricity, so drifting particles could short computer equipment. The flammability of wood and graphite proved dangerous in pure oxygen atmospheres present in pre-Apollo manned space missions.

"The solution patented by Paul C. Fisher was a pressurized cartridge of thixotropic ink. His 'astronaut pen' worked at any angle, underwater, and in extreme temperatures—with a shelf life of a hundred years. He understood that oftentimes the easy design—in this case, pencil graphite—introduces a host of undesirable consequences. The engineer's challenge is to foresee the consequences; his art is to adapt with all achievable simplicity."

Dr. Malcolm Clare was a man with a kind of star power that intimidated most students. From 1971 to 1974, he had served as a flight test engineer at NASA's High-Speed Flight Station. He had worked on eleven projects, including a number of spin tests for fighter jets, before moving to Mojave. He had founded Malfactory in the California desert, an enterprise that designed aircraft and spacecraft prototypes. He later developed the company into ClareCraft, one of the world's leading prototyping facilities, headquartered at the Mojave Spaceport. During his time he'd been responsible for the design and oversight of forty-one aircraft and four rockets.

Clare's spaceplane, Spica, had earned a five-million-dollar prize for its novel engine. At full thrust, most combustion chambers reached temperatures upward of 3,000 degrees Celsius, enough to melt the heat-resistant sidewalls. The traditional solution had been to lay in networks of cooling tubes, whereby heat-absorbing liquid fuels would abduct thermal energy, but such "regenerative cooling" systems added mass, expense, and complexity. Clare's design employed a novel configuration and material for the tubing that contained the blaze and its damage to achieve breakthrough weight and efficiency.

Dr. Clare had joined the Stanford faculty in 1981, where he taught advanced courses in aerospace engineering. He spent his years alternating between innovation at ClareCraft, research at Stanford, and consultation at Pasadena's Jet Propulsion Laboratory as a technical advisor to NASA's Deep Space Network supporting interplanetary spacecraft missions. Students welcomed his regular guest lectures at Caltech. In 1992, he had earned the Royal Aeronautical Society's Gold Medal for "pioneering experimental contributions to modeling transonic wave drag," as the official text put it. By the early nineties, his contributions to aerospace engineering had become legendary.

In 1994 Clare's celebrity nosedived. The face of aeronautics had vanished from the press and television. Interviews and guest lectures had come to a halt as Stanford's most visible professor withdrew into reclusion. His inexplicable departure from the headlines had created fodder for detractors. "It appears the great innovator's spigot has run dry!" critics had chided as conjectures abounded.

Yet as a magician harbors mystery behind his curtain, Malcolm Clare continued to baffle students with his eccentricities and prowess.

Ten minutes late, Austin parked his bike and dashed across the courtyard between the Hewlett and Packard buildings. He ran up the stairs and entered the amphitheater, taking a seat in the back under a hanging periodic table. He entered quietly, careful to avoid the professor's notice. At the bottom of the room, Clare paced the floor.

"To continue our theme of parables," he said, "there's a story told by the painter Giorgio Vasari in his biographical history of artists. In his tale, city officials asked to see the Florentine architect Filippo Brunelleschi's design for a cathedral dome. Filippo instead proposed that whosoever could make an egg stand upright on flat marble, without aid, should be hired to build the cupola. When none could find a way, he lightly smashed one end on the marble, making the egg stand on its flattened shell. Rival architects argued they could have easily done the same. Filippo said they could have also built the dome, if they had seen his model. He earned the commission."

There were chuckles.

"You may wonder why I've chosen these stories to stress the power and pitfalls of simplicity. The answer is, your midterm scores. I was impressed by your ability to apply textbook theorems and formulas. Nonetheless, the average was quite low. Success on this test took creativity. You were evidently pressed for time. Some students left pages unanswered. In posted solutions, you'll see much of the algebraic busywork was avoidable if you'd viewed problems through a simpler lens.

"Don't worry about grades. This is only a gauge of your preparedness for the quals. I encourage you to visit me during office hours to discuss how you might better employ your scientific intuition. That's enough on the test.

"Let's continue where the last class ended. I believe we were discussing the principles governing hypersonic combustion in scramjet engines. We'd seen how these engines require few moving parts, since the aircraft itself uses speed to compress air. Who can tell me why a hybrid ramjet/scramjet engine would have a lower minimal functional Mach number?"

That concludes today's material. Thanks for your attention. As you know, I don't like slideshows, so rather than post a PowerPoint, I'll email out my lecture notes. See you next time. Oh, and I'd like to see Austin Hardy in my office. Right now."

Austin felt a pang of guilt. He wasn't sure if the professor had noticed his tardiness. No one missed a minute of Clare's class. The professor had made clear that attendance and punctuality were required of students wishing to master advanced aerospace studies.

Austin wasn't the type to show up late. Today was a rare exception. As he descended the amphitheater steps toward the professor, he fretted over the reception of his apology.

"Sorry," he said. "No excuse for the delay."

Malcolm Clare almost laughed. "You think that's what this is about?"

"What else?"

The professor had an odd wrinkle to his face. "Let's walk to my office."

The two had become well acquainted, developing a mutual appreciation and respect for each other's intelligence and company. Austin was outspoken in class. His habit of extracting double meaning from scientific jargon had earned him a reputation for adding levity to lectures. Clare had adapted his own arsenal of retaliatory wordplay. Austin was also known to challenge the professor on occasion, highlighting potential snares in the theories presented, which they often discussed over drinks outside of class.

The professor led Austin to the top floor of Gates, where he was consumed by the spectacle that was Office 317. Toy rockets stood poised for launch on wall outcroppings. Perched model planes tilted back on their wheels, angled for takeoff. A bat-winged ornithopter dangled from string beside an American WWII fighter; the fighter was a Vultee XP-54, a radical design whose elongated nose had given rise to its moniker—the *Swoose Goose*. Suspended at the center of the room was a Douglas B-18 Bolo, an American bomber of the late 1930s, entangled with a Nakajima Ki-27, a low-wing monoplane of the Imperial Japanese Army Air Force.

The décor reminded Austin of his own working models and the reason he'd built them. At age ten he'd been flying alone to meet his father in Lisbon. His airliner had experienced a midflight explosive decompression over the Atlantic Ocean, coupled with a hydraulic systems failure. The pilot had successfully forced a belly landing on the island of Terceira in the Azores. Despite the trauma, his fear of flying had been short-lived; rather, he'd become fixated with building planes that wouldn't fail. He had begun studying ways to create small flying machines, first from kits, and later from everyday materials. His motors were constructed from magnets, nails, coiled wire, and car batteries. Using more compact batteries, he had integrated smaller, lighter propellers into balsa-wood airframes. Homemade radios became transmitters and receivers that controlled the planes' servomechanisms. By his early teens, his planes were delivering paper messages and light objects to kids in his neighborhood.

He continued his sweep of the professor's office. A gilded telescope and a pair of British pilot goggles served as paperweights beside a biplane, carved of black walnut, its propeller blades creating a room fan. Inflated dirigibles hung suspended by invisible thread, among them the *Norge*, the first uncontested airship to fly over the North Pole. A glass sheet protected a fifteenth-century map of the world on Clare's desktop, along with scrolls of Ptolemaic and Copernican planetary cartography. Da Vincian flight experiments adorned the shelves as bookends. A number of tomes caught Austin's interest, among them a volume on Norse mythology.

Clare hung his coat in an armoire and took a seat at his desk.

"Hope I'm not keeping you from any prior engagement. If at any point you have to leave, I won't be offended."

Austin hadn't expected geniality, much less an invitation to the inventor's inner sanctum.

"Thanks. I'm free most of the evening," he said, sitting.

"Any idea why I called you in?"

"I'm guessing it wasn't to share your collection of artifacts."

Malcolm shook his head. "The midterm average was fifty-three percent, with a standard deviation of seven. Scores were tightly clustered around the mean. There were some outliers, but none as striking as yours." He placed an exam on the table. "You scored a ninety-five, and if you hadn't forgotten how to add and subtract, you might have aced it."

Austin smiled. "Always the arithmetic."

The professor reclined in his chair, smoothing out his brown flannel shirt. "You have a gift. In my years of teaching, there have been few like you. I asked you in to get to know you a little better, discuss your career, and submit a modest proposal, if your ears are open."

"Sure."

"In all the times we've met after class, I've never asked you what you see yourself doing with your degree."

"Tough question for a first-year," Austin said.

"No need to commit."

"If it were in private industry, I'd probably try to build portable, amphibious sports aircraft. But the military has its appeal. I've thought about becoming a flight test engineer at Edwards Air Force Base."

"Sounds like one thing you'll never do is sit under the fluorescent lights of an office cubicle."

"My feet would itch."

"Don't blame you. There was nothing better than working in the Mojave heat. Is that what you always wanted to do? Build planes?"

"Unless you count my adolescent infatuation with espionage," Austin said.

The lines of Clare's face creased into a smile. "Elaborate."

It was a strange tangent, but he was used to Clare's surprises. Austin thought about his answer. Growing up, he had often constructed Rube Goldberg contraptions using objects around the house. The kitchen had become a series of concealed electrolytic reactions and mechanical processes that rallied to prepare hot chocolate in cold temperatures. Soon he had undertaken more practical designs, selling homemade radios to neighborhood friends. He had buried a network of small electric cables so they could communicate via Morse code from their bedrooms. By eleven, he and his friends had become conversant in a number of ciphers, most of which Austin had created and documented in a classified handbook of cryptographs.

"The kids in my neighborhood loved coding messages to each other," he said with a lilt of nostalgia. "You could say that lured me into the technical side of espionage."

"Not your typical childhood fantasy," Clare pointed out. He seemed to be finding genuine humor. "What did your parents make of this?"

"They indulged me. My dad joined the U.S. Navy Reserve during the Vietnam War, spent two years as a lieutenant. He later worked as a secretary to Senator Abbott Botulga of California, and served as a U.S. ambassador to several European countries. My mom's a biologist at the Malibu Aquaculture Research Institute. She has ongoing projects in coastal communities in Indonesia and Timor-Leste. Sometimes they'd create stories of political espionage based on their travels. Or play games."

"Games? What kind?"

The professor was certainly taking every opportunity to learn about him. Austin wondered what this was really about and felt a bit irritated by the lack of candor. For now he was willing to go along. He admired Malcolm Clare, and felt confident the man's interrogation was calculated.

"Whenever we dined out, some minutes after we were seated, my mom and dad would tell me to close my eyes. They'd ask me things about the environment—things like, what color is the ceiling? How many chandeliers are in the room? What's in the painting to your left? It's funny how quickly the mind discards details like that. I guess the idea was to hone visual memory and observational skills."

Clare stood and lifted a red model biplane from its string, twirling the burnished propeller. A full minute of silence passed as the man toyed with his aircraft. Austin waited for the professor to speak, wishing for a way into his thoughts. Usually perceptive of people's intentions, Austin realized he was clueless, and aware only that there seemed to be a number of things on Clare's mind. The man was present with his words, but Austin had the impression he was torn by distractions.

Clare let the plane dangle by its string again, and gave the tail a gentle push so it flew in circles.

"You said you had interest in becoming a military flight test engineer," he said. "Let's assume for a moment you didn't go this route. Would indirect military involvement interest you?"

"What do you mean?"

"Let's say you were in a position to assist the military while retaining civilian status."

"You'd have to tell me more."

"Unfortunately I can't be more specific," Clare said. "I assure you my questions are carefully phrased."

Austin didn't doubt it.

"I'm flattered by your interest in me, Professor. With all due respect, I'd like to know where this is leading."

Clare chuckled. Most students would have answered any question he asked. Austin was another matter.

"Mr. Hardy, I'm offering you a job."

Austin tried not to look too questioning, nor did he allow himself any premature eagerness. "I'm assuming this isn't research assistance."

"Right."

The biplane came to a stop. Clare's presence seemed to swell and occupy the entire room.

"I know how peculiar it must sound, but there is little concrete I can tell you," the professor added. "It would be unwise, even dangerous for me to share much without a pledge of commitment."

"To what?"

Clare seemed to talk over the question. "Regrettably, secrecy only makes your decision harder. Forgive me if it's all too abstract, but you'll have to determine . . . you'll face a hazy crossroad, and have to decide, from limited knowledge, whether the work interests you. Decline, and I'll ask for your discretion, but no more. Accept, and I will tell you everything, knowing your agreement entails nothing short of full dedication."

"How abstract are we talking? What *can* you tell me?"

"You'd learn national defense secrets as you cultivate relationships with military leaders as an engineer. Your travel schedule would have you so busy, you'd likely need passport inserts within two years. You'd associate with a preexisting organization but operate as an independent entity. And you'd need more than a sharp mind. An athletic body would serve you well."

"For a minute there, I thought you were talking politics."

"Mr. Hardy, I'd like to elevate you, not sentence you."

Austin let out an earnest laugh, then tilted his head sideways. "You mentioned defense secrets."

"With secondary, albeit profound, political consequences."

"Any more you can say about that?"

"I'm afraid not."

"Why me? Don't you have any better qualified candidates than a first-year doctoral student?"

"Don't think you're the only mental acrobat I have my eyes on."

Austin bit his tongue, humbled. "But my hopes are high for you. I saw an exceptional student—outspoken, bright—and wondered if he's for hire. Don't get any ideas because I brought up defense secrets. This isn't your childhood fantasy. The work is scientific. But it has benefits. A salary, for one. You'd start out around three hundred thousand, with room to grow."

For a student, it was unheard of. Still, Austin was surprised and a tad annoyed the professor would presume to propose something so important and explain so little.

"Mind if I ask more questions?" he asked.

"Go ahead."

"How long would my employment last?"

"You would sign on for four years. With luck, you'd want to stay indefinitely."

"How many have you recruited?"

"Personally, a few dozen. But there are hundreds in the workforce."

"All university students?"

"You'd be among the first your age."

"Could I tell people about this? Friends, family?"

"You could tell them you were a private military consultant, no more."

"A private military consultant."

Clare fogged his glasses with a warm breath and polished the lenses, his expression unreadable as stone. "Someone who works with heads of the Defense Department as a creative builder."

"A builder. Of what?" He saw from Clare's face that the question would go unanswered. He tried a new tack. "What use could a first-year grad student offer a general?"

"You wouldn't work for any general. You'd work for me. People would listen. People in high places."

"Would the job be dangerous?"

"For you, no. You'd be perfectly safe."

Austin felt a twinge of discomfort. Apart from the obvious omissions, there was something the professor wasn't sharing—something pivotal.

"You've been doing more than teaching," he said. "Sounds like Stanford has been kept in the dark about something."

"It's no secret to my closest faculty friends. But their knowledge is limited. Not even my daughter knows everything I do."

"You have a daughter?"

The news certainly didn't break the day's pattern of revelations.

"Due to the nature of my work the last few years, not all those in my life have remained safe. My daughter is an example. I've kept her well protected."

"I had no idea."

"Then I've done well. When she was young, I had to watch her closely. She was an old soul, that much was always obvious—but I knew she couldn't grasp the extent of her vulnerability. Now that she's grown, she understands the need to keep to herself." His eyes misted with pride. "Talk about killer smarts. She's just like her mother. Plays piano like her, too." His grin began to vanish. "If only they'd known each other. They're similar in almost every way."

"I didn't realize you had married."

Clare nodded toward a small picture frame on his desk. He was about twenty-five years younger, sporting a bomber jacket and standing next to a dark-haired lady on a cobbled street. They were surrounded by colored lights. The woman peeked through a feathered mask encrusted with rhinestones in the shape of a fleur-de-lis. Her neck was strung with Mardi Gras beads, and her legs were wrapped around the younger Malcolm's. She was beaming, her golden suntan setting the picture aglow. Austin blinked twice, taken by the photo. "She's drop-dead gorgeous."

"Angelica Francesca Freire," said Clare. "That was at Rio Carnival."

"How did you meet?" Austin asked, not really expecting the professor to answer.

But Clare surprised him. "In Brazil. Soon after I formally left Clare-Craft for Stanford, I started getting speaking invitations to universities around the world. Met Angelica at the Federal University of Rio de Janeiro. She taught math there. Funny, I kept finding reasons to fly back. We married in eighty-three."

"Does she still teach?"

He knew he was pushing his luck with curiosity.

"The next year, she grew fatally ill after giving birth."

Austin felt stricken for having asked him to talk about it. "I'm sorry."

"I didn't invite you here to commiserate. You've just heard an unusual proposal, and I'd like to know what's going through your mind."

Austin allowed himself time to ponder. "You've given me a lot to think about," he said. "And I'm honored by your trust in me. You have to understand, I struggle with secrecy. The idea of keeping things from loved ones could never be comfortable for me."

"Understandable."

"On the other hand, from what little I know of it, the job seems tailor-made to my interests. I'd like time to decide."

"No need for promises tonight. How's one week?"

Austin didn't expect much sleep the next seven nights.

"One week," he said. "Okay."

Clare stood. He rested a reassuring hand on Austin's shoulder before gesturing toward the door. "Don't kill yourself over this. If you have more questions, ask. I'll be in my office from eight a.m. till nine p.m. all week."

"You practically live here."

"And you're always welcome to visit."

"Thank you, Professor."

As he headed out, Clare's voice caught him in the hallway. He glanced back. The inventor's clouded gaze seemed to have given way to a skittish excitement. Austin returned to Clare's office and reconnoitered the room once more, which for all its model planes and zeppelins looked like a chamber in Santa's factory.

"One more thing," Clare said.

"Yes?"

"A fun little perk. Those who work for me learn to fly. Private pilot lessons with my compliments."

"Who's the instructor?"

"You're looking at him."

THREE

Man's natural response to the unknown was fear, Clare mused. Of course Austin wouldn't jump at the offer.

The discussion had gone well enough. Though his student's acceptance wasn't mission critical, he had sensed something exceptional and wanted to get to it early.

After Austin left, Clare closed the door and reclined in his desk chair.

Organizing his mental to-do list, he realized he'd reached a rare lull in activity. It wouldn't be long before the action picked up again—twenty-four hours, tops—but he welcomed the break. He had only to wait.

And drink. Within hours, he expected cause to celebrate.

He took a champagne bottle out of a small refrigerator near his desk, popped the cork, and poured a glass. The flute paused at his chin.

He flipped open his cell phone and speed-dialed a number.

"How's everything?" he asked. "Good . . . Yes, they always do that, standard protocol. . . . Don't worry, they'll have it under control. . . . Ha! Of course not. That will probably come as a shock. . . . You know I'd be there myself, if I could. . . . Take pictures, if you can, square on the belly of the beast. . . . Agreed. We'll talk soon. Safe journey."

Clare snapped his phone shut and placed it at the edge of his desk.

The crystal felt cool on his lips, the champagne thrilling his palette with a refreshing kick. It was the glory of achieving yet another milestone. One empty glass became a second, then a third.

He idled away time by skimming headlines on his laptop. Finding little of interest, he shut it down and placed the computer in his padded briefcase. He flipped on the news from a miniature television he often played on mute. If only the media knew, he thought, presses would fly hot.

His attention drifted to a different photograph on his desk. He gazed at the image for a few minutes in quiet reminiscence, seeing his happy younger self, trying to remember the carefree days before his present responsibilities. It had been a less complicated time, and he had been a simpler man. He sighed as he looked through the mask at Angelica, and for a moment he could hear her; she spoke gently, and as the alcohol saturated his veins, she began to caress him. Memories flashed like images from an old film projector. He wanted to see her again, to run his hands through her hair, to feel those endless legs wrapped around him. He pinched his forearm for entertaining the impossible.

A rumble in his stomach escalated to a growl. He drank the remainder of his champagne, save one glass, which he vowed to finish after getting food.

He placed his briefcase against his desk and walked into the darkened corridor, locking the door behind him. He stopped. Had he heard something? A fleeting sound—or was it the champagne buzz? He turned a corner and descended the stairs, his thoughts now on the choice of cuisine.

In his office, his mobile phone began to vibrate, its screen displaying an incoming call from a restricted number. The phone jittered on his desk, moving millimeters at a time, until slipping off and dropping onto the floor. For seconds it lay still. Then it shook once more.

Outside, Clare breathed in the cool air. Cloudless skies revealed clusters of stars winking down on the university's quad. A black sedan was parked to the north. A fountain sprang to his right, splashing over a mound of rocks and creating a rhythm of water breaking against water. A family of raccoons stole into the bushes, staring at him. Crossing the street, he strode toward the iconic cloistered quadrangle. Something shifted in the darkness. A shadow flitted.

Sharp-edged pain shot through his skull. His teeth clamped to compensate. Scores of lights flared in his head, blinding at first, revolving in strange constellations and whisking away his sense of up and down. His strength waned, and his knees gave. Night closed in on him like a shroud. The stars faded. He fell limp, grappling with an enveloping black void.

FOUR

S he was a fortress on water.

Her smokestacks seemed to tilt with the passing clouds as the man gazed up from the dock. The largest ship in its fleet, the *Pearl Enchantress* housed a small city. She was over one thousand feet long and nineteen stories high, dwarfing other ships in the Port of Miami.

Garbed in a Cuban-style guayabera, former Air Force combat weatherman Jacob Rove climbed the gangway toward the cruise liner. He had traveled aboard many vessels during his service, never for leisure.

He reached a line of passengers waiting to board. A toddler peered at him from behind his mother's leg, smiling. Children's reactions to his appearance had always puzzled him; they were more often fascinated than afraid. He looked rigid as brickwork and older than his forty-eight years, with wide shoulders and a stocky frame comparable to a middleweight boxer's. The tattoo on his left deltoid was a crude, grinning toucan. Shadows clung to the grooves of a craggy face, one bearing traces of cynicism and fatigue. Missions overseas had led to physical erosion, just as training good men—and watching many die— had left emotional damage difficult to quantify. Telltale scars around his collarbone attested to his acquaintance with physical pain.

Some perceived a facade of cold granite when they looked at him. Others saw through this mask into a kind soul. Though he spoke little, there was a friendly humor in his voice when he did, one that offset the gravity of his expression. His father had come from a Scottish family of devout Catholics, and his mother from a Polish family of Orthodox Jews. They had eloped to Nevada, where his dad had joined the Sparks Police Department as a patrolman. Wounded by family hostility between faiths, they had reared Jacob without religion. Before his fourteenth birthday, Jake's father had been killed in a gang shootout and left in an icy lake. In his sleep, Jake would see the gleam of a police badge sinking in the deep; two arms would reach from a cold murk, and the sight of a white, bloated face would haunt him. Fearful their family had been targeted, his mother had insisted they move in with her sister in Houston. At fifteen, Jake had been forced to confront his terror of swimming when asked to help at his uncle's dive shop. He had spent hours filling tanks, disinfecting regulators, selling gear, feeding fish in the aquarium, and restocking inventory. He and his uncle would dive every day after school until Jake was ready to assist teaching scuba classes at sixteen.

The apprenticeship had kindled Jake's interest in oceanography. At seventeen he had earned a scholarship to UC San Diego, where he'd double-majored in marine biology and meteorology. After graduating, he had joined the Hubbs–SeaWorld Research Institute as an assistant to Dr. Boyd Bowles, director of the Bioacoustics Laboratory, and collected data for the analysis of animal sound perception and dispersion. Jake had helped Dr. Bowles study vocal learning in gray whales and killer whales under contract to the U.S. Air Force and Coast Guard. It was at the institute in 1982 that Jake had learned of the budding Law Enforcement Detachment (LEDET) program, its mission to deploy aboard naval vessels and conduct maritime security and interdiction operations. He'd enlisted in the Coast Guard as a living marine resources specialist.

Following the National Defense Authorization Act of 1989—which tasked the Department of Defense with monitoring maritime drug trafficking—the Coast Guard was chosen as the principal agency for interdicting and apprehending drug traffickers on the high seas. The Defense Department fulfilled its statutory responsibility by deploying ships to support Coast Guard counter-narcotics operations. Among them was the USS *Cohoon,* aboard which then-Lieutenant Rove earned his first LEDET assignment following extensive training in close-quarters combat, precision marksmanship, and vertical insertion techniques.

Rove's first success had resulted in the seizure of a sixty-three-foot semi-submersible vessel 360 miles southwest of Nicaragua. Two smallboats had been launched to intercept the craft, where his team had surprised the crew by boarding under cover of night. In an effort to shake the boarding team, the smugglers had attempted to scuttle the vessel by opening sea cocks, but eventually surrendered contraband amounting to eight tons of cocaine. The same year in the Eastern Pacific Ocean, Rove utilized an MQ-8 Fire Scout—an unmanned autonomous helicopter used for reconnaissance and precision targeting—to interdict a cigarette boat carrying over five hundred kilos of cocaine. After gathering video evidence of a rendezvous with a refueling vessel, Rove's team detained the go-fast boat and further discovered munitions and robotic spy technologies belonging to the U.S. military. Ensuing interrogations furnished evidence used to indict a mole at Marine Corps Logistics Base Albany, along with two other infiltrators, who had been supplying equipment to a drug syndicate.

Following his promotion, Rove had deployed as a LEDET aboard multiple foreign vessels, including the HNLMS *Onbevreesd* of the Royal Netherlands Navy. There he'd conducted operations in the Gulf of Aden as part of Combined Task Force 151, an international naval coalition established to fight piracy and terrorism in shipping lanes off the Somali coast. Rove had led the first capture of a pirate mother ship. Accompanied by a Scout Sniper Platoon, his LEDETs had boarded a dhow in response to a distress signal originating from a French yacht, one that had been picked up by a local U.S. Navy helicopter. They apprehended over thirty pirates, confiscating dozens of assault rifles and rocket-propelled grenade launchers—but only after a shrapnel blast had ripped through the lateen sails, torn his back open, and killed his two youngest soldiers.

Rove had spent four months in rehabilitation at a naval hospital in Bahrain before his transfer to Bethesda. When his doctors had deemed him incapable of a swift recovery, despite his furious appeals to resume service as a LEDET, he took station at the Navy's Meteorological and Oceanographic Command at Stennis Space Center in Hancock County, Mississippi. A sonar research lab utilized his expertise to crack underwater acoustic transmissions mimicking mammalian and other marine vocalizations. To add insult to injury, they had knocked him up a pay grade.

Fully recovered three years after the shrapnel injury, he was asked to accompany a team of combat weathermen through Operation Brother Vigil, an effort to locate and detain a suspected narco-submarine off the coast of Guatemala. Rove was tasked with training the squadron to discern disguised human signals from naturally occurring signals, advising soldiers on the production and propagation of cetacean sounds. The sub was found with several tons of cocaine and 178 illegal migrants on board. The mission proved to Rove not only how much he missed the sun, but what value his training could offer service weathermen. Aware of his likely confinement to the laboratory otherwise, he discharged from the Coast Guard, forfeiting rank and pay to become an Air Force Special Operations Weather Technician (SOWT). Earning his crest and pewter beret at Pope Air Force Base in North Carolina after sixty-one weeks of training, he'd been stationed at Hurlburt Field as a member of the 10th Combat Weather Squadron.

Rove's military career had ended in the nineties with a full medical discharge after he'd been captured and tortured in a Colombian cocaine plant. "You wouldn't fire a missile without fins or a guidance system, would you?" his doctors had said. "Your first recovery was miraculous. Now you've been seriously injured a second time. You have to accept it. You won't be a full-up round again." Soon after he returned home, his mother died of a stroke. He rented out her suburban apartment and bought supplies to build a new home, feeling the physical activity would help him heal.

The home would be on the beach in Mazatlán, Mexico. Construction had taken four months. Though hardly bigger than a shanty, it could have withstood a hurricane when he finished it. During summers, the home became a part-time fishing and dive shop. He offered scuba lessons and maintained a small stock of gear for sale. After six years he bought a small catamaran. He sailed alone, riding in waves as high as fifteen feet—or drifting between two islands off the coast. He'd often bring a bottle from his collection of mezcal to sip by sunset.

"Para todo mal, mezcal, y para todo bien también," a friend at a local liquor store had always said: For everything bad, mezcal, and for everything good, too.

He spent most evenings watching an orange sun give way to a drape of cobalt. Shaped like pearls on a neckline, new lights would come alive throughout the bay and stretch south to El Faro, the city's lighthouse of the late 1800s. He would often stroll along the beach there. Some nights he'd join the crowds watching divers leap from a high tower into violent waters. Waves raged against rocks below, and riptides threatened to claim any amateur who mistimed a plunge.

One evening, as he had waited for the divers to arrive, he had observed a group of inebriated teens mingling with a crowd gathering for the show. He had watched as a local bon vivant approached and schmoozed with the girls, offering to drive them around the city on a barhopping spree. The party boy had led the girls to the other side of the bay while Rove tailed them. Joined by three friends, the man had shepherded the girls to a dock, where a speedboat awaited their arrival. Before they could make a getaway, the girls' impromptu guardian had lunged from the shadows. Soon the traffickers had lain comatose on the planks.

The father of one of the girls was a wealthy banker, who had asked to compensate Rove with a blank check in return for having saved his daughter. Rove had declined; he had all he needed to enjoy a retirement spent sailing and diving. But the father had insisted on remuneration. "Have you explored the Great Barrier Reef?" the man had asked. "How about Bonaire? The Grand Cayman? Mr. Rove, I'm sending you on a world cruise, and I'm booking the penthouse. Don't argue. The decision is made. The ticket is in your name and your name only. Use it or not—that's your choice."

Rove had researched the cruise ship, which according to brochures offered a "symphony of lavishness and sublime comfort." The dolphin-nosed *Pearl Enchantress* was the grand crown of Pearl Voyages, a cruise line internationally acclaimed for exceptional quality and culinary delicacy. The ship had received highest accolades by readers of *Condé Nast Traveler* and other magazines as a haven of serenity. Pearl's company attracted award-winning stage talent, gourmet chefs, virtuosic musicians, and a host of capable engineers responsible for maintaining functionality across a spectrum of modern technology. Rove had regarded the touted extravagance with disinterest, if not a sad patience. But the itinerary had included a number of colorful dive locales, which had been enough to sell him on the cruise.

Rove looked up at the behemoth of a ship and began estimating its mass and displacement tonnage. How many kilograms of opulence did it take to make these people happy? Luxury was as foreign to him as it was inessential, and he wondered if the look of belonging aboard a vessel like this would ever come. He'd never risen to warm slippers and foamy baths. His mornings had more often opened with gunfire and centipedes. An eighty-pound backpack was more familiar to him than a tuxedo, a soldier's stridence more comfortable than a butler's genteel courtesy. In Rove's mind, luxury entailed an abdication of the very responsibility that had kept him alive. His instincts rejected it.

He feared he'd grow restless during the first weeks of cruising. If he did, he could always abandon ship and fly home, he thought. Spas and massages, champagne fountains, tanning decks, scented steam baths, and infinity pools did little to excite him. Still, he walked the gangway with buoyancy in his stride, if only for the dive tour.

An attractive blonde greeted him at the ship's entrance.

"Welcome aboard!" she said. "May I see your cruise pass?" He handed her a gold, wallet-sized card, one that had been given to him inside a thin metallic box imprinted with the Pearl logo. "This will be your door key, charge card, shore identification, and overall handy friend throughout your cruise. Don't lose it! Now please look into the camera. Every passenger gets a picture. Perfect. Now, smile . . . Mr. Rove, we're thrilled to have you aboard. Enjoy your one hundred twenty-five days of escape."

"Thanks," Rove said. "Which way to my quarters?"

"May I see your pass again, please?"

He showed her the card. His weathered look didn't fit the usual profile of a penthouse guest. Her politeness turned to genuine interest. "Forward end of deck fifteen," she said. "You have yourself an excellent stay, Mr. Rove."

The entrance hall fed into a piazza-style grand atrium. Two cherry-carpeted staircases climbed in half-spirals around a central waterfall, cascades gushed in alcoves around the room, and lights that waxed and waned on the ceiling created a starry effect. A string quartet filled the ship's spacious centerpiece with Pachelbel, whose repetitious Canon clashed against jazz chords emanating from a distant lounge. Painters displayed their works on the second of the atrium's three levels, their easels and wall mountings lighted for viewing. Passengers greeted one another in the gathering area, taking drinks and hors d'oeuvres from waiters ambling with trays.

"Foie gras mousse with quince marmalade *en croûton*?"

The French words did nothing to hide a Scandinavian inflection.

Rove took in the assailing presence of the waiter. The man was a bulging tuxedo; Rove had to tilt his head back to see the malicious blue circles that were his eyes, and the sardonic line for a mouth that looked incapable of breaking its horizontal. The square of his face was almost geometrically precise, his blond hair drawn in a ponytail. The server's body looked fit to wrestle any beast in the Serengeti.

He carried a tray of canapés in one hand. There was a diamond ring flashing on his other hand. Rove watched as the man's fingers, moving nimbly and without conscious direction, made the ring vanish from one finger and reappear on another.

"You'll have to forgive my impoverished gastronomical heritage and deliver that in my native tongue," Rove said.

The server's mouth remained flat.

"Duck liver on bread," he said.

Rove detected an air of condescension.

"I'll take two."

The server looked down in a half-nod. His fingers began playing with the ring faster, almost twitching.

"Pretty piece of jewelry you have. You practice sleight of hand?"

"A small hobby. Have a nice evening."

Biting into a savory topping, Rove nodded.

He climbed the aft staircase and passed a library, eyeballing the interior chocolate suede walls and wine-red upholstery. Next to catch his notice was an expansive Dolby-equipped Hollywood Theater, set near a Mediterranean bistro and card lounge occupied by eight bridge players sweltering in the heat of concentration. He climbed higher still and emerged on the open lido deck, where the buffet of the Century Oasis restaurant, as much a feast for the imagination as the gullet, exerted an inescapable pull on him. Chefs displayed an international assortment of steaming entrees, desserts, and carved fruits. Avian ice sculptures spread their wings over garnished dishes and vegetable figurines crafted from Arcimboldian inspiration. Rove sampled a dish of mango with raspberry sauce as he made his way outside to resume his inspection of the ship. Habit demanded he locate the gym. He found the workout room on the forward end beyond two main pool areas, the Seahorse Lagoon and Neptune's Sanctuary. A brief look at the facilities proved them ample.

He dropped down a deck to find his room. The hallways reminded him of those on aircraft carriers: Four lines converging on a single point gave the illusion of infinite length. As he walked toward the forward end, the hum of revolving laundry emanated from a "Crew Only" sector, as did snippets of conversations in Tagalog.

Letters on a mailbox beside a white wooden door read, *Clifford Pearl Presidential Penthouse*. He inserted the keycard and removed it. A light flashed green. The latch clicked.

Shielding himself from a chandelier bursting with refracted light, he proceeded with soft feet so as not to disturb the sheen of the rug. Wall sconces, shaped like bow maidens of warships, clutched candles in the vestibule and welcomed him with visions of conquest. Gowns billowed on the feminine figures, matching the satin drapes that framed a blue panorama. There were rays of sunlight streaming through the windows and beveled mirrors on opposing walls that extended the cabin's perceived space.

Rove opened a sliding closet, and chuckled. Inside were three plush Frette robes and accompanying silk kimonos. Just what he needed. He visited the bathroom; from a steaming whirlpool tub, he could soon lie back and enjoy the moving azure seascape. Egyptian cotton bath towels dangled from a golden bar. Furnishing the main bedroom were maritime tokens, including shadow boxes of sailor's knots and antique compasses. A tablet engraved with names of former *Pearl Enchantress* captains rested above a model helm.

Above the king bed hung a portrait of a man in uniform, an officer with one hand at his sword's scabbard and the other on his vessel's wheel. His baldness was offset by a tapered beard. Medallions decorated his outfit alongside a sash, while scarlet epaulets confirmed his rank as highest in the cruise fleet. Rove admired the dignity of the painting's subject, noting a resemblance to the infamous Captain Bligh. A plaque beneath the portrait read, *Clifford Pearl, Founder of the Intercontinental Line.*

Rove lay across the bed, staring up at the white ceiling. Strange as it felt, luxury was his.

A rap at the door roused him.

He squinted through the peephole and saw an elderly man standing outside, a pair of horn-rimmed spectacles perched low on his nose. Age had worn traces of kindness into the crevices of his face. His head was encased in sterling hair. A tailored three-piece suit gave him a spry look and accentuated a chest that was permanently inflated like a puffin's. His sleeves tapered to white gloves and hung at his side, his right cuff scraping the chain of a pocket watch.

Rove opened the door and took an instant liking to the stranger.

"*Bonjour,* Monsieur Rove!" the man said, his voice somewhere in the registers of a didgeridoo. "*Hola, y bienvenido a la magnífica* Pearl Enchantress. *Ni hao.* My name is Lachlan Fawkes, and I will be your faithful, devoted steward for the next hundred and twenty-five days. I have come to make my . . . *gran introducción.*"

The man bowed at the waist, holding his left arm bent and tracing circles in front of his upper torso with his right. The sight of this spritely old man put a smile on Rove's face.

"Pleasure to meet you, Mr. Fawkes. Word on the street is the United Nations still hires translators."

"Every day a new surprise, mate. Call me Lachlan. The pleasure's all mine, and I'm honored to serve you on this most *tremendous* voyage. I've brought up your luggage on my petite dolly." He gestured grandly, imitating a pontifical French accent. Then he dropped the accent and staged a deadpan. "Which, I must say, was almost too heavy for me to even hoist onto this bloody hauler. You must be taking your whole damned mansion with you."

"Close," Rove said. "Scuba gear."

"Ever heard of equipment rentals?"

"I prefer my own."

"Ding-a-ling!" crooned the man. "Folks, we've got a curious case on our hands. Brings his own diving gear to save a little moolah, blows it all on the penthouse. I smell a puzzle"—he winked playfully—"or a dotty bloke indeed."

"I'm riding courtesy of a friend."

"If only my friends were as generous as yours."

"We didn't know each other long."

"What did you do? Ransom his kid?"

"Something like that."

The old man whistled. "Really, now? This cruise turns out to be more than I bargained for." Fawkes captured the air of performing before a rolling movie camera, yet Rove appreciated the sincerity of his warmth. "Where do you hail from?"

"Sometimes Texas, sometimes Mexico." He paused, looking over his steward from head to toe. "And despite your near-perfect accent, you are certainly no Frenchman. I'm guessing you're from Down Under."

"Aussie all the way," Fawkes said. He turned sly. "A tasty slice of the Outback, say the sheilas."

"Wouldn't doubt it. Before boarding, I didn't realize I'd have a butler."

"*Steward,* good friend. I abhor the other term."

"Pardon me."

"No worries, mate. There's plenty of us onboard, but only the high rollers get their own *personal* steward. It's not a one-to-one ratio for everyone, you see. So love me while you got me." Fawkes placed a hand on the dolly. "I'm on call for you twenty-four-seven. My quarters are right beside yours. If you need me, all you have to do is press the button on your phone or knock at my door, and your wish is my command. Or just bloody bang on the wall. I'll hear you. Before anything else, let me unload your baggage."

"I can do it," Rove said.

"Hands off. They have to pay me for something." With little strain, Fawkes hoisted Rove's suitcases upright and rolled them into the cabin. "Might I interest you in a creamy Kahlúa cocktail?"

"Perhaps in a bit."

"A punchy Kahlúa cocktail?"

"No Kahlúa for now. Thanks."

"Tequila then? Or just plain ol' Adam's ale?"

"Appreciated, just not thirsty yet." Few people made Rove as curious as his new steward, and even fewer so immediately. "How long have you worked for Pearl Voyages?" Rove asked him.

Fawkes pursed his lips. "Since the start of the company."

"You must know the founder."

"Knew him before he became a maritime icon. Cliffy and I go back. The nice thing about knowing a bloke before he makes it big: You still get to use his cute old nickname."

That was interesting, Rove thought. He was vaguely familiar with the line's beginnings. Pearl Voyages had formed during a time of consolidation in the shipping industry, by a man reputed as a ruthless opportunist with unusual devices. Biographies indicated Clifford Pearl had kept a Rolodex full of private investigators he employed to blackmail competitors. Lawsuits had been filed against him in the sixties; allegedly, he would gather destructive corporate evidence and tip select investment banks to short-sell stock. Cases were either dismissed or settled quietly.

"What did you do before stewarding?" Rove asked.

"Oh, I worked all sorts of odd jobs in my youth, from packing meat to tarring roofs to conducting locomotives. You could say I was a nomad. After moving to the States, I settled. No more drifting. Met Cliffy in Manhattan. He was the president of Wilkenson and Company, an old transporter of petrochemicals."

"I've heard of them."

"Bet you have. In sixty-four Cliffy bought three competing businesses and turned them into Pearl Voyages. The line put its first ship, the *Prince Toreador*, into service within two years. Looked more like a tugboat or a dinky yacht if you ask me. He needed workers to clean it up. With enough elbow grease shed by yours truly under a burning sun, we turned that woeful, barnacle-skinned bath-duck into a love boat for the starry-eyed."

Rove wondered how well the steward had known Pearl, and how much truth there was to his reputation. He felt it would have been rude to ask.

"And soon he had a small navy to his name," Rove said.

"Oh, yes. The line's capacity doubled with the addition of the *Savoir Swift*. By 1972 the Pearl fleet held the second and third largest passenger vessels afloat, among a total of six ships."

"Impressive. Did you ever captain any of them?"

"Me? Heavens, no! I had no sailing experience and wasn't about to learn. But I could clean up hell's pits and make 'em glisten. I was the handyman, the waiter, the brass-shiner, whatever he needed. That's how I made a quid."

"And here you are, steward of the presidential suite."

"Penthouse, my friend. Cliffy was always good to me. His blood's worth bottling, that man. He could have left me to sneeze in the dust, but he kept me under his payroll. Otherwise . . ." Fawkes clapped his hands loudly. "I'd not have had a brass razoo! But there I go again, getting all windy about myself. I should write a book, *Memoirs of a Deck Swab*."

"A well-dressed deck swab, I'd add. I'll look for your memoir when it hits the shelves."

"Let's have your story then, mate. Retired, by the looks of you?"

"A former Coast Guard LEDET and Air Force combat weatherman."

"Ah! Rambo the news forecaster, I picture."

"Not for news," Rove said. "For air and ground forces."

Tactical observers known as Special Operations Weather Technicians deployed into hostile and denied territories to gather and assess meteorological data. Trained in combat, these Battlefield Airmen were among the military's most highly skilled warfighters. Their analysis and forecasts were provided in support of counter-terrorism, short-duration strikes, search and rescue, reconnaissance, foreign internal defense, and humanitarian aid. They were experts in land navigation, overland travel, and surface water operations employing amphibious techniques. They were trained in snowmobiling, precision parachuting, motorcycling, rappelling, and fast-rope procedures—all ways to penetrate hostile territories to collect upper air, snow, ocean, river, and terrain intelligence used in mission planning and route forecasting.

"Never heard of such a thing, anyhow," Fawkes said.

"Most civilians haven't, but we've been around since World War Two."

The Air Force had deployed special operations weathermen in the European Theater of Operations at Normandy Beach, and earlier in the China-Burma-India Theater against the Japanese. In 1966 the 10th Weather Squadron began operating at Udorn Royal Thai Air Force Base, instructing native meteorologists and establishing covert weather observation networks. Their presence proved vital to Operation Ivory Coast, an albeit failed effort to rescue sixty-one American POWs from the Son Tay prison camp near Hanoi. The squadron also positioned along the Ho Chi Minh trail in support of strafing missions against Viet Cong guerrillas and North Vietnamese Army soldiers using those jungle paths. Since the U.S. invasion of Grenada, combat weathermen would directly partake in most modern special operations worldwide.

"Suppose I should mind my own bizzo," Fawkes said, "but I reckon you've a wealth of stories to share. Forgive me if I pester you about them." He adjusted his spectacles, reached into his breast pocket, and brandished an envelope with Rove's name inscribed in ornamental cursive. "Almost forgot. A delivery for you."

Rove broke the seal and removed a folded piece of paper bearing a handwritten message:

Major Rove,

It is our great honor to welcome you to the Pearl Enchantress. *We trust your journey aboard the fleet's prized ship will be filled with adventure and relaxation. As a presidential passenger, you have access to all elite amenities and services. A personal steward has been assigned to fulfill your round-the-clock needs.*

It's with pleasure that I invite you for a private tour of the bridge tomorrow evening, followed by dinner with me and my First Officer, Trevor Kent. Il Ristorante Della Maschera Veneziana has never been known to disappoint. Guests are welcome. If you accept, please meet by the deck fourteen elevators, forward end, at seven o' clock. A bridge hand will escort you to the ship's command center. We hope we can count on your visit.

Sincerely,
Captain Giacomo Selvaggio

"Exciting, isn't it?" Fawkes said. "Traditionally, the invitation goes to the guests of the penthouse."

"I've always wanted to see the bridge of one of these mammoths," Rove said.

Fawkes cleared his throat, a twinkle leaping to his eye. "If you don't mind, mate. You seem to be traveling alone, and the letter does specify guests are welcome."

"Who did you have in mind?"

"You could bring me along."

The request seemed brazen, though he saw no reason to refuse.

"I'd be surprised if you found it interesting, Lachlan. You've been with the company so long, you've probably seen the bridge countless times."

"Ha! But it's been ages since my last lobster in the Venetian Mask restaurant. And I'll bet you ten to one it's on the menu. We stewards dine from a different galley. A bodgy one. We don't always get a fair crack of the whip, and I'm fed up to the back teeth with our chow. If I've known Chef Piero Greco for a day, lobster would be quite a treat."

Rove didn't mind at all. "I'll inform the captain that my steward will be my guest."

"*Prego,*" Fawkes said. "I'm delighted. Can't wait to sink my teeth into that succulent sea critter. Now, let's see. I was off to fetch you a creamy Kahlúa cocktail, wasn't I? Excuse me. Better skedaddle."

The furniture shuddered. Decks below, doors clanged shut as more rumbles emanated from the engine room.

A team of dock hands cast off the mooring lines, and the *Pearl Enchantress* drifted from its berth. A horn shook the marina, sending flocks of gulls into a squawking tizzy. Echoes of the blare ricocheted between piers while bystanders on land waved from afar, bidding the travelers bon voyage. Two labored brays followed the initial horn blast. The floating city began a slow sail toward the harbor's edge.

"We're off!" Fawkes shouted. "Underway—shift colors!"

FIVE

Austin doused himself with cold water. He'd found rest elusive during the first half of the night. Morning found him battling a cloak of grogginess that took more than a yawn and a stretch to shake. He had promised himself he wouldn't lose any sleep over Clare's offer—a promise he found exceedingly difficult to keep. A desire to doze off followed him through his morning classes. He sat in the back of the auditoriums in case fatigue got the best of him.

At lunchtime he found Ichiro Yamada and Rachel Mason sharing lunch at Stanford's largest cafeteria at Wilbur Hall. He joined them in their chat about upcoming sports games and soon felt his weariness lifting. During the autumn quarter, Stanford and Berkeley's football teams would fight their most fierce battle in the Big Game, the annual culmination of rivalry between the two schools. Anticipation abounded, as this year's clash would take place on Stanford turf, or "the Farm," as the campus was nicknamed. The feud between Stanford and Cal Berkeley went back as far as 1892, when Stanford won the first game 14 to 10 under the management of President Herbert Hoover.

Big Game Week was imminent. Excitement and rancor fermented, leading to a climax that would determine who celebrated and who languished. Stanford marked the week with an all-school pep rally, a bawdy theater performance called *Gaieties,* a reading called the "Bearial at the Claw" of macabre wishes against Cal's mascot, Oskie the Bear, and gleeful irreverence designed to inject venom into the hearts of participants. For Rachel and Ichiro, it was the most exciting week of the quarter.

Earlier that year, Stanford had achieved victory against the University of Southern California in a remarkable upset. Austin had been coming home from San Francisco at the time. He'd spent the day in the city participating in the university's notorious team-based scavenger hunt. On the returning Caltrain ride he'd received regular updates from a Trojan friend who was watching the game live at the Coliseum. The messages, initially bombastic, took on a sour tone by half-time. In the fourth quarter, they continued to deflate into despondency and, after the final pass, anguish.

Despite jubilation at the Farm over the recent upset, the most meaningful challenge still loomed. The Cardinal had trounced a daunting opponent, but no archrival. The Big Game's victor remained yet undetermined. Losing to Berkeley meant losing the Axe, a symbolic trophy dating to the late 1800s. The Axe was awarded each year to the winning team—that is, unless someone stole it.

This had happened multiple times; one heist was famous. Leery Berkeley authorities had fortified defenses, stowing the Axe in a bank vault and guarding it in an armored vehicle for appearances during rallies. On April 3, 1930, soon after a spring rally at Cal's Greek Theater, four Cardinals posing as Berkeley photographers had bombarded Norm Horner, the grand custodian of the Axe, with camera flashes. Mayhem had ensued. The "photographers" seized the trophy while other Cardinals in disguise hurled a smoke bomb into the heart of the chaos. The thieves sprinted toward one of several cars waiting to whiz off in random directions. Stanford's charlatans had caused further delays by organizing false search parties pursuing decoys. Though some of the Cardinals were found out, the plan had succeeded. Stanford's twenty-one conspirators, later known there as the "Immortal 21"—or the "Immoral 21" at Cal—had reclaimed the Axe.

Generations after the heist, the rivals prepared to face off again.

"So," Rachel said. "Game day plans?"

"Sure," Ichiro said. "Win."

"And if we don't?"

"I don't waste brain space on irrelevant hypotheticals."

"Pretty cocky given the strength of Cal's team. You willing to bet?"

"You'll bet *against* the Cardinal?"

"I'll take an insurance policy in case we lose."

"Austin, what do you make of this? Rachel seems to have little faith in our team." He looked lost in thought. Ichiro nudged him. "Hey, space cadet, back me on this or you'll owe me a rib-eye."

"Careful, Rachel," Austin said. "When it comes to games and betting, you'd be surprised what Itchy's capable of."

"You guys seriously need to come up with a new nickname."

Ichiro, Austin's roommate, was a second-year doctoral student in mathematics and a competitive programmer. Like Austin and Rachel, he had completed his undergraduate studies at Stanford. His education had been fully funded through a scholarship afforded him by a Japanese electronics company. While he was a senior in high school, the company had awarded him the gold medal in its annual game coding competition. Throughout his academic career, Ichiro had earned a number of other honors. In the world finals of the ACM International Collegiate Programming Contest, he had earned nineteenth and fifteenth place in consecutive years, following second and first place in the Pacific Northwest regionals. His team had earned honorable mention in the William Lowell Putnam Mathematical Competition, placing fifth. He had earned silver and gold medals in the International Olympiad in Informatics, placing seventh and second. He also participated in a number of Internet coding and problem solving contests, and coached teams back at home.

He thrived on strategy games. His dissertation research would examine multiple interfaces between computer science and game theory. The past two years, he had worked as a teacher's assistant in Programming Abstractions, an introductory course in the Computer Science Department. Students tried hard to be assigned to his section. He wasn't sure if it was his funny accent, Hawaiian shirts, or admittedly lax grading style. His undergrads sometimes joined him on Friday afternoons to play bughouse chess, a variant with double boards and four players; captured pieces could be placed on a teammate's board, and the game ended at the first checkmate. He was never good enough to compete formally, but the mental sport fascinated him. It was fast, chaotic, unpredictable, aggressive, and the tides could turn with a single placement.

Ichiro and Austin had met as sophomores in a project-based class designed for collaboration among computer science, physics, and aeronautics students. There they created computerized aircraft models, which they flight-tested using simulation software built from scratch. When their third team member dropped the class, the two were forced to pull a series of all-nighters at the lab, trading shifts napping in sleeping bags to meet deadlines. Their friendship had grown out of mutual dedication to the project. They'd often celebrate milestones at The Counter, a design-your-own burger joint on California Avenue. It was there they had discovered something else in common— carnivorous palates. Henceforth they traded favors using the promise of steaks as currency. Denominations varied according to tenderness and flavor. One or the other would often find the word "YOMAR" written in his lab book: *You owe me a rib-eye*.

Also a second-year grad student, Rachel had been one of Ichiro's closest friends since they were undergraduates. The two remained inseparable, though she and Ichiro were made of altogether different stuff. Rachel had been an English major, expending most of her energy on creative journalism. Her cheeky, nuanced column for the *Stanford Chronicle,* "Muse Me," had made her famous among humanities students, as each week she'd offer reviews of philharmonic performances, theatrical productions, and art exhibitions in San Francisco. Ichiro had sought her out as a freshman in response to her blurb in the *Chronicle* advertising services as a "proofreader for engineers and other English-challenged students." He had needed help with an essay for a required writing course. He remembered two things about his first encounter with her. First, her candor—"Your words really jump off the page, perhaps to escape torture"—and second, the way she made him want to come back with new essays that might actually impress her.

"If you could learn to profit from your mistakes," she'd said of his second attempt, "you'd be a rich man."

Their banter was usually fueled by the division between brain hemispheres. The majority of disputes were contests in the merits of logic and science versus language and creativity. Without mathematics, he would argue, man could not have engineered civilization. She would say that it wasn't for lack of math that the Tower of Babel fell.

"Typical fuzzy logic," he once said, "citing fiction to promote fiction."

"And what would life be without stories and art to ignite the soul?" she'd retorted. "How else could you fathom the depths of your own humanity?"

"The deepest part of me is my belly button."

"Then good luck trying to ever fathom the depths of a female."

Equations were Ichiro's fascinations; people were hers. She took another's shyness as a challenge, a challenge to open a person and learn what was inside. She had a gift for earning trust. She also spoke her mind with little filter, and her brazenness could make Ichiro uncomfortable. If ever he seemed timid or anxious, she took outright pleasure in making him confront his nerves. She had even been known to push Austin's envelope at times.

Now she was looking at Ichiro, who seemed to be reading her thoughts.

"Austin, you're in another world," she said, turning to face him. "Care to invite us?"

"Sorry, guys," he said, coming into focus. "Just thinking through a puzzle."

"Is it Professor Clare? Did he give you an assignment right after the exam?"

"In a way."

"Only he would do that."

"The stories you tell," Ichiro said. "Strange bird, that man."

"But the best professor I've had," Austin said. "And the clearest, until now."

By the time lunch ended, he felt rejuvenated, his mind at least temporarily relieved. But, as he'd expected, when he left his friends, nagging questions edged back into his thoughts.

The uncertainty was too great. Before he could decide, he had to talk to Malcolm Clare one more time.

A ustin arrived at his aeronautics class early and chose a seat at the front. Clare never entered. Instead, a lanky grad student, arms poking out from an oversized sport coat, took center stage in Hewlett Auditorium.

He paced without direction, appearing to shrink into corners as the students entered and chattered away, paying no attention to him, his presence as unassailably awe-inspiring as the flakes of chalk dusting the floor.

He cleared his throat. No one heard him. He held up a hand, whistled, and waved, swelling his body to fill the space, and failing. Capturing the attention of perhaps ten percent of his audience, he began speaking.

"Hi, class." He backed against the whiteboard. "My name's . . ." Voices died throughout the room. Austin watched in pain, half-expecting him to pronounce the words Ichabod Crane. "I'm Walter . . . Rosekind. As you know, I'm one of the TAs for this class." His voice cracked, and he hesitated to regain it, cowering under the collective glare of the class. "Yesterday, I received an email from Dr. Clare informing me of an unanticipated and extended research leave. He didn't say where he was going or when he'd return. He asked that I instruct the class until . . . further notice."

For the most part, the students showed little surprise. The call for a substitute might have generated curiosity if it were any other professor, but Clare was impossible to predict, last-minute disappearances not beyond him. A few students looked disappointed, but they took the news at face value—except Austin, who realized the departure didn't jibe with yesterday's conversation.

"Let's begin. Forgive me: Where'd we leave off?" A student raised her hand and filled him in. "Okay. Thanks. Let's . . . ah, let's go back to the subject of torque." He began scribbling on the whiteboard.

When class ended, Austin approached the front of the room.

"Thank you for subbing," he said. "Must have felt like standing in for a rock star."

"Hope everything was clear," answered Rosekind.

"Yes, it was," Austin assured him. "Listen, Walter, I need to ask you something. What did Professor Clare say in his email to you?"

The TA frowned. "I told you. He said he was leaving for research purposes. Nothing beyond that."

"Any mention of his destination? Do we know if he's still in California?"

"No. I don't know anything. All the TAs are baffled. Professors shouldn't jump ship like this."

"Clare's an eccentric with a lot of irons in the fire. I'm curious if he left any clue as to which of his projects pulled him away."

"Zilch," Rosekind said.

"What was the tone of his email? Did it sound urgent?"

"Not really. His message was plain. Matter-of-fact."

"Did he sound like himself?"

The grad scratched his forehead. "Uh, we don't communicate by email very often."

"How do you usually talk?"

"By phone or in person."

"Give it your best shot. Based on your communication with him, did he sound normal?"

Rosekind shrugged. "Sort of. His statements were straightforward. Reading between the lines, I got the feeling . . . yeah, things seemed normal." He then huffed, "But burdening a TA with an advanced class is not acceptable. I'm going to talk to the Provost."

"Be careful."

Austin felt his stomach sinking. Clare had told Austin he would hold nighttime office hours all week.

"Careful about what?"

"I'm not sure, but I have a feeling it might be better for you to let this rest for now, and keep teaching as normal."

"You can't be serious," Rosekind said. "He can't just, without warning, saddle me with part-time professorship or extended subbing or whatever you want to call it. He's placed the class on my shoulders. It's not reasonable."

Austin agreed, but in light of the dangers Clare had alluded to, it would probably be best if this episode stayed as quiet as possible. "I understand your frustration, but you might not want to make a big scene."

"Why not?"

"I have a feeling that whatever Clare's up to, it's worthwhile."

Recognition leapt into Rosekind's speckled face. "You're the guy who almost got a hundred on the midterm. What did he want to talk to you about yesterday?"

"I'm afraid that's between us."

"Figured you'd say that. Come on, I'd like to learn Dr. Clare's whereabouts as much as you would."

Austin concealed his growing impatience. "He wanted to congratulate me, and ask if I might help as a research assistant. One more question for you. When did you receive his email?"

"I don't know. Recently."

"What time exactly?"

"Who are you, the Grand Inquisitor?"

"Hey, we're on the same side here."

"I don't have to answer to you. It's none of your business." Feeling the heat of the fire he'd kindled, Austin inched back a few steps. His retreat seemed to achieve its desired effect. Rosekind sighed. "Well, I suppose it couldn't hurt." He opened his laptop to check his inbox. "If you must know, I got the email at six fifty-five p.m. yesterday."

Austin flushed scarlet. At 6:55 p.m., he had been sitting across from Malcolm Clare. The professor hadn't used his laptop to send any emails during their conversation.

"Thanks for your help," he said.

Austin slung his backpack over a shoulder and left the building.

Unlocking his bike, he raced east along Serra Mall, the street running perpendicular to the picturesque Palm Drive. He dialed his roommate as he pedaled. Ichiro answered after a few rings.

"Hey. You sound out of breath."

"I'm biking," Austin said. "Itchy, quick question. Did you know Malcolm Clare has a daughter?"

Ichiro burst out laughing. "You may be obsessed with the hard to get, but, my friend, some are downright unattainable."

"So you know her."

"Sure. We're in the same math program. She's in my differential geometry class and kind of hard to miss. Apparently you think so, too."

"I'm not looking for a date. I've never met her."

"Uh-huh," Ichiro said with a purr. "Victoria Clare's a knockout."

"I have a favor to ask."

"You sound frazzled. What's up, roomie?"

"Do you know anything about her schedule?"

"Ah, so Casanova *is* looking for a date!" Ichiro needled. "Helpful hint: Stalking won't get you any warm and fuzzies."

"Before yesterday, I didn't even know the girl existed," Austin said. "Help me out."

Ichiro heaved a sigh. "Sorry to disappoint. We only have one class together, which she seems to be doing exceedingly well in. That's all I know of her schedule. She probably has plenty of secret admirers you could ask for a play-by-play of her routine. I'm not your man. Although I did just see the ice queen in question at the Axe and Palm five minutes ago."

Austin pedaled faster, steering south around the history corner.

"Austin, I don't know what you're after, but be careful with this one. She's kind of a loner, has a reputation for being an antisocial bookworm. My feeling is she has a massive superiority complex, and from what I hear, no interest in playing the field. If it seems at all like you're coming on to her . . ."

A dial tone interrupted his admonition.

"Suit yourself," Ichiro said.

SIX

The Axe and Palm was the closest thing Stanford had to a burger joint. Austin surveyed the room. Most students were congregated around tall tables, chatting, nibbling, waiting for food. He ordered a dish of crepes and scanned the crowd for Clare's daughter, spotting the most likely contender sipping a smoothie.

She sat alone at the counter, and looked to be about twenty-three. Shiny aviators left her eyes to Austin's imagination as he struggled to decide whether she more closely resembled a Bouguereau portrait or a creature from the untamed tropics. Panting from his bike ride, he studied the planes of her face. They were soft and still, gilded by past summers and tanned to a burnished glow. Her lips were restful, sphinx-like, perhaps even stubborn. A jacket of black Italian lambskin was zipped over the curve of her chest. Its color matched the obsidian of her hair, which was full and draped in layers over a straight shoulder line. White linen slacks concealed her legs, which Austin envisioned as long and firm and copper-colored.

He admired her conservative, self-styled brand of chic. Days ago he hadn't known this prodigy existed, let alone as the daughter of an aeronautics legend. Gathering his composure, he pulled out a chair beside her.

"This seat taken?"

She took an unhurried sip, contemplating the question without comment. Nor did she glance at him, apparently preferring to receive strangers by sound of voice.

She replied at last. "It is now."

Austin detected a subtle whiff of perfume, clean and oceanic, and resisted the temptation to lean closer.

"My name is Austin Hardy. I'm a student in your father's class."

"Victoria Clare. Apparently you knew that."

"Not until yesterday. Your dad mentioned you. But . . . no one has seen him today." He expected her to say something. She didn't. A waitress delivered his crepes. He tasted a spoonful of sliced bananas smeared in melted chocolate. "Any idea why?"

"No."

She sounded American, though he detected hints of her father's posh British intonation.

"I realize I'm a stranger to you. But I've come to alert you to something potentially worrisome."

A gleam of amusement shone through her apparent boredom. "Oh?"

"Maybe you could answer some questions."

"Why is that?"

"You'll see why."

There wasn't a speck of curiosity in her reply.

"Shoot."

"Have you spoken to your father recently?"

"How is that relevant?"

"He didn't teach today. The TA said he'd left on a sudden research trip, but he hadn't mentioned anything to me."

"Does my father usually share his travel schedule with you?"

He tried not to let her chilliness peeve him, and wondered if there was any mirth behind the reflective aviators. "I know more than you might think, Victoria." As far as he could tell, she was an emotional desert. "Your father confided in me. He told me you and he never feel truly safe in this world."

She leaned back against her chair, but said not a word.

"Why not talk to me?"

"To answer your question, I haven't spoken with him recently."

"Did he tell you he'd be taking any research trips? Any idea where he is?"

"No."

"Does he vanish frequently?"

"He's done it before."

"Does he usually tell you first, or does he just slip away?"

"Sometimes he tells me. Sometimes not." She sighed in reproach. "Mr. Hardy, I wonder why you sat down."

"Hang with me. There's something weird I'm getting at. I was in your father's office yesterday, and I didn't leave until after seven. The TA said he received an email from him at exactly six fifty-five p.m.

Not possible. I was with him at the time. He wasn't sending emails. Strange, no?"

"No."

Her patent lack of concern staggered him.

"You're serious?"

"There are things about my father that you'll never know. His affairs are none of your concern. I know nothing about you, whether you have his best interest in mind, or whether you cooked up a sham to get laid. Excuse me. I'm busy."

"You really think that's what I'm after? God. I've never met anyone as self-absorbed in my life." She remained motionless, no evidence of surprise—no evidence of anything. He let the silence linger a moment before continuing, his tone less confrontational. "I'd like to help you, Victoria. I saw a problem and came straight to you. The least you can do is hear me out. Evidently you're not interested. If you change your mind, here's my number. If you'd rather find me in person, I live in Escondido Village. Think it over. More importantly," he paused, "try reaching your dad." He jotted his digits on a napkin and slid them to her.

He trashed his remaining crepes and mounted his bike outside. Sour thoughts consumed him as he pedaled toward his dormitory on the east side of campus. If there were a way to the professor, it would be through his daughter, but he was far from earning her trust.

He steered onto a path between the post office and the bookstore, climbed a slight hill, and coasted down around Meyer Library. A breeze calmed him, distracting him from the day's puzzle. He slipped into a dispassionate state of problem-solving.

Slowly his initial pang of dislike for Victoria dissolved into understanding. Malcolm had warned that his daughter kept to herself, that she lived under the constant threat of some unnamed danger. By the sound of it, she spoke with few people and trusted even fewer. It shouldn't have surprised him that she'd turn away an unfamiliar face. Victoria Clare had to know her looks were a powerful weapon, but for someone living under threat of some unnamed peril, attention had drawbacks. Beauty was incompatible with anonymity, and Austin figured it was anonymity she desired most.

He sighed. No wonder she'd brushed him off. Chances were he was just another drooling male, or worse, a threat to her safety. Dropping her guard could mean inviting an enemy closer.

The sun retired. Stars peeked through an indigo canopy that faded to the horizon's blue pastels.

Austin coasted along Escondido Road. Before he reached his apartment complex, he had an idea. If Dr. Clare were still around, there was one place worth checking. Austin swerved across the road, biked through a parking lot, and headed northwest.

A shortcut took him around Branner Hall, a large freshman dormitory. Named for the university's second president, John Casper Branner, the hall originally built to ease a campus housing crunch now gleamed after recent renovation, its buttery, cream-colored walls and enhanced woodwork giving the impression of historic grandeur. Outside, students played games around a birdbath centered in a magnolia-shaded courtyard.

Austin cut into a parking lot, his path feeding into a street that ran before a palatial building one might expect tucked away in the Catalonian Mountains. This was Toyon Hall, a Spanish-villa-style dorm that housed sophomores, and a smattering of juniors and seniors. Beyond the dorm's manicured lawn, an archway framed a trickling fountain in the inner court, around which winding staircases coiled up to higher levels. To Austin, Toyon's architecture had more charisma than that of any other dorm on campus.

He turned left at an intersection, heading toward the school's largest fountain, a column of water that would soon run a grisly crimson—symbolically, with Oskie's blood. Lapping water would kick up a layer of red mist through Big Game Week. Within a stone's throw, the iconic Hoover Tower, overlooking campus from soaring heights, would also glow an ominous red. In a night of tradition and lore, hundreds would soon rally at the foot of the tower before the football team waged battle for the Axe.

Beyond the fountain's circle, the street continued across from the main quad. A stretch of sandstone walls and Mission Revival architecture unfolded under the moon's glow. The courtyard inside was a serene and mystical place at night, the walls a stronghold for Stanford's spiritual sanctuary, Memorial Church. Austin admired the triangular Romanesque form of the church whenever he passed by. He often entered the quadrangle after dark to sit on the large, circular planters and marvel at the facade's mosaic. Sometimes he would lie on the grass and stargaze. Palms would stir under a gentle zephyr as he paid homage to the university's founders.

Tonight, choral echoes emanated from the sandstone archways. Sixteen tones blended as one, weaving the rumbles of the basses, the harmonies of the baritones, the melodies of the leads, and the high chimes of the tenors into rich textures. An a cappella rendition of *My Romance* resonated from a group of tuxedoed young men huddling in a circle.

A few hundred yards ahead, the sound of yet another fountain signaled that he had neared his destination. When he reached the engineering quad, Austin parked his bike in a rack, secured the frame to a metal bar, and tried the front door of the Gates building. As he had guessed, it was locked.

He trekked around the periphery, checking other doors, his mind exploring new conduits. Maintenance had secured the building. He tried the windows, most of them sealed shut. Again he circled, yanking the panes with greater force. When one pried open, he hoisted himself up and stole into a dark classroom. He cleared the window and offered his pupils time to adjust to the darkness. The halls beyond were lit. His jeans scuffed as he walked into the hallway. Distracted momentarily by his own noise, he snagged a foot on a stray chair and landed on his elbow, the pain in his arm not half the pain in his ankle. Bad time to be a klutz, he thought. When the tenderness subsided, he located the main lobby, summoned the elevator, and pushed the third-floor button.

When the doors opened, he considered removing his shoes; socks would mute the footsteps. He weighed the benefits against the risk of someone finding his abandoned footwear in the corridor. He kept them on and trod lightly. Rounding a corner, he passed a row of cubicles.

He depressed the handle to Clare's study, but it hardly budged. Everything was locked. What did he expect? He improvised by visiting the nearest cubicle and opening a drawer to find a plastic jar of desk supplies. He removed a heavy paper clip and bobby pin, unfolding the paper clip into an L-shaped tension wrench that he inserted at the bottom of the keyhole. Next he inserted the wavy side of the pin, and after minutes of raking, he fooled the lock into thinking the flimsy tool was a key.

Malcolm Clare's office was a new animal at nighttime. The model planes dangled without motion, ghostly craft in the shadows, formless but for the spectral outlines of their wings. Zeppelin silhouettes flickered under the light of a muted mini-TV showing the news.

Austin shut the door, lowered the window blinds, and flipped on the light.

When the room sprang to life, he noticed a collection of oddities. For all he knew, the television had been on for hours. The professor's briefcase lay propped against his desk; he hadn't taken it with him. A crystal flute rested on the desktop, its amber liquid tepid and deprived of fizz. Reading the label on the empty bottle next to the glass, Austin wondered why the professor would let a vintage champagne go sour. Maybe he had left in a rush.

Austin began snooping through the professor's sanctum for any indication of his whereabouts. A chrome-colored object beside the wheels of the professor's swivel chair caught his eye. Austin dropped to his knees and discovered it was Clare's cell phone.

None of it added up. If the professor had taken an extended trip, he'd have taken his phone and briefcase. Fastidiously neat, he would have also tidied his office before leaving. Austin pocketed the cell phone and began opening drawers. He found paper clips, rubber bands, a stapler, tape. In another cabinet he rummaged through envelopes, stationery, and other office supplies all neatly compartmentalized. Until reaching the last pullout, he found nothing of interest.

The bottom drawer was empty but for a thumb-sized flash drive.

He cradled the device in his palm and removed the cap to reveal a USB plug, wondering what data could be stored within its circuitry. Averse as he was to violating the professor's privacy, Austin made a mental note to explore the chip's contents at home. He capped the drive and placed it in his pocket with the phone.

He continued searching through items on the desktop. Any clue would have sufficed—a scribbled note indicating his plans, a letter, a Post-it. Clare had left not a shred of indication.

Austin resorted to leafing through folders in the professor's file cabinet. Old exams, lecture notes, and slides proved of little use. He skimmed the tabs and found nothing of relevance. Air pockets between sheets kicked up puffs of dust as he flipped through files. He battled the urge to sneeze.

A folder at the back of the drawer caught his attention. The contents were light, the file thin. The tab at the top had one word written on it: *Baldr.*

He set the folder on the desk and opened the front cover. Other folders in the drawer stored stacks of text-heavy documents. This one did not. It contained sheets of blue diagrams. The illustrations ranged in quality, some computerized and some drawn by hand with a ruler and compass.

Austin's mind churned as he studied the images. Cryptic, the drawings were poorly labeled, offering obscure combinations of scribbles, faint doodles, and computer graphics. He projected shapes onto the diagrams, dissecting the geometry and probing for patterns between angles, cross sections, and arcs. He spread out the papers, arranging them in various positions, and recognized a few schematic elements borrowed from technologies he'd studied in class. The rest was indecipherable.

Footsteps echoed in the corridor.

Instinct broke his initial paralysis, a knot twisting in his gut as he shuffled the papers and stuffed them into the folder before tucking the file under his arm. He flipped off the lights and threw himself into the professor's armoire, contorting his body to fit behind a rack of coats. He muttered a plea that the doors whine quietly as he closed them, and he left a sliver of space between the edges for a peephole.

The steps grew hard and brittle, each one more defined than the last. He hoped it was the janitor, though he heard no maintenance cart. The steps slowed to a halt outside the office. Austin wondered if a camera had revealed his break-in. Had a security guard come to grab him? He ran through the array of possible consequences for trespassing in a professor's office. Expulsion was a certainty.

A key slid into the lock, and the portal swung open.

The door frame could hardly contain the shoulders of the hulk that entered. Austin caught a glimpse of the newcomer. Bones jutted from his face like crags, his leathery skin threatening to fray under the pressure of the protrusions. One eye wilted slightly under a faded pink scar. Light projecting from the television fell over his biceps, defining sinews so strung they looked ready to snap as the massive arms shifted. One arm bore writing and a pattern. Through the peephole Austin couldn't distinguish ink from shadow.

The man struck Austin as Gothic incarnate. His face was a primitive cave carving, whose sculptor had clomped on fistfuls of clay without smoothing the edges. His hair was a dark flame of red. Austin was certain he'd seen the man before. It was a wonder someone this size had approached with a nearly soundless gait. He watched as the intruder set the professor's briefcase by the door. Next the man went straight for the bottom drawer. Finding it empty, he grimaced.

Austin played out the scene where he hurled himself at the redhead. He would swipe the telescope or empty champagne bottle on Clare's desk. With enough power and precision behind a blow, along with the strategic element of surprise, he could inflict severe damage. He could conceivably burst from the closet and lunge with a crude weapon in fractions of a second. His timing would have to be perfect. Hesitate, and he'd fail. He might also stumble—easy enough to do in the dark, as he'd discovered. After recovering from the shock, the redhead would have the clear advantage of his size. Austin opted to wait.

Watching the man, he realized he'd left the file cabinet open. Spirits sinking, he could only hope the anomaly would go unnoticed.

The intruder combed through every drawer, his fingers searching out small nooks to no avail. Austin fingered the flash drive in his pocket, willing his cell phone not to ring, dreading any urges to sneeze. He discarded the idea of assaulting the man when the champagne bottle landed in the trash. The redhead held up the flute, balancing the neck between two steady fingers. He guzzled the liquid and placed the crystal piece inside the small refrigerator.

His eyes roved around the room, darting from model rocket to airship before coming to rest on a burgundy-colored model with double wings. Austin recognized the biplane. It was the model Clare had played with during their conversation. The prowler ogled the plane with deference, as if it were a relic from a shrine, taking it in his hands and feeling the weight of the wings with open palms. His fingers quivered with indecision, and for a moment Austin suspected he would crush the fuselage. The man's pensive look yielded to melancholy, then to torment. His two heavy claws lingered on the craft, their trembles faint but discernible, ready to shatter the model into shards of wood, metal scraps, and cracked paint.

They never did. The man let go of the biplane and grunted before rummaging through more drawers. He continued for a while, apparently failing to locate what he had come for. Then he stopped.

Crouching, Austin felt a sudden inertia that seized him like rigor mortis. The prowler's head had snapped to the armoire.

Austin knew he'd made no sound, but he was caught in a riptide of panic. The man was approaching his hiding spot, leaving him approximately five seconds to act. He yanked a hanger down from the crossbar and twisted it sideways, the suspended blazer now serving as a curtain. He quietly jammed himself into the least conspicuous position, his limbs searching for gaps between coats while the bulk of his body remained invisible.

The doors swung open, and a big paw reached inward, grasping at space. Mentally preparing himself for a scuffle, Austin tried to avoid the intruding hand as it groped the blazer. If he'd need to fight, he'd be sure to deliver the first blow; he had no chance otherwise against this mountain of muscle. One strike was all he could hope for, one deliberately placed strike, buying him scant seconds to flee before the other could retaliate.

He suddenly wished what he'd seen in movies were true, that one upward strike to the nose with enough force could incapacitate a man by driving the septum into the brain, causing blackout and, moments later, death. Yet the anatomical impossibility was fundamental enough, the nose built with only two bones, both small and fragile. The rest was cartilage, too pliable to exploit. Austin considered a similar maneuver, one a friend and martial artist had once described. The idea was to strike the philtrum, that soft spot under the nose and above the upper lip, with the heel of a palm. When applied with accuracy to such a vulnerable area, the arm's thrust had the power to confound and destabilize a victim, at least momentarily, earning time for the assailant to plan his next move. Then there was the classic attack on the carotid artery. The potential for lethal damage seemed farfetched, as did the notion that one quick chop to the neck could disrupt blood flow to the brain and lead to unconsciousness—but Austin didn't doubt that a shock to the carotid could decommission a person. Finally, fumbling at the limits of a narrow repertoire, he contemplated a third frontal assault, this one a blunt blow to the chest designed to disturb, or even stop altogether, the regular rhythm of the heart. Such trauma was called commotio cordis, a rare but potentially fatal shock induced by impact to the precordium. Again, this seemed farfetched, if not impossible, given the thick barrier of muscle between Austin's hand and the intruder's heart.

Not yet sensing opportunity, Austin saved his attack. The hand felt its way up the blazer and reached into the pockets. Finding them empty, it moved to the adjacent coat, then to another, discovering nothing but loose change. For a moment the giant fingers brushed Austin's skin—in its heightened sensitivity, his body tensed like a drawn cord—but then they moved on and took hold of other garments, shuffling through coats for what seemed an eternity as Austin watched the hangers sliding along the crossbar.

Finally the prowler gave up and shut the doors. He powered off the mini-TV, then picked up the briefcase and left the office, leaving no trace of his visit.

The door to the office latched shut.

For thirty full seconds, Austin remained crouched in breathless silence. He shifted his weight after the footsteps grew distant. When the sound had faded, he climbed out of the wardrobe and dusted himself off.

He was tempted to call the police and report the trespasser, but what would the police say? He was guilty of the same intrusion. Besides, if the man was as practiced a criminal as Austin supposed, he'd have left no hint of a destination. Reporting the incident would be counterproductive. Austin would be charged with trespassing, and the prowler would disappear.

This was a story meant for Victoria's ears.

She wasn't going to like it, but that wouldn't stop him from telling her. Clutching the file folder, he swiped the spyglass from Clare's desk and left the room. He descended the stairs to the first floor, certain the prowler had elected the same route.

He faced two exits, one on the side of the building, the other feeding into the engineering quad. He chose the side outlet, which provided faster access to the bushes. Darting outside, he hid within a blanket of foliage, listening for footsteps. He gauged himself at a safe twenty-five seconds behind the other man, who was now finding it easier to blend in with the evening's cyclists and passersby.

But some were too big to hide, Austin thought, peering through brambles in the underbrush. At first he saw nothing. He checked his watch. Time was running short. The longer he waited, the more easily the intruder would evade detection.

He zeroed in on the noise of a car door opening. Not fifty yards away, he spotted the prowler's thick arm, his hand clasped on the handle of Clare's briefcase as he stepped into a black sedan. It was parked in the Oval, the road looping at the university's entrance. The engine rumbled to life, and the automobile backed out.

Austin scrambled away from the bushes and jogged toward the Oval for a better view. He was safe now. From behind a tree he expanded the telescope and trained it on the sedan's license plate. Three strips of duct tape covered the plate.

The road folded back on itself and became Palm Drive, a main artery. The sedan sped away, mingling with traffic until Austin could no longer distinguish it. He lost track of the car at the intersection with Campus Drive.

The faraway hum of passing cars punctuated an occasional horn blare as he stared at the intersection. Desperation grabbed hold of him. The license plate was his only connection to the prowler. Now he doubted he'd see the sedan again. He found the prospect haunting as he stood behind the tree.

Malcolm Clare's cell phone vibrated inside his pocket.

He checked the caller identification and let out a sigh of relief. He recognized the voice on the other end.

"Dad?"

"Victoria, this isn't your dad," he said. "This is Austin Hardy."

"From the Axe and Palm?"

"Yes. We need to talk."

"Clearly. You have my dad's phone."

"I found it in his office, and I wasn't alone. Can we meet?" He took her silence as a sign of indecision. He searched for words, which usually came to him so swiftly. "I know it's strange, but I need you to hear me out." He didn't know how else to say it. "I just witnessed a break-in. I don't think your father is safe."

"I know," she said.

"You do?"

"My dad carries an emergency pager. I doubted your story back at the restaurant but figured it wouldn't hurt to verify what you'd said. He never called back."

"Believe me now?"

There was another pause. "Let's meet," she said. "Someplace private."

"Better not be my place. I have a roommate. He'll hear everything."

"Come to Roble. I have a single."

"See you in five."

SEVEN

A jet wheeled to a stop on a tiny runway in the Central Pacific. The hatch clicked open, and a stairwell appeared. Dan Chatham stepped onto the landing and let the warm breeze of the equator embrace him.

"*Yokwe*, Omelek Island," he muttered. *Hello, Omelek Island.*

He swept the terrain with gray, baggy eyes that moved erratically. He was a thickset man who looked as if he'd played professional football early on and escaped any form of physical exertion since. It was just an appearance; he'd never actually set foot on a gridiron.

Scraggly trees covered the island, a sheet of green growing on reef rock somewhere between Hawaii and Australia. Over time, coral, mollusks, and other remnants of marine life had accumulated to form the island. A bent road carved through its eight acres.

Chatham glanced up at a cloudless sky and surveyed the stars, a thousand lights winking back at him.

A voice broke his meditation.

"Mr. Chatham, sir?" At the base of the stairs stood a young man in uniform, his expression stiff as his spine. "Airman Gibbs. Welcome to the Marshall Islands, sir."

"Thank you," Chatham replied, adjusting his suit. "At ease, soldier, or you'll fall over."

"Yes, sir." The airman bowed his head with no change in posture. "We didn't expect you this early. Luckily we're ahead of schedule. I'm assigned to escort you to the control room, where you'll be able to watch the process."

"You don't expect me to watch this from behind glass, do you?"

"I'm sorry, sir. Standard protocol. You read the manual."

The flight had been rough, all ten hours spent reading reports of previous successes.

Responsibility rested in the hands of his contractor, giving him a well-anticipated break after years of preparation. He had worked tirelessly, spending more hours over the past months in the cabin of a jetliner than in the comfort of his Virginia office.

"I'm sure you make allowances every now and then," Chatham said. He climbed down the stairs and shook hands with his escort. "Take me to the control room, Airman Gibbs."

Over the dying hum of his jet, Chatham heard a voice crackle through the airman's walkie-talkie. It was cool and efficient. "Gibbs, have you greeted the Glitnir president?"

"Yes, Colonel. Mr. Chatham and I are on our way." He clicked off and beckoned the new arrival. "Follow me, sir."

Chatham noted the difference in perspective as he experienced the terrain from ground level. His aerial view had given him a sense of the island's small size—it was no more than a speck in the great blue—but as he'd gazed out the window of the jet, the nighttime darkness had shrouded all hints of Omelek's flatness. Now he wondered what happened when storms struck. It seemed a ten-foot wave would wash right over the landmass. So shallow was the island's perimeter that its gently sloping edges were visible beneath the water as low as a gull's view.

Omelek was a part of the Kwajalein Atoll, a crescent-shaped ring stretching over sixty nautical miles within the Marshall Islands. The atoll was home to many military launch areas, among them the Ronald Reagan Ballistic Missile Defense Site. This zone belonged to Skyvault, a private space transport company that launched reusable, liquid-propelled carrier rockets into low-Earth orbit. The company had recently launched its Griffin-7 vehicle for the fourth time, achieving a new milestone in the reliability of private spacecraft. The first successful Griffin prototype had thrust its own thirty thousand kilograms into the sky with a simulated payload of over a metric ton. Since then, the rocket's family had been responsible for fifteen commercial launches. Relying on state-of-the-art avionics and an equally cutting-edge computing infrastructure, the Griffin-7's design exemplified simplicity as elegance. Skyvault had also achieved breakthrough modernization of space access with its Cricket capsule, offering trustworthy shipment of crew and cargo to the International Space Station. Having taken a personal interest in the company, Chatham felt assured its technology would protect tonight's haul.

Another warm gust swept over the land. He removed his jacket and flung it over a shoulder. When the wind died, the air fell silent. He knew the hush wouldn't last. He focused on the sound of his own footsteps crunching on gravel. It took his mind off a puzzling, insidious anxiety that had wormed into his sleep the night before and nagged at him the past ten hours. Strange, the thought hadn't bothered him in the years building up to tonight. But he couldn't ignore the fact that he'd been thinking of the myth of Prometheus. Maybe some gifts were never meant to be given, some things never meant to be built. Funny how he hadn't felt the butterflies till now.

As they rounded the bend, a white structure cut a sliver of smooth curvature out of the nightfall. The slender construction reached skyward like a spout of light from a springhead, supported by meshes of ultramodern scaffolding, its naked beams careening in a web of severe angles. The frame looked physically cold, mounted around a tapering pillar drenched in the light. Reinforced concrete at the base of the figure was charred, brutalized by the extreme temperatures of past launches.

The path wound about a cluster of trees. The rocket loomed over them, towering like a sequoia over surrounding woodland, its surface reflecting a pearly sheen over space-grade aluminum alloy. Chatham admired its luster.

"Something so sleek was never meant to stay grounded."

Gibbs didn't comment. He gestured toward a building shaped like a greenhouse. "This way, sir."

Chatham followed. Inside the building, fifteen scientists typed into computers and spoke into headsets, their desks united by a single panel running along the wall, above which hung monitors displaying images of the rocket from eight angles. Staff manipulated the images from their computers, zeroing in on any details requiring attention. Hours earlier, the room had been abuzz with activity. A stillness had since settled, but the intensity persisted.

A man at the far end of the room approached. His hand shot out and enveloped Chatham's with a crushing shake.

"An honor to meet you, Mr. Chatham. I'm Colonel Rumby, the launch director on Omelek. I'll be conducting tonight's operation." The colonel had a wiry build, crew cut, and polite demeanor. Chatham had the feeling he was a man who did not like to be disturbed from his work. "We've eagerly anticipated your arrival." He did not smile when he greeted Chatham, but his greeting sounded heartfelt.

"That's nice of you, Colonel," Chatham replied, rubbing his knuckles.

"Wouldn't miss it for the world. I've looked forward to this for some time. Years, actually."

"I only wish I knew what was inside the rocket. Corporate's kept me in the dark."

"Sorry to hear that, Colonel." He felt a peculiar pleasure at withholding information he knew would have left the man dumbfounded. "I wish I could tell you, and I wish I could have introduced you to the designer. He wanted to be here tonight, but couldn't." Chatham added believably, but untruthfully, "Depending on how tonight goes, maybe soon you'll know what's inside."

If Rumby was disappointed, he was not letting it show. "My job is to facilitate. Our team has prepared the Griffin's flight."

Gibbs chimed in. "Mr. Chatham, these headphones are for your protection. With a missile over 21 meters tall, 1.7 meters wide, requiring 347 kilo-Newtons of thrust on liftoff, you can imagine how earsplitting launches can be. If you're not careful, even deafening. Propellant feeds down a shaft, which is part of the 'turbo-pump' controlling a cycle of gas generation. Kerosene flows into a combustion chamber, where it ignites and eventually—"

"That's all right," said Chatham, patting the airman's shoulder. He seated the headphones around his neck. "I gathered enough in the reading material your company sent me. Right about now, I'm ready to watch this megalith soar."

Rumby gave a curt nod to his team and ran through one final checklist.

"Initialize launch sequence."

Outside, the Griffin-7's scaffolding shifted with a metallic groan. Two clawlike arms released their grip on the missile they'd been hugging.

Under Rumby's oversight in the control room, the squad of scientists studied the monitors for any sign of error. The building had fallen quiet but for the hum of electronics.

While the task of launch distracted the Skyvault employees, Chatham made for the door and found a sheltered alcove from which to observe. This was the inauguration of a new age, he thought. The metal frame quavered, and he listened as the thrusters mounted from a steady growl to a heroic bellow.

Blinding light emanated from the regeneratively cooled engines. Clouds of dust and leaves kicked across the launch pad, bending the surrounding trees outward as the white missile lifted off and joined the stars.

Climbing higher, the rocket left behind a small silver halo. The shell broke away, somewhere a parachute opened, and the airborne beast unfurled its wings.

EIGHT

Rove cinched a half-Windsor in front of the mirror, the gold buttons of his jacket shining from recent polish. Rounding out his look with khaki slacks and Sperry Top-Siders, he could have passed for a yachtsman.

He checked his watch. Five minutes till he met the escort. He ran a comb through his short hair and walked over to Fawkes's stateroom. Through the walls he heard faint crooning, the lyrics and melody improvised on the subject of a scrumptious meal.

Rove knocked.

"Coming!" the old man croaked. "Be there in a moment, cowbells and all."

The ship listed starboard as he waited. He'd rarely set foot on vessels large enough to dispel the sway. He'd grown used to the perpetual motion, which now afforded him a degree of comfort.

He checked his watch again. The hands nearly marked the hour. His steward's door opened.

"Ready as they come," Fawkes said, grinning through his spectacles and fixing a pair of onyx studs that matched his cuff links. He brushed the tails of his tuxedo, and with an agility that belied his years, threw up his hand as if conducting an orchestra. A pleated cummerbund complemented the waves of his silver hair.

"Very sharp," Rove replied. "Should I have worn a tux?"

"Not unless you want to. I've a particularly good reason to dress tonight: a dinner date with a lovely, stalk-eyed crustacean. And perhaps others in her family."

"Does her family approve?" Rove asked.

A few hours playing cards with Fawkes the night before, and the steward had already broken the barriers of Rove's humor—one that had lain dormant for a while.

"The Homaridae adore me as I do them. I've seen quite a few get steamy. Perhaps I could introduce you to a few decadent decapods. But first, the tour. To deck fourteen we go."

They descended a flight of stairs, and a junior officer waited by the elevators.

"Good evening, gentlemen," he said.

Rove unfolded his invitation and handed it to the man.

"I'm Jake Rove. My guest is my steward, Lachlan Fawkes."

"Pleased to meet you, Major Rove and Mr. Fawkes. The captain will now see you for a private tour of the bridge. Right this way." The escort ushered them through a vestibule beyond a *Crew Only* portal. They passed a row of officers' quarters before the maze of corridors led them to a new entrance. "Here we are."

The door opened to a panorama of seascape as seen through a 180-degree arc of clear panels. There was an island of computers behind which the bridge officers monitored systems. The staff looked relaxed; much of their work was automated. The wall of shelves behind them stored maps, star charts, an array of special cruise documents, as well as the flags of every country they would visit tucked neatly into individual cubbyholes. In the center of the room stood two uniformed men, hands at their sides, expressions cordial. The taller of the two, a man of stocky build and olive complexion, wore a mustache level with the bottom of his meticulously groomed sideburns, stray whiskers pruned to avoid disrupting the line of curls.

"Welcome, Major Rove. I am Giacomo Selvaggio, proud captain of this ship. The man beside me is my first officer, Trevor Kent."

"I'm honored by your tour and dinner invitation," Rove said. "You're giving me a trip down Memory Lane. Seeing the bridge reminds me of my Coast Guard days." They shook hands. "This is my guest, Lachlan Fawkes. Seeing as we have four months at sea, I thought this would be a good way to get to know my steward."

The captain nodded and smiled at the old man. "Good to see you again, Mr. Fawkes. We met a few years ago while I was captaining a ship through the Greek Islands. As I remember, you attracted a harem of Mikonos goddesses who could hardly hold back their tears by departure time."

"You sure that was me?" Fawkes said with feigned ignorance.

"A shame we had to leave port, if your luck by day foretold your luck by night. Heh!"

"Guilty as charged, I suppose," Fawkes muttered.

Selvaggio motioned to his counterpart. "Mr. Kent is my right-hand man. Without him, captaining the *Pearl Enchantress* would be impossible."

"Nice to have you on the bridge," Kent said.

His hair was parted at the side over a stern face with vestiges of a German heritage. He stood at stiff attention relative to Selvaggio's ease.

"Right now you're standing in the humble control room of a 114-kiloton piece of machinery," said the captain. "Registered in Bermuda, the *Pearl Enchantress* is one of the largest cruise vessels on the seas. Her nineteen decks can house 3,600 passengers and 1,300 crew. She's more than 120 feet in beam, and three and a half football fields in length."

"Impressive," Rove said, mentally comparing the ship with an aircraft carrier. "How fast is she?"

"Twenty-four knots, max. She's equipped with diesel electric propulsion."

"How many hands usually man the bridge?"

"Our deck officers man the bridge on a twenty-four-hour basis. It's imperative that the operational center of the ship, accountable for all navigational and chief safety systems, remain under constant supervision. Every four hours, we introduce a new shift—a pair of deck officers and a pair of Able Seamen. Responsibility for the ship's safe navigation lies in the hands of the officer of the watch while the Able Seamen keep lookout and report to the officer. The Able Seamen also direct the helm. When heavy traffic, stormy weather, or difficult maneuvering call for additional hands, Mr. Kent and I join the fray."

Selvaggio preened, smoothing his mustache with a forefinger, and continued his practiced monologue. "Information from six main data sources displays on one easy-to-read console. With real-time figures streaming in from multiple sources, the computer consolidates data for the officer of the watch to avoid information overload."

Rove glanced over at the console, where an officer stared at a green line rotating around a sprinkling of dots.

"That's the radar, one of the six main sources/sensors along with the gyro compass, speed log, satellite nav, echo sounder, and ECDIS, or electronic chart display and information system. As I'm sure you know, radar helps us monitor proximity to other ships, up to one hundred fifty kilometers, allowing us to travel in zero visibility. The tallest navigation mast holds three radar scanners. The other two are located at the bow and the stern. We also have an automatic identification system that taps into the Maritime Domain Awareness network. It tells us about other vessels in our immediate vicinity. For example, by using this click-down screen, I can tell that this little green dot"—he pointed over the officer's shoulder at the screen—"is a small merchant ship thirty nautical miles to our west, delivering cargo to Aruba with an expected arrival in sixteen days. This one right here is a logging craft sailing to the Baltic. And this one is a survey ship researching an endangered marine mammal."

"What do you do if a vessel shows up unidentified?" Rove asked.

Selvaggio jerked his thumb over his shoulder. "Stay far, far away."

Kent chuckled as the captain meandered over to a device in a corner of the room, an object with a series of concentric rings on a pedestal.

"Here's one of the ship's most sophisticated pieces of equipment, the gyro compass. A spinning disc rotating in azimuth ensures that the compass needle always points to a location in space directly above the Earth's meridian. The compass seldom exceeds a single degree in error. In case of gyro failures, we also have backup magnetic compasses.

"While the compass aids helmsmen with bearings, most of the ship's navigation happens through auto-steering. We can preprogram way-points into the system, plug in our desired arrival time, and the internal programming directs the ship according to our specifications, stopping at each waypoint.

"In a sense, the autopilot has its own intelligence. It adapts to weather, sensing how storms, winds, currents, or choppy seas affect cruising. Sensors relay the information to the central system, which compensates by adjusting rudders. If we plug in a waypoint but a storm interferes, autopilot computes our drift and the corresponding required rudder correction, sending a signal to the vessel's steering motors. The bridge team can monitor any of this, since the console indicates rudder angles."

Selvaggio beckoned their small group to one of the wings of the bridge. They came close to the window, standing on a ledge protruding over water. "In the side wings here, we can observe the ship lengthwise, making our job easier when we intend to pull into port or, when maneuvering a ship that can fit, pass through the Panama Canal. For angular control, we can adjust the side propellers to spin in opposite directions. Funny thing about that. I park a floating city for a living, yet my wife won't let me drive our car into the garage because I scrape the paint."

Fawkes sniggered.

"Now if you'll focus your attention here, this monitor shows the depth of the ship, and by live video feed, the keel. It's important to keep close watch on those, particularly when entering shallow ports. Scraping the bottom would be a bit more costly than a new paint job on a car."

"I'm stonkered," Fawkes said. "It doesn't make sense they'd be in the bridge. Depth monitors should be placed in the galley."

"Oh?" Selvaggio said.

"It's a simple study of variable weight. The biggest cause of mass fluctuation stems from the kitchen. Chefs prepare food, which passengers eat, making the ship heavier."

"A very astute observation, Mr. Fawkes." The captain played along. "Would you care to venture a guess as to our maximum food capacity?"

"It would be a shot in the dark."

"Four hundred tons."

"Then I raise a valid point," Fawkes said.

Rove asked, "What's your most difficult port of entry?"

"Fjords are often dicey; Oslo can be a challenge. Under windy conditions, I personally find navigating the narrow channel into Saint Petersburg the most difficult. But nothing is ever too bad. I grew up in Sicily. Watching the ships sail by the island, I knew the ocean was my life. I always wanted to be a sailor. Naturally, I started small, working on tugboats and schooners before moving to larger ships. There's no preparation like experience, yet I had it easy compared to the new generation of officers. Cruise lines place rookies through intense training simulators before they ever set foot on the bridge.

"If you were wondering about safety onboard the *Pearl Enchantress,* I should mention that one of the most interesting aspects of our ship's safety protocol is our method of responding to fire. The ship contains 6,500 smoke and heat detectors, one in each stateroom, as well as 800 call points. Our Hi-Fog System provides 14,000 sprayers, which extinguish fires by injecting dense, highly pressurized water into the air, thereby reducing oxygen levels to squelch flames but still allowing people to breathe should they tread in an area of fire. Think of them as advanced sprinkler heads. This network of foggers supplements the 824 water, power, foam, and carbon dioxide fire extinguishers onboard. We have a total of 635 fire hoses—that's eight miles in length—and almost 900 fire doors. Drenchers stand at the ready to douse fires on any balcony. Fire doors, both sliding and hinged, assist in containment."

"And if you have a fire in the engine room?" Rove queried.

"Cylinders containing halon occupy machinery space, electrical substations, galley hoods, and ducts."

Fawkes said, "In other words, there's a snowball's chance in hell of a fire on this cruise ship."

"To put it mildly. So what about flooding? Watertight doors and cross-sectional dividers prevent flow from one side of the ship to the other. Then you ask, what if we're slow to shut the doors? What if crew members don't recognize the disaster until too late? Have a look. This computer receives live data from our smoke and heat detectors. We can hone in on any one of thousands." He jiggled a mouse and in a series of clicks called up the penthouse. "Here's your stateroom. If a problem came up, a red light would blink in the exact location of the threat, instantly alerting us. Looks like your stateroom is safe and sound.

"Should the need to abandon ship arise, a near impossibility, our lifeboats, tenders, and other rescue vessels would carry passengers to safety. A marine evacuation system drops inflatable rafts, which float alongside the ship. The rafts alone, not counting lifeboats, are enough to float eighteen hundred people."

"Have you ever needed to deploy lifeboats?" Rove asked.

"Never in my career. Several years ago, I captained a ship that caught fire in one of the live theaters. The company should never have allowed pyrotechnics aboard a ship. Anyway, personnel didn't even require an audience evacuation before gaining control over the flames. A minor incident, and the worst I've encountered."

"You're lucky. Have you ever encountered pirates?"

"Pirates are generally more interested in seizing merchant ships than cruise liners. They want cargo. But even if they did try to hijack a ship, our helo deck is equipped with a high-power parabolic sound reflector, a long-range acoustic device or 'sonic gun.' If we sensed a threat, we could aim it at any oncoming craft. No one outside the target line would feel anything abnormal, but the pirates would hear a piercing shriek. The deafening sound, calibrated to match the resonant frequency of the human skull, would cause the bone in their heads to rattle in a most painful way. If they continued pursuit, the amplified sound waves would eventually split their eardrums and cause disorientation."

Rove nodded. "The Coast Guard and Navy use the same technology, often for a different purpose. Handheld sound reflectors have helped us communicate on deck when machinery noise gets loud."

"It's an ingenious tool, but Pearl Voyages has never encountered any hostile vessels. To date, no reason to use the reflector. But I've heard stories from friends at other cruise lines. For instance, before buying out Pearl Voyages, our competitor at the time had a ship touring the Hawaiian Islands when a group of eco-terrorists in a speedboat threatened to fire shotgun shells into the ship's hull. The fanatics were protesting the pollution caused by large vessels. This happened to the company Sapphire Pacific, who now owns Pearl Voyages."

"I wasn't aware Pearl Voyages had been sold."

"Happened four years ago, against the wishes of Clifford Pearl. Since they started capturing market share, he'd been obsessed with beating them. Sapphire Pacific made attempts to acquire Pearl Voyages as early as the eighties. Our board of directors wanted it to happen. Pearl was so stubborn on the issue—said they'd ruin the reputation he'd built—that he was finally ousted. Not much changed. Anyway, Sapphire Pacific's ship, the *Meridian Maiden,* focused the parabolic sound dish toward the approaching speedboat. It wasn't long before the environmentalists veered away.

"Another event happened five years ago, when a madman flying a seaplane came frighteningly close to my Alaska cruiser. Loungers on the sundeck reported seeing a passenger curled into a ball, poised to somersault out and land in our ship's pool. Thank goodness he never jumped. Imagine cleaning up that mess."

"Poor soul didn't realize there's no such thing as a free buffet," Fawkes said.

"How did you handle the plane?" Rove asked.

"We barely had time to react. The plane came out of nowhere, climbing over the hill of a tiny Alaskan islet. By the time we noticed, the seaplane was practically scraping our mast. Under normal circumstances, if we can see the oncoming planes in advance, we notify the military. We're prepared to respond to anything. And there's a near-zero probability we'd even need to." Selvaggio paced back to the center of the room and clapped an Able Seaman's shoulders. "You rest in capable hands, friends. Our bridge team trains diligently to earn the honor of serving here."

"Aside from simulators, how do deck officers train?" Rove asked. "Do they still study celestial navigation?"

Selvaggio looked entertained. "Tell me, is the Coast Guard stuck in the age of Columbus? I suppose next you'll ask whether we teach recruits to read sextants. We store star charts for good measure, but I doubt the modern training mandates learning to read them. Advanced GPS has rendered celestial navigation obsolete. To be fair, all senior officers onboard know how to read the charts. It's the new generation who rely almost entirely on global positioning satellites and electronic charting."

Adjusting his spectacles, Fawkes approached the navigation console and ogled the main joystick, a stub no larger than a pen cap. "It's hard to believe this floating colossus bends at the will of a twig."

"You get used to it."

Fawkes piped in again, with a look that boded wit. "Imagine the navigational nightmare if every passenger stood on one side of the ship. We'd sail in circles."

"Not if we threw them overboard," Kent said, his intended comedy lost in the grimness of his expression.

Selvaggio said, "In all seriousness, it wouldn't make a difference if a parade of elephants mobbed one side of the ship. Stabilizers keep us level, and the mass of fuel and water onboard far outweighs our passengers, even after they've gone to the buffet."

"What about power?" asked Rove. "How big are your generators?"

"Large enough to power a city of sixty thousand people. I would take you to the engine room to show you firsthand with the chief technical officer, but I'm afraid that's no longer allowed for safety reasons. I doubt you'd want to go down there anyway. It feels more like a jail than a cruise ship. No passenger ever goes below deck four."

"I don't imagine you find any plush carpets down there."

"Up here, it's nice. I can't complain about my work. Twenty-four-hour food, a private swimming pool for crew."

"And a postcard view of the sea."

"We do enjoy a remarkable view," Selvaggio said. "Thirteen nautical miles to the horizon from deck fourteen. At any rate, I've gotten carried away. You've heard nothing but numbers for the past half hour. Could I interest either of you in a cigar? Nothing like lighting up at the bow."

Rove said, "Maybe after dinner."

"Ah, yes. You must be famished. Our private dining room in the Venetian Mask restaurant awaits. Shall we?"

Fawkes asked, "Dare I ask what Chef Greco has prepared?"

"Stuffed lobster tails, Mr. Fawkes."

The steward pinched his fingers together, kissed them, then threw them open.

"*Aragosta, ma certo.*"

NINE

Austin's bike skidded to a halt in front of Stanford's largest dormitory. Located between a small forested area and a lake, Roble Hall felt secluded despite its central location. He jogged up the steps and peered inside to find Victoria waiting in the lounge. Hearing his knock, she answered.

Unshielded by her aviators, the aquamarine of her irises reflected a deeper sapphire when shadows darkened them, shocking against her black hair and delicate golden tan. Catching their glints, Austin felt like a patron admiring stones in a jewelry display. He sensed an iron will and a voracious lust for living.

A nightgown of silk chiffon with ivory lacing outlined a svelte figure of six feet, one with hips that swayed ever so slightly, gracefully, as she walked. The arch of her back held an immovable shoulder line. He'd seen many slender bodies in the student population, but few as lithe or lofty. Her standing height took him by surprise.

Austin had expected the same glacial remoteness from her. It wasn't melted butter, but her voice carried more warmth than he had hoped for.

"I'm ready to listen," she said. "Come in. We had a bad start."

"I laid into you like an interrogator. Could have shown a little more tact."

"I could have listened."

"Don't blame you for your reluctance. Frankly, I was curious to meet the daughter of a genius. You know, to see if she had giant glasses, red freckles, and buckteeth."

"The verdict?"

"It was hard to say at the time. You did have giant glasses, which could have been hiding the red freckles, and I didn't know if you had buckteeth because you never turned my way."

"Very entertaining."

Smells of burned popcorn and microwaveable pizza accosted him when he entered the lounge, as did the noise. Undergraduates crowded around a high-definition television, spellbound by their movie, watching as a torpedo closed in on a submarine on-screen. "We have no more decoys!" a panicked crewman, sweat rolling down his cheeks, was shouting over an epic soundtrack. "What do we do now?" The scene cut back to the cigar-shaped missile only meters from its target. "Now?" came a relaxed German voice. "Now, we die." Water burst through the bulkhead. A chorus of cheers erupted when the villains' vessel was no more.

She took him past a theater room, where a student was practicing Liszt's third *Liebestraum*. The notes were technically perfect, the tempo strict—too perfect, too strict, like a pneumatic player fed by paper. Victoria's fingers twitched, perhaps at the sound of mechanized Romanticism. She moved on, continuing up a small flight of stairs that led into a hallway.

"How'd you end up in an undergrad dorm?" Austin asked.

"Housing mix-up. This is temporary."

She sounded indifferent, though he guessed the situation was one that regularly tested her patience. He hid his smile. There was something funny about this girl as a fish out of water.

"You must be the life of the party," he said.

"Look out!" a male voice exclaimed.

A disc sped toward them, and they ducked in time to avoid impact. Then a soccer ball whooshed past, bouncing off a drinking fountain and rebounding through the hall.

"Sorry about that," said the freshman who caught the Frisbee. "Two games in one hallway means bad news for pedestrians without helmets."

"You guys wanna play some Ultimate?" asked the thrower, a beach-blond sophomore with hair below his shoulders.

"Any other night," Austin said.

"Live a little!"

"Big paper due tomorrow."

"That's like twelve hours from now."

"A fifteen-pager."

"Yeah, so do the math."

"Sleep would also be nice."

"Boring," said the freshman. "Good luck, though!"

Following Victoria around a corner at the end of the hall, Austin heard the whistles and catcalls of the boys, presumably under the impression they'd left earshot. Nothing registered on Victoria's face, though Austin was certain she'd heard them.

They came to her room, a modest rectangular space on the third floor. She had decorated the walls with oil paintings—one of a red 1929 Model J Duesenberg motorcar, one of tango dancers embraced in a fiery Corte, and one of a Mardi Gras headpiece, and all of them red, black, and white in theme.

"Nice artwork," Austin said. "Did you paint those?"

"A long time ago. My dad owns the Duesy," Victoria explained. "We call it our Cardinal car. I'd like to learn to tango, and my Brazilian mother loved the Rio Carnival."

"That says a lot about you, I'm sure." He gestured toward one of her shelves, packed full of colorful booklets. He couldn't make out the series. "Wouldn't have pegged you for a comic book nerd."

She dismissed the comment and pulled up a spare chair. "What is it you came to tell me?"

"It's been quite an evening. Better brace yourself."

Austin recounted the story in detail. He explained how he'd broken into Clare's office and snooped for evidence her father might have left behind, and finally how he'd scrambled into the closet when the intruder had entered, rummaged, and pilfered Clare's briefcase. He was struck by her remarkable calm. She listened intently but showed no sign of agitation. Instead, she took in the details as if she had expected that something like this might happen, and had spent years preparing.

He concluded. "I watched the man pull away in a black sedan. Using your father's telescope, I tried to read the license plate, but the letters were covered by duct tape."

"It probably wouldn't have made a difference," she said. "No way we're going to see that car again. If he has my dad's briefcase, the prowler won't be back."

"Victoria, there's another thing I haven't told you." Austin took in a deep breath, contemplating whether he should expound upon his meeting with Dr. Clare, and in how much detail. It might shed further light, and she'd be the only one he'd tell. Given the circumstances, it felt like a necessary breach in confidence. Nonetheless, he felt a deepseated guilt. "Yesterday, I didn't just see your dad for extra tutoring. He asked *me* to come in. To offer me a job."

Again, her cool confounded him.

"I'm guessing it wasn't to TA his class."

"He didn't explain exactly what I'd be doing, but it definitely wasn't that. He said I'd learn national secrets, build things, and travel frequently. He didn't reveal much more."

"Did he reference any connection to the military?"

"He said I'd be working closely with the Pentagon."

"Pay grade?"

"As a starter, beyond my wildest dreams."

"Privacy?"

"He said I'd have to be fairly discreet. My family couldn't know any details of the work."

Victoria exhaled sharply. "Can't say exactly what position my dad had in mind, because I don't know. But I can say with ninety-nine percent certainty what line of work it would be." She looked suddenly distraught. "I can't tell you."

"It may be important in finding your dad, Victoria."

"It's one of his best-kept secrets."

"Maybe this will change your mind." Austin tossed the folder from Clare's cabinet onto her bed, then reached into his pocket and dangled the flash drive.

"What are those?" she asked.

"That's for us to figure out together. The man skulking around your dad's office was looking for this drive. He got angry when he couldn't find it. As for trying to understand the diagrams in the folder, I'd have better luck proving the Hodge conjecture. Now, if you please, I'd like to hear your interpretation of Professor Clare's proposal." When Victoria reached for the flash drive, Austin snatched it back. She looked mildly annoyed.

"If you're going to play cat-and-mouse with information, I could have you arrested for breaking into a professor's office."

"That won't get us anywhere. Look, I understand your paranoia. You hardly know me. But we're both concerned, and curious. I'll show you mine if you tell me yours."

"I know you better than you think, Austin Hardy, born February second at the Long Beach Miller Children's Hospital. Father Derek Cadman Hardy, former U.S. Ambassador to Portugal, Italy, and San Marino, and currently Greece; attended Wesleyan University with a degree in public administration. Mother Sophia Madison Hardy, senior research biologist at the Malibu Aquaculture Research Institute, studied microbiology at UCLA. I wouldn't be sharing *anything* without a background check. Want to hear your favorite ice cream flavor?"

Austin backed off a little. "All right, I'm spooked. You know this how?"

"Part network, part nepotism." She remained withholding and opaque.

"You have my attention. I assume your 'network' relates to your father's secret?"

"In a way. You know my dad as a scientist. He's also . . ." She looked as if she were still deciding whether this was a good idea. "He's a philosopher, deeply concerned with the protection of individual rights. In 1994, he chose a new way to apply his scientific knowledge to protect American lives." Her lips tightened, indicating remorse for what she was about to disclose. "My dad founded an aerospace and special projects corporation called Glitnir Defense. Its goal is to fortify homeland defenses with innovative warfare technologies. There are two main headquarters. One's just outside Harrisonburg, Virginia. That's the operations and administrative center, with a number of task forces: counterintelligence, logistics, counterterror, geospatial surveillance, the list goes on. They interface with the Pentagon. The other's in Mojave, used for testing and prototyping alongside ClareCraft."

"So back in the nineties, when the media slammed your dad and called him all kinds of crazy over his 'reclusiveness,' he was actually working to protect the very critics disparaging him."

"Yes. Dad's last decade has been his most productive. He's designed breakthrough ground weapons used by Special Forces, ballistics, navigation systems, stealth microbots, reconnaissance devices, new programming methodologies, missiles—you name it."

"Missiles, what kind of missiles?"

"In that arena he focuses mostly on refining the next generation of guidance systems. He works with infrared optics, accelerometers, global positioning systems, and gyroscopes—all the things that help guide the missile toward its target."

"Why so secret?"

"What's the alternative? Become a walking target? Terrorists could cut off a major source of progress in American military technology. A bullet to the head would do the trick. Worse, they might try to steal Glitnir technology. Besides, lots of his projects are geared for one-time use in operations the CIA wouldn't call newsworthy."

"Black ops?"

"Right."

"Glitnir Defense," Austin repeated. "Your dad's private defense contractor. Must be hard for him to find time to teach."

"Time's never an obstacle for him. He designs and researches, and delegates the administrative and contractual work to the Virginia branch. His friendly college rival from MIT is president of the company. Dad minimizes personal contact with bureaucrats and does what he loves. My guess is, he wanted to hire you as a projects engineer, or as a liaison between Glitnir and the Defense Department."

"Now I see why he couldn't explain my role. At the risk I'd turn away the job, it would have meant compromising his own safety, and the secrecy of his company."

She grew somber. "As well as my safety, and the safety of our country. See why I was so cautious at the Axe and Palm? I had no idea whose camp you were in. You might have been hired to kidnap me. There have been attempts before. Imagine the ransom opportunities. 'This instrument for your daughter, Malcolm Clare.' I have to live with that fear."

"You were smart." He glanced at the folder on the bed. "You've clarified a lot. Thanks. Guess I better hold up my end of the deal and show you what I found. Let's start with this." He opened the folder and spread the thin sheaf of papers on the floor.

"What are they?"

"Blueprints. Maybe for your dad's latest development. I don't know."

"What does the tab say?"

"B-A-L-D-R. Baldr."

"These diagrams look like schematics for a new technology."

"How do you know?"

"He names all his inventions after people and places in Norse mythology. Glitnir, for example, was the hall belonging to Forseti, the god of law and justice. As a young girl, I adored mythology. Dad read stories to me before bedtime. The Norse tales were my favorite."

"What's the Baldr project?"

She shrugged. "You know as much as I do. He doesn't share classified information with me. Let's have a look at the diagrams." She studied the drawings, absorbing the scribbled words, making a first attempt at deciphering the formulas. "I'm a math student, and these symbols don't mean a thing to me."

"I'm just as baffled," Austin said. "My roommate's a whiz with codes and numbers. If only I could show him."

"No one else can know about Glitnir."

Austin gave her a severe look. "I understand."

Judging by her expression, his severity gave her relief.

He went back to the items in front of them, running a hand along the edge of a penciled outline. "Look at this linear form. Based on the slopes of the edges and his mention of RP-1 in the sidelines, I'd say these shapes are thrusters."

"You think it could be a propulsion system?"

"Best guess."

"Why do you say that?"

"RP stands for 'refined petroleum.' It's a particular kerosene used as rocket fuel. As to what the propellant is intended for, I could only speculate. Notice this. The diagrams are marked in stages. Like they describe an evolving process. Whatever these blueprints map out has several rotation points. You can tell by the arrows which parts are meant to revolve."

"There seem to be vectors drawn in," she said. "The spinning of the arms seems to be linked to speed and direction."

Austin frowned. "What confuses me are those stages. With each stage, the diagrams take on a smaller shape. And in stage three, the lines disperse. They seem to be in two places, like something dropped away from the main frame."

"A casing?"

"Maybe. That would explain the changing size. But stage three is different. That separate body doesn't look like a shell."

Victoria studied the images under a magnifying glass, then narrowed her eyes. "I don't think this is the right approach."

"What isn't?"

"Trying to crack these diagrams. In his rougher designs, my dad includes only very basic elements, and in his own notation."

"Why not make them more universal?"

"To prevent what we're trying to do. He'll modify them eventually, but this sketch is probably chock-full of red herrings."

"So we'll have to track him another way. I assume Glitnir has no website."

"Of course not. It's a secret company."

"Then let's see what's on this flash drive."

He handed her the device. She plugged it in and waited for it to load. After a few seconds, a prompt appeared asking for a password to open the contents. She tried some of her father's regulars, and got through after a few tries.

A single folder popped up, titled *Baldr*. She double-clicked it.

"The Baldr folder contains one Word document," she said. "It's called *Maritime Radio Transmission*."

"Open it."

The file came up. "It's a short document. Quarter of a page." She began reading the text out loud:

> The way is off my ship! *[Static]* I am altering my course to port, over . . . *[Muffled noise]* Man overboard! *[Static]* Keep clear of me; I am maneuvering with difficulty, over . . . *[Muddled voices]* I am now altering course to starboard, over . . . *[Shouts]* . . . My ship is on fire, and I have dangerous cargo onboard—a naval mine shipment. Keep well clear . . . *[Static]* I have a diver down to assess propeller damage; keep well clear at low speed, over. *[More shrieks]* Negative! I am altering my course to starboard. I already tried altering my course to port. I repeat, the way is off my ship. You may feel your way past me. Man overboard! *[Overpowering static. End transmission.]*

When she finished reading the script, she asked, "What do you make of it?"

"Seems like another dead end." Austin massaged his temples, willing fatigue out of his system. "The transmission seems unrelated to Glitnir. Where does it come from? What does it mean? Who sent it, and to whom?"

"There's no time stamp or identification," she said. "The sender sounds frantic. Incoherent. What does he mean, 'The way is off my ship?' And he can't seem to make up his mind which direction he's going."

"Seems full of non sequiturs. It's also bizarre the sender would have a diver down while his ship blazes with dangerous cargo. The ship must have ignited while the diver was under."

"Maybe the communication has some historical significance. A famous ship that sank. Regardless, we have no guarantee this Baldr trail even leads us in the right direction."

Austin perked up a little, not ready to abandon this route.

"True. But I have a hunch it does. Why else could the office prowler so desperately want the flash drive?"

Victoria paused. "You may be right. I should have connected the dots when you first rolled out the diagrams. Dad recently told me he'd completed a project long in the making—one of his most important yet—and said it had crippling abilities. Judging by the date the Baldr file was last modified, this must be one."

"Did he mention any specifics?"

She shook her head. "He just reminded me to look out for myself."

"This leaves us with only one more avenue." Austin placed Dr. Clare's cell phone in Victoria's hands. "When you called your dad, I noticed he had one unheard voicemail message. Maybe we should check it."

She nodded and dialed her father's voicemail, keying in the password and turning on the speakerphone.

A guttural voice spoke.

"You did it, Malcolm—congratulations! I won't forget the honor of having worked with you on this one. Sorry to say, this has to be brief. I'm calling to warn you. Yesterday I found a bug in my telephone. I can only guess what you may encounter. Careful, Mal, and talk soon."

Recognition sparked in Victoria's eyes.

"You'd better pack your bags and grab a passport," she said.

"What are you talking about?"

"You're in it this far. Tell your roommate you'll be gone a few days. My dad said you'll be traveling? It starts now."

Her insistence was as encouraging as it was bewildering.

"You're a high-pressure saleswoman," Austin said, "and I'm listening, but a little lost."

"We've found our lead. The voice in that message belongs to my honorary uncle, Fyodor Avdeenko. He's a nuclear physicist at Saint Petersburg State University, a consultant to many of Glitnir's projects, and a dear friend of my dad's."

"You can't just call him?"

"This isn't the sort of thing you discuss on a nonsecure line. Plus, we can learn more in person."

"You know where he lives?"

"He's practically family. I've been to his home lots of times." Victoria closed her eyes a moment. For the first time, her face registered the stress of the situation. "This is about my dad, Austin. He must have seen real promise to offer that job. He trusts you. You've already gone to exceptional lengths. I could use a capable partner in finding him. It's a lot to ask."

Her face was a study in tenacity and, despite her appeal for help, self-reliance. Austin knew his answer made no difference to her plans. She would go with or without him.

He saw beyond the attraction of an escape with an enchanting young female. He was watching her sense of security unravel; she could only be wondering when they'd come after her. He also realized there was more at stake than the lives of Malcolm Clare and his daughter. Much more. Whoever was behind the professor's disappearance, whoever the red-haired prowler was linked with, didn't want the man for his blood. Someone was after his ideas.

He softly squeezed her shoulder.

"I want to go with you," he said, "but you should know why. As much as I'd hate to see a girl orphaned, I'm doing this because an enemy of your father is an enemy of mine. Clear?"

A twitch moved her lips, and he understood the comfort his selfishness afforded her. "Clear."

"Now, a few minor obstacles."

"Yes?"

"My passport's expired."

"I'll snap a picture, send it in. Your documents will be waiting at the airport."

He tried to keep the pessimism from his chuckle, didn't want to sound dismissive. "You're kidding, right?"

"Did you hear anything I told you about my father's line of work?"

"Okay, say your connections come through. How do you expect to finance this trip? We don't know what we'll run into."

Victoria was already reaching for her wallet. It was in her pocket, not in a purse. "This will do." She spun a black card of anodized titanium between her thumb and middle finger, holding it under the light.

"Is that . . ."

"An AMEX Centurion? Yes, it is."

"*Yours?*"

"As I said, it will do." She returned the charge card to her wallet. "Any more obstacles I should know about?"

"Let's check available flights to Saint Petersburg," Austin said.

I get it," Ichiro said smugly, pacing the floor. "You're failing Clare's class, so to get on his good side you're taking his daughter on a trip. If all goes according to plan, sparks fly between you, and you cozy right up to Clare."

"Very perceptive," Austin replied, stuffing his backpack with gear.

"Ichiro the Clairvoyant knows all, sees all." He slapped a palm with his other fist. "I just can't believe you made it this far with that frigid—"

"Sure, Victoria's a pistol. She warms up when you get to know her. A little. You might describe her as a . . . what did Hitchcock say of Grace Kelly in *Rear Window*?" He remembered. "A snow-covered volcano."

"Let's call that a euphemism for another word I had in mind. Where are you going with her, anyway?"

"Telling you wouldn't be such a smart idea. You might show up and ruin our fun."

Ichiro snapped his fingers. "And you're going to drop all your classes, just like that?"

"Midterms are over, no assignments due. I can watch lectures online later." Ichiro shook his head, looking incredulous as Austin loaded his pack, then zipped it up and flung it over by the door. "By the way, I've got a project for you to work on while I'm gone, if you're up for it."

"Oh, really?"

Austin handed him a printed transcript of the document from the flash drive. "This is a radio transmission from an unknown ship at sea. I need you to find out what it means—where it came from, who received it, what the context is. Don't show it around."

Ichiro grabbed the paper, read it to himself, and scoffed. "This is nonsense. Why should I do this for you?"

"It will help you solve the mystery of my 'impulsive' departure." Austin landed like a barbell on his mattress. "Time for me to hit the hay. Big day tomorrow."

Ichiro's brows drew together as he watched his roommate pull the covers over his head. He had never known Austin to be anything other than a lucid pragmatist.

"There's no logic in this," Ichiro insisted. "I know what you're doing. 'Live every day as if it were your last, because one of these days, it will be.' That stupid rule is going to hurt you."

"Maybe it would, if I ever followed it."

"Oh. So now you're gonna tell me you follow some other rule." Austin spoke with his head between pillows.

"Live your *life* as if it were your last, because it *is*."

"Brilliant," Ichiro said. "Any other enlightened Hardyisms I should know about?"

"Only the most ancient, mystical of all," Austin said. "He who first explains radio transmission shall feast on rib-eye."

TEN

A Porsche rumbled into the driveway of a modern home tucked in the Virginia forest. The structure's chaotic geometry and fragmented panels clashed with the surrounding hills and greenery. The owner called it enlightened deconstructivism. Neighbors called it litter in the virgin woodland.

Dan Chatham climbed out of the Porsche, closed the garage, and made a beeline for the bedroom. He tossed his clothes onto the bed and began filling his bathtub with water. A high-pressure faucet thundered against the basin.

Chatham stretched his arms, mouth widening in a yawn. The trip to the Marshall Islands had taken a lot out of him. He hadn't stayed but a few hours on Omelek before turning around and making the arduous flight home. Despite the comforts of a private jet, his muscles still ached from sitting in the same position.

It had been worth it, if for no other reason than to witness the initial blast. Images of the rocket's contrail against a black sky still haunted him.

It was done, the negotiation sealed. No more signatures. The rocket had left his domain the minute it had reached space.

He clambered into the tub, memories playing through him in vivid detail. He let them fade away as steaming water rose around him. His thoughts drifted. Heat eased the tension in his body. He focused on the sound of water spilling into the tub, his mind a thoughtless vacuum stimulated only by the blissful bodily sensations.

There was something satisfying in the thought that he, not Malcolm Clare, had witnessed the launch. It gave him an ownership—at least an illusion of it—that somehow made them equals. It's like Malcolm works for *me* now, he thought.

He'd known Malcolm almost fifty years. They'd shared an apartment as undergrads at MIT. Dan had been inspired by Malcolm's ability to excel in both physics and mechanical engineering—two difficult majors. Ambitious and competitive, he'd tried to do the same, but his performance had fallen. He'd resorted secretly to copying Malcolm's assignments and lying about marks to stay respected. Malcolm never learned of the subterfuge; he was busy corresponding with the British government to free relatives detained during the Cold War. Malcolm had wanted to trust him, Dan realized. The support of friends would carry him through his hardship. Malcolm needed him, too, he'd always said to himself.

During their third year, Dan had concealed from Malcolm that he'd been placed on academic probation. The work had been impossible. How did his roommate ace classes with so little effort? He probably cheated, too, Dan thought; no one could be that good. The worst of it was, women rarely gravitated to Dan when Malcolm was around. Why? Dan always fancied himself better-looking.

When he'd learned Malcolm had applied to MIT's graduate program in aeronautics, Dan had also quietly submitted his own name. He wasn't accepted. Instead he attended Columbia for dual law and business degrees. At least the decision had practically guaranteed better wages than Malcolm would ever earn. Dan had graduated in 1970 and aligned himself with a small team of engineers starting a robotics company. In five years the project fell apart.

Malcolm had invited him to Mojave to act as legal counsel for his new enterprise, Malfactory, a company that designed and prototyped aircraft for amateur builders. Despite his aversion to working for Clare, Dan had few better options. He retained an executive role during the company's expansion into ClareCraft, and became the vice president of operations. Clare had placed great trust in him, and in 1994 asked him to help start Glitnir Defense. When Clare resumed teaching, he'd passed on leadership to Dan, who would preside over the company while Clare contributed designs from the sidelines.

Chatham hadn't felt such ownership of a Glitnir project until this launch. The designs had been Malcolm Clare's, but not the execution. It seemed the company could perform without Malcolm.

He gunned the jets and poured in two scented oils that blended in an aromatic mélange, delighting in the fragrances as the Jacuzzi massaged his tender spots. He drifted into existential rapture.

A harsh noise interrupted his moment.

He jerked his head, banging it against tile. Muttering a curse, he sat upright. Water sloshed out of the tub. Just what he needed: another damned phone call.

A wireless set buzzed outside the tub. It rang through one cycle, then began another. Where can a man find peace these days?

He answered the call.

"Chatham here," he said irritably. "This better be good."

"Oh, it's good," came the voice on the line, deep and resonant, a growl in a cave.

"Who is this?"

"You're a devious man. Nearly covered all your footsteps." Chatham's heart quickened. He could feel the thumping in his chest. "Don't worry. Your secret can stay safe."

"What the hell?" Chatham said. Now finding the temperature unpleasant, he twisted the knob for a stream of cold. "Who is this?"

"The man who will make you very miserable . . . or very rich."

ELEVEN

There was light in the void, and he reached for it.

Malcolm Clare awoke to a throbbing head. With effort he lifted his eyelids for a blurry view of his surroundings. They fell back down again, cemented shut, and after a few attempts he finally pried them open. He didn't know where he was at first. His vision was a watercolor left in the rain, the pigments blotted and diluted. He could focus only on the tingling soreness between his ears.

He was seated. Was he in his office? He tried to massage his aching skull, and a searing pain lanced through his arm. Had he any wind in his lungs, he'd have let out a moan.

He sat still, waiting for the stinging to subside. He fluttered his eyelids to clear his vision. This was difficult. Light only aggravated the pain in his head.

It was daytime. He wished it weren't.

Dazed, he tried to make sense of his environment. He sat by a window. Not one, but many windows, and there were seats. A bus? No . . .

He combated dizziness, struggling for control, bringing his world from its violent spin to a slow, carousel-like motion. Something told him he wasn't supposed to be conscious. I've been drugged, he thought, fighting a wave of nausea.

He tried to stand, but couldn't. Again a burning pain shot through his left arm. He could hardly move his wrists and realized they were tied down by rope. What were they tied to? The armrest felt familiar.

A sluggish transition to consciousness challenged him to distinguish reality from the last remnants of sleep. Wherever he was, the place was loud, full of white noise, and oppressive. The sound was not shrill, not distinct, but full and rounded, as if his ears were at the mercy not of a needle, but a hammer. He felt immersed in the noise, drowning under its pressure. It was a sound he recognized.

He looked out the window. Outside, colors shifted between blues and patchy grays. He searched for the ground but didn't find it, more aware of his location with each passing second. He was moving, fast.

A minibar with an assortment of wine bottles and liquors faced his seat. Leaning closer, he detected the sweet fragrance of maraschino cherries. Embossed on the crystal glasses beside the wine bottles was a familiar slogan: "Justice from a Forge."

He was riding in one of his own private jets, used by his own company. *How?* The last he remembered, he'd been walking along Serra Mall toward the Stanford quad.

His questions would have to be answered later. Right now, he needed a way out. He checked the cabin but found no sign of anyone else onboard. He was alone, as far as he knew, and strapped to the seat.

He kicked at the top of the minibar, and the bottles and glasses came crashing down on the floor. He caught a crystal glass between his knees, pinched the edges with enough force to break it, and used the rough surface to cut himself free. Banging on the cockpit door, he wielded the jagged edge like a weapon. No answer. He tried the hatch. It was locked. Then he remembered. At the back of every plane he had stored a crowbar in case of emergency. He searched through every compartment and found it behind the bulkhead along with other supplies—a first-aid kit, a flashlight, life vests, and an inflatable raft.

He jammed the crowbar into the cockpit door. Still dizzy from sedation, he lost his footing. . . .

When he woke again, he was on the floor, the pain in his head worse than before. The crowbar had landed on his body and knocked him back to sleep. He controlled his breaths, counting them, and listened to his own voice say: "I'm awake." Taking a moment to regain his balance, he stood and said it again: "I'm awake."

He wedged the tool into the door frame and pried it open.

A single pilot sat there, unperturbed. Malcolm Clare held the crowbar over his shoulder.

"Step away from the controls, or I'll hit a home run."

The pilot stared serenely into the clouds.

"What's the matter with you?" Clare said. "Step away. *Now.*"

The pilot didn't move and didn't say a word. The professor prodded him in the neck, not to provoke but to elicit some sort of reaction. Still no response. Was this a product of his own delirium? Finally he brought the crowbar down on the pilot's ribs. The pilot slid off to the side and landed with his head in the flight controls, colliding against knobs, dials, and switches.

It was then that Clare noticed the pilot's ashen skin tones. He lowered the crowbar and put a hand to the man's neck. It was cold. No pulse.

Thinking fast, he shoved the body out of the seat and assumed control. The needle on the altimeter was dropping. He yanked the throttle, expecting a harsh ascension from the abruptness of his pull. The plane surprised him by continuing on its trajectory. He flipped three switches and tried again, certain he had disabled the autopilot. Still, he had no control of the jet.

"Boot voice command," he enunciated clearly. The jet was designed to offer multiple solutions to a problem. He hoped his captors were unfamiliar with the intricacies of its programming.

A female voice responded through the jet's speakers. "Voice recognized: Doctor Malcolm Ian Clare."

"Computer, where are we going?"

"Destination unknown."

"Why is it unknown?"

"Our destination has not been programmed into the database of known locations. Would you like coordinates?"

"No. How long until we arrive?"

"Expected arrival at destination in three minutes."

"*Three* minutes?" Through the window, he scoped wide stretches of blue with no sign of land. The altimeter continued to drop at a frightening rate. The jet had passed below the cloud line. "Computer, change destination."

"Where would you like to go?"

"Calculate approximate distance to nearest landmass."

"Nearest land is 92.4 nautical miles away."

"How much fuel do we have?"

"Thirty pounds of fuel remain."

"Disregard change of destination command. Computer, why don't I have manual control of the plane?"

"Unable to process command. Please rephrase."

"Diagnose problem with throttle."

"Throttle is a part of the manual control system. Manual control was disabled in preflight specifications."

"Who made preflight specifications?"

"You do not have access to that information."

"I programmed this jet! Tell me, who tampered with the plane?"

"You do not have access to that information."

Clare slammed a fist into a wall of switches. "Computer, send out a Mayday signal immediately."

"Unable to issue distress call."

"Why the hell not?"

"Unable to process command. Please rephrase."

"Diagnose problem issuing distress call."

"You do not have permission to issue a distress call."

The altimeter dropped to one thousand feet. "Computer, where are we now?"

"Our current location has not been programmed into the database of known locations."

"So we're just going to crash somewhere over open water, in the middle of nowhere, with no ability to send out a distress call?"

The computer bleeped. "Unable to process command. Please rephrase."

"A scrap of information, that's all I'm looking for . . . just a scrap! Computer, state pilot's name."

"Pilot identity unknown. Pilot's name was not entered with pre-flight specifications."

"I programmed you never to allow takeoff without knowing the pilot or the destination. . . ."

"Unable to process command. Please rephrase."

The world began to recede under his heavy eyelids. He grappled for control, refusing to succumb to the darkness edging back into his vision. His thoughts were running along new channels. Who had knowledge deep enough to tinker with the jet's programming? He pulled the pilot upright and searched through the man's pockets. He found a wallet but no license or identification. There was an Air Force pin on the pilot's shirt. Clare noticed a mark on the man's wrist. He yanked up the sleeve to reveal a crude picture of a helmet and two protruding horns, drawn with a black marker. Clare shuddered; the hands were white, the knuckles cold.

"Computer, how long have we been flying?"

"Fourteen hours, thirty-six minutes."

The altimeter now hovered at the 800-foot mark.

"From which airport did we depart?"

"San Francisco International Airport."

"How long have we been on autopilot?"

"Autopilot has been active for twelve hours, thirty minutes."

"List the passengers onboard."

"There is currently one passenger onboard. Doctor Malcolm Ian Clare. There is currently one pilot onboard. Pilot identity unknown. Pilot's name was not entered with preflight specifications." The altimeter needle began to accelerate. "Warning. Low on fuel. Time to destination: two minutes."

A rosy estimate, Clare thought. He knew all evidence of his disaster would rot with him on the ocean floor unless he acted before the altimeter hit zero. He toggled switches and pushed buttons methodically. Nothing worked.

Another bolt of pain assailed his left arm. He looked down and saw a large gash in his bicep. How had he not noticed it before? Someone must have administered an analgesic that was beginning to wear off. The evenness of the cut suggested it was intentional. Bleeding had stopped, but the wound was big enough to open up again later. He tore off the pilot's shirt and wrapped the fabric around his wound in a tourniquet, then left the cockpit to see what he could scavenge in the cabin. He checked for parachutes, but they had been removed. He found a backpack, which he stuffed with water bottles and a knife from the kitchenette. He grabbed the inflatable raft from the emergency bulkhead.

Heading back to the cockpit he noticed three words written on the white carpet of his plane, not more than a yard from the seat he'd been strapped to. The words were spotty, written in blood from his gash. The sight of them triggered a buried memory.

They read, *Remember the Firecat.*

"What in the world . . ."

Denying the urge to linger and ponder the message, he returned to the cockpit, where he learned the altimeter had dropped below three hundred feet. If I'm in for a crash landing, he thought, I'll at least try to control it.

"Computer," he said. "Reduce speed by forty percent. Stall plane."

The droning engine seemed to sputter as the plane decelerated. Hitting an air pocket, the jet wavered and encountered a period of turbulence before smoothing out again.

"Reduce speed by another twenty percent. Prepare for emergency aquatic landing."

Using a piece of the rope that had been used to tie him down, he fastened a knot around the cockpit's door and held on to the end while inching toward the exit hatch. Wind blasted through his ears, pulling him outward, but he held tight, smelling a salty breeze.

"Computer, what's our current altitude?"

"One hundred feet."

He felt as though he could reach out and touch the water. It was odd, he thought, to perceive so intimately what was to become his grave. Sun reflected from the ocean's surface in countless shimmers. If this was his death, he was at peace knowing it would be at the ocean's gallows. But he had no intention of resigning from life until it was wrenched away from him.

The rope began slipping through his fingers. He held on as the descent steepened.

"Altitude!"

"Seventy-five feet."

"Reduce speed to forty knots! Stall plane!"

The aircraft could no longer fly. Plummeting toward the water, the jet was seconds from impact. Holding the backpack and inflatable raft under his arm, he curled into a ball and let go of the rope, letting wind sweep him from the cabin. Before surrendering to the waves, he experienced a few seconds of peace. The noise of the jet engines faded to silence, and the plane became no more than a passing shadow.

Water rushed in around Clare, invading his every sense, the pressure nearly rupturing his eardrums as he plunged headfirst. He fell instantly blind, deaf, and cold.

TWELVE

Days had passed since his tour of the bridge, and Rove had settled into a routine. He awoke early on sea days to jog the upper decks, after which he would refuel at the Century Oasis buffet and dine alfresco. He would lift weights for two hours before eating again. After his morning workout, he'd visit the library to continue reading a collection of history books he had started on day three. He'd nap, then spend quiet evenings strolling the lido deck. Occasionally Fawkes would invite him to play poker in the card lounge.

His favorite locale so far had been the Cayman Islands. He'd rented a boat and dived along colorful reefs, exploring a metropolis of undersea activity in waters clear enough for him to read a newspaper at eighty-foot depths. The fearless gliders of Stingray City had engulfed him, stroking his wetsuit with their smooth underbellies. Rove looked forward to an eventual first dive along the Great Barrier Reef when the ship reached Australia, and in Bonaire when the ship would return to the Caribbean at the end of the cruise.

When night fell, Rove would suit up and enjoy a full-course dinner with unlimited entrees. He'd have a drink on the veranda before retiring. The routine grew on him.

On the bridge, Trevor Kent stared at the computer monitor.

"Captain, you'd better have a look at this."

Selvaggio sauntered over to the console, a cup of coffee in hand. "What is it, Trev?"

"It's the auto identification system."

"What about it?"

"We seem to have lost actionable intelligence from Maritime Domain Awareness. Look at these ships here." He pointed to three dots on the screen. "Number one, a freighter headed for Aruba, ETA in sixteen days. Number two, a logging craft bound for the Baltic Sea.

Number three, a research vessel looking for an endangered marine mammal. Any of those ring a bell?"

"Those were the ships that appeared during the bridge tour. At the time, I found it strange a ship would take sixteen days to reach Aruba from anywhere in the West Indies."

"That's right, Captain. Now click around on the other ships."

Selvaggio did as told. His brows furrowed.

"Impossible," he said. "The specs are the same. Each ship is one of three, either Aruba-bound merchants, Baltic-bound loggers, or surveyors for endangered marine life. The auto ID must be malfunctioning."

"Every ship appearing on-screen is a carbon copy of one in the trio," said Kent. "And if that ruined your day, this will make it worse. At three this afternoon, the radar showed us coming within ten nautical miles of one of the ships. From the bridge, we can see thirteen nautical miles. There was nothing off the port side but leagues of empty sea."

"Any guesses as to the reason?"

"Not yet. I'm hoping it's just a minor hiccup, and that systems will soon function normally again."

Selvaggio let the news sink in for a moment.

"Log a glitch in the radar," he said. "Call a technician and see what he can do. Closely monitor all personnel who sit in front of this screen. I'm hoping we can rule out tampering. Let's be sure."

THIRTEEN

S verre, Jorgen—this box to the *Baduhenna,* the other to the *Jarn-saxa.*"

Ragnar paced the docks, overseeing dozens of husky workers loading contraband onto double-masted corsairs. Their arms bore the insignia of a horned helmet over a double-sided ax.

Hidden in Norwegian fjords miles above the Arctic Circle, their convoy would set sail by nightfall.

The boxes were light enough to hoist onto their shoulders. The men moved as if they treated every second as precious. They never looked at Ragnar, and they said little as they transported cargo. They knew he was watching.

He was aware of the respect he commanded. He'd been with them a long time, and they knew his beginnings. His father, Ernst Stahl, had been a decorated aviator and pilot of VIP aircraft—a regular for the Swedish prime minister and the royal family. After the birth of their third child, Ernst had bludgeoned his wife to death and left the infant to perish. He'd fled with his two toddlers, Ragnar and Benedikt, to a countryside retreat in the far north of Sweden, where the three had resided in a summer house on the banks of Lake Torneträsk. After nine years in seclusion, Ragnar had shot his father with a hunting rifle to protect Benedikt from Ernst's beatings. The boys were found by a local Sami reindeer herder and fur trapper. They had helped chop lumber, tend to animals, and build fishing canoes, growing tough working through winters until the herder had fallen ill. Benedikt had wanted to stay in Sweden to become a pilot like his father. Ragnar had crossed the border to Norway to avoid foster care. He'd survived on his own in Narvik, inhabiting a manor's detached wine cellar until roving criminals had invaded the home and incorporated him into their band at eighteen.

Ragnar checked his watch and dialed a number. The answer came immediately.

"I'm here."

"Viking. We leave dock within the hour," Ragnar said.

"How was your trip?"

"The professor remained asleep throughout the flight. I watched his plane go down minutes after I parachuted out. A group of my men awaited my arrival in a Zodiac. They took me back to our dock, where I've been able to supervise the loading of weaponry."

"You're certain you saw the plane go down?"

"There's no mistaking a splash that size."

"We only await your arrival, Ragnar. I've spoken with the president of Glitnir. Soon he will recover from his shock, and I'll make my first call to the company directly. I've asked Vasya to begin his assignments. First he'll remove the nuclear physicist from the picture. Then he'll meet with our biggest potential buyer, Farzad Deeb, to negotiate a starting bid. They will convene in Bruges."

Ragnar didn't like the idea of a change in plan.

"Bruges?"

"Deeb's request. He's visiting a partner in Brussels and wants to attend a festival in Bruges shortly after. Crowds attracted by the festival will make the meeting safer for both. Besides, I doubt Vasya would want to visit Deeb's home near Tripoli. Considering the degenerates he associates with, we benefit by the relocation. I wouldn't trust Deeb in the comfort of his home. I need my soldier."

"Vasya's capable of defending himself."

"He's nonetheless safer away from Deeb's turf. You've given the briefcase to Vasya, yes? Deeb will require the demonstration."

"I'll soon hand it over."

"I also assume you found the passkey without difficulty."

Hearing the inevitable question, Ragnar clenched a fist. "The drawer you had described . . . was empty."

Disquiet coiled within a silent phone line.

"This was supposed to be simple."

"Not only was it missing from the drawer, but it was nowhere in the office. The professor must have given it to someone."

"No, Ragnar." The Viking's snarl was fierce but regulated. "Malcolm Clare doesn't trust a soul in this world. He wouldn't entrust the passkey to anyone but his own daughter, and she knows nothing of Baldr. The key must have been in his office, where it's always been."

"It wasn't there."

"Vasya has spent the last ten months observing interactions between

Clare, Chatham, Avdeenko, and the Glitnir headquarters. His interceptions of relevant communications have led us to know the password. Problems would arise should someone else discover it. Lifting the flash drive was not necessary for Baldr's acquisition. It was necessary to prevent retrieval. The key is to be destroyed."

"Our plans shouldn't change. For someone to reclaim Baldr, he would have to appropriate the briefcase from Vasya—a trained assassin—interpret the transmission, and enter the passkey. The odds border on the impossible."

"I don't roll dice. This operation was designed to leave nothing to chance."

"The key wasn't there." This was a bark, not a statement.

"You should have kept looking. Fail me again, and I'll be forced to lessen your share."

"Our agreement holds. Betray me or my men, and I'll hurt you. You won't exactly be in a position to defend yourself."

The Viking disregarded the comment. "Contact me when you've left Norway. You've a long voyage ahead."

"When does the bidding begin?"

"Tomorrow."

"I hope your rat is as good an actor as he is a turncoat."

"He will be. Now finish preparing your ships. Your crew needs you."

Ragnar ended the call and replayed the conversation in his head. The Viking owed him a greater debt than he could imagine. If he double-crossed Ragnar, he would pay with his life.

His mood didn't improve when he spotted a man waiting for him at the end of the jetty. He was swarthy and handsome, his lips curled into a smile as sharp as his widow's peak. He looked amused as he watched the sailors lifting heavy cargo. This angered Ragnar; he could see the man's hands were smooth, uncalloused—perhaps a little physical labor would humble him, if there were time to put him to work. The man approached, and Ragnar realized the smile was pigmented with unease, probably owing to their difference in size. Suddenly he felt he had the upper hand, even as the man confidently clasped his shoulder.

"I believe you have something for me," said the man.

"Vasya. Follow me."

As he led the newcomer aboard the tallest corsair, Ragnar cautioned him about its billowing sails, which in windy weather had been known to strike the unmindful. They descended a compact staircase to a chamber below the weather deck, where a lantern dangled from the ceiling and maps were rolled out on a table, held in place by littered paperweights, sextants, and a mariner's compass. A vault was recessed over a bed next to a wall-mounted marine chronometer. There were no decorations; every object in the chamber had some utility.

"A captain's quarters," Vasya said. "A privilege."

Ragnar ignored the flattery and pointed to a spot on the map. "When the *Pearl Enchantress* arrives at the given coordinates, begin the demonstration." Ragnar opened the vault and handed Clare's briefcase to Vasya, who took it with both hands. "For now, Baldr is yours. Use it well."

When they returned to the main deck, a handshake affirmed their devotion to the mission, and Vasya walked ashore. A car waited around a bend. He took the driver's seat. The vehicle began a long, twisting journey to a distant airport.

"Godspeed," Ragnar said.

The corsairs were fully loaded when night fell. Darkness would obscure passage. Winds picked up as if to beckon the fleet seaward. Crewmen untied the lines and cast off. The ships began to creep away from the hideout, transporting sealed boxes and identically tattooed sailors down the main channel.

Still waters stirred as five corsairs departed from Ragnar's cove. The fjordal walls rose sharply. Foliage grew from clefts and crags to coat stone with green. After sundown, the sheer faces became jagged shapes lacking definition or dimension, detectable only by the blotting of stars. Norse warriors had used these clandestine waterways to hide vessels during the Middle Ages, and had gazed up at the same mountainous teeth connecting the earth with the heavens.

Breeze turned to gale as they ventured into the open, and Ragnar stood at his ship's bow, hand clasped to the forward mast. Forecasting a squall, he leaned into the wind, tasting the air, and let his mind unreel under the sound of the buffeting sails. He was going home.

PART II

PULSE

FOURTEEN

P ulkovo International Airport bustled with activity as tourists dis-
embarked and cleared customs. To obtain visas, Austin and Victoria had visited a special bureau, where a disagreeable officer
had raised doubts as to whether they'd be able to set foot outside the
airport. Unsatisfied with their answers to his questions, he had dele-
gated the decision to second and third representatives, who had repeated the questions and insisted upon thorough bag inspections. After
two painful hours of standing at the counter, they had been granted
the necessary documents.

They had slept soundly during the first leg of their journey to London and entered an even deeper slumber, albeit brief, heading northeast to Saint Petersburg. They'd awakened to the thud of the aircraft's
wheels making contact with the runway.

Groggy, they stood outside the terminal and hailed a cab. Victoria
indicated a point on a map, and the driver accelerated toward an
apartment complex off Nevsky Prospekt, the city's main thorough-
fare. Twenty minutes later they arrived at the city center.

For more than two hundred years, Saint Petersburg—formerly
known as Petrograd and Leningrad—had been the capital of the Russian Empire. In 1703, Tsar Peter the Great founded the city during the
Great Northern War with Sweden, building the Peter and Paul Fortress,
which would stand as the first brick and stone building. For all its grandeur, the city could not claim a pleasant past. Austin gazed out the
window and spotted peddlers selling crafts on the sidewalk. They bore
signs of oppression: sunken, spiritless faces, lumbering gaits, haggard
dress. Vagabonds slumped on street corners by shambling structures.
Fortune did not favor the elderly.

Victoria stared out the other window, lost in her own reflections.

"Penny for your thoughts," Austin said.

He was sure she had heard him, but she took her time to answer.

"Just imagining," she said, "what it must have been like for my dad
living here."

"I wasn't aware he'd spent time in Russia."

Austin realized how little he knew about the professor's personal life.

"Long story," she said.

It was always hard to read her. There was no telling what she was inclined to share, and when curiosity might offend. He decided not to ask, but she seemed willing to volunteer more.

"You might have heard of my paternal grandfather, Hugh."

"Of course I know that name."

Hugh Saxon Clare was a well-known British physical chemist and metallurgist who had advanced the understanding of solid-state materials. He had studied the effects of atomic-level imperfections on the properties of metals and alloys, publishing his work in the seminal book *Thermodynamics of Solid State Reactions*. Hugh's father, Rupert Clare, had been involved in developing poisonous gases used in World War One.

"His wife was Doreen, my grandmother," Victoria explained. "She worked for Vancuso Wireless Telegraph Company, a British telecommunications enterprise. As a logistics coordinator, she helped establish a network of coastal radio stations for ship-to-shore communications."

Austin listened. Serving as a scientific advisor to the Royal Air Force, Hugh had been invited to attend a chemistry conference at Moscow State University. Soon after he arrived, Doreen was mailed a telegram stating her husband had been killed in a Moscow car crash. After two years spent believing the telegram, she received a coded letter from Hugh informing her that he was alive: The Soviets had faked his accident and forced him to advise Air Defence Forces on the construction of robust aircraft. Hugh's letter warned Doreen not to inform the British government, lest he be killed and the family targeted by Soviets.

In an effort to find him, Doreen left her job. A series of petitions and bribes earned her unauthorized entrance into the USSR. Malcolm and Barrington, her two children, came with her. After a year of searching, she learned Hugh was detained at a military base in Lipetsk, but her attempts to make contact were foiled by police guards. She was forced to work as an English typist for a KGB officer under threat of her husband's execution. The boys had no means of communicating with their father, and soon Doreen was resigned to accepting their separation.

Malcolm often threw rocks at the police for mistreating his mother.

Barrington kept a low profile; he also never came home with bruises on his face. Doreen would scold Malcolm for his insubordination, telling him to accept life under strict control, but he would sneak by the base in Lipetsk hoping to glimpse his father. Usually he saw nothing but a field lined with Soviet fighter craft. He spent his nights dreaming that Hugh would commandeer one of them and soar into freedom. He conceived of unconventional aircraft and made sketches in his free time, regarding the plane as a symbol of liberty and autonomy.

At fourteen, he finally did see his father. Hugh had been sitting at a table of officers. He'd put a finger to his lips and greeted Malcolm at the fence. There he'd instructed the boy to take his mother and brother and return to England—and if she refused, to go himself.

Believing they would kill Hugh if she did, Doreen refused to leave. At fourteen, Malcolm was afraid to go without her, so he stayed in Lipetsk. He and Barrington remained unschooled for three years, but they would often visit the home of a local scientist whose son they'd befriended. The man's name was Andrei Avdeenko. His boy was Fyodor. Aware of their interest and acumen, Andrei would tutor the children in physics. When they weren't studying or playing, Fyodor would share his collection of comic books featuring Norse deities.

"Andrei had purchased them as a gift from a Danish merchant," Victoria said. "The boys couldn't understand the language, but they followed the pictures."

"Hence the lasting interest in Norse mythology," Austin said. "And the names of all the Glitnir projects. Those comics, could they be—"

"The ones in my dorm room? Yes. Fyodor gave them to me when I was five. A family relic."

"So what happened to Doreen?"

"In the early winter of 1958, she was contacted by a member of MI6 saying they'd decrypted a letter from the Lipetsk base. It was from Hugh. A vehicle was sent to drive Doreen and the children to Finland, where they'd catch a plane to London."

"Imagine her relief."

"For the children, yes. But she stayed in the Soviet Union, fearing they'd kill Hugh otherwise. My dad and Barrington returned to England alone to live with my great-aunt Susan. After studying at the Harrow School, my dad was accepted to MIT. As an undergrad he made frequent trips to London to help the British locate the Clares. The Secret Intelligence Service got them back in sixty-six."

The taxi passed a row of breweries along the tree-lined canals before veering onto Nevsky Prospekt. They reached an intersection and waited at the signal. A neon orange car whizzed through the junction and nearly caused an accident. The driver barked something about New Russians.

"So Hugh was held in the Soviet Union for fourteen years."

"And the boys, four. In the early eighties, my dad learned Fyodor had become a professor of nuclear physics at Leningrad State University. That's when they reconnected."

They turned onto a dimly lit street, and the cabbie pulled to the curb. Austin paid the fare. The taxi drove away, leaving them at the entrance of a dilapidated apartment complex.

Victoria pushed a button by the door, and they were buzzed in. Fetid odors assailed their nostrils in the lobby, if it could be called that. It was a dark cavity that smelled of urine. Pipe drips landed on their heads. Wrinkled newspapers lay scattered on the ground, soaking in the moisture. The plaster of the walls was not merely chipped but gouged, leaving exposed the building's plumbing. The sight conjured an ugly metaphor in Austin's head: the building was a body, and he was staring at its entrails.

"You sure this is the right place?" he asked.

Victoria nodded. "Hard to believe anyone could let a home decay to this extent, much less live here. Tenants feel no sense of ownership. Most of these apartments are communal. No one takes responsibility if the building rots."

They stepped onto an elevator with scarcely enough room for the two of them. A collapsible door sealed them from the shaft, and the box began an upward crawl.

"To think a nuclear physicist lives like this."

"Talk to people in the city," she answered. "You'll find many people hold advanced degrees, yet they're selling trinkets on street corners—more profitable than the careers their degrees afford." The elevator screeched to a stop, and the door folded open. "This way. Fyodor is expecting us."

They knocked on an old, beaten door and heard movement on the other side, followed by clinks of shifting bolts. In the crack of the doorway stood a man of medium height with curly hair, a flimsy build, and distinct Slavic features, the slant of his forehead continuing the line of his nose. Squinty, magnified eyes blinked behind thick glasses that gave him a permanent look of intense scrutiny. His shirt was half buttoned and half tucked.

The apartment's cheerful décor seemed unbefitting of the complex. Scant, but bright furnishings invited a measure of warmth into a clean, humble residence. A painting of an Italian hillside rested over an oak rocking chair. A basket teeming with red flowers hung on a kitchen wall. Shelves were stacked full of black-and-white photographs of late relatives, including Andrei, and the living room was rich with foliage.

Avdeenko opened his arms and embraced Victoria.

"My dear girl!" he said. He kissed her left cheek, then her right, then her left again. "I can't tell you how pleased your visit makes me. And this time you flatter me by bringing a friend."

She returned his embrace. "Wonderful to see you, Uncle Fyodor. I've missed you. This is my classmate, Austin Hardy."

Austin offered a hand and said with a grin, "Victoria hasn't stopped talking about you."

"Only good things, I hope."

"You can be sure of that. Thank you for your hospitality."

"A student of science is always welcome here. So you take aeronautics with Malcolm. A challenging course, I imagine." His cheery tone took a dive. "If only we were meeting under happier circumstances. Victoria, I worry for your father. It is a good thing you have come. Both of you, please step inside. May I pour some drinks?"

"Tea would be nice. Thank you," she said.

"I'm fine, thanks," Austin said.

Avdeenko put a kettle on the stove while Victoria sank onto the sofa. Admiring the old photographs, Austin found a stuffed animal sitting on the shelf.

"A wolf," he said. "There must be a story here. Do you have children?"

"That's Sköll. And no, I do not," Avdeenko said from the kitchen. "That was a birthday gift from Victoria ten years ago. I'm sure she's shared her appreciation for Norse mythology."

"Sköll is the wolf who chases two horses carrying a chariot holding the sun," said Victoria. "I thought it was the perfect gift for a physicist, a man who spends his life hunting answers to the cosmos."

"You have both come a long way for answers tonight," said Avdeenko. "I'm ready for questions."

Austin brought him up to speed on his night in Clare's office, and how he'd found the professor's cell phone lying on the ground. "We connected with you when we heard your voicemail message. You'd mentioned finding bugs. Where exactly did you find them?"

"There were two. I first discovered one in my mobile device. My cell phone had been running out of battery faster, despite indications of strong charge on the display screen. It was getting hotter than usual and made little buzzing noises before I'd make a call or immediately after I'd hang up. Usually, the buzzing and the static don't start till the phone starts dialing. It was the buzzing that finally clued me to the fact that someone might have installed a program. Sure enough, someone was intercepting my calls remotely. Later I dissected my landline and found evidence of wiretapping."

"So what did you do?" asked Victoria.

"I reformatted my cell phone to wipe the bug. As for the landline, I installed a scrambler, and usually leave the earpiece off the hook to waste time on the interceptors' recorders. When the replays aren't filled with static, they will be stuffed full of gibberish."

Austin said, "We have a theory as to why someone tapped you."

"I'm all ears," Avdeenko said.

"You'll have to excuse some gaps and holes in our knowledge. Hopefully you can fill those in."

"I will try."

"It sounds from your voicemail message like you consulted for Professor Clare on his most recent project, Baldr."

Avdeenko looked alarmed. "You know about it?"

"Not much, but we suspect the tapping was an effort to learn about the technology and monitor its progress. We think someone wanted to overhear your conversations with Clare. When the time was right, the interceptors sent an agent to kidnap the professor and steal his technology. The briefcase must have had something to do with it. Stealing Baldr had to be a slick in-and-out. The kidnappers had to move before the technology could be transferred to the military. Your collaboration kept them apprised of the project's timeline."

"It's plausible."

"But now to why we're here: What exactly is Baldr?"

The kettle began to whistle, and Avdeenko filled Victoria's cup. He sat in a chair opposite them, looking troubled.

"You can trust Austin, Uncle Fyodor," Victoria assured him, sipping her tea. "Dad did. He knows about Glitnir Defense and Dad's real line of work. Only one aspect is still foggy to both of us—the inventions themselves. We're only asking about the latest."

"You don't have to persuade me," said the physicist. "Under ordinary circumstances, my lips would be sealed. But judging now . . . Malcolm's life, and a great many more . . . Wait here."

Avdeenko disappeared into his bedroom and returned with a box-shaped apparatus of naked wires and circuitry behind a funnel-shaped tube. He placed the contraption on the floor.

"This is my Herf Gun," he said. "A home-built High Energy Radio Frequency weapon constructed using my own microwave oven. Do you want to see me use it?"

Austin eyed the machine warily. "Do we?"

"I think you do. Remember, this is just the preamble to a full explanation."

Avdeenko opened a cabinet filled with small electronic toys. He pulled out a remote-controlled car and set it on the ground next to the contraption, handing the control to Austin.

"Turn it on," he instructed. "Take her for a spin. Just don't crash into my microwave."

Austin took the control and flipped the switch. The car reacted with a click. He oriented the automobile down a clear path and accelerated. Before the car hit the other wall, he jammed the stick to the left. The car spun out and circled back toward them. He began steering in circles and figure eights.

"Now," Avdeenko pronounced, "watch this."

He aimed the contraption's funnel at the car and pulled a trigger.

The car rolled to an immediate stop.

There had been no sputtering, as they might expect from a drained battery. It had merely died.

Austin jiggled the controls, holding down the accelerator. No response from the car. "It's broken," he said.

"More than that," Avdeenko said. "It's fried."

"What happened?" Victoria asked.

"The Herf Gun's high-intensity waves, focused by a parabolic reflector, induced destructive voltage spikes within the car's circuitry, disrupting its electronics. The toy's cooked. It will never work again."

Austin set down the remote and took a closer look at the car. "Fascinating."

"It's hard for us to fathom what we cannot see or hear. For instance, the myriad radio waves and particles bombarding our bodies every instant of every day. We can't escape them, nor do we perceive them. The car, on the other hand, did experience the consequences of the waves I shot through it."

"So that's what Baldr is? A Herf Gun?"

"Far from it," Avdeenko said. "The Herf Gun is an approximation, a gadget that creates an effect similar to Baldr's on a microscale. And you wouldn't want me to point the Herf Gun at you. It would probably damage your nervous system. You'd hardly know up from down. The vertigo, motion sickness, and nausea would be terrible. You'd have trouble breathing. High energy waves would damage tissue. It would be a very painful experience." He tossed the toy car into the trash. "Baldr would have the same effect the Herf Gun had on my toy car, but on a larger scale, and without physically harming humans."

"What exactly is it?" Victoria asked.

"Baldr is a weapons satellite, an arsenal of nuclear weapons orbiting Earth."

"I thought it wouldn't harm humans," said Austin.

"Not physical harm. Economically, culturally, and politically, it could mean life and death." This was a circuitous route to addressing their confusion, but Austin was sure it would pay off with clarity. "You assume the nuclear warheads are intended for detonation on Earth."

"As opposed to?"

"Space," Avdeenko said. "Or high in the atmosphere, witnessed from one very dark piece of land."

Victoria shook her head. "I don't understand how a nuclear explosion in space could have the same effect as your contraption."

"I haven't explained it yet." As Avdeenko filled her teacup with more hot water, Austin glanced at the bared fangs of the toy wolf, Sköll, on the shelf. Had it been alive, the animal would have been bounding straight at him. Austin's attention returned to Avdeenko's voice. "When a nuclear weapon detonates, it creates a burst of radiation called EMP, or an electromagnetic pulse. Coupled with a fluctuating magnetic field, the shockwave creates voltage surges and a destructive current within electronics, frying the circuitry."

"How long have scientists known about these pulses?" Victoria asked.

"Since early nuclear tests, but not until conducting further research did we realize the magnitude of the effects. The Starfish Prime test of 1962 sent ripples through nuclear physics intelligence circles at the time of its detonation, far surpassing calculated consequences. The nearly one-and-a-half-megaton weapon exploded four hundred kilometers above the mid-Pacific, burning out streetlamps and setting off burglar alarms as far as Hawaii, thirteen hundred kilometers away. The bomb would have had even greater effects had it gone off over a point on Earth with a stronger magnetic field.

"Around the same time, the USSR produced three pulses during nuclear tests over Kazakhstan. These tests were smaller, but they were far more damaging because of their proximity to civilization. Several factors determine the shockwave's destructive power. First is the altitude of detonation. A nuclear explosion fifty kilometers above the North American continent could affect five or six states, whereas an explosion five hundred kilometers above land could wipe out all of the country's electricity, and bring the economy of the United States to a standstill.

"Can you imagine the ramifications? Since the Cold War, our civilizations have grown increasingly dependent upon electronics for communication and data storage. Dependence translates to vulnerability. Consider the upshot of even a localized attack. A strike to the New York Stock Exchange would halt a sizeable fraction of world financial trading. A strike on an airport would render air traffic controllers incapable of guiding planes to safe landings. Aircraft would collide or continue to glide until they ran out of fuel. Now imagine the outcome of a nationwide attack, a space blast over Kansas. Telecommunications, industrial, and transportation networks would shut down. Cars and buses would stop on busy highways. Passengers would be trapped in subway tunnels without working cell phones. No computers, no landlines, no radio, no television or Internet access. A person couldn't communicate with a friend a hundred meters away, let alone kilometers apart or across states. Hospitals would no longer function. Supermarkets couldn't refrigerate food. There would be no heat for homes. People would starve and freeze. Emergency relief agencies would have no way of mobilizing response teams. The power grid is unprotected. Hierarchy would become anarchy. Infrastructure would collapse."

"We've learned a bit about EMP bursts in class," said Austin. "The consequences have always sounded farfetched."

"I don't exaggerate. The technology is real," Avdeenko countered, "and it's capable of stopping the motor of modern Western civilization. An electromagnetic tsunami formed at the right altitude could bring a country as large as the United States to its knees. Nuclear explosions generate cascades of X-rays and gamma rays, which interact with molecules in the upper atmosphere to generate a pulsed, oscillating current of electrons. The electrons interact with Earth's magnetic field. Invisible waves stream out, a million times as strong as normal radio signals, and devastate all unprotected electronics within the blast's line of sight on land, at sea, and in the air. The flux can wipe out circuits, silicon chips, transistors, diodes, inductors, and electric motors."

"What about vacuum tubes?" Victoria asked with sarcasm.

"Those would be relatively safe."

"So if you're living in the early nineteen hundreds, you're home free."

"Five variables determine the magnitude of a pulse's effects," Avdeenko continued. "So far, I've talked about altitude. Second is the actual potency of the bomb. As we saw from the comparison between America's Starfish Prime and Russia's 'K Project' over Kazakhstan, proximity to civilization introduces a third. You must also consider geography and strength of the local magnetic field, a fourth and fifth.

"As you saw with my Herf Gun, it is possible to generate the same effect without a nuclear blast. We can create other electromagnetic bombs, called e-bombs, although their effects are usually limited to a radius of ten kilometers from the blast. We can also focus high-intensity rays on targets using parabolic reflectors. Militaries would use these weapons for disabling localized targets, like moving vehicles. For broader impact, nuclear warheads are ideal."

Victoria's eyes narrowed to a squint. "The sun burns by nuclear fusion, right? It's as if the sun is nothing but billions of nuclear bombs going off at once. You'd think that with all that power, the sun might wreak the same havoc on our planet."

"Disturbances in space weather caused by the sun *have* disrupted power on Earth. Geomagnetic storms, caused by solar wind shockwaves linked with flares, coronal holes, or other anomalies, can create temporary changes in Earth's magnetosphere. In 1989, one such electromagnetic storm affected power throughout Quebec. The storm knocked out their power grid, leaving six million people without electricity for nine hours. People witnessed auroras in the sky as far south as Texas. Later that year, as if Canada hadn't suffered enough, another storm put Toronto's stock market on hiatus by widely damaging microchips."

"So there's nothing we can do to prevent disruptive solar phenomena," Victoria said. "But what if a rogue state obtained the technology required to detonate a nuke in space over the States?"

"Your government established an EMP commission to assess the threat and recommend defenses against hostile states. It is possible, though expensive, to protect systems from an EMP attack. The process would entail encasing every electronic component with a metallic cage to block out electromagnetic radiation. A ballistic missile defense system would help safeguard the electronic infrastructure, as well. Your question is particularly relevant today. Concerns for an attack abounded during the Cold War, then diminished. Now there is concern over Pakistan, Iran, North Korea, and a few other countries, particularly since North Korea has expressed willingness to sell its nuclear weapons to terrorist organizations.

"Which leads us to Malcolm's latest development: the Baldr satellite." Avdeenko interlaced his fingers and pushed his wrists together, stretching his palms. "Satellites come in many forms, shapes, and sizes with a wide range of purposes. Technically, a satellite doesn't have to be manmade. A satellite is anything that orbits a planet or large body. The moon, for example, is a natural satellite. We distinguish manmade satellites by calling them artificial. The first successful manmade satellite was launched in 1957 by the USSR."

"Sputnik One," said Austin.

"Correct. The event marked the start of the Space Race between Soviets and Americans. Decades later, thousands of satellites and pieces of 'space junk' orbit Earth. These satellites serve a wide scope of functions. Some are astronomical, used to observe stars, planets, and galaxies. Telephone companies use private satellites for communication. Meteorologists use Earth observation satellites to monitor the environment and weather. Cartographers use them for mapmaking. GPS systems receive key information from navigational satellites.

"The military has its own reasons for launching satellites, among them reconnaissance. Spy satellites collect intelligence overseas and send classified data to agencies. And then . . . you have killer satellites: orbiting arsenals designed to eliminate other threatening satellites, hostile warheads, et cetera.

"Malcolm designed Baldr as an armed killer satellite loaded with nuclear missiles. The missiles range in yield and can be detonated from any preselected altitude.

"In plain English, it's a floating armory that can drop a bomb of any size wherever it wants. Mind you, Baldr's purpose is not to incinerate land or people. It is intended for the EMP effects. It can also deploy non-nuclear EMP missiles for localized targets. Anything the U.S. wants to shut down, whether it's an armed vehicle, nuclear facility, battlefield, village, city, or portion of a continent, it can.

"The nation that owns Baldr has great power over any other country. Most pertinently, I would hope, for preventive defense. Who would threaten to launch a missile against the United States? The U.S. could quickly cut enemy power, and even localize EMP shockwaves to specific arsenals or nuclear facilities. The U.S. would suffer none of the typical political consequences associated with preemptive strike or the killing of innocent civilians. America could mitigate any threat with clean hands.

"In terms of ground warfare and special operations, Baldr can effectively neutralize even fortified opponents with advanced defense systems. Say the U.S. wants to capture a drug lord in dense jungles that are difficult to navigate and infested with armed mercenaries. On a criminal's turf, the criminal has the advantage. Take out his power, and you level the playing field. The same applies to the sea.

"Reconnaissance tools built into Baldr reduce the perils of gathering intelligence on enemy soil. The terrorist trail often leads your foot soldiers to arid deserts, hidden caves, and other harsh terrains. Baldr's spy technology helps locate targets. Once it's found any hostile combatants, Baldr can isolate whichever region the military wishes to immobilize, knock out electricity, and put a crimp on the enemy's ability to organize. The military can then advance swiftly and with greater safety.

"There you have Malcolm's work in a nutshell. Victoria, I imagine you have already discovered the mythological connection. How did the satellite get its name? In a sense, your father's invention is an absolute master of light. With its all-seeing electronic scanners, the satellite can gaze directly into enemy territory, illuminating its controller's foes. It has the power to give light. It also has the power to remove light, and cast vast regions into total darkness. That is why Baldr was named after the Old Norse god of light."

"Why doesn't the satellite destroy or depower itself after detonating a nuclear missile in the near vicinity?" Austin asked.

"Warheads never blow in the satellite's vicinity. They travel great distances before detonating to avoid direct damage to the missile carrier caused by the heat of the explosion. And the exterior is covered by a heavy shield of conducting material, preventing electromagnetic radiation from damaging the satellite's core. This shield is called a Faraday cage."

"Doesn't the launch of the Baldr satellite violate any sort of international space law?" Victoria asked.

"It does," said Avdeenko. "Namely, the Registration Convention and the Outer Space Treaty. The former, adopted in the mid-seventies, requires countries to provide the United Nations with information about the orbit of all space objects. The latter, signed in 1967, forbids states party to the treaty from launching nuclear weapons or any weapons of mass destruction into Earth's orbit—among other rules. But remember your Defense Department's logic, and your father's. Used for its disruptive rather than destructive potential, Baldr enables a more surgical form of warfare, one that spares lives, minimizing physical harm to American soldiers and civilians in hostile territory. It was largely for this advantage that the satellite was contracted, despite its violation of space laws; and it is in part because of those laws that the satellite must remain top secret."

Austin leaned back on the sofa, cupping his hands on his knees. "It's astounding such unthinkable power can be unleashed at the flick of a button. Also makes sense why any number of extremist groups would want to steal it."

Somber, Avdeenko shook his head. "Based on what you witnessed in Malcolm's office, it may be too late. Someone out there must have done more than plant bugs in my telephone to learn the ways of Malcolm Clare."

"What do you mean?" Victoria asked. "All they took was a briefcase."

"A briefcase with Malcolm's laptop inside," Avdeenko answered.

"And in that laptop he installed a copy of the program that operates Baldr—all the basic functions. From his own office, he could transmit, or uplink, any command he desired."

Paling, Victoria said, "Why would he do that?"

"Malcolm wanted to ensure the ethical use of Baldr. A tool this powerful . . . he knew it could easily fall into the wrong hands, perhaps some political loon either too afraid to use it or too trigger-happy. Closer to home, he worried about moles at Glitnir. The only solution was to duplicate the controls and allow himself overriding authority unbeknownst to anyone but me. A moral failsafe. He never thought this action would compromise us. Of course he protected the overriding program with various security measures. Any false attempts or efforts to crack the program's password—just a single misstroke—would cause the duplicate program to erase itself from his hard drive."

"Dad could never have anticipated someone stealing his backup control," Victoria said in his defense. "Not if no one knew about it."

"That's right."

"Then apparently our thieves do careful homework," Austin said. "It's safe to assume they've kidnapped Clare and stolen his copy of the satellite's command controls. They must have been watching a long time, studying his and your every move to find an Achilles' heel."

"We didn't think there was one," Avdeenko said. "But we were wrong. We can only hope they have yet to discover the password."

"Do you have any idea who might have taken Baldr?" Austin asked. "While you collaborated with Professor Clare, did anyone express interest in the project? Any other physicists or colleagues?"

"I kept my consultation private. Unfortunately, despite his talents, Malcolm was never the best judge of character. He's too trusting." Victoria arched a brow at Austin, who shrugged. "My leading suspicion is that a Glitnir insider has been gathering information. I believe a mole from within his company had something to do with it." The physicist's head sank into his shoulders. "I simply can't wrap my head around the notion of a heist."

"Clever criminals," Victoria said. "They seized the project soon before its official reveal, during a time of ambiguous ownership. Surely the Defense Department was about to assume control. Before the transfer, the satellite disappeared, and all that remains is that obscure radio transmission on the flash drive Austin found in my dad's cabinet."

"Just a gut feeling, but I don't think Baldr rests in the hands of the end user . . . yet," said Austin.

Avdeenko looked skeptical. "What leads you to that hunch?"

"Terrorists tend to be poor organizers. That's not true across the board, but in general they tend to be scattered. No harebrained fanatic could have easily found the resources to keep you, Clare, and Glitnir under close surveillance and execute the robbery of such an important technology without someone hearing about it. I agree the existence of an insider seems a likely explanation. Of course, a defense corporation like Glitnir thoroughly investigates the backgrounds of its employees. Anyone with the remotest link to an extremist group would never make the cut. That means whoever stole Baldr probably intends to sell it rather than use it, unless the thieves have some very large target in mind—some very large chips to fry."

"A logical conjecture. And for God's sake, I hope you're right. If Baldr does indeed rest in the hands of middlemen, then we might still be able to keep it from truly dangerous hands."

Victoria exchanged fretful looks with Avdeenko as she walked to his side. She had never seen him so forlorn. Fear was etched into the wrinkles around his eyes, which had begun to dampen.

"Uncle Fyodor," she said, embracing him, "you've been so helpful. We'd better leave you now. I've made reservations at the Hotel Dostoevsky, and I don't want them to give our room away at this late hour."

"You are welcome to stay here, Victoria. You, too, Mr. Hardy. That is, if you don't mind sleeping on the floor. I have but one mattress." He looked embarrassed. "And one key."

"Thank you," Victoria said. "We wouldn't want to burden you. You probably need to return to the university in the morning. We don't have plans yet. Not knowing where today would lead us, we left tomorrow open."

"You've given us much to think about," Austin added.

"Run off and sleep, then," Avdeenko said as he led them out. "I will place some calls to Glitnir and begin an investigation of my own. Any leads I find, I will pass on to you. Believe me, something like this cannot happen without a fight on my end. If anything comes up, call me."

"We will," Victoria said. "Good night, Uncle Fyodor."

Avdeenko closed the door and heaved a sigh. He poured the remaining tea, drank it, and crashed on the sofa.

Despite all the security measures, he couldn't help but think Clare had been careless to let the satellite escape him.

Planning a course of inquiry, Avdeenko reviewed the calls he would make the next day. Then, grudgingly, he let himself sleep. On his shelf, the wolf idled in the dust. It hadn't missed a word.

FIFTEEN

On the street outside the apartment complex, a swarthy man waited in the front seat of a rental car. You found the first two bugs, he thought, but not the third.

He clicked off the recording device and removed his earpiece, watching the apartment's entrance. Soon two young figures exited the building and flagged a taxi at the corner. They were next, he decided. After admitting to holding the passkey, they had told him exactly where they'd be spending the night.

When the taxi drove away, the man climbed out of his car and rang the bell. Probably assuming his recent guests had forgotten something, Avdeenko buzzed open the main door.

The man called the elevator. When the unit started its ascent, he took a 9mm Makarov from his pocket and in one smooth motion began screwing in a silencer. When he reached the top, he knocked on the physicist's door. He heard scuffling feet and shifting deadbolts.

The door opened.

A face as handsome as his seldom elicited panic, but the man at the door was dizzy and trembling. The curly-haired physicist tottered backward, staring down the hole of the Mak's barrel.

"Good night, Dr. Avdeenko."

The taxi pulled alongside the Hotel Dostoevsky and dropped them off. Austin tipped the driver before he drove away. They entered the lobby and checked in at the reception desk.

"We have a reservation for two, one night," said Victoria.

The receptionist was a young brunette wearing a tag that read "Svetlana." She was pretty, hiding glances at Austin beneath ripples of chestnut hair. "Name, please?"

"Clare," Victoria answered.

The receptionist scrolled down on her computer. "Victoria?"

"That's right."

"How many beds?"

"Two," she blurted.

The receptionist repressed a grin.

"Smoking or nonsmoking?" Svetlana asked, venturing another glimpse at Austin. Victoria's female instinct told her the receptionist was mentally undressing him. She felt a little irritated, only because she couldn't wait to get to sleep, and the receptionist seemed to be working slowly.

"Nonsmoking."

Victoria signed a paper and handed over the black Centurion Card.

"I see it's your dad's," Austin said, glimpsing the name.

"He lent it to me," she said. "Tell me you didn't believe a poor, starving grad student actually owned one."

"You never know when it comes to poor, starving daughters of billionaires."

Svetlana set two keycards on the counter. "For your room," she said. "Our restaurant serves a buffet breakfast from seven to ten-thirty a.m. Would you like a bellboy to help you with luggage?"

"We're traveling light," Austin said. "It's all on our backs."

"Americans?" He nodded. "Have a pleasant stay. Your room number is 405."

"Thank you, Svetlana."

They heard a slight giggle as the elevator doors closed.

Austin and Victoria went up to the room and sprawled out on their beds. With little discussion they brushed their teeth and took turns showering, then lay under the covers in silence. Austin shut off his thoughts, his mind awash with exhaustion. He practically jumped into a disturbed slumber.

Vasya parked his car near the back of the hotel, and pulled down the flaps of his black fur cap. He flicked on his pistol's safety and concealed the gun in an inner pocket of his trench coat.

He brushed aside the doors, passed through the lobby, and walked directly to the second floor.

He found what he was looking for. Starting at the farthest end of the hall, he collected all the used room service food trays from the corridor. He found three, then did the same on the third, fourth, and fifth floors. Soon he had gathered a large stack.

Along with each serving dish came a small glass vase containing an orchid. He removed the flowers from each tray and put them in one vase, forming a bouquet. He took the vase with him.

Returning to the lobby, he pinched a business card from the front desk before going back to his car. In the parking lot, he flipped open his cell phone and dialed the number on the card.

"Thank you for calling Hotel Dostoevsky," answered a voice in Russian. "You have reached the concierge. How may I help you?"

He replied. "Hello, I am just arriving in your back lot. I have some heavy bags. Would you send someone to help me carry them?"

"Right away."

Vasya leaned against his car, roll-tapping his fingers across its fender. The lot was empty. Not a soul in sight. Idle minutes in the cool air tempted him to light a cigarette. Before he had the chance, a young bellhop appeared wearing a crimson double-breasted jacket with golden buttons.

"You called for help with your baggage?"

"I did," Vasya said. "Let me pop the trunk."

He pushed a button. The latch clicked, and the bellboy lifted the rear open. He looked surprised.

"Sir, I don't see any bags."

Facing the empty trunk, the bellboy froze as cold metal dug into his spine. His knees buckled slightly and his legs quavered, the metal prodding him forcefully. He sensed a capable hand behind the trigger.

"Strip down."

The bellboy began to shake. "You want money? I have two thousand rubles in my wallet! Oh, God, please!"

"Shut up and strip."

The boy's quivering fingers made it nearly impossible to unfasten the buttons. Sweaty palms didn't help. His assailant waited patiently as he undressed. Had he been facing the other direction, his fear might have boiled over into full-blown terror at the sight of his attacker disrobing, too.

Vasya flung his trench coat into the car. Keeping the muzzle steady, he slipped on the bellboy's uniform.

"Get in the trunk," he told the boy.

Crouched in the trunk, the boy curled into a ball.

"Are you going to kill me?"

"Not if you are quiet."

The trunk's slam squelched his sobs. Now in uniform, Vasya tucked the handgun away and returned to the lobby. He passed the concierge desk, picked up the vase of orchids, and approached reception.

Folding his new white gloves on the counter, he said, "Hello, Svetlana."

The brunette studied him without recognition. She seemed to be noticing his apparel's ill fit, but forgave the shortcoming as soon as she got lost in his smile. She let a few seconds pass to take in his features at her own pace.

"I didn't know we'd hired a new bellman," she said.

"Just part-time, during the nights," he said.

She let linger a beguiling grin. "Do you need help with something?"

"I am to deliver these flowers. A man ordered them to surprise his girlfriend. It was just the two of them, young Americans. I don't remember their room number."

Svetlana looked a tad doubtful, but he sensed she was easily swayed. "Are they a couple? The lady asked for two beds."

"Maybe the flowers are supposed to help with that."

She shrugged. "They checked in a few minutes ago. Room 405."

"Do you have a spare key in case they've gone out? I'm to leave the flowers on the nightstand." Seeing her mistrust, he added, "The young man asked as a special favor."

Svetlana punched some numbers, swiped a fresh card, and handed it to him. "Fine, here."

His manner and appearance continued to charm. "For the sweethearts," he said.

Treading gingerly, Vasya walked down the hallway and inserted the keycard. The room opened to darkness and the silence of sleep.

"Wake up," he hissed.

There was movement under the sheets of both beds. Austin and Victoria sprang upright.

The intruder set the flowers on their nightstand. "Quietly rise, keeping your hands on your heads," he told them.

Victoria rose to her feet by the closet. She had often experienced the harsh transition from nightmare to consciousness. This felt like the reverse.

"What's going on?" Austin said.

When Vasya's silhouette loomed over him and he felt the icy barrel on his cheek, it became clear. He studied the intruder's shape. The man was lean and small compared to the prowler in Dr. Clare's office.

"If I shoot," whispered the man, "no one will hear. Do as I say, and you will live."

They complied, but knew better than to trust the promise. Without light the man stood faceless, and the room seemed to close in around them.

"Stay there," said the man. "I will not hesitate to shoot."

Victoria stared straight at the man. "Who are you?"

"For your sake, I won't answer that."

"What do you want?"

He ignored her. "I know what you're both thinking. You're imagining ways to best me—wondering if you should dial the front desk, or attack me and try to knock the gun from my hands. You will fail. Do only as I say."

Victoria glanced at Austin. He seemed unfazed, and this calmed her a little. "Tell us why you're here," he said.

The man backed away from their beds, giving them space. "I believe you saw my colleague a few days ago."

"You mean the big hairy office creeper?" Austin said. "You and your friends have a knack for showing up uninvited."

"In the office you found a small flash drive," the man said. He sounded patient. "Do you remember any of the sentences stored on it?"

Austin's chest clenched with the realization that this was a test, and his answer would determine whether or not the assassin spared them. He had the feeling this man's guiding principle in killing was necessity. "I'd help if I could," Austin said. "Believe me, your gun is persuasive. But the flash drive was password protected. We couldn't get in."

The man's quiet told them he was judging the veracity of Austin's excuse. Austin felt glad the room was dark, so his face couldn't expose the lie.

"Give me the drive," said the man.

"Is that all you want?"

"I won't ask twice."

Anger brimmed inside Victoria, along with surprise as Austin reached into his backpack and retrieved the device. She was watching him relinquish their only hope of finding her father and bringing an end to this catastrophe. A voice inside her screamed in protest; how dare he just hand over her father's property!

She drew back her leg, preparing a kick to the man's groin. It would be so easy. He was almost within reach, as was Austin, and she could thwack either of them before they could make the exchange. But reason told her it was too risky to try to stop Austin. The man had warned he was prepared to shoot.

Austin handed over the flash drive. So he had deserted her. Loathing welled inside her, loathing toward the man with the pistol—but more so toward her double-crossing partner, who had so readily acquiesced. No fight, no questions, no thought to alternatives. The drive was gone.

The man dropped the flash drive onto the floor and stomped on it. The casing cracked. He squashed it again with his heel for good measure, then slipped the remains into his pocket. Victoria shuddered with revulsion toward both men. She had to stop this.

The man sensed her imminent attack.

"Don't do it," he said.

She found the voice to be eerily contained.

"The information is destroyed. Accept it. Don't make me cause more damage."

She retreated.

"Is that all?" said Austin, still sounding calm.

"Unplug your telephone. I don't want you calling the front desk before I get down there."

Austin tore off the receiver and yanked several other cords from the wall. The intruder moved to the door. He stood not ten feet away from them, and still neither could see his face. "Do not come after me," he said. "If you do, I will be forced to come after you."

The man drove to a nearby alley, took off his clothes, and opened his trunk. He handed the uniform to the bellboy, who shivered.

"Please don't take my life! Please don't take it!"

"Drink this," Vasya said, drawing a flask from his trench coat.

The bellboy whisked it from his hands, unscrewed the lid, and guzzled—not out of thirst, but compliance. He choked on his first swig, spouting a bit. Soon the alcohol smothered him in warmth and dulled his shock.

"Drink it all," said Vasya.

The boy didn't seem to mind.

Vasya lit a cigarette. He inhaled deeply, then let it all out in slow, irregular puffs. They sat there together a few moments, without rush, the man and his captive. He smoked half the cigarette and handed the rest to the bellboy.

Then he sped away, leaving the boy in the alley.

G ather your stuff," Austin said. "We're leaving."

He chucked his backpack over a shoulder and wiped the bleariness from his eyes. Sleep would have to wait. He flipped on the bathroom lights and splashed his face with cold water.

Victoria came to the doorway.

"I'd more happily kill you."

He turned to face her.

"What's the matter?"

"From here I go alone."

He was mystified. Her sincerity reminded him of the iciness of their first meeting. There was a new distance between them. They were no longer partners on a team.

"What's bothering you?"

"I can't believe you gave him the flash drive," she said. "It was our only lead."

Relief washed over him.

"If that's what's upsetting you, you can relax. But there's no time to talk details now."

"Details?" Victoria snapped. "You consider this a minor mishap?"

"We have to follow that man. *He's* the new trail."

"I told you, I'm going alone. And now I'll have no idea how crucial that radio transmission may have been in recovering Baldr."

"Not yet."

"What do you mean, not yet? It's gone. Destroyed."

"The flash drive is," said Austin. "Not the contents. I left a copy of the transmission with my roommate. If I know Ichiro, he's been working to decipher its meaning since we left Stanford."

She retained her hostility, not ready to admit she'd misjudged. He approached her cautiously, as he would a rattlesnake.

"If you'll let me past this door," he said, "we can follow this man together." Then he added with a quiet warmth, "You'll find me helpful. I have a merit badge in hunting and stalking."

She looked away in what he realized was an effort to hide embarrassment.

"I'm sorry," he continued. "Must have given you a real scare."

"Damn you, Hardy." She shook her head, wearing the look of someone finally grasping she wasn't alone. "Hang on while I get my backpack."

The man with the Makarov dialed a new number, juggling his phone and the steering wheel.

"Hello, Vasya," answered a bassoon-like voice.

"Viking. I've recovered and destroyed the missing passkey."

"Good. That blunder could have been costly."

"I'm heading to my meeting with Deeb now."

"Remember not to show too much interest in his bid up front."

"I'll give him time to consider the satellite's worth before exerting pressure. Are we ready to initialize Baldr?"

"Wait two hours before sending the pulse."

"Why the delay?" Vasya asked.

"The corsairs need time to sail into closer range."

"Not too close. We don't want to cripple Ragnar's ships."

"Start a timer then. I'll send you the coordinates now."

They had left their room and crossed through the hotel lobby. Austin was scanning the streets. The man had left no trace.

"It's useless," Victoria said. "All we have is a voice. We don't even have a face."

"I'm not looking for a person."

"Then what?"

"A speeding car. A taxi weaving lanes. Anything."

"Where would he go?"

"His hotel. The airport. Another city."

Austin thought back on squinting through Clare's spyglass when he'd been trying to read the license plate of the sedan speeding down Palm Drive. He recalled the same sense of futility.

"Help, please!" came a meek snivel.

Victoria spun around. A young, uniformed boy staggered toward them, an empty flask in his hand. His hair was ruffled, his face pallid. Tears had hardened on his cheeks and left a crusty residue in his lashes. His golden buttons were undone, his outfit creased.

"Help, please!" he repeated, reeling forward. He retched on the sidewalk.

"What is it? What's the matter?" Victoria said.

He lurched into her arms and coughed.

"Back trunk." His words were slurred. "He put me in trunk. He took my clothes and put me in trunk."

"Who put you in a trunk?" Austin said.

"He held gun to my back and told me strip, then he put me in trunk. I said please, don't take my life!"

Austin felt hope. "Who was it?" he asked. "Try to remember."

"Oh, God, I need hospital," the bellboy groaned.

"Are you hurt?" Victoria asked.

"No, he did not do anything. Not yet . . . I need hospital. I could barely breathe in trunk. . . . Please, don't take my life . . ."

"We're not going to hurt you," Austin said. "We want to find the man who did this to you. Can you remember what he looked like?"

Translating the mumbles on top of his Russian accent was a challenge all its own. "I did not see him. I told you, he put me in trunk. I could not see."

"What about when he released you?"

"No, I did not see. I think he was about my size. . . . That is all I know. Please, it was not my fault! He just came and stole my clothes."

"We know it wasn't your fault," Victoria said.

"He gave me this. Made me drink. I do not think he really wanted to kill me."

Austin took the flask and turned to Victoria. "Forcing this guy to down the alcohol was a calculated move. Our man wanted him to stumble back drunk, so people would doubt his story."

"It is true story," said the bellboy. "No lies."

"Did he give you anything else?" Victoria queried.

"A cigarette. He gave me cigarette. I could hardly breathe in back trunk, but I felt around clothes he had dressed in. I reached into pockets. I found these."

The bellboy handed them several passports and some papers. Austin shuffled through them.

"Anything useful?" Victoria asked.

"This man has more IDs than the Department of Motor Vehicles," Austin said. "But there's one thing he can't lie about: his destination."

"How do you know?"

"Train ticket receipts. He's leaving tonight by rail, making several transfers en route to Bruges."

Victoria turned to the bellboy. "Get back inside the hotel. Stay warm. Tell them what happened. If you're too soused to make it home, stay in our room tonight. It's 405. Here's the key." She turned to Austin. "Do you know which tracks he's leaving from?"

"The receipts are basically copies of his tickets. We have tracks and departure times."

"When does the first one leave?"

"We'd better find the station. It leaves in less than an hour."

SIXTEEN

Whistling "Mack the Knife" in the twilight, Rove leaned over the portside bulwark and watched the Atlantic waters roll past the hull. Like he did most nights, he had come to find peace in solitude. The sundeck was nearly empty. A few passengers lounged outside, reading on reclining chairs and soaking in Jacuzzis, but most had retired to dinner and various evening shows. Musical performances could be heard in decks below. Rove listened to his own melody and let the ship's gentle rocking soothe him. A few mojitos had given his cheeks a rosy tinge. The buzz was slight, enough to pacify him before bedtime.

The ship had lit up for the night's passage. From an aerial view, he thought, the craft must have resembled a parade of drifting candelabras.

Skies of molten amber emphasized a sharp horizon line. That morning, sunrise had projected a gradient of ruby shades into the heavens. He recalled the old mantra, "Red sky at night, sailor's delight; red sky at morning, sailors take warning." There was truth to the adage, and he wondered what sort of weather the red sky forecasted.

He predicted a storm. Cumulus clouds mushroomed into anvils, cotton-topped with gray undersides. Waters had grown choppy, crowned in whitecaps. The ship canted sharply. The ship's staff had covered the pools with nets to prevent swimmers from entering as waves slammed against the tile edges. If conditions worsened, they'd have to drain the water until weather improved.

Rove found the prospect of a storm thrilling. As it had so often done in his years of service, the sea would test man, and man would win. He'd never subscribed to the theory that man was a helpless gnat in a vast macrocosm, powerless and small. To him, man was capable of heroic ends, among them defying nature's worst. He looked out at the brewing tempest, watching the waves rage against the steel hull—and he thought, here's nature's finest creation against its strongest creation: man versus the sea.

The ship rocked steeply again. At least he thought so. Maybe it was the drink. If it had been, he sobered quickly when a voice crackled through the ship's PA system.

"Passengers. This is your captain speaking, Giacomo Selvaggio. We are about to experience a ship-wide power outage. Do not be alarmed. We seem to be having trouble with one of our generators in the engine room. Our technicians are addressing the problem. Rather than have you ambling in darkness, I ask that you all return to your staterooms immediately. I apologize for the inconvenience this will cause. There is no need for distress. Please report to your cabins. Crew, please assist passengers, then return to your own quarters. Remain there until further notice."

The message jarred him from his thoughts. There was a foreboding tone to the captain's voice that made his chest grow heavy. The voice had indeed belonged to Selvaggio, but not the blithe, easygoing Selvaggio he'd met on the bridge.

Several things happened at once.

Glass shattered near the bow. A panel of the bridge side-wing window blasted outward and fell into the frothing waters below. A human form rammed through the glass, limbs flailing, teetering on the precipice before plummeting toward the sea.

Rove's clasp tightened on the rail, nerves firing throughout his body. He glanced skyward. A storm cloud loomed over the ship, blotting out the remaining yellow hues. He could have sworn he saw a brilliant flash of light, something like an aurora, but it passed in microseconds, hardly leaving an impression.

Deck lights flicked out. Vibrations emanating from the engine room, hardly noticeable before, suddenly seemed conspicuously absent. Water lapped against the hull. Beyond that there was silence. The regular hum of the generators faded, and at once Rove felt as though he were riding a dead whale.

SEVENTEEN

The orange raft rose and sank in choppy waters, the crests ever higher and troughs ever deeper. Clinging inside, Malcolm Clare felt like a bobbing buoy.

Days had passed in this empty panorama. A few craft had sailed by, too distant to hear his cries or observe his flags. He had prayed for a barge or a cargo ship. None came. His only companion was the open sea.

Huddled on one side of the inflatable raft, he shook in the cold. The last few days had entailed the severest physical pain of his life. Though he'd stopped the bleeding early, his bandaged arm still throbbed. Hypothermia plagued him day and night, depriving him of sleep. He'd lost all bearings, had no idea how far he'd drifted. Saltwater sores stung him. The sun exposure wreaked havoc on his skin, scorching his neck and forearms, leaving him practically reptilian for all the peeling and flaking.

He knew dehydration posed both lethal threat and irony. To a man dying of thirst, the infinite supply of water was there to tempt him. Several times he'd cupped his hands and held small pools between them, longing to smother his lips and gulp handfuls. But the salinity would desiccate him all the more; he'd shrivel like a raisin.

Along with sleeplessness, the dehydration had begun to affect him in ways he hadn't expected so soon. Random visions, often in the shape of people, came and went. He'd pinched himself whenever they appeared, forcing away the hysteria. It disturbed him that his mind was beginning to run amuck before even a week had passed.

He'd been using a knife from his first-aid kit to spear fish. Trapping them proved tricky at first, but he'd adapted to the learning curve his survival demanded. He'd devoured even the skin and eyes, knowing they had valuable nutrients and fluids.

Right now, he was simply waiting and thinking. His throat clawed at him, parched, a dry cave that led to an empty stomach. When the sun fell, he rested against the raft's fabric coating. He'd grown accustomed to the water sloshing in his ear.

He had resigned himself to the certainty of death, but not to the curiosity over his killers. He often meditated on his circumstances and looked more deeply into possible motives. He pictured the headlines: "Stanford Inventor Crashes Private Plane." Conspiracy theories would run thick as oil; his death would provide all kinds of fodder for a scandal-starved media. He worried for Victoria, whom they could easily entangle in their investigations. She, too, would always wonder.

The worst thing they'd stolen from him was the chance to say good-bye, and explain. He'd spent his days of isolation wondering whether it had been wise all these years, keeping her so in the dark.

As he rested, an image of the pilot's corpse played through his mind. He entertained the idea that his murder had been made to look like suicide. It would be the perfect scenario, he thought as he grasped his bandage. Someone had left a gash on his arm to give the impression he'd tried to commandeer the plane, but had been held at bay by the pilot, whom he'd eventually killed before sinking them both.

He abandoned the idea, remembering he'd been tied to a chair.

He replayed those frenzied minutes in his head, from the moment he'd woken up in a stupor to the moment he'd barreled out the door. The wind had seized him and battered him, had flung him like debris. He'd lost all orientation. He remembered a second of peace before tumbling into the water. He'd surfaced in time to see the enormous splash. Had he forgotten anything else?

It struck him.

The hatch had been open.

Someone else must have been there. Not the pilot, but a third passenger.

He had never opened the hatch. Someone else must have done it and parachuted out. For all he knew, the "pilot" had been dead the entire flight, or no pilot at all. Someone else had navigated the plane while a dead man sat there. This would pin disaster on accident.

Unless the pilot had opened the door midflight, then returned to the cockpit to his death by heart attack or poison . . . but why would the pilot have opened the hatch, only to remain inside?

Someone else must have opened it. The same sadist who'd cut a rut in his arm.

He remembered the three words written in his own blood. The memory chilled him.

Someone with a warped sense of history.

A noise stirred him from his speculation. Something was moving through the water. Hopeful, he stood for a better view, dancing on the raft to keep his balance. He blinked. Was it real? He pinched himself again, wondering if madness had finally got the better of him. What he was seeing had more definition than any hallucination. They were phantom shapes at first, bearing a faint resemblance to skewers. The image cleared. He realized the shapes were bowsprits cutting a path through the fog. There were several of them, vessels approaching from the northeast on a direct route toward his raft. He tottered backward in astonishment.

"Here I am!" he rasped, words scratching their way out of a throat that felt like parchment.

He tore off his shirt and waved it.

"Please help me!"

He feared the ships would disappear at any moment, melting away like everything else, pointing the way to greater dementia. But he wasn't about to let a new hope slip his grasp.

"Ahoy! Lost sailor ahead!" *Flyer, rather,* he thought. "Ahoy!"

The ships maintained course. He continued flapping his shirt around, spouting feeble calls. As of yet he had discerned no human forms on-board the vessels. Not until the ships steered closer.

The flotilla had five long, narrow craft. Double-masted with triangular rigs, the ships maintained a swift slice through the water.

"Keep coming!" he shouted. "You see me."

He saw cargo boxes piled near the sterns, and studied the ships harder.

Corsairs?

He felt a twinge of dread. Corsairs had a history riddled with violence dating back centuries to the Middle Ages, and even the Crusades. Pirates sailed corsairs, relying on the maneuverable designs for speedy assaults and quick getaways. Shallow drafts helped traverse shoal waters. Bladelike bowsprits sparred with the breeze and pierced any wave that challenged the forepeak.

The ships came within a hundred-foot range. Clare slid his shirt back on and kneeled on the floor of the raft. The center corsair pointed right at him.

He paddled, trying to move himself out of the ship's line of passage, but his attempt was in vain; he was no match for its speed. The flagship closed in at fifty feet, then thirty. He paddled furiously, shouting for attention. The corsair would soon destroy his raft.

He eyed the flagship's bowsprit and considered grabbing hold. No, he was too weak.

"Please, look out . . ."

He could almost kiss the bow of the oncoming vessel. It plowed forward, the shaft only seconds from impaling him. He braced for impact, vaulting over the edge of his raft with what little strength remained. The corsair rammed his float and punctured a hole. The raft deflated and sagged, filling with water.

"I'm right here!" Clare shouted. "Starboard side!"

He thrashed his arms, not merely treading water but kicking up buckets. The ship didn't stop. He sensed his only chance of survival slipping away. Searching for handholds, he clawed at the hull as it sailed on. A coiled rope, partially frayed, unraveled out of nowhere and splashed next to him. He grabbed hold and wrapped several loops around his wrists. His frail fingers could hardly maintain a grip. The rope began to slide away.

On deck, a pair of hands reeled in the catch. Clare didn't let go. A powerful arm reached over the side of the ship and hoisted him out of the water by the collar. He collapsed, coughing and spewing seawater over the deck.

Finally able to breathe, he took a moment to find his bearings.

He glanced upward at a hulking mass crowned in red hair. The site of a familiar emblem caused him to blink twice, but he didn't cower, even as his ribs caved under the weight of a heavy boot. A host of men surrounded him.

"It's him," the leader said. "Put him in the brig."

EIGHTEEN

Welcome to *Glitnir Defense,* read the topmost sign over the elevator of the building's lobby, and below it, *Justice from a Forge.* As he stepped inside, Dan Chatham dabbed the sweat on his forehead with a sleeve. His spine had the unnatural stiffness of someone who usually slumped when no one was watching.

"Everything okay, Mr. Chatham?" asked the receptionist as she scanned his ID card.

"Dandy," he said, looking past her.

The main office looked like the sales and trade floor of an investment bank. Scores of desks were lined in rows, each one equipped with a quintuple monitor set. Engineers operated satellite stations of clustered computers. Switching between keyboards and separate touch-screens, their fingers were never still.

Eyes followed Chatham as he crossed the floor and entered his office. He usually drew attention. He was a portly fellow, but not obese, and walked with a slight waddle that suggested he was heavier than the reading on his scale. Today his presence had a silencing effect on his Glitnir subordinates—all but one.

"Mr. Chatham."

The voice belonged to Kathryn Dirgo, the operations director. The sound of her deliberate, brusque strides had announced her approach. People well knew that tempo. Authoritative by design, her executive wool suit of slate blue, worn with a gray blouse, captured the rank and dignity of a general's uniform. She wore it with grace, but not with a feminine grace. She was a petite woman in her late thirties, and neither attractive nor unappealing. By virtue of professional decorum, she remained outwardly sexless. Her cropped hair masculinized a set of features that might have otherwise turned heads.

She had spent several years as a Marine captain in a St. Louis facility for the National Geospatial-Intelligence Agency. She had joined Glitnir Defense during its establishment and become operations director after six years. Among the things Dirgo didn't tolerate was incompetence.

When Chatham wasn't in, she ran the floor with clean efficiency, her tactics scarcely short of the jackboot. She delivered results. When he was present, she maintained a thin veneer of subservience. No one took issue with her leadership style. It was effective. She was appreciated among those who reported to her, not for her congeniality, but for the productive, meritocratic atmosphere she fostered and for the initiative she inspired.

"Morning, Kate," said the president. "How's the dame of steel?"

If there was a wince, it didn't show. She was used to Chatham's chauvinism.

"We have a problem."

"Oh?"

"We've lost control of it."

"Control of what?"

"Baldr."

The president stopped and turned around to face Dirgo. Personnel on the floor looked on, watching his reactions.

"What do you mean, you've lost control of it?"

"Exactly that—and that's *we*, not *me*. Hours ago the satellite deviated from its normal trajectory. We don't know why."

"Have you tried compensating?"

"Naturally."

"And?"

"So far, nothing has worked to realign the satellite with its intended orbital path."

"Where is it now?"

"Somewhere over the North Atlantic."

"What do you mean, somewhere? Speak precisely, Kate."

"Simultaneously with the satellite's orbital deviation, we lost contact with the navigation system."

"Jesus."

The color left his cheeks. He slid his hand into his pocket to hide a tremor.

Dirgo said, "I've contacted our programming engineers. They'll be here soon."

"Have you called anyone else?"

"Malcolm's nuclear consultant in Saint Petersburg."

"Avdeenko?"

"Yes."

"What did he say?"

"I couldn't get through."

"Why not?"

"No answer."

"Which numbers did you try?"

"Both his home number and his university office. His phone's been ringing off the hook."

"Why hasn't he answered calls from Glitnir? Is he traveling?"

"No explanation."

Chatham wiped his brow. "Someone get me a cup of ice water."

He registered an uncomfortable invasion of personal space as Dirgo edged closer and nearly scraped the overhang of his stomach. When his secretary brought him a drink, he used the opportunity to take a step backward.

Dirgo said confrontationally, "Well?"

"Well, what?"

Her voice filled a room that had come to a hush. "What are we going to do?"

"What we always do. Call Malcolm."

"You don't think we've tried that?" Dirgo snapped. "I called his Stanford office. No answer. Voicemail. No response. No one in his department knows his whereabouts. One of his teaching assistants, Walter Rosekind, wrote back and said he'd claimed to have gone on a research excursion. Of course, he told no one where he was going and left no forwarding or contact information. I had people call San Francisco Airport this morning to see if our plane there took off. Guess what? It did."

"With Malcolm in it."

"Who else?"

"Did they have access to any flight logs? Could they tell where he was going?"

"No access."

"That's impossible."

"Air traffic staff report the log was erased an hour after it was entered."

"Logs don't just get erased, Kate."

"This one did."

"Who'd you speak with?"

"Two tower controllers, as well as the traffic management coordinator."

"Did they explain the data omission?"

"If they did, I'd have said so. This is Malcolm we're talking about. If he's intent on covering his tracks, he'll find a way."

"I want you to keep investigating. Find out where he was going."

"I think we have a bigger problem on our hands."

"You said you couldn't reach Avdeenko, and our programming engineers couldn't figure it out. Who else can we count on?"

"I said our programming engineers will be here soon. They haven't tried. They may uncover something useful."

Chatham knew it wouldn't make a difference. Calling in more engineers was a waste, but saying so wouldn't gain anything. To placate Dirgo, he knew he had to create the image of a clockwork solution. Damn it, why was he always pleasing her? She reported to *him*.

He stood on a chair. The legs buckled under his weight.

"All right, everyone," he announced, clapping his hands. "You've all heard what's going on. Our latest launch seems to have a will of its own. Baldr's navigation system's gone haywire. She's hovering a little south of the Arctic Circle." A collective murmur filled the room. Chatham raised a hand, and the buzz died. He continued. "As you well know, Baldr is our most prized piece of weaponry to date. It belongs in the hands of the Defense Department. We're going to give it to them."

Dirgo's expression added, *come hell or high water.* It wasn't a smile or even the hint of one, but a contented look that crossed her face as he spoke—perhaps the satisfaction of seeing proper urgency conveyed.

"There's no time for sermons about teamwork," Chatham continued. "Just do what needs to be done. Do it well, and fast. As of now, your prior assignments take the back burner till we resolve this. These are your new tasks. People in customer engineering, make phone calls to determine Malcolm's whereabouts. He's the best man to help us. Radio and transmit-station personnel, your new assignment is to search for glitches in our navigational uplink program. Sift through lines of code if you must till you learn whether the problem's on the ground or in the sky. People in the applied mathematics department, figure out how much power was required to alter course to Baldr's current location. Everyone else—"

Chatham's secretary tapped his shoulder.

"Sir, it's for you."

"Who is it?"

"He didn't give a name."

Staring at the phone in her hands, he began to feel nauseated. "Tell whoever it is I need a name."

"Sir . . ."

"What?"

"He seemed adamant."

"Do you expect me to talk to a no-name caller?"

"I . . . I really think you'd better answer."

Chatham grabbed the phone from her hands and barked into it, "Hello?"

A familiar baritone drawl greeted him. "Turn on the speakerphone. Do it, Dan."

Reluctantly he did as instructed.

Chatham glared at his secretary and mouthed the words, *Trace the call.*

The secretary shook her head. "The caller's using VoIP," she whispered—that was, Voice over Internet Protocol. "But it's IP-spoofed. The information packets are falsified and shifting rapidly. The call appears to originate from Colorado . . . now Bolivia . . . now Hong Kong. It's going to keep shifting."

When the voice on the line spoke, workers sat motionless, apparently fearful of any sound that might provoke Chatham.

"Employees of Glitnir Defense," said the voice, "no doubt you've spent the morning in a dither over a certain missing satellite. Not to worry. You have the power to win it back."

Center stage, Chatham held the phone over his head. Engineers and other Glitnir employees in proximity leaned in from behind their desks, keying in on the call.

"Who is this?" Chatham demanded.

"I am the man who has taken the satellite from you. My ownership is temporary. In several days' time it can be yours again."

"I require a name. A name, an organization, a cause. I refuse to speak with an anonymous terrorist."

"I am no terrorist," said the voice. "You may call me 'the Viking.'"

B aldr is safe," the Viking declared after his summary, "but depending on who wins the auction, your homeland may not be."

"Let me get this straight," Chatham said. "You've stolen our technology, and now you're auctioning it off? Who are we playing against?"

"Several bidders. Your biggest rival is a former Algerian oil minister now residing in Tripoli. He is the primary financier of a radical terrorist army called al-Nar. The army prides itself on being a new breed of religious revolutionaries, an intellectual breed. They are striving to harness advanced weaponry to establish a worldwide caliphate ruled by sharia law."

"I'm perfectly familiar with al-Nar, thank you," Chatham spat.

Quickly usurping an engineer's computer, Dirgo tried to contain her alarm as she refreshed her memory with a search on al-Nar. Founded by Othman al-Zayfi, the group called for global jihad beginning in Algeria, and had made several attempts to replace the Algerian government with an Islamic state. In response to unheeded demands in 1998, al-Nar had initiated a campaign of civilian exterminations in satellite villages to Algiers, the bloodiest of which took place in Casbah. Cloaked guerrillas had reportedly arrived at two A.M. in trucks and cars, armed with machetes, shotguns, and grenades. They had systematically murdered men, women, and children for five hours, cutting throats of animals and leaving pyres of corpses. Most young girls were abducted rather than immediately killed. Severed limbs and mutilated bodies were thrown through windows, infants flung against walls. Homes were burned and bombed. Females both living and dead were raped, the stomachs of pregnant women machine-gunned. Amnesty International had reported a death toll of 429.

Dirgo kept reading. In 1999, in response to Algeria's recommendation that other states make aggressive efforts to disable al-Zayfi's networks abroad, al-Nar had conducted a series of bombings in France and the United States. During this time, they were responsible for the hijacking of a ferry between Belgium and England; seventy-nine were killed. In 2000 Othman al-Zayfi's soldiers had created and dispersed a video intended to be seen by the entire Islamic world, in which he condemned his own army's past massacres: "Small arms are ineffective. We will not make progress raiding a village or blowing up a bus. We must strive for technology that can dismember perennial powers of the Western Crusader world."

Dirgo printed off the page and wrote in felt marker at the top: *Other bidders*. She tried to hand the paper to Chatham, who waved it away.

"You said they're financed by a former oil minister?" Chatham said into the phone.

"Correct. One of my agents, a facilitator of this auction, will soon meet with him. He will want to know your starting bid. That is why I call."

Chatham could hardly think over the drumming pulse in his head. It was hard enough to admit to himself that he needed Malcolm's help.

"Which minister?" he said.

"I have agreed to bidder privacy, but you might deduce his identity. His days with OPEC were marked with turbulence."

"I'll give you an answer now," Chatham said. "The answer is no. Our company designed and built the satellite. Baldr belongs to us."

"Seems not," said the Viking. "Refusal to comply is the natural response to a sudden demand like this one. But think it over, and you should come around. It's in your best interest to offer a bid. And I can recommend a reasonable start."

"What?"

"Eight hundred million."

"Outrageous."

"The figure doesn't far exceed your expenses. If you factor in your cost of materials, launch, manpower, and nuclear warheads alone, you arrive at a number close to that."

"That's irrelevant."

"Ah, but how about value to country? I'm sure I needn't explain the ramifications of losing this auction. The millions you'd save would mean little without an economic infrastructure. I encourage you to bargain seriously."

"Is this how you make a living? Nuclear blackmail?"

"I haven't blackmailed anyone, nor have I threatened injury. I've done you favors by informing you of your opponent's affluence and mind-set. I have no intention of using Baldr against the United States."

"There's not a court in the country that wouldn't call you a terrorist."

"I have no interest in international politics. My actions are in the name of no religious jihad or revolution. I have no ideology, and I promise violence can be avoided."

"What are you after then?"

"Money, Mr. Chatham. Whether it's yours or the minister's, I'm after money. I assure you and everyone listening, I am a man of my word. Bid highest, and Baldr will return to Glitnir. I'll simply deliver a laptop and pass-code, returning control to you. I will not inflate your rivals' bids when relaying them. I promise to conduct a fair auction, as one would a piece of art. Frankly, I hope Glitnir wins. A shift in political and economic power so large would unsettle me."

Chatham spoke through a tight jaw. "You've stolen our weaponry and offered to give it to a terrorist organization."

"Not give. Sell."

"You're no better than they are."

"What I've done is create a market. You and the minister have been offered the same opportunity to participate. No gifts in my repertoire, Mr. Chatham." He paused, then continued. "I congratulate you on a masterful engineering feat. Baldr works beautifully."

"How do you know?"

"I've used it."

Chatham fought off full-blown panic. "Where? On whom?"

"The al-Nar sponsor asked for a demonstration," the Viking said. "I gave him one. I could tell you the location if you accepted my suggested starting bid." Chatham turned to his secretary and started to mouth, *Turn on the news,* but was cut off by a disturbingly prescient remark: "You won't find reports on any channel."

As Chatham scanned the room for help, it was no coincidence he didn't cross eyes with Dirgo; hers were too penetrating, too severe—too judgmental. He never turned to her when searching for an emotional crutch. Finding no inspiration, he sipped his water.

"I remind you, Mr. Chatham," Dirgo said from the sidelines, "our nation does not negotiate with—"

"What the hell do you suggest I do?" he retorted. "Do you see what's at stake here?" And why did Kate always think she could do his job better than he? Maybe the stupid Marine wanted it. He turned to the phone. "Goddamn it, tell me what you've done."

"I take it you're offering the bid?" said the Viking.

Chatham ignored Dirgo's wrathful crossfire. "Just . . . tell me the damages."

"Very well. I acknowledge your initial offer of eight hundred million. Rather than inflict damage on land, I decided to conduct a smaller experiment at sea by disabling a cruise ship. A group of seafaring mercenaries will soon arrive to keep order on the luxury liner. I chose to experiment on the high seas so as not to provoke war or political skirmish, which could only complicate my bottom line."

"What bottom line?"

"My auction."

"Where's the ship?"

"I won't tell you that," the Viking said. "It's not in your interest that I do. Neither of us wants an unwarranted military response."

"Someone's going to find you."

"The ship is uniquely positioned near little traffic. I doubt it will get much attention from other vessels. And if the auction goes quickly, the cruise ship needn't remain there long."

"If you dare harm anyone onboard—"

The Viking went on. "You'll take the blame for whatever happens at home or at sea. Baldr belongs to your company. How will you explain to your government and people that you lost it? Should another bidder win the auction, how will you explain that your people's safety wasn't worth the cost? Failure to partake in this auction will expose your secret 'defense' corporation. Millions of Americans will learn Glitnir was too cheap to protect them. And they'll find out it was you who refused to buy their lives, Mr. Chatham."

Chatham hated perspiring while standing perfectly still. It was mortifying. A pool had collected under his chin, and it was no use trying to hide the stains under his armpits or the new ones that were beginning to bleed from his chest and back.

"You heard my colleague," he said. "The United States does not negotiate with terrorists."

"You can spare me the bromide, Dan. Terrorists negotiate with me."

"How can we even be sure you'll return the satellite if we transfer funds?"

"Trust."

"Not a chance."

"I don't think you understand. You don't need to trust in my conscience. I'll be trusting in yours."

"What gives you faith in me?"

"My mercenaries have been instructed to place several dozen explosive charges around the hull of the cruise ship . . ." Dirgo's eyebrows leapt. She stared at Chatham in apparent shock as the Viking resumed speaking. ". . . And I will be inclined to detonate should I meet resistance on your end. I now speak to everyone in Glitnir. This is your warning: Don't cross me. I'm a simple auctioneer, but I have terms."

"What terms?" Chatham asked.

"No doubt you've considered pinpointing Baldr's location and shooting it out of the sky. You may have contemplated getting the Department of Defense involved. Don't try either. The moment I smell military cooperation, I sink the cruise liner."

"What happened to no violence?"

"No outside parties means no necessary violence. Complicate things, and I'll know. Alert the Navy or the Coast Guard, and you'll wish you hadn't. Do you understand?"

"Yes . . ." Chatham began to say. "But you can't—"

"Thank you for submitting your starting bid of eight hundred million USD. My facilitator will convey your offer to the Algerian minister and other players. After their meeting, I will notify you of the counteroffer. The whole process may take a few days. I will only call you during regular business hours. Whenever I do, I expect you to put the phone on speaker. I want everyone in Glitnir headquarters privy to our parley . . . and your promises. Good-bye."

Click.

There was no pity in Dirgo's glower at Chatham. He stared back, empty and out of focus, feeling the weight of a look he couldn't avoid.

"What could I do?" he said to her, suddenly aware of his own pallor. "He's a lunatic."

Dirgo crossed her arms, pursed her lips. "You're doing business with him."

"He has us in tight clutches."

"So what are you going to do about it?"

"Play his game. That's the only way. We have to bargain."

"With what? Glitnir's piggy bank?"

"We'll come to a compromise."

Her eyes drilled into his as if glazed with kerosene. She must have been aware of how it made him feel—that her glare nearly caused his knees to fold.

"You won't do that," she declared.

"There's no other way."

"You aren't thinking very clearly. Or have you ignored the responsibility of thinking altogether?"

"It's not exactly easy when . . . why are you being so hostile?"

"I don't appreciate the fact that bending over is your default."

"Stop antagonizing me. We need to work together here."

"Oh, I'm sorry. Let's hold hands and smile at the situation we're in. Give in to his demands, that's all we have to do."

"Jesus, Kate, I have no recourse. Never pick a fight with someone who *wants* a fight."

"He doesn't want a fight. He wants money. We can stop him." She pressed a stiff forefinger to his abdomen. "Take control. What would Malcolm do?"

Her question angered him. He wanted to ball a fist and punch her. She could take it, if she wanted to be such a man.

He felt too crowded by thoughts to care that the entire office was listening to her rebukes. He slid his feet together to determine whether he had regained physical balance, deciding he had.

Chatham opened his eyes for a pronouncement.

"I need everyone to listen. This lunatic is determined to squeeze us for every penny we've got. He's using thousands of innocent lives as leverage to broker a deal. I need information before the bidding gets out of hand. If we're to determine the magnitude of the effects of the pulse he's unleashed, we need to know where and when he detonated the nuclear warhead in space. Folks, I want to know the exact coordinates of the Baldr satellite. Find it."

NINETEEN

A chunk of driftwood would have had its benefits over a cruise liner without power—maneuverability, for one, the ability actually to paddle somewhere. Leaning over the rail, Jake Rove felt like a castaway, the *Pearl Enchantress* his island.

The alcohol had begun to wear off, and he returned to his senses. He paced the deck, mentally replaying phrases from the ship-wide announcement.

This is your captain speaking ... we are about to experience a power outage ... trouble with one of our generators ... technicians are addressing the problem ... return to your staterooms immediately ... remain there until further notice.

The message had filled him with doubt. Did it make sense? He remembered Selvaggio saying the generators could power a city of sixty thousand, but they didn't power everything. He walked to the nearest bar. The bartender had returned to his cabin. Rove hopped behind the counter and pushed a button on the soda fountain. The faucet gurgled, and a few drips spurted before the pressure ran out. He tasted the cola. There was little sweetness; the electronic valves hadn't dispensed any syrup.

He judged by the fading daylight he had less than an hour before the ship's corridors would become too dark to navigate. He jogged to the buffet at the Century Oasis. Passengers had begun to stream out. The staff were ushering guests to the exit, shrugging and shaking their heads at people asking what the fuss was about. Some crew appeared unfazed, as if the blackout were a routine drill, while others stood wary.

Ducking and squeezing through the throng, muttering half-formed apologies to those he jostled, Rove worked his way upstream into the restaurant. It was hard to move; guests were vacating in mass exodus.

The serrated edges of a familiar voice caught him.

"We're on cabin lockdown. You're going the wrong way."

Rove stared back at the flat lips that had pronounced the words, then at the malevolent blue eyes that echoed them. The blond, tuxe-doed wall of a man registered in Rove's index of faces. The diamond ring seated on the waiter's middle finger confirmed his memory.

"No more canapés, I see," Rove said.

"We're closed. Go to your cabin."

"My wife left her diamond bracelet at the dinner table."

"You boarded alone."

"We didn't board together."

Rove made a motion to circumvent the obstacle and felt a clamp of flesh around his forearm.

"I think you're a liar," the man said.

Rove's thumb shot into the crewman's wrist and pinched a nerve into a bone. The tendons in the crewman's arm tightened. He jerked away, his lips breaking their perpetual flatness.

"And I think you're a lousy waiter," Rove said. "Step aside. I'll return to my cabin after getting the bracelet."

Distance grew between them as the crowd kept moving. Rove ducked down and continued working against the outward flow. He cast a sidelong glance at a sign that read *Buffet Open 24 Hours* and noted the irony. The crowds soon thinned, and he realized he probably looked like a jewelry thief scouring the restaurant for dropped valuables. Sure enough, he found what he was looking for. On one of the tables sat someone's forgotten camera. He picked it up and pushed the "on" button. Nothing happened—no lens movement, no power light. He set it back on the table.

He made his way to the galley, where cooks and busboys were salting meats and wrapping foods in foil and cellophane. They could hardly see their own hands, it was so dark inside. Light was fading fast. They opened refrigerators sparingly to preserve the cold.

"What are you doing here?" a waitress asked behind him.

Rove glanced over his shoulder. "Finding out what's wrong."

"Please return to your cabin."

"You sure are an adamant bunch. It's not fully dark yet."

"It will be soon."

"I'll go in a minute. Quickly, do you have any electric can openers?"

"Sir, I'd rather not have to ask you again. Please return to your—"

"Miss, please bring me a damned can opener."

She fetched the tool from the kitchen and huffed, "Here you are."

He knew the situation had probably made her nervous, and the last thing she needed was an unruly passenger. He tried not to upset her, but he didn't want to have to explain.

Rove tried it. The blade wouldn't spin. "This doesn't work. Do you have another? How about an electric cork remover? This is actually important."

"Sir, this can't possibly—"

"Just find it!"

His outburst made her curious. The waitress returned with a second electric can opener. "Try this one."

Rove pushed the button. "Doesn't work." He tossed it onto the counter.

She escorted him out. "Go directly back. Please follow our emergency protocols."

He descended one flight below the lido deck. If it weren't for the portholes, the halls would have been pitch black. A din of voices followed the tightly packed river of people, elbows jamming against one another as passengers made for their staterooms. He kept wondering, what could cause every electronic device onboard to die? Built-in components had failed—but so had remote ones.

An unseen force, surely nothing inadvertent, had laid siege to the ship. His next observation confirmed the hunch. Despite the power breakdown, people had no trouble accessing their staterooms through keycard scanners. He noticed a fortified metal sheath encasing the locking mechanism. Somehow the doors' electrical components remained unaffected. Rove read into the clue. If his theory were correct, shielded keycard scanners would have indeed been impervious to damage, along with the cards themselves, which had been issued at the departure port inside thin titanium protectors.

Had there been an unauthorized weapons test? The location didn't make sense. They were too close to the Baltic. Maybe the outage was a calculated element of an attack. If someone had planned to take over the ship, disabling power would be a good start. But who? As Selvaggio had pointed out, few pirates raided cruise ships. They had better luck with freighters. And what pirates could afford equipment powerful enough to black out a cruise liner? Few had the capital or internal organization required for an attack on that scale.

If an attack were forthcoming, it would happen soon. Confused prey meant easy prey. Hardly five minutes had passed since the outage, and near pandemonium had broken loose. It was an ideal time to strike.

Two crewmen had tried to stop his queries. If he hoped to investigate further, he'd have to blend in with them. Nudging his way through the crowd, Rove descended several flights toward the bottommost decks and entered a staff-only zone.

He walked with authority, and people were too harried to question him. He turned into a hall lined with crew members' staterooms. A man about Rove's size was leaving his cabin. The man brushed by, and Rove caught the portal with a toe before it closed. He sidled through the doorway and changed into a uniform.

He returned to the sundeck, where starlight illuminated a strange spectacle to the northeast. Rove trained on a spot midway from the horizon. There were five shapes, five wakes. He didn't need binoculars to appreciate their speed.

A hook snagged the rail next to Rove.

They're preparing to board, he reasoned as he observed the foreign crewmen from the bulwarks. The corsairs had pulled alongside the *Pearl Enchantress,* their crew unraveling ropes with grappling hooks, extending ladders, and dropping anchors off both port and starboard sides of the cruise liner. These heavyset minions were unscrewing lids to cargo boxes.

By now the lido deck was clear. No one else roamed the walkways.

Keeping safely out of sight, he peered over the bulwark and noted details pertaining to the five ships and their crew. More than half of them blond, the sailors spoke a language he couldn't understand. A Scandinavian tongue, he guessed. He leaned toward Norwegian.

The contents of the boxes came as no shock to him. They had guns. Automatics. Each man strapped a firearm around his torso before beginning the climb by rope ladder to the lido deck. The men looked fit to hoist at least twice their own weight.

Rove guessed each corsair could house thirty men; together, it meant there were around a hundred and fifty armed soldiers. Dispersed over twenty levels, between seven and eight armed hijackers would cover each deck, or maybe a few more, since only fourteen levels had cabins. Three thousand passengers could surely resist a hundred and fifty armed hijackers, though not without bloodshed and coordination. The latter was the limiting factor. Rove had faith in man's bravery. No doubt there were enough passengers willing to fight to reclaim the ship. But being confined to cabins, they had no way of organizing their resistance.

The grapplers clanged against metal rails, showing the *Pearl Enchantress* to be surrounded. The hook nearest Rove jangled as a climber ascended. He considered casting off the hooks. He would foil a few climbers, but invite retaliation from the rest. There were too many of them, climbing too fast.

Expecting soon to see fingers and faces appearing over the ledge, he took cover inside and peered through a window as their boots hit the deck. The invaders gathered and stood at attention beside the Neptune's Sanctuary pool, waiting for their chief to arrive with instructions. They pointed flashlights haphazardly, forcing Rove to duck to avoid catching any beams.

The leader appeared, and the lights steadied. Rove peeked up again and took in the man's height and girth. He was built like a wrestler without the chiseling, the muscular bulges smeared around a torso in top-heavy proportion. The cheekbones were obtrusive to the point of looking primitive. Rove noticed the red hair, the *Firecat* tattoo on his bicep, the latent violence behind a sullen expression. Despite his unsightly features, the man had a graceful gait and bearing.

Unprepared for an encounter, Rove located the nearest stairway and dropped one flight. He found a canvas fire hose coiled behind a glass panel near the elevator doors. He shattered the glass and strapped the hose over an arm, using a pocketknife to slice through the canvas. His blade was small and rusty, the canvas rugged and durable, making for slow cutting. When he finally got through, he looped the severed coil over a shoulder.

The closed door of the penthouse beckoned him—he knew he'd be safe inside—but first he checked on Fawkes. Hearing his knock, the steward let him in at once, wearing the look of a kid who'd crept into a cemetery on a midnight dare. Tiny shards of glass dusted his trousers.

"Jake, what the devil?" he asked. "I heard banging against the window. When I looked out, I saw rope and feet. Something's wrong, Jake. The captain hasn't told us everything."

"I know. I was just on the lido deck. We're being boarded by about a hundred and fifty Scandinavian pirates. Their vessels have moored off both sides of our ship."

Fawkes blinked rapidly through his spectacles. "*Pirates?* But Selvaggio said . . ."

"I know what Selvaggio said, and it made sense. These guys obviously have access to more resources than your average hijacker. Where and how they got them, I don't know."

"Where'd you get that uniform? And why the fire hose?"

"I grabbed the uniform from a crewman's closet on a lower deck. Good for accessing private areas without hassle, though it may prove unnecessary with the crew confined. The fire hose will come in handy soon enough."

"But you cut it!"

"It's not for putting out fires."

"Whatever you say, mate." Fawkes pulled a flashlight from his pocket and flipped the switch back and forth. "My beamer doesn't work. This is no simple blackout. I don't know what Selvaggio's keeping from us, or why."

"He probably wants to prevent panic."

Fawkes grumbled, "I'm not panicking. I just want to know what's amiss."

"So do I," Rove said. "Something tells me we'll find out soon."

"Look out for yourself, mate. Perhaps you'd like to stay in here with me?"

"I better not. Just checking on you. If anything bad happens, bang the wall. It's important you stay in your cabin as Selvaggio said. These pirates have weapons, maybe for stray passengers."

"What's going to happen to us?"

"I don't know, Lachlan. But I'll be damned if I let them ruin my vacation."

PART III

NIGHT DIVE

Hurtling like a spearhead, the train blasted along steel rails and pitched left through mustard plains. Bearing southwest, fifteen cars coasted through the European countryside, making a sound like a horse's gallop as the wheels hit the rail joints. Austin was reminded of a nineteenth-century locomotive.

He stared out the coach window. Ahead, flat meadows sloped into gently rolling hills. Victoria reclined in the bed of her sleeper, studying the collection of fake passports the bellboy had found in the assassin's trunk.

"Let's see," she said. "We've got United Kingdom, Canada, France, Slovenia, Russia, and the Czech Republic. Think any are real?"

"I doubt he's British," Austin answered. "His accent seemed fairly neutral. Can't say anything about the others."

"I'll bet one is legitimate."

"Why's that?"

"To have been able to penetrate Glitnir and learn about Baldr, he's no amateur. Probably trained by a government intelligence agency, maybe still working for one. But I don't think any government's behind the heist. Stealing Baldr is a brazen move, enough to provoke serious conflict."

"Which means he's playing for a second team, maybe for hire."

"Right, and if that's the case, he wouldn't give them everything about himself. Maybe a few aliases, but he'd keep his real identity with him as a firebreak. In case he had to cut and run."

The sleeper car went black for several seconds as the train entered a tunnel. When they came out, a ticket collector passed through the car and punched their stubs.

"I still see no guarantee they're not all bogus," Austin said when the collector left. "We can't be sure he ever worked for an intelligence agency."

"No, but remember the flask he gave the bellboy?"

"What about it?"

"The flask bears a coat of arms with a shield and sword," she said, passing it to him. "Notice the red star in the middle, with a hammer and sickle inside it. It's the KGB insignia."

He examined the flask.

"I doubt these were ever handed out like candy," he said. "A keen observation, Nancy Drew. You suspect he's ex-KGB?"

"Why else would he carry it? Which leads me to my belief that his real identity would be the Russian one."

"What's the name?"

"Vasya Kaslov," she said.

Austin polished the vessel's silver with his shirt. "You may be right. There's something on the bottom."

"What is it?"

"An engraving. Initials, I'd guess. V.A.K. What's the middle name on Vasya's passport?"

"Anatolievich."

"I'd say it's a match. Let's verify with a little experiment. Can I see those passports?" She handed them over. "Have you jotted down the information from each?"

She held up a notepad. "It's all here. Where are you going?"

"To chat with the train conductor. Back in a flash."

Austin made his way into the adjacent car and found the man wearing a black cap, gold-trimmed visor, and whistle. The conductor was leaning out between cars, fixated on the passing terrain. His badge read, "Yuri."

"Excuse me," Austin said.

"Hello," the conductor replied.

"May I ask a favor . . . Yuri?"

"What?"

"At the last train station, someone tried to pick my pocket. He wasn't quick enough, and I scared him off. After he tried to rob me, I followed the guy and managed to swipe a few passports from his bag of stolen goodies."

Yuri shrugged. "What you want me to do?"

"Help return the stolen IDs," Austin said.

He fanned out the passports like a hand of cards.

"Why not do yourself?"

"I don't want anyone to think I stole them." The conductor obviously didn't want to be bothered. "You wear the uniform," Austin added. "Besides, the top passport looks like it might be yours."

"Mine?"

Yuri looked at him strangely, then opened the passport to find a folded bill inside. His disinterest gave way to what looked like real concern as he slipped the bribe into his pocket.

"Sorry about thief," he said. "I will try and return passports."

"No need to credit the Good Samaritan who gave those to you," Austin said. "In fact, he didn't even board the train. Understood?"

"Okay, yes," Yuri answered.

"I'll be waiting here after you've scoured the train."

Victoria had allowed herself to become mesmerized by the railcar's steady cadence, its rhythm complemented by the occasional screech of steel on steel. Austin walked in holding an imaginary pipe and magnifying glass.

"Your intuition was correct," he said. "If our midnight assassin does carry his true identity with him, then he is indeed a Russian citizen by the name of Vasya Anatolievich Kaslov."

"How do you know?"

"Child's play, my dear Watson." He handed her five out of the six passports, then explained his ploy with Yuri's help. "Our man must have felt a small shock when the conductor presented him with all six passports, of which he could keep one. And so we learn from his choice which is most important to him. Not only that, but we also know where he sleeps. His car is second to last. We'll be able to follow him to his hotel. All of that for five hundred rubles."

Victoria pressed her thumb and forefinger to her chin. "Nice sleuthing."

"I humbly agree, but the initial hunch was yours."

"Only because I noticed the flask, which seems even more relevant now."

"We have yet to prove your KGB theory. Does Fyodor have any connections to the Russian government? Might he be able to search any databases for the name Vasya Kaslov?"

"I don't think so, but I'll call him and ask. He'd probably want to search for 'Vasily,' not the nickname."

Victoria dialed the number from her international phone. It rang a few times. When someone else picked up, she blanched.

"This is who? . . . You're doing what? . . . No, I was not aware. Who let you into his apartment? . . . This is a dear friend of his. He and my father—" She shook her head in disbelief. Austin leaned in closer. "I'm sorry, I couldn't understand you. . . . No, I don't speak Russian. . . . No, I don't know . . . I don't know how it could have happened. . . . Yes, I understand you are busy. . . . Please, continue your investigation. Bye." She turned to Austin, shaking her head. "That was a Russian police officer. Fyodor is dead."

He leaned toward her. "I can't believe it! How?"

"A bullet to the neck. Someone reported blood leaking under his door. The police found his body this morning."

Austin cast a mournful look out the window, then sat beside her, placing a hand over hers. "Victoria, I'm so sorry."

She turned away from him, resting her head against the pillow in a struggle against tears. The phone conversation had siphoned away her spirit, leaving her distant, enervated. Austin wanted to tell her it was okay to cry, she shouldn't fight the sobs, she should weep before the pent-up sorrow ate away at her—but he knew it wasn't in her nature. She was the type who refused to be pitied or to appear pathetic.

Then, something changed in her. The despondence began to evaporate. Her misty eyes dried like puddles in the midday heat, the lines of her face hardening with an unrealized objective.

"I could tell he loved you very much," Austin said, lacing his fingers between hers and squeezing tightly.

"My dad knew him a long time. Longer than I ever did." Her lip twitched. "Kaslov killed him. It had to have been this Vasya Kaslov."

"Why?"

Victoria shook her head, staring with determination at nothing, her expression conjuring in Austin's mind the image of a bloody cavalry charge. "There must have been a third bug in the apartment. That's led Vasya to us. Fyodor was already dead by the time we had reached our hotel in Saint Petersburg. Vasya shot him with the same gun that nearly ended us."

"And now we're riding a few cars ahead of the same killer . . ."

Victoria's nod was bleak, her words resolute. "We'll bring this Vasya Kaslov down. I'll kill him myself if I get to."

Getting to know Victoria was like opening a set of Russian *matry-*

oshka dolls, Austin thought. There was always another shell to be removed, a deeper layer to be seen. He sensed newfound strength in her. If the murder of a family friend had elicited this reaction, he could only imagine how she'd behave if the victim had been her father. He admired her passion, but remained mindful that obsession could become hazardous. A certain unholy desire could be healthy, as long as it didn't jeopardize their purpose.

No words passed between them for hours. When night fell, they stretched out in their fold-down beds and slept, lulled by the rocking, bumping train car. They awoke the next morning to squeaking wheels as the train pulled into the Belgian railway station. They thanked the conductor and stepped out of their car into the cool of dawn, min-gling with the crowd to remain invisible.

Austin kept his vision glued to the penultimate railcar. Having donned her leather jacket and aviators, Victoria hailed a cab while Austin watched and waited for the assassin to emerge. It would be his first good look at the man who had leveled a pistol on his chest. He expected a chill to pass over him at the sight and was surprised when none came.

There he was.

A man of average height, stepping out near the last car. Handsome, with the swarthy look of a gypsy. Broad shoulders, a sharp widow's peak in his hairline. There was something in his hand—a briefcase.

Austin followed the man outside the station, watched him flag a cab, then located Victoria, who had begun negotiating with a taxi driver. They both looked irritated, apparently at a stalemate, when Austin appeared.

"Just get in," he said. "We've found our man." He pointed down the road and said to the driver, a squat, bushy, ill-tempered fellow, "Fol-low that cab. Don't be obvious." He turned to Victoria. "Good news."

"Really?"

"Vasya's carrying a leather briefcase."

"And?"

"It's your dad's."

"How do you know?"

"I recognized the shape and color. Somewhere along the way, there was a switch. The office prowler must have given it to him."

The news lifted Victoria from her gloom. "His laptop! It's probably still inside."

"My thoughts exactly." Vasya's taxi zoomed by, and their furry driver stepped on the accelerator. "Just maybe . . . Baldr's in there."

"All we need is that laptop and the password. Question is, how do we get them? Vasya clearly knows what he's doing, and he won't like learning we've followed him."

"We outfox him."

"Not going to be easy."

"We can take tonight to brainstorm."

Their tires jounced on marble cobblestones, and the cab turned into a network of boulevards winding through the heart of Bruges. Austin looked out the window at a street fair, captivated by the city's preserved medieval character—moats, carriages, neo-Gothic structures, steeply sloping roofs, merchant rows. Horse stomps and exhaust pipes were heard together in a strange coincidence of the modern and the archaic. It was a town from the Middle Ages, he thought, though he knew little of its two millennia of history. Beginning as an anti-pirate fortification built by Romans near the edge of the Flemish coastal plain, Bruges would develop an important harbor for trade with Scandinavia. The city's name had come from the Old Norse word *Bryggja,* meaning "landing stage." Ninth-century Viking raids had prompted the reinforcement of Roman military fortifications and the city's main citadel, enabling trade to continue with little fear of incursion.

Their path meandered in a labyrinthine circuit. Austin hoped the driver knew these streets well. They could easily get trapped in a maze of one-way roads and cordons that blockaded festival territory. The taxi passed the Sint-Salvator Cathedral and crossed a bridge spanning a waterway that encircled the town. Following Vasya's lead, they approached a bell tower rising from the central square. The tower was one of Bruges's most popular landmarks and attracted climbers to tackle its 366 steps. The belfry featured four minarets that pierced up toward the main carillon, housing a clock mechanism and ancient treasury. Flying buttresses supported an octagonal upper structure from which bell-ringers would peer through lancet windows, spying on the market square on one end and a courtyard on the other. Forty-seven bells were now chiming to Beethoven's Ninth.

Austin's imagination ran free as he envisioned knights on horseback galloping through the streets and reptiles slithering through the canal system; shirts and jeans of street vendors became coifs and tunics in his mind. Victoria's voice dispelled his fantasy.

"He's pulling in."

"Where?" he asked.

"A hotel."

Austin tapped the cabbie's shoulder. "Keep driving slowly. Don't let him know he has a tail."

The cabdriver tapped the brakes and kept his distance, just far enough to offer a view of Vasya as he paid his driver and walked inside.

"He went to Boterhuis Hotel," their driver said. "I saw. Boterhuis in Flemish, it mean *butter house* in English. I saw him go. Historic place."

Austin said, "Move in a little closer."

They crouched low in their seats so as not to rouse suspicion. Peering out the window, Victoria said, "I don't think he's spotted us. He's talking with the receptionist. She's giving him a room key . . ."

"Can you see any numbers?"

Her eyes narrowed behind the aviators. "No. There's too much glare, even with these on."

"That's okay. Keep moving, driver. There's a place straight across from the Boterhuis." He pointed to a building on the other side of the street. Over the doorway he could see the words *Hotel Navarra*. "We can track him from there. Whenever he leaves, we'll know."

"Let's drive around the block a few more times," Victoria suggested. "I don't want him coming back to the lobby and seeing us. Let him settle. Then we'll check into the Navarra."

Their room was well suited for surveillance. Windows overlooking the street provided a perfect view of the Boterhuis. They'd pinpointed Vasya's room on the top floor and could observe his motions through a window. Not a hundred yards separated them, and they had a visual line into his room.

Her aim steady, Victoria positioned herself near the windowpanes, kneeling for comfort and drawing the curtains together to hide her face and body. She tweaked the focus on her binocular lenses and didn't leave the viewfinder. "He's talking on the phone," she relayed as Austin brushed his teeth. "He looks calm. He's sitting on the bed. . . . I'm looking around the room for objects he was carrying. He travels light . . ." She rubbed one of the lenses for a better view. "Still talking . . . He seems absorbed in something. . . . Now he's walking over to the window . . ."

"Don't let him see you," Austin said from the bathroom.

"He won't. I've pulled the drapes around me."

"Is he still on the phone?"

"Yes, chatting with someone . . . He seems to be watching the traffic below, or maybe he's just staring into space. I'm looking for the— come on, it has to be there somewhere . . . Okay, there it is. He's hung up the phone. He's pulling out the briefcase. He's opening it, and . . ."

"And what?"

There was no response.

"What is it?" Austin mumbled through his toothbrush.

"Dad's laptop is definitely inside. You were right. Somewhere along the way, there was a switch. He picked it up from one of his friends."

Austin turned on the faucet and rinsed. "Then we're only one hotel away from the answer. If we could get him to leave his room without taking the computer with him, if only for a matter of seconds, we could break in and—"

"Shhh. Don't distract me. . . . I'm trying to see where he puts the laptop. He opened it and typed a few things, as if he was checking something. . . . Now he's slipping it back into the briefcase. He's standing up . . ." She lowered her binoculars and narrowed the blinds even more before glancing up again. "He's making for the exit . . ."

She said nothing for a while.

"What now?" said Austin.

"Lights out. He's on the move."

TWENTY-ONE

Greetings, luxury lovers,

This message comes from your hijacker. Read carefully and entirely.

Power will not return.

My reasons for disabling this ship do not involve and should not concern you. I am no petty thief. Armed guards patrolling the halls will not come after your jewelry. Given your cooperation, we will not confiscate your valuables or threaten your lives individually.

Cancellations have been made at future ports. Foreign port authorities no longer expect your arrival. A virus infecting computers at the main offices of Pearl Voyages will falsely report our location. A dot representing the Pearl Enchantress will appear on a map and move according to the planned itinerary. "Official" calls will be made to assuage doubts. Corporate headquarters will detect nothing abnormal and find no reason to investigate.

It is regretful my negotiations should disrupt your vacations. Do not panic. If my associates adhere to plan, nothing will compromise your safety.

I have three rules.

One. Do not leave your cabins. Your doors will remain closed and locked at all times, unless you hear the knock of a guard delivering rations. Violators caught loitering or skulking will be shot. Anyone responsible for or complicit in organizing a counterattack will be shot. Anyone who communicates with passengers in another cabin will be shot. Anyone who physically assaults a guard will be shot. Anyone who riles a guard will be shot. Anyone who causes unnecessary disturbance will be shot. Stay in your cabins. You, too, crew members.

Two. Passengers with balcony rooms may jump ship without fear of pursuit. Several hundred miles separate us from land. Happy swimming.

Three. Obey Ragnar Stahl. He is my strong right arm, my fidus Achates. He currently commands the ship. You will recognize him if and when you see him.

The Pearl Enchantress *is mine.*

I wish the best for you, truly.

Regards,
The Viking

A patroller had slipped the letter-sized message under Rove's door. No doubt the hijackers were distributing thousands of copies. He folded the paper and set it on his nightstand.

His initial energy had dulled to restlessness. He squinted through his door's peephole, hearing voices and shouts that abated in time. Occasionally he'd hear lumbering footsteps and see one of the guards up close. They were gold-haired Goliaths, bred for piracy. Despite his excellent shape, Rove knew he was no match for their raw strength. If he stood a chance in hand-to-hand combat, it would be agility against size.

A rifle butt clicked against the outside wall railing as one of them paced near. Rove barely glimpsed the face, but he did notice the guard's bicep. For the first time he had a clear view of the tattoo. He studied the design, trying to place it, then copied the pattern onto a notepad for later reference—a horned helmet and double-edged ax.

He ogled the gun slung over the patroller's shoulder and recognized the classic automatic assault rifle. The gas-operated weapon was originally developed in the Soviet Union for the Red Army. Over sixty years later, regular armed forces, as well as revolutionaries and terrorist groups around the world, still fired its 7.62x39mm cartridges.

Rove jotted down the detail. *They carry AKs.*

These weren't their only weapons. He'd seen others, among them Uzi submachine guns, and he'd recognized their Belgian make: Fabrique Nationale d'Herstal. This he jotted, too; the pirates had access to quality arms dealers.

He reread the Viking's note at his bedside. Who was this joker? He looked up at the portrait of Clifford Pearl hanging over his bed, taking in the regal uniform, picturing that severe face colored with rage. If only Pearl knew what was happening on his ship, he thought, and for a moment he imagined something in the solemnity of the captain's expression—a dare, a nod of permission that said: *No harm goes unpunished.*

Rove retrieved a map of the *Pearl Enchantress* from a drawer and slipped it into his pocket for safekeeping. Then he tapped on Fawkes's wall, punctuating his taps with breaks to spell out a message. After ten seconds of silence, he heard tapping from the other side and decrypted the answer.

Yes, I know Morse.

Rove tapped a few more sentences. They took a painfully long time to convert, as neither was an expert. But the messages were unmistakable, nothing lost in translation.

Will communicate this way, Rove encoded. *May need your help soon.*

For what?

Don't know yet. Must work together.

Could rig rope chute outside for note passing.

Dangerous. They might see. Letter said no communication.

True.

Stay tuned for my taps. Back later.

TWENTY-TWO

Negotiations would take place in the heart of medieval charm at La Taverne Brugeoise. Austin and Victoria had followed the man to a small restaurant with a tearoom and outside seating. The setting provided a clear view of the bell tower, while the din of the marketplace made eavesdropping difficult.

Briefcase in hand, Vasya took a seat beside a dark, oversized man. His neck was covered in a checkered keffiyeh, his skin deeply pocked and flecked with birthmarks. His beard was tamed but thick, the kind that grew scraggly in a day. And his nose slanted gently before ending at a radical hook, as if a wood plank had smacked him at childbirth and forever disturbed the natural slope.

After shaking hands with Vasya, the man pulled up a chair, filling it with his mass. Austin and Victoria observed the interaction from the market square.

"Let's move in closer," Austin said. "I'd like to hear what they say."

Victoria glanced at the lunch companions, who had begun to converse. "Vasya might recognize us," she said.

"We'll sit behind him. We'll be fine. Remember, he only saw us in the dark."

"You don't know that. He might have seen our faces before the run-in at the Hotel Dostoevsky."

"Then we'll be careful."

They moved in toward the tavern, Austin taking a seat at a table not ten feet from Vasya. He had a clear view of Vasya's companion. Victoria joined him moments later. They went through the motions of reading the menu.

A waiter came to their table and greeted them. "Welcome to La Taverne Brugeoise. Would you like to start with drinks?"

"Just water for me," Victoria said.

"I'll have a Sam Adams," Austin said.

"Sorry, we don't—"

"How about a Grolsch?"

The waiter bowed his head. "On its way."

They watched peripherally as Vasya opened the briefcase and removed Malcolm Clare's laptop along with a satellite uplink device. He booted the computer and placed it on the table. Austin and Victoria tried to filter out extraneous noise and capture snippets of the conversation. Vasya was speaking, his demeanor genuine—too genuine, his affectation and oversold sincerity what one would expect of a fly-by-night charlatan.

This was given to me by Ragnar at the fjords after he obtained it from Stanford University," Vasya said to the man across from him. "I would like to see how it works."

"Sure, Farzad."

"Have you tested it yet?"

"The demonstration you asked for has shown Baldr to live up to expectations. Have a look." Vasya tapped the keys. "Here you input coordinates, adjust altitude, et cetera—or you click on the world map, zooming here, and the satellite will alter course, compensating for the presence of other objects in space to avoid collision. Data required for safe navigation feeds from the United States Strategic Command, an agency that tracks satellites and orbital debris." Vasya pointed to a spot on the screen. "Here you select the desired yield. Based on your inputs, the program will extrapolate expected damages, shading a region on the map most likely to be affected. Alternatively, you can highlight an area of geography, and the Baldr program will compute the detonation coordinates, altitude, and yield necessary to address the selected region."

"What does Glitnir offer?"

"Eager, I see."

"It's for my own good."

Vasya nodded. Having researched all participants in the auction, he was well aware of Farzad Deeb's reasons for being here. Originally from Oran, Deeb had worked at the World Bank on petrochemical projects for five years before joining a large Algerian oil consortium created to exploit the country's hydrocarbon resources. He had spent twelve years there, becoming the vice president of operations at the Hassi Messaoud oil refinery, before his election to the People's National Assembly of Algeria. In 1983 he was appointed Minister of

Energy and Mines and became an oil minister for OPEC living in Algiers. His years in OPEC had been marked by disintegrating cohesion among participating states. The First Persian Gulf War and the Iraqi invasion of Kuwait led to divisive fears over a massive supply disruption. Deeb's proposed reductions in production quotas—which would bolster Algerian revenues in the short term—had conflicted with the Saudi concern that raising prices would compel nations to cultivate petroleum alternatives.

Deeb had dissented against Saudi policies. In 1996 Saudi intelligence had accused him of employing al-Nar operatives to infiltrate and sabotage Saudi Arabia's Ghawar and Shaybah oil fields—attacks which had caused $320 million in damage. The claims were substantiated by evidence confirming he had contributed $100 million of his own to support the group's activities. Deeb had denied allegations but resigned from office, moving to Tripoli to escape imprisonment. He had bribed away most Algerian investigations, but remained among Saudi Arabia's most wanted.

In Tripoli he'd befriended Othman al-Zayfi, the founder of al-Nar, and sponsored the group's endeavors as a means of protection and power. Though he remained apathetic toward the group's religious motives, in return for money and armaments, they would defend him from the Saudis and implement his wishes abroad.

Vasya leaned in. "Glitnir bid eight hundred million."

The bushes that were the former minister's eyebrows crawled like mice when he moved his forehead. "I will take them higher."

"How much?"

Deeb's fingers were hidden in his beard. Before he answered, the waiter returned to Austin and Victoria's table with their drinks, blocking their view.

"Ready to order?" he asked.

"We're just having drinks," Victoria said.

"You sure? We have some really fabulous entrees."

"Drinks will do for now, but thank you."

"Okay," said the waiter. "Enjoy."

They isolated the two voices again, trying to fill in the gap in continuity.

". . . healthy offer, Farzad."

"I think it will send the company a message of my intent."

"Glitnir faces serious competition."

"Something that worries me," said Deeb. "There is a chance Glitnir would try to shoot down the satellite before I could use it. How can I be assured of its safety?"

"The satellite's designer, Malcolm Clare, built in a safety provision," Vasya answered. "Glitnir lost its trace on Baldr the moment I opened the overriding program. They won't be able to find it. And even if they did, the Viking has spun your demonstration into a bargaining tool."

Austin was revolted by the feral look on Deeb's face. And who was this "Viking"?

"I see," the man said.

The dialogue continued for minutes. Vasya closed the laptop and locked it in the briefcase. The same waiter tended to their table, jotting down their orders, then disappeared into the kitchen. To Austin and Victoria's chagrin, a gang of tourists moved in between their tables, filling the tavern with spates of laughter and clamoring silverware. She frowned at them. Austin shifted in his seat to get a better look at Deeb, who had folded his fingers on the tablecloth and begun to glance about with the paranoia of a man who didn't want to be found.

"The briefcase is between Vasya's feet," Austin said. "It's so close. If we could give him a reason to leave the table for a second, I'd have time to grab it."

Victoria saw that he was right.

He tried to be inconspicuous as he watched Farzad Deeb fingering his fork and gawking at the dishes being served around him. Apparently the sweet concoction of aromas, combined with wafts from the tavern's brew, were difficult for the man to endure.

Deeb's gaze fell upon Austin, who looked away. He still sensed the Algerian's stare boring a hole into his profile, weighing and measuring him.

"What's the matter?" Victoria asked.

"Don't turn back. He saw me."

"Who, Vasya?"

"The man he's with, this Farzad Deeb." Austin sipped his Grolsch. "He's watching me right now."

"Do you think he suspects anything?"

"Maybe. He just turned away, but he studied me a good while."

Victoria cast a quick glance in their direction.

"Now he's muttering something to Vasya," she said. "They don't look happy."

"Bad sign."

"They're still talking about us. I can see them."

"Keep your voice down."

"That night, remember what Vasya told us would happen if we followed him?"

Austin felt a momentary relief as the bells of the tower began to toll, now certain they could not be heard. "Not the sort of thing one forgets."

"This means we're on his target list. The moment we get up and leave, he'll tail us. Luckily, he doesn't know where we're staying. We're probably safe as long as we can leave the tavern without him following."

"Not exactly," Austin said. "Close your eyes."

"Why?"

"Just do it. Fast."

"Okay. Closed."

"Without opening, what color is the chair you're sitting on? Don't peek."

"This isn't a good time for games, Austin."

"Just go along with it. Keep those eyes closed. What color is the chair?"

She thought a moment, then ventured, "Brown."

"Good guess. Is there a small bouquet of flowers on the table?"

"Yes," she murmured.

"How about a salt or pepper shaker?"

She shrugged. "Probably."

"Yes or no?"

"Yes."

"Now open."

Victoria surveyed the tabletop, shocked by the degree of her inaccuracy. "A red chair, no flowers on the table, and I got lucky with the salt and pepper." She looked annoyed. "What's your point?"

"It's a little game my parents used to play with me. You'd be amazed how basic elements of your environment slip your mind if you don't pay attention. They simply don't register to the untrained observer. Take a better look around for a few seconds, and let's try again."

Victoria reexamined the table, the tavern, and the marketplace, taking mental snapshots and storing them. She took in the entire restaurant with a full pan of her head, noticing everything from the tessellated patterns on the floor to the number of chandeliers to the color of the bartender's facial hair. She closed her eyes. "Shoot."

"What color is the overhead awning?"

"Green," she said with confidence.

"What's on the wall opposite you?"

"An oil painting of a young peasant boy."

"Good," Austin said. "Last question. Ready?"

"Yes."

His voice fell to a faint whisper as the bells stopped pealing. "Who are the men at the table to your left, and why do they keep listening to us?"

Victoria's eyelids fluttered; she could no longer force them to stay closed. She casually peeked to the side and observed two surly-looking hoodlums swigging ale. They set their drinks on the table and stared indiscreetly at Austin and Victoria, not caring to avert their attention despite having locked eyes.

Austin let the realization sink in before adding, "Two more at the bar, far side of the tavern. They've been watching us and every other patron since we arrived."

"Probably Deeb's goons," Victoria surmised, watching foam trickle over the lips of the men's steins. "They look like real tough customers."

"I'll say."

"You think they're on to us?"

"Undoubtedly. Two minutes ago I saw them signaling to each other and shooting glances at their boss, who's looked this way more than once. You said we're safe as long as we can leave the tavern without any tails. Losing these guys may be a different ball game."

Victoria thought fast. "I have an idea."

She caught the waiter's attention and flagged him down. He smiled and sped to their tableside with his notepad. "Decided you'd like a bite to eat after all?"

"Nothing to eat," Victoria replied. "But we could use your help."

"What can I do for you?"

"Please speak quietly. The gentlemen behind you, and several others, are listening."

His elbow jerked back. "Why? Who? Are you sure?"

"One hundred percent," Victoria said. "We don't appreciate the attention. We're ready to pay and leave, and we don't want them following us out."

"What can I do?" the waiter asked.

"Bring out a tray or platter from the kitchen. Fill it with silverware and dishes. Act like you're in a hurry, then trip over a leg of their chair and drop the tray. Make lots of noise."

"I'll be reprimanded!"

"Shhh. Softly, please."

"Have you thought about calling the police?"

"They haven't committed any crimes."

The waiter shook his head. "I can't do this."

Victoria slipped him one of the hundred-euro bills she'd acquired at the train station's exchange booth. Bribes had been effective thus far.

"We can't get out of here without your help," she said.

The waiter looked torn, but he accepted the bill and groaned. "If I'm fired for this, a hundred euros won't make a difference."

"We'll explain the situation to your manager later. We think these men are dangerous."

The waiter vanished into the kitchen and returned with a tray of forks, spoons, knives, and stacked ceramic plates. He also carried several full glasses of water. At a brisk pace, he headed straight for Deeb's men and snagged his foot on a stool. The tray went down with a raucous clatter. Heaps of utensils went flying, rattling and clinking against shattered ceramic. Kitchenware spilled over the table, and the glasses drenched the patrons in water. The waiter went sprawling onto the floor.

"Watch where you're going, hammerhead!" one of Deeb's bodyguards snarled.

Farzad Deeb shoved his chair aside and stood straight as a ramrod, jarred by the disturbance. The tourists kept chattering. Briefcase still pinched between his legs, Vasya surveyed the fallen waiter and the trail of broken dishware. The waiter clambered to his feet, uttering a stream of apologies as he collected shards from the ground. One of the tourists lent a hand.

Vasya gritted his teeth. Deeb cast a scornful look at his men, who shrugged back at him as he motioned to the set of empty chairs that had been occupied by Austin and Victoria.

TWENTY-THREE

Rove still remembered his first plunge into that murky oblivion. He'd been fifteen. Since watching police divers scour the bottom of that lake for his father's body, he'd been petrified of all things aquatic, but was forced to confront his fear after relocating to Texas. He'd been asked to help at his uncle's scuba shop and take lessons in preparation for becoming an assistant scuba instructor. His first night dive had been a terrifying encounter with the dark. Little could be as eerie as feeling one's body suspended in a void, he'd thought, or wondering what predators lurked outside the light beam. His mind had built a fragile fort, looped a soundtrack of rational mantras—*I'm okay, there's nothing to be afraid of, it'll be over soon.* But every sound or ripple or brush of seaweed had crumbled the fort, turning the mantras into wails. Only time and experience had pacified his nerves and reined in the frightful images that would unreel on the backs of his closed eyelids. He'd later come to thrive on the exhilaration of viewing the nocturnal world, where corals bloomed and reefs came alive with a different cast of characters.

Years in the Coast Guard and Air Force had further worked to dispel his phobia. There had always been distractions—namely the mission at hand—to stand in the way of his apprehension. He would simply put the regulator in his mouth and dive.

He was lugging the severed fire hose onto the balcony of his suite. Standing at the ledge, he tied one end to a firm, steel beam and let go of the spool. The coil spun downward and splashed into the water stories below.

He unzipped his equipment bag and stripped off his clothes. The yellow toucan on Rove's deltoid smiled in the mirror, an unsettling reminder of his last experience behind enemy lines. In the late nineties, his squadron had begun establishing a series of clandestine weather observation networks throughout Colombia, Peru, and Bolivia. The networks were leveraged in operations to suppress violence originating in Cali and Medellín, where rival drug cartels had earned the enmity of the Colombian and U.S. government by gunning down high-ranking police officers and ministers of justice. As a combat weatherman, Rove had been attached to Navy SEAL Team Four. He was to collect environmental intelligence from forward deployed locations.

He had been shot and captured during a route-forecasting mission in the Andes jungle. Mercenaries had taken their prisoner to the inner chambers of an underground production plant, where he had been drugged, bound, gagged, beaten, and tortured for hours. They had fractured his legs and inflicted lacerations, cauterizing the wounds with a blowtorch. He still wore scars on his chest and legs, along with the tattoo they had given him. It was the smiling toucan, two inches square, emblazoned in red and yellow on his shoulder.

"You're a quiet man," his tormenter had said. "Don't say much. But the toucan craves attention. He will give you color in death. The devil will find you and know you died in Colombia—more toucans than any country on his earth. The bird will be your pet in hell."

He'd been battered into unconsciousness by the time the SEALs had infiltrated the plant and rescued him. He was rushed to the Soto Cano Air Base in Honduras for emergency care. Fractures healing in his left tibia had left him limping for years.

Rove donned his wetsuit, covering the bird. He was not about to be captured again. He fastened the jacket of his buoyancy compensator after affixing a tank he'd refilled at the last port, and he slipped a rubber mask and snorkel around his neck. He considered bringing a speargun—ship security had given him a hard time over it, and still he hadn't used it—but he couldn't foresee needing the weapon. Instead he strapped a knife to his ankle. Clasping his fins against his chest, he grabbed hold of the fire hose and began a slow descent, struggling to counterbalance the weight of his air tank without banging too loudly against the hull. At such heights, letting go of the hose prematurely would mean death, given the heavy gear attached to his body. He trusted the canvas wouldn't tear. He also knew descending was only the half of it. Later he'd have to climb up, though he intended to lose the cumbersome tank beforehand.

His biceps burned in protest with every inch of the climb, and as the feeling spread to his shoulders, he realized how glad he was to have stayed true to his fitness routine. With the full force of the wind astern of him, he held fast.

A cool wave washed over his aching muscles when he entered the water. These waters were meant for a dry suit, not a wetsuit; he would soon become hypothermic. He purged his regulator a few seconds, then began to breathe through the mouthpiece, his lungs taking in a full load of air. He placed the mask over his forehead and strapped the fins to his feet. Before he submerged, the last he saw of the world above was the silhouette of the *Pearl Enchantress* hiding the stars.

He cracked a glow stick, illuminating a tight radius, and descended toward the ship's keel.

Every few seconds he'd glimpse a darting fish. A conger eel slinked its body past him, exposing a row of snaggle-teeth, its beady eyes measuring him for a meal. A pattern of leafy green and black would disguise its skin in any reef. Rove held its glance. Finding nothing worthy, the eel slithered away.

Keeping an eye on his pressure gauge, Rove released a gradual stream of bubbles from his BC and descended another ten feet. He fluttered his fins, propelling himself horizontally at constant depth.

A phrase in the Viking's letter played in his head. *We will not threaten your lives individually.* Rove puzzled over the sentence. What did it mean? No individual would be singled out, but passengers as a whole would be threatened? There was one conceivable way the hijackers could imperil thousands at once, and Rove needed answers. He glided along the ship's hull, the glow stick casting a ghostly penumbra against the steel plates, and he steepened his angle once more to leave the shallow depths. With every exhale, a swarm of bubbles engulfed him. He hoped none of the hijackers stood guard on any weather decks, lest they spy the bubbles at the surface. He took shorter, less frequent breaths.

A Portuguese dogfish sauntered within his stick's scope, followed by a fanged, fork-tailed creature with luminescent organs. A cod fluttered by. Visibility didn't compare to Cayman waters in this unfamiliar dominion; darkness covered all. With poor range, he could hardly tell up from down, nor did he have the usual tug of gravity to orient him. After a while, water began seeping into his mask. He tilted his head back and lifted the mask slightly, blowing a steady stream from his nostrils to expel the leakage.

He coasted clockwise around the ship. Minutes passed like hours without turning up anything anomalous. The hull had no hidden crevices; he'd assumed the hunt would be easy, but his confidence began to wane, and he worried he'd wasted an air tank looking for something that wasn't there.

A current swept his knees sideways. Something thumped against the hull. The sound had been quick and dull, like a grunt. He whirled around, waving the glow stick, his left hand gravitating toward the knife at his ankle. He didn't unclasp it, but he was ready to. He swam on with more determined vigilance, wishing he'd brought the speargun.

Hovering along the hull of the *Pearl Enchantress* made him feel like he was gliding over a barren seafloor, no carnival of marine life to admire, just a smooth, gray surface and endless stretch of wall. He plunged deeper yet, level with the upper keel, and drifted between two propeller blades. Over eighteen feet in diameter, the propellers had once whipped a force that could move megatons. Now they lay dormant.

Thoroughly he searched every blade. Nothing there. He checked his air gauge and figured he had twenty minutes to spare. He hadn't descended below thirty feet and wouldn't need much time to decompress. With an extra cylinder in tow, he had a few good breaths before he would be forced to surface. He ascended on the port side and resumed his examination of the hull, his light guiding the way. Occasional gold shimmers floated by his mask, reflections of plankton, debris, and other particles.

His hand struck something, making him pause. Circling back, he held the glow stick closer to the ship.

There it was, finally, as he'd suspected. No wonder he hadn't seen it before: The gray of the ship's plates had camouflaged its color. He defogged his mask again to allow for better scrutiny, then eyeballed his find, assessing the power of the explosive device.

One blast would hardly be enough to take down the cruise liner. Larger cruise ships were divided by watertight bulkheads into six or more flood-proof sections, preventing horizontal flow along lower decks in case of a breached hull. The craft could endure a single mighty explosion without sinking, but multiple discharges, yield and placement calculated correctly, could do her in. Rove noted the depth of the device, then swam on with renewed purpose.

A hundred feet forward, he found another. Sure enough, someone had placed charges around the perimeter. He examined the device up close, wondering if he could disarm it.

He stopped.

A foreign light emanated from the distance, the rays perpendicular to the ship. Judging by the clarity and brilliance, Rove guessed it was coming from a probe.

Swimming nearer, he discovered otherwise. Someone was hard at work, fixing more explosive charges to the hull.

Rove knew his glow stick would give him away. He considered tucking it into his vest but decided against it. There were spares if he needed them. Unstrapping a lead weight from his waist, he hooked it to the rod, then let the stick plummet, watching the glow fade like a firefly in fog. Altering his angle of approach, he took a diagonal route around the back of the light. He had no idea whether the other diver was armed, but there was no reason to risk it. The surprise factor was his, so he moved in.

His body parallel with the seafloor, Rove chose an attack depth level with the other diver's shoulders. He kicked his fins and drifted until he could reach out and touch the man, making sure to hold his breath to remain soundless. As the man worked, Rove studied the fastening method, memorizing how the charges were being fixed to the ship's plating.

After a few moments, he'd seen enough; soon he would need to exhale. The buildup in his lungs left little time to devise an assault. He had options, the best of which did not involve letting the man bleed. He had no idea what predators infested these waters. He considered using the man's regulator as a garrote, or turning his own breathing device into one. Throttling the other man would be easy if Rove could position himself well. Or he could simply slice the cords of the hijacker's regulator and puncture his vest, then hold him submerged, forcing the hijacker to inhale that painful lungful of water . . .

The scuba light swung around and shone into Rove's eyes, momentarily frying his optic nerve. Suddenly all bets were off. His first impulse was to reach out and grab the light. His arm was met with a yank, and the light flung out of both their hands, hovering a yard away and gradually sinking.

Were his retinas not suffering from the flash, he'd have been able to form a clear visual of the diver, but the effects persisted, and he wasn't quick enough. An elbow dug into his stomach. He recoiled, lurching toward the light, then reached for it again. A fin knocked his arm out of the way.

Rove blinked in his mask, still blinded. He looked left and right, unable to find the scuba-jacker. The man had fled, possibly for a better vantage point. He was still out of sight, and Rove was working without any sense of cardinal direction or up and down.

He had to move fast; the other diver would descend upon him. He fluttered his fins and jetted seven feet outward. A three-sixty degree pan of his surroundings revealed nothing. Somewhere in the third dimension the hijacker waited, planning a move.

The knuckles came fast and hard. A sidelong blow sent pain spearing through Rove's neck, and was followed by a kick that jarred his rib cage and nearly splintered bone. A hand clenched his hair and tugged hard while the other wrenched off his mask and snorkel, leaving him blinder than before.

A skilled fighter would have gone straight for his regulator and probably killed him already. This enemy was no trained professional. Rove focused, reining in his pulse. He had forfeited the element of surprise; the mistake had been his, though his opponent hadn't fully taken advantage of it.

He needed a swift recovery. He squinted, seeing only a blur, then grabbed a spare glow stick and cracked it, allowing him to discern a long, pointed object in the hijacker's hands. The object rotated to face him. He thrust himself out of the way in time to evade the speargun's projectile.

Ducking, Rove realized he had literally brought a knife to a gunfight—but, for all he knew, his aggressor might have just wasted his only shot. Maneuvering to the hijacker's back side, Rove rammed a fist into the man's spine and seized his regulator. He wrenched out the mouthpiece and used the tube as a noose, cutting off the air supply. The hijacker thrashed, flailing the waters in search of his spare. Rove snatched it away and held the tube out of reach. His face changing from bright red to blue, the hijacker wrestled with Rove for control of the regulator. Edging his fingers between his neck and the tubes for leverage, he finally wriggled free of the stranglehold and buried his nose in the bubbles of a purging mouthpiece. Not about to lose his advantage, Rove thrust a knee against the man's tailbone, buying time to unclasp his knife and drive his blade through the man's vest.

His BC torn, the hijacker scissor-kicked, shooting toward the surface. Rove grabbed hold of an ankle and yanked him down, while reducing his own buoyancy. The hijacker threw a cascade of punches, whipping the water like a blender yet striking nothing. Still recuperating from the blinding flash and the loss of his mask, Rove retained his rear position and sealed off the man's air valve.

The hijacker's bubbles stopped streaming. The man resorted to poking Rove with the empty speargun. Rove jabbed back with his knife, slashing into the man's dry suit over his arm. Torn neoprene pulled away, and Rove caught a flash of the horned helmet insignia.

A cloud of blood was oozing from the wound. So much for the clean attack, he realized.

Apparently recognizing he had thirty seconds or less until he had to breathe, the hijacker turned around and began wrestling with Rove for the knife. It was oxygen against sight; Rove had the air supply, his opponent a mask. The hijacker's hands clenched around Rove's wrist as the man cast his worthless regulator aside and made for another assault.

He pulled Rove's palm toward his open jaw and tried to sink his molars into a finger. Rove bashed him in the nose before he could break flesh. Still gnashing his teeth, the hijacker managed to loosen the knife from Rove's grip.

The blade glimmered, its edge reflecting the sinking light. Now armed and poised to lacerate, the hijacker drew near and swung the knife wildly. In an effort to stop the blade, Rove reached forward and clasped the man's forearm, at the same time letting go of his spare regulator. The man took hold of it and stole a breath. In that moment of confidence, the man had relieved his lungs but forfeited position, giving Rove the angle he needed.

The hijacker had moved dangerously close to his opponent and suddenly lost sight of him. Rove clamped his arms around the man's neck, constricting in an irreversible headlock. The hijacker grappled, but Rove was too powerful and too carefully placed. His thumb, bent into a small hook, reached under the man's mask and gouged a path through an eye socket.

His face contorting, the hijacker writhed, letting out a muffled scream as his eye began to hemorrhage. Rove released his lock, retrieved his knife and suspended mask, and swam slowly away, leaving his foe sightless, airless, disoriented, and floundering in a pall of crimson water.

Rove's victory had not gone as planned. The scent of open flesh had long since drifted, and he knew it. The waters had the illusion of chilling and congealing around him. He wasn't sure why; perhaps the scuffle had drained him of strength and fatigue had turned the water into molasses—or perhaps it had been the sight of death where he'd always imagined it, in the deep. Whatever the cause, he felt a violent desire to flee and kicked out of there as fast as he could. He glanced back in time to witness the materialization of a razor-like dorsal fin and a pair of sunken eyes, eyes without comprehension or malice. A whiplash snapped through the porbeagle's body, and the hijacker's screams were subdued.

Rove's tank had run out, and he'd swapped it for his spare minicylinder. The spare had given him a few extra breaths, and he'd made the best of them. It was time to leave these waters. He looked up, shivering. A shadow loomed over him. He skirted the iceberg and surfaced where he'd begun his dive, stories below his suite.

His head came up in a tangle. He peeled off his mask and understood the folly. The fire hose had been untied and tossed over the balcony's edge. In all likelihood, a guard delivering food had missed his answer at the door, broken into his room, and discovered the rope. He'd lost his only way of reboarding the *Pearl Enchantress*.

One option remained.

Someone had to be waiting for the scuba-jacker to finish planting explosives. Rove would find a welcoming committee on one of the corsairs.

TWENTY-FOUR

Shh, shh, shh."

An infant's wails filled the darkness of a cabin. A mother sat on the edge of the bed and formed a burrow of blankets for her child. She rocked him, her lips resting on the baby's cheek, the warmth of her breath soothing the baby between her hushes.

"Is he all right, my love?" asked the father in Dutch. As long as he remained motionless, he remained invisible. Though their pupils had adapted to nightfall, it wasn't until he sat beside his wife that he could see her move. He closed a hand around hers. The hand was as cold as the room, but she welcomed the assurance.

"He's hungry," said the mother. She tried not to let her tears fall upon the cheeks of her infant.

The father stroked the mother's neck.

"The rations they give us are too small," he said. "We're out of food."

The mother wept on her husband's shoulder.

* * *

Don't kill Daphne, kill me!" exclaimed Detective Sylvester Rogers, stretching open the arms of his trench coat.

"Why should I do that," cackled Dr. Headstrong, his finger almost at the blinking button, "when I can end you both?"

A loud crack of thunder replied before the detective could.

"Because I love her more than life itself."

"Oh, Sylvester!" cried the lovely Daphne, writhing over the pit of hungry, greedy crocodiles. "I love you, too, but do something!"

Dr. Headstrong laughed maniacally. "You'll both be fodder for my crocs!"

Just as the evil scientist's finger pushed the button, the brave detective's lightning-fast hands—

The cabin went dark, filling it with an odor of smoky sulfur dioxide as the match went out.

"What's the matter, Grandpa?" came the eager voice of a ten-year-old. "Don't you want to finish the story?"

"Of course I do, champ," said the graying man at his bedside, setting the book on his nightstand. "But the detective has almost solved the case. If we finish it now, there won't be any left for tomorrow."

"Does that mean it's bedtime?" asked the boy.

"You bet, champ."

"Can I go get some cereal at the twenty-four-hour restaurant?"

"Not tonight."

"But I'm hungry."

"Sleep is more important right now."

"Why?"

"The restaurant had to close tonight."

"You seem scared."

"Not at all. Now you just lay your head down and try to sleep."

"Okay."

"Rest your head. I'm watching you, young man." He smiled.

"Good night, Grandma and Grandpa."

The boy pulled the covers over his ears and fell asleep dreaming about how he would have rescued Daphne from Headstrong's crocodiles.

"He loves those Detective Rogers books, doesn't he?" said the grandmother.

"He certainly does," her husband answered.

"Why'd you stop reading?"

"That was my last match."

The grandmother looked troubled.

"Les, what's happened to this ship? What's happened to us?"

"I wonder if we'll ever find out."

"We can't let him know how much we worry. You'll have to read to him during the day. I don't want our grandson to fear anything. I don't want him to feel like we're prisoners in our own room."

*　*　*

I'm sorry, Grace—but I won't be a hostage."

"Derek, don't! They'll kill you. They said to stay in our cabins."

A man stood at the door of his stateroom with a firm hold on his girlfriend. She was half bawling, half yelling for him to stay, her words no longer comprehensible beneath the sobs. He tried to wipe the wetness from her face; he only smeared it around.

"I can't stay in a room like this—I *won't* stay in a room like this—and have them tell us what to do. I'm going to find out what the hijackers want and give it to them."

"Derek . . . no . . . you don't have what they . . . *stop!*"

He shoved her back into the cabin as he opened the door. He stepped into the hall, his body soaked in a flood of light.

She screamed for him to retreat, then watched as he sat down on the floor, grasping his thigh and convulsing. His surrender was a painful roll back into the stateroom. She shut the door and felt his skin with her hands, searching his body in the dark, trembling because he trembled.

"Oh, God, oh, God . . ."

"Grab a bath towel," he gasped. "I'm shot."

*　 * 　 *

Two crewmen stared out through their porthole. One was a chef, the other an actor who performed with the ship's theatrical troop. They were roommates.

They had raided their own closets for as many warm layers as they could find. Now there was nothing to do but sit and wait in the silent stateroom, trying not to shiver.

"Strange, isn't it?" said the chef.

"What?"

"Feeling like a passenger again. I mean, we're not really crew anymore."

"What do you mean?"

"We're just people, floating on the same vessel, spread out over almost two thousand cabins . . . all asking the same question."

TWENTY-FIVE

Viking, I have news."

"Yes?"

Entering a cobbled alleyway at dusk, Vasya pressed his cell against his ear. "Deeb has offered a counterbid. He wants to intimidate the Americans, and has raised them a hundred million higher than we expected."

"Excellent work, Vasya."

"It took little convincing on my part. When he saw the extensiveness of Baldr's functionality, he tendered the offer without reserve."

"My next conversation with Chatham ought to be interesting."

"He faces determined competition. Deeb might actually win."

"Have you emailed the other players?"

"I will tomorrow."

"What's the delay?"

Vasya lowered his voice. "A minor distraction. Remember when I told you I retrieved the passkey?"

"Of course."

"I had found it with two Stanford students."

"And?"

"Somehow they managed to follow me from Saint Petersburg to Bruges, despite my warnings. I believe one of them is Malcolm Clare's daughter."

"Interesting."

"I doubt they could jeopardize any plans on our part, but we do want to avoid a media upset, and this is Clare's daughter we're talking about. She may stop at nothing to find her father. She might act irrationally, and you know what they say about loose lips." He added stonily, "We can prevent damage. I did warn them."

"Yes, you did."

*　*　*

Austin and Victoria had agreed to rest and use some alone time to think. She had gone to the steam room to decompress, but the heat had made her restless. After drying off she headed to an Internet café, dialing a Virginia number as she walked. If Fyodor was no longer there to help, maybe she could glean something closer to home.

"You've reached a private Glitnir line," an operator answered. "We recognize this number and require authentication with a voice biometric. Please state your full name and birthdate."

"Victoria Catherine Clare. September 1, 1984."

She waited for her vocal patterns to be recognized.

"Thank you. Go ahead."

"I need a personal file on someone."

"Connecting. This may take a while—hectic day."

She was on hold ten minutes.

"Counterintelligence," a lady answered.

"Victoria Clare here. I need a record on a man called Vasily Anatolievich Kaslov." She spelled the name, heard the keys being punched in.

"Most of that record is classified beyond your authorization level."

"Please tell me what you can."

She pinched the phone between her ear and shoulder, filling a notepad as she walked.

"Born in 1961 in Minsk, then the Soviet Socialist Republic of Belarus. His mother was a 'Ruska Roma,' a Russian gypsy of Romanian decent, and a horse trader. His father remained a factory worker until his conscription to the Soviet Navy. Served in the submarine fleet. Vasily Kaslov moved to the USSR in 1979 to study history and politology at Perm State University, becoming a fluent English speaker. After graduating, he joined the KGB and trained at the 401st KGB school in Okhta, Leningrad."

Victoria felt encouraged. They actually had a file on him! "What can you say about his career?" she asked.

"We know he spent half a year in counterintelligence at the Second Chief Directorate. In 1985 he transferred to Kiev to continue his studies in British English. Next year he was stationed in Ottawa under the alias Christian Lefevre. He substantiated his false identity by living it: Lefevre spent one year working at the Canadian National Department of Defence, and two more at a private international security consulting company specializing in risk management. In 1989 Lefevre immigrated to the United States and used his legend to acquire a job at a leading defense contractor. He worked as a finance analyst and spent his years stealing and photographing documents."

She was surprised by how much information was in his file.

"So he was caught?"

"Yes."

"How?"

"When the KGB dissolved, he continued channeling information to the new Russian Foreign Intelligence Service. He became part of a military technology procurement network that exported high-tech microelectronics—detonation triggers, radar and surveillance systems, weapons guidance systems—to the Russian military. In 1994 he learned of the founding of Glitnir Defense. Earned a job here as a low-level contracts manager."

Victoria's voice conveyed shock.

"He worked at *Glitnir*?"

That explained it—though given her father's rigorous security measures, it seemed preposterous to think a mole had been allowed to burrow.

"Briefly, until his efforts to hack our computer systems were detected by Kathryn Dirgo. He was deported in ninety-six. We suspect he remained assigned to his directorate responsible for scientific and technical intelligence."

"What more can you share?"

"None. Sorry."

It was still a lot.

"Okay," Victoria said. "Thanks for your help."

The more she learned about Vasya, the more he frightened her. She didn't feel safe walking the streets of Bruges alone, but there was still more to be learned.

TWENTY-SIX

Austin used the privacy of the Hotel Navarra's indoor swimming pool to collect his thoughts and penetrate the meaning behind what he'd overheard at the tavern.

He pushed off the wall and dolphin-kicked to the opposite end, then shot himself backward in a streamline. He rebounded and began alternating between a breaststroke and a sidestroke, concentrating on form.

The water felt cool against his skin. He exhaled and allowed his travel-worn body to sink. Sitting cross-legged on the pool floor, he reveled in the stillness. After a few seconds he came to the surface and shook out his hair.

A wave of heat rolled through the room, followed by thick clouds of fog and wafting herbal scents. Someone had exited the steam bath, toweled off, and left the secluded spa area. A little sweating sounded attractive to Austin. He submerged himself again, coasting along the floor of the pool with smooth, broad strokes and a frog kick. He came up at the far end.

"I told you not to follow me," came a voice.

Rubbing away the water, he distinguished a man's shape as the vapors receded. He couldn't see it, but he imagined there was a pistol.

"You're in Bruges, too?" Austin said, backstroking toward the ledge. "What a coincidence."

Vasya stepped closer until the handgun came into view. "As if I wouldn't notice the reflection off your binoculars as you spied on me from your hotel room. Get out of the water. Let's not sully a clean pool."

"So who is he?" Austin asked. He realized delay tactics could only get him so far.

"Who?"

"Your charming lunch companion, Farzad Deeb."

"He's an industrialist, and a wealthy one."

"So that's what you're after."

"Get out of the pool."

Austin took his time to obey. He contemplated remaining submerged as long as possible, hoping someone might come to the pool area and call the police. Water was practically bulletproof even at shallow depths. At most firing angles, high-caliber rifles could only penetrate a few feet and remain lethal. But if no one came, his fate would be sealed the moment he rose for air. He chose to talk. "What about the 'Viking'? Who's that? Does he plunder villages and scourge the sea?"

"He is of no consequence to you."

"I'd send my regards if I spoke Old Norse. Clever scheme of his, I admit, auctioning off a nuclear weapons satellite."

"You must think you know a lot. Your meddling is your undoing."

"Curiosity always gets the better of me."

"Shut up and stand in the corner. Let's get this over with." He motioned with his Mak. Austin noticed the screwed-in silencer, the same one he'd encountered before.

"What do you care if I live or die? I already gave you the flash drive."

"It's complicated."

Austin grabbed his towel and began drying off. He unclipped his watch, spotting a small exit door behind him. He began thinking of ways to distract Vasya. All he needed was a moment's diversion, but the man's eyes showed no sign of peeling away.

"Just give me a minute, old pal. Any civilized executioner would have the decency to send his victim into the afterlife with pants on. Tell me, how many have you killed since Avdeenko? And who's next after me?"

"You should know," Vasya said. "You've been following."

"Lunch was hours ago. For all I know, you've worked up a tally by now."

"I took no pleasure in my evening's work."

Austin paused, his face growing hot. He left his trousers on the floor. "What?"

"I appreciate beauty just as you do." Vasya inched closer yet, his outline fully visible and his shoes squeaking against the wet tile. "The girl you were with. You should have protected her. To maim the daughter of a legendary intellect . . . and furthermore an exquisite creature . . . I took no pleasure in it."

Austin was left in a whiteout. The steam seemed to thicken, the gray puffs hardening around him, blinding him like a blizzard and leaving him without reference points. He felt a surge of heat, like the opening of a kiln.

"What did you do?" he said, slamming the wall. "*What did you do?*" His fingers trembled with the urge to throttle, the handgun centered on his chest scarcely deterring him from lunging.

"Did you think I would come after you first? You're a no-name. She's much more important."

Austin forced himself to blink. His eyes felt like they were searing, his throat constricting. "You twisted bastard!"

"She didn't suffer long. I shut her up quickly. She kept calling your name. She didn't understand why you weren't there to protect her." Vasya stepped closer still, the details of his visage breaking through the steam and revealing a grimace. His tone remained at a simmer, soft and mocking. "If only she had known you were playing in the pool."

Vasya's finger flickered over the trigger. Staring into the barrel, Austin stood stock-still.

"The three of you will pay for the murder of the Clare family," he said. "You, Farzad Deeb, and the Viking—whoever he is—will all suffer."

"We'll see."

The muscles of his face relaxed, and Austin continued to stare down the shaft of the silencer. He still wore the look of pain, but it was now mixed with an emerging tranquility justified by the certainty he would deliver on his promise.

"Next time you see either of your colleagues, why don't you tell them they're running quickly out of this . . ."

In one swift motion Austin slid his gold watch over his wrist and tossed it at Vasya, who stole a glance at the timepiece as it arced toward him. Vasya reached outward and caught the watch with his free hand, throwing off his aim slightly. Austin dove for the exit. From Vasya's angle in the steam it appeared his victim had jumped straight at the wall. It was all the time Austin needed to push through the emergency door.

A bullet whizzed behind him but struck only wood, splintering the portal.

Vasya sprinted.

The door opened to a staircase. Panting, Austin flew up the stairs and landed in a patch of bushes. He plowed through the greenery and turned onto the main street. It was almost midnight. The market, once teeming with people, had been vacated. Vendors had long since left their stalls and locked down their shops. A few pedestrians strolled the avenues, wrapped in scarves; otherwise, the streets were empty.

Austin's bare feet pounded against the cobblestone. He winced as every step left tiny cuts and scrapes on his skin. His mental compass was spinning. The moonlight and lanterns would guide him through the maze that was Bruges, but they were not enough to orient him.

After a two-minute dash, he paused to look back. Had he lost his tail? The zing of a projectile striking a lamppost gave him his answer. The bullet ricocheted off the post and clanged against a bronze pot. If he didn't move, more rounds would follow. Austin darted into a side street connecting two major boulevards, searching for an alcove where he could hide; he doubted he could outrun Vasya without shoes. Nothing seemed suitable. He looked for gates or recesses. Nothing. Beads of sweat rolled down his neck and his spine.

He grated his teeth to cope with the smarting in his feet. Landing on a rugged, irregular surface was only half the challenge; tiny pebbles had begun to embed themselves in his flesh. He veered right at the intersection with a major lane. A wooden stepladder leaned against the wall, tempting him to see where it might lead—perhaps he could climb it and find a way onto a roof—but the sound of Vasya closing in forced him to scrap the idea. Instead, he grabbed the ladder and hastened into another street. As he expected, the unwieldy frame took a toll on his speed. He could only hope the measure would pay off.

A stone wall blocked his path ahead. He set the ladder against the partition and scaled the steps. At the top, he lifted the ladder and tossed it out of reach in time to see the assassin come into view. Before Vasya could take aim, Austin jumped from the edge.

His feet splashed in muck. He'd landed in a canal. He waded through a furrow of foul-smelling grime and algae that felt more like a sewage culvert. When he reached the other side, he slipped on the mud banks but quickly regained balance, figuring the ladder ploy had bought him an extra twenty seconds.

The sound of feet running over a drawbridge told him he'd made a gross overestimation.

The Russian loomed over him, standing on the wooden planks.

Reflex launched Austin at the assassin, and he hurled a fist into the man's thigh, causing him to stumble backward. Austin fell to his knees on the drawbridge. Dropping low, he seized Vasya's ankles as the man teetered, and he yanked hard. The Russian lurched and fell, but never lost his hold on the pistol. Austin clambered to his feet, only to have Vasya knock him down with a kick that buckled his knees. Austin slammed a hand on the Mak before it could find him. When Vasya tried to free it, Austin planted a foot on his cheek and thrust outward.

The blow bought Austin the time he needed to scramble upright and sprint back into town. He entered through the gate and disappeared around a corner, hearing mutters of anger from Vasya, who had recommenced the hunt.

Austin took a new direction, toward the cathedral, in hope of finding refuge. He had calculated the odds. It was useless to head anywhere else. A wake of dripping water left an obvious trail.

As he ran, he could think only of Victoria.

TWENTY-SEVEN

Rage and fear make a deadly combination," the Viking said. "Try to calm yourself, Mr. Chatham."

Once again, the phone on speaker held the attention of the entire office. Standing at the forefront, Chatham wanted to slam a hammer onto the receiver as his world collapsed to an even lower rung of hell.

"Why are you doing this to me?"

"It's not about you. You're just a middleman."

"It has everything to do with me," Chatham said. "I handled the negotiations with the Pentagon. I sat in the defense secretary's office to close the Baldr deal. I oversaw the project. No, I didn't design it—but someone had to make it and sell it. It's because of me the satellite orbits. I earned the money for this company. Now you're going to sap us dry."

"No one is forcing you to bid higher."

"Force has everything to do with it! You know damn well I have no choice. I *must* bid."

"In that case, your primary contender has proffered a counterbid of one point two billion."

"Jesus Christ. What's he trying to do?" Chatham shook his head. "His damn oil revenues . . . and in all likelihood, we discovered his fields for him. American prospectors! Look, you've stolen our invention, and now you've pitted us against our own rightful returns. Our money against our innovation . . . The injustice is inestimable!"

"If you wish to preach ethics to me, Chatham, I could point to a dearth of character inside Glitnir."

Chatham looked at Kate Dirgo as he spoke. "What are you talking about?"

"Take a closer look," the Viking said. "Within your own agency, integrity seems to have taken a vacation." He offered nothing more. "I'll have your next bid."

Dirgo stepped aside for a moment to take a phone call. When she returned, she showed Chatham a note on which she'd scribbled a message: *Software engineers arrived. Will begin working to see if they can determine Baldr's location.* Chatham nodded.

"What's the minimum increment?"

"One hundred million, until we reach a standstill. Then I change the rules."

"Tell that arrogant sheik he'll have to beat one point three billion."

"One small step to glory," said the Viking. "Until next time."

TWENTY-EIGHT

The seas had grown more turbulent, the swells unpredictable.

Two hijackers waited on a corsair. They had not boarded the *Pearl Enchantress* with their colleagues. Instead, they had moored near her stern, waiting for their diver.

Rove came up wearing his snorkel. He blew the water out and swam toward the corsair. When he saw the men, he felt a wave of relief at what was possibly his only good fortune the entire day. The men were hardly standing watch. They carried no weapons and appeared to be staring into space, bored. When he reached the ship, he banged the hull and threw his fins onto the deck. One of the guards tossed a mesh of rope over the gunwale. Rove climbed aloft and grasped the Norwegian crewman's assisting hand when he reached the top. The second guard relieved him of his tank and BC.

Without removing his mask, Rove flattened his palm and drove the edge into the first man's carotid artery. Before the second guard could react, he connected his other fist with the man's cheekbone. The watchmen collapsed. Giving them no time to recuperate, he grabbed a nearby coil of rope and proceeded to bind them.

Leaving them on the open deck would be too risky. He also didn't know if anyone else was onboard. Not taking any chances, he descended a staircase and surveyed the lower decks for other crew. The ship was empty. These men appeared to be the only two on watch. Using his leash of rope, he dragged them into the closed space below deck.

"Who are you?" he asked.

A ball of saliva landed in his face.

"Dra til helvete!"

"Kyss meg i ræva, din drittsekk!"

Rove kicked them solidly, his expression devoid of sympathy, then held a firm ankle against the solar plexus of the man who'd spit at him. "There's a hungry shark in the water who just had an appetizer. He's ready for the main course."

The men strained against the ropes. One of them let out a stream of unsavory shouts.

"Du er faen meg det styggeste jeg har sett, ditt fittetryne!"

Rove pushed harder, feeling the man's heartbeat. "Who are you? Why are you here?"

"Ditt helvetes grisetryne!"

This was going nowhere. Rove gagged them and knocked them unconscious with two measured blows, leaving them slumped against the wall.

He explored the enclosed area and entered a cabin. The room was tidy. On a desk lay a map, pinned down by a mariner's compass and a few stones. A lantern swung as the ship rocked, and the wood creaked. Rove took it as a sign of the brewing tempest. He examined the map, following a trail of dots that began in the fjords of northern Norway, crossed the Arctic Circle, ducked under Iceland, and faded without a clear terminus. He put them somewhere near Canada or Greenland. Whoever had been plotting the dots had given up before reaching a destination, or at least failed to mark any current coordinates.

A leather, diary-sized logbook rested against the compass. Rove opened it and read the scrawled handwriting, a mixture of Norwegian and English. The owner had written little, not enough to fill two pages. Rove read the entries he could understand.

> *Phone call with Viking ended approximately 16:00. Vasya left with briefcase soon after. Left cove at 20:32. Viking cannot be trusted on agreement.*
> *We found him drifting. Miracle he survived crash. Viking thinks dead—a good thing—will keep alive now for bargaining. Job can be finished later.*
> *Beginning to regret detaining old man, his screeches and yells . . .*
> *Storm on way but nearing coordinates. Expected arrival 18:30.*
> *How long will this traitor remain committed? Will the insider keep promise? So much rests on his ability to act . . .*

All else was in Norwegian.

Rove closed the book. Who was this insider? What promise had he made? Who had the author found drifting in the water?

He soon learned one of the answers.

"Is someone there?"

The voice had come from another hall. He thought he'd checked every room.

"Do I hear someone?" the voice rang out. It was physically weak and careworn, made of hoarse croaks. But an underlying grittiness was still audible.

The English language in itself put him at ease. He proceeded with caution, holding his knife at the ready. He stepped out of the captain's quarters and entered a vestibule. Turning left, he discovered a new corridor.

"Wish you bastards would feed me," came the voice.

Rove rounded the corner and entered a tiny rectangular chamber ridden with a dank, stale smell. A row of steel bars sealed off access; he could move no farther. Behind the obstruction rested a copper pot. He leaned in closer and regretted his curiosity when a collection of odors stabbed his nose. On a shelf behind the bars was a candle burning over a cascade of wax that had melted and solidified into a stalactite. The flame illuminated a frail, beaten body capped in a thick mound of wispy white hair.

"You're not one of them," rasped the man. Apparently elated, he wrapped his fingers around the bars and leaned in for a closer look. "What's your name? How did you get here?"

"With difficulty. I'm Jake Rove, a bioacoustical oceanographer. I served as a Coast Guard LEDET and Air Force combat weatherman. Who are you?"

The captive didn't answer yet. "They've called in the military?"

"Unfortunately, no. I'm a passenger aboard the *Pearl Enchantress*."

"The *Pearl Enchantress*?"

"A cruise ship from the Pearl fleet."

"Forgive me. I've literally been kept in the dark. Haven't a clue where I am." He coughed.

"Don't waste your breath on apologies. You're weak."

"So they've taken over a Pearl ship, have they? What are you doing here?"

"Stopping them."

"And they haven't killed you? Do they know where you are?"

"Only the ones I've knocked out. I'm learning what I can of their motives, and surprisingly advanced resources."

"Well, Jake Rove, I could use a friend. I've jumped out of the frying pan, into the fire, and back into the frying pan. The last few days have been hellish. You're the best thing that's happened. I'd try to shake your hand, but mine are quite dirty." Instead, he offered a salute and a canny smile that suggested an inner waywardness.

"I'll try to get you out."

"That's impossible at this time. Only Ragnar Stahl has the key. In case you didn't know, he's the ringleader."

"I know." Rove scratched his head, hearing the English accent. "This may sound strange, but have we met before?"

"No. But you've may have seen me. My name is Malcolm."

Rove drew back. "Malcolm *Clare*?"

"That's the one."

Rove bowed his head. "I'm honored."

"Likewise."

"Don't mean to sound maudlin, but to the men and women of uniform, you're a hero."

Clare chuckled mirthlessly. "Only high-level strategists are supposed to know where my military innovations come from. You're telling me you've heard of . . ."

"Glitnir Defense? I'm among a privileged few. Assisted some platoons that used Glitnir technology." Rove examined the lock on the cell. "You're sure this Ragnar doesn't keep a spare key?"

"I don't know. This lock is no easy pick. Then again, I haven't had much to work with."

"How long have you been here?"

"I've lost track of time. Days, at least. They found me floating at sea after my plane went down."

"What caused the crash?"

"It was an assassination attempt. Not the cleverest idea to try staging an accident in a plane programmed by the victim. I managed to escape relatively unscathed. Now they've got me here after finding me adrift. For a while I thought my days were numbered."

"Not anymore."

"Who are these people? Pirates?"

"A safe bet, but I don't know much."

"And Ragnar hasn't discovered you?"

"No. I've only encountered three of his men so far. One's dead, two unconscious."

"Might I ask where these hijackers have all gone? This corsair was crawling just hours ago."

"They've boarded the cruise ship and distributed themselves throughout the decks on patrol. The vessel has ceased all operation. It's completely blacked out."

"Something to do with the generators?"

"More serious. All handheld electronics, all things detached from the main power grid, have failed. The hijackers must have used an EMP device to eliminate power."

Clare looked as if those words had tortured him.

"I know where they got it."

"How do you know?"

"I designed it."

"That must be why they tried to kill you. To prevent you from intervening after they'd stolen the EMP device. But who, and why?"

"There's a way to get answers," Clare said. "I'd do it myself, but I'm behind bars, and my fingers are shaky. Down the hall, you'll find Ragnar's quarters."

"I was just there."

"As they dragged me into this cell, I think I saw a smartphone on his desk. If it's still there, you can use it to send a message."

"We're on the open sea, middle of nowhere."

"I think the phone's linked to a two-way satellite communicator."

"And if we have trouble connecting?"

"The pulse came from a special satellite that can connect you. You'll have to enter a numerical access code, which I will give you."

"I should contact a naval base. They'll prepare an emergency dispatch."

"That's already being done," Clare said.

"By whom?"

"My company, Glitnir. I guarantee they're working with the military now to pinpoint us. What we need is information about our hijackers. I'm going to give you an email address. Write as much information about the hijackers as you can: defining features, their language, what their ships look like, and so on. Tell her what's going on. Just remember—you're using Ragnar's phone, so whatever you send might be read by him, his underlings, or his superiors. Don't write anything too sensitive about yourself."

"Who's the recipient?"

"My daughter," Clare said. "Now go send the message."

TWENTY-NINE

The main entrance was locked.

Austin ran around the cathedral trying every door. All were locked. It was how he wanted them, as long as he could find one way in.

He sidestepped a circular enclosure of gravel, wary of the jagged edges on his tender feet. He jogged to the back of the church and began banging on the wooden doors. It was past midnight. The chances were dismal, but it was worth a try.

Vasya had entered earshot. The footsteps stopped, alerting Austin to danger. It was either a reassuring sign or a foreboding one; either Vasya had lost track of him or paused to take aim. The former was unlikely. Austin was still dripping a trail of water from the canal.

Austin bolted as Vasya pulled the trigger. A bullet grazed his shoulder, slicing away the top few layers of skin. He winced, counting himself lucky. With newfound stamina he dashed around the periphery and continued pounding on doors.

Ahead, someone was leaving the Sint-Salvator. A side door pushed open, and a robed cleric crossed the threshold.

"Wait! Hold it!" Austin cried. The priest froze as Austin bounded toward him. "Keep the door open!"

He could see the cleric was debating retreat. When Austin reached the door, he grabbed the priest by the waist, pulled him inside, and slammed the door shut. The lock clinked.

"What is going on?" the priest demanded. "The cathedral is closed! You're filthy, and wearing—"

"There's a man out there. He wants to kill me," Austin explained.

The priest flinched, the lines on his forehead drawing together in both exasperation and pity for what appeared to be a case of lunacy.

Austin brushed past rows of empty pews toward the main altar, and looked up at the organ and surrounding wall tapestries. Only hours ago the pipes' chords had filled the cavernous space. "Are you sure all the doors are securely locked?"

"Yes. I was just leaving."

"Does the second story have windows?"

"Look around. There's plenty of stained glass."

"I mean to the outside. Windows that open."

"Near the back, yes, if you climb the spiral staircase to the clerestory. Please, dear boy, try to calm yourself."

Austin caught his breath. "You can help me."

"I'm not the right person for that."

"It's very easy. The man outside is a trained killer. He'll follow any sound he hears. Go up to the second story, find an open window, and start throwing things into the bushes. Books, candles, whatever you can find. Don't let him see you. When he approaches, start yelling at him. If he points a gun at you—though I doubt he will—duck inside. I'll exit the cathedral from the opposite end."

The cleric shook his head, as if his suspicions of psychosis were no longer mere suspicions.

"Your feet look terribly bloody, and you've a hurt shoulder. Please rest on a bench while I call a doctor."

"How do you think this happened? Please do as I said! We're losing time."

"Look, boy, I don't even know who you are. Why don't we start with that?"

"Did you not hear pistol shots?"

The priest shook his head. "I did hear *something*. I just don't see—"

Two loud bangs rang out, and a door swung open. The priest yelped, withdrawing into a transept, his sanctuary now a battleground. Austin darted to the back side of a column supporting an archway. He peeked around the edge to see Vasya entering the nave.

"Come out," Vasya said. "Let's talk."

It was an ultimatum, not an invitation. Austin clung to the pillar, adjusting his position as Vasya's footsteps traveled. Isolating their source in the hollow cathedral was like pinpointing a voice in a dark echo chamber. Vasya spoke again.

"I'll let you live."

Austin dropped to his knees and crab-walked between two benches, behind Vasya, toward an exit door. He peered up every few seconds, glimpsing the silencer's muzzle.

A guest at the evening's service must have dropped loose change on the floor. Austin gathered the coins and flung them into an alcove enclosing a shrine. Vasya's ears pricked up, and he approached the recess as Austin inched toward the door.

Vasya strengthened his grip on the Makarov and leapt into the alcove, his smirk at once replaced by a look of conflict. He whirled around in time to see the far door slam. Making for the portal, he was greeted by a stiff breeze when he opened it. He looked out into the night, searching the darkness, unable to find his target.

Austin pinched his nose and prepared to hurl. His stomach climbed into his throat, but he forced it back down again, keeping his mouth dry. The nausea gave way to a milder form of queasiness, and soon he regained control of his insides. He replaced the manhole cover above him and followed a conduit toward a sound like gurgling sludge. As if the streets aboveground weren't perplexing enough, the network of subterranean passageways wove a conundrum navigable only to travelers bearing a map. The light was no help; it was worse than dim, virtually nonexistent. He kept a hand on the walls and took careful steps to avoid tripping over pipelines.

He negotiated the underground with no particular bearing in mind. His first priority was to go far from the Sint-Salvator. The conduit brought him to a river of sewage in a vein the size of a subway tunnel, large enough to fit a raft or small boat. Keeping to a footpath, he continued straight for thirty yards, crossed the river of waste on a concrete bridge, and turned into a small offshoot. The ceiling was lower there, and he had to duck. A few more yards into the passage, he turned into another tunnel and followed a pipe as far as it took him, which must have been over a mile. He was thoroughly lost, but it didn't matter; he had shaken his tail.

He entered a cavity that housed some rusty machinery. A sliver of light shone from above, through a finger hole on the lid accessing the utility chamber. He climbed the ladder and peered through the hole, checking for passersby who might have been able to spot his ascent. He could see little as he lifted the cover, careful to place his fingers where they wouldn't get crushed by the tires of any passing vehicle. The crack afforded him a wider pan of his surroundings. He spotted a few people: a couple embracing, a haggard woman wrapped in shawls, a throng of teenage boys snickering at the lip-locked lovers, daring each other to whistle. Austin waited for them to pass, by which time the elderly woman had advanced no more than a few feet. He had to move, regardless. He popped off the manhole cover and hoisted himself onto the street. The lovers were too distracted to notice, and the old woman cast an unconcerned glance his way.

His relief was short-lived. Voices carried from behind him, harsh voices, one of them barking commands. He spun around, hearing loud steps, the boots drawing nearer, already so close he could see crisscrossing flashlight beams emanating from an alley. The priest must have called the police. What a conversation that must have been, Austin thought. *He was a lunatic, bloodied and wet, fraught with paranoia, stubbornly insistent I let him into the cathedral. . . . Someone followed. . . . There was fighting. . . . This is a sanctuary, not a combat zone. . . . Yes, a crazy man running through my church in a swimsuit, bringing a gun battle!*

Immediate on his list was finding the Navarra. He studied the pattern of intersecting alleyways in an attempt to create a mental map with his place on it relative to the bell tower. This was impossible; the night shrouded all, including the landmarks he'd noted during the day. The flashlights nearly upon him, he chose a street at random and followed it to an intersection. He turned onto a boulevard snaking alongside a canal, then stopped atop a crossing marked *Bridge Langerei.*

Having sprinted without a break, he leaned over the bridge rails in an effort to control a cramp in his diaphragm. It was a poor place for someone hoping to escape detection, but a good one for someone trying to breathe. He took a moment to cleanse his airway of the lingering stink of sewage. He couldn't stay long. He heard the voices again, saw the lights. They were coming from either side of the bridge. He was trapped.

He paced, and a brass-jacketed hollow point shattered the wood rail near him. The bullet hadn't come from a policeman; the police wouldn't have shot without warning. Somewhere along the canal, Vasya must have caught up to him, spotted him, and pulled the trigger—probably attracted by the authorities. Austin had no choice but to dive before the second round finished him. The channel was shallow. He made as small a splash as possible and broke the surface at a near horizontal to avoid striking the bottom. The water lit up around him, then faded to blackness again as a flashlight passed over the canal. He heard clanks on wood and scuffles of feet above. He could feel the vibrations as he braced himself under an arch of the Bridge Langerei. The police had converged on his position. They were on the crossing, probably now seeing the splintered guardrail.

With a tilt of his nose toward the surface, Austin took advantage of one last breath before using the Langerei's brickwork as a springboard and jetting himself downstream. The natural current carried him in part, while his own kick carried him farther. When the impetus of his launch diminished, he turned his palms out and thrust the water back in a breaststroke. The conditions were poor to travel far without breathing. Adrenaline, together with his lengthy sprint, had already elevated his pulse. Not ten seconds passed before he felt the urge to resurface and hyperventilate. Twenty seconds, and the inclination verged on uncontrollable, but he knew breathing was suicide. He was still too close to the bridge. The police were on the lookout, and Vasya would be skimming the water to see how far he'd traveled.

Bubbles seeped from his lips, not large enough to be seen from the surface, yet significant by implication, he realized. His body was warning him he'd have to breathe soon. Forty seconds, fifty seconds, one minute . . . starting from rest, holding in the lungful would be easy until now; as a swimmer, he had a developed lung capacity. But he'd been out of breath from the beginning, and a rocketing heartbeat didn't help. He kept swimming, tracking fractional seconds, each one a feat of endurance. When the initial stages of blackout crept into his vision, he knew it was time. He expelled a stream of bubbles. Then he rolled onto his back, pushed his lips forward, and inhaled, temporarily exposing himself.

He went under again, and after five minutes of rationed breathing he left the canal and followed another boulevard. The police were far behind, though he wasn't sure about Vasya. He read the street name: *Carmersstraat*. From here he could see the bell tower—finally a landmark. He followed the street toward the central market square, now dimly certain of a route to his hotel. Two policemen stood watch in the square, facing opposite directions, each on horseback. Given the modest number of people moving through the square, he thought about walking straight to the other side. But he was dripping again, his clothing scant, and he stood out.

Clicks and clacks caught his attention—wooden wheels rolling over uneven ground, and hooves meeting cobbles. A horse and carriage approached along the vein that would feed into the market. Austin stepped up on the ledge and took a seat within the canvas-covered compartment. There were two passengers inside, a man and a woman, young and dressed to the nines, holding hands, her head wrapped in the hood of a shearling toggle coat and leaning on his shoulder. Honeymooners, Austin suspected. They shrank away when he entered. The woman looked as if she might have screamed had her husband not drawn her closer and tightened his grip on her hand.

"I am Valentino Strongbottom, and I am ready to please," Austin said. He ran five fingers through his hair and let his hand follow down to the nape of his neck before gliding to rest on his upper chest. "Which one of you frisky newlyweds rang for a three-way?"

The couple eyed their hop-on with apparent despair. Neither answered, perhaps afraid he might be dangerous or deranged, and seemed mystified by the accent he had affected—an impromtu potpourri of European articulations.

"Don't be timid," he said. "There's nothing you can say I haven't heard before."

Obviously more than apprehensive, the husband and wife looked at each other, then back at Austin, who was barely paying attention to them; he was busy calculating the number of seconds needed to reach the other end of the square. Now sheltered from the police as they passed through the marketplace, he estimated the crossing would take thirty seconds. Thirty seconds under the protection of the canvas were all he needed. He had little confidence in his own ploy, but figured it sounded better than *Don't let the police find me* or *There's a man out there trying to kill me.*

He glanced at the woman's watch, a mother-of-pearl face set in a golden rectangle. He synchronized his mental count to the movement of the watch's second hand, his fascination with her jewelry causing the woman apparent anguish. With her eyes, she seemed to be pleading with him not to steal. She jerked her wrist away and hid the watch under her coat. Aware of her distress, he redirected his gaze, continuing the countdown.

"There's no need to be bashful," Austin said. "I go by the hour. The longer we wait before someone fesses to their whimsies, the lighter your pockets, and the less fun we share."

"Please, don't harm us," whispered the man. His cheeks twitched, and there was no mistaking the tremble in his Mancunian dialect. "Is it money you're after?"

"Not until we've had a good time. I wouldn't try to cheat you."

The woman spoke next. Her accent was the same as her husband's, the vowels over-enunciated, a few glottal consonants colored with non-rhotic R's.

"What is that awful stench?" she blurted.

"Only the award-winning Eau d'Égout, from the Scintillant collection by Yves Duval," Austin countered. "It's all the rage in Paris, but no doubt an acquired taste."

"Please leave."

"I am sure you will come to enjoy the latest addition to Monsieur Duval's fragrance collection. Particularly as we become more familiar." Fifteen seconds, Austin estimated. "Might I ask to which hotel we are headed?"

The husband tightened his hold on his lady. "Get to the point! What do you want from us?"

"Of greater relevance is what you want from me. But as we have yet to establish which of you called for my services, it seems we're far from arriving there. You have ten seconds to start explaining before I double my price. Time is money in my line of business. Ten . . . nine . . ."

"Neither of us—at least . . . well, I didn't . . ." said the man with a disbelieving, though questioning, look at his spouse.

"Absolutely not!" she shot back.

"Really, there's nothing to be ashamed of," Austin cut in. The woman pressed her head into her husband's chest, which had swollen noticeably since Austin's intrusion. "You eat when you're hungry, don't you? You drink when you're thirsty, don't you? I'm a professional offering a gourmet assortment. And what better way to seal the bonds of marriage?"

"Get out!"

"But I—" Austin paused. "You are Mr. and Mrs. Vanderhort, whom I was to meet in the middle of the square, are you not?"

"No!"

"Forgive me," said Austin. "Do remember, though, that variety is the spice of life."

Having cleared the market square, he leapt from the carriage and ran into a nearby lane. Two turns later, he spotted the Navarra and raced up the stairs, knowing he had little time before Vasya would look for him there.

The lights were on when Austin opened the door to the hotel room. "Finally! Where have you been, and what have you been doing?" The reproach caught him by surprise, but he couldn't have been happier to hear it. "That's a hell of a long time to be swimming, and by the looks of it, you could still afford a shower with a dozen lathers."

"Victoria!" He rushed forward. "You're here."

She looked radiant under the light, glowing as if she'd just emerged from soapy bathwater. His eyes traced the line of her collarbone and stopped at the confluence of her chest and neck. He became suddenly aware of the warmth and shape of his own lips.

"Where else would I be?" Smiling, she crossed her arms and read the depth of his concern. "Where on earth have you been? You look terrible. Why didn't you tell me you'd left the pool? I was worried."

"*You* were worried. I've been playing hide-and-seek with Mr. Kaslov and the police for the past hour. The malicious bastard told me he'd hurt you."

Her smile vanished. "It's a good thing I walked out when I did. I'd be dead."

"Where did you go?"

"I made a brief visit to the steam room, then went to an Internet café to check my email. You'll never guess what I found there."

"Tell me later. Vasya's on his way."

She spotted his shoulder.

"Shit."

"What?"

"You're bleeding. It looks terrible."

"Doesn't hurt too much," he said. "Not like my feet, anyway."

"It looks *really* bad. You're still gushing."

"I'll deal with it later. We better move."

"Where are we going?"

"The Boterhuis."

"Are you crazy? That's where he's staying!"

"I know."

"What's your logic?"

"Haven't you read *The Godfather*?"

"Enlighten me."

"Keep your friends close, but your enemies closer. He won't suspect us there."

The need to speak in whispers and check in under a false name made their small room at the Boterhuis Hotel, directly below Vasya's, feel more incarcerating than hospitable. As the owner had wished to preserve the historical integrity of the hotel, it had no elevator, but rather a winding staircase with steep, creaking steps that would give Vasya away when he moved.

"You said you learned something interesting at the Internet café," Austin called from the bathroom. He was putting a complimentary sewing kit to use, stitching the gash on his shoulder.

"If you call pillaging, plundering, and pirating interesting, then yes," she replied, moseying into the bathroom. "Playing surgeon, huh? That looks painful. Let me help you."

"I can do it."

"Don't be a hero."

The needle plunged. He squeezed his teeth together, otherwise concealing the pain.

"Sew it poorly, and the scar will end up worse," she said.

"Am I that bad?"

"Not bad, but not good." She took the needle and held it under a match to sterilize it, then rubbed it in soap and ran it under the faucet. "Hold still. Hopefully this will ward off infection until you can see a real doctor."

"You win, Nurse Victoria."

Her fingers felt smooth on his skin. He no longer winced when the needle pierced the edges of his wound. Her touch had a warming effect on more than his shoulder. Despite his pain, the sensation spread down his arm and into his chest, relaxing him like a poultice, and made its way down his abdomen and thighs. Aware of the need for an unclouded mind, he tried to resist.

"Better?" she said.

"Without a doubt. Thanks."

"Two hands are better than one." She grinned in amusement. "So, hot jock streaking through Bruges in a Speedo, huh? You didn't strike me as an exhibitionist."

"I was underground or underwater half the time."

"A timid exhibitionist, then. Cute."

"You should have seen my Lothario act," he said. "Now what was it about the three *P*'s?"

First she filled him in on what she'd learned of Vasya Kaslov. Then she handed him a rolled paper from her pocket and resumed suturing. "This new email was sitting in my inbox, received this afternoon. I printed it out."

Austin's brain switched on when he began reading. "Dear Victoria . . ."

"Read the whole thing aloud," she said. "I want to hear it again."

He did.

> "*Message comes from* Pearl Enchantress *luxury cruise liner. Ship lost power from detonated EMP device called Baldr. Defenseless and hijacked by foreign vessels, total five corsairs. Scandinavian crew who appear and speak Norwegian have threatened to sink ship. Carry AK-47 assault rifles, Uzi submachine guns, few other weapons I don't recognize. All wear tattoos on arms of horned helmet with double-edged ax. Principle hijacker and leader named Ragnar Stahl: big man, red hair. Mastermind uses alias Viking. Recent acquisition of Pearl Voyages by competing cruise corporation, Sapphire Pacific. Don't know current coordinates exactly. Will send soon. Approximation: North Atlantic, near Iceland. Please investigate information. Reply soon. You can trust me. Your father sends his love. He says this is no carnival. Jake.*"

Austin looked at a reinvigorated Victoria and said, "Your dad's alive!"

"Yes, he is. And soon we'll know where."

"Must be friendly captors if they took him to a cruise ship," Austin said. "That's not kidnapping. That's a holiday."

"I doubt he's eating cake."

"Doesn't sound like any of the passengers are, either. It's coming together, Victoria. The demonstration Deeb and Vasya were talking about? This must be it. They used Baldr to take out a cruise ship's power. And the man he describes, this Ragnar Stahl, sounds like the intruder I saw in your dad's office."

"My thoughts exactly."

"But who's this Jake, and can we trust him? They could be baiting you."

"The message is real."

"How do you know?"

"The last line. *He says this is no carnival.* It's a code my dad and I use. As I was growing up, Dad warned me of the dangers that went along with his business. We both knew what he was worth dead to terrorists and what I was worth in ransom."

"What a warm, fuzzy talk that must have been with you as a ten-year-old."

"He said if either of us were ever being forced to speak under duress, we'd use the word 'festival.' Otherwise, we'd say 'carnival.' We can trust the message."

"Clever."

Austin reached into her pocket and removed her phone.

"What are you doing?" she asked.

"Your cell is international. We need facts. I'm calling Ichiro. He'll do a little research for us."

Before she could object, his roommate picked up.

"Yamada's palace."

"Have you been renovating?" Austin asked.

Ichiro's resentment was palpable through the line. "Where the hell have *you* been?"

"I told you to take comfort in the fact it was a romantic escapade."

"Do I sound like an idiot? I can only believe absurdities for so long. You don't return my calls, I don't have a clue where you are, you vanish off the face of the earth, leave me in the dark. . . . Rachel and I have nearly lost our minds. And have you totally forgotten your schoolwork? It's not like you're taking basket weaving courses, you big slacker. What the hell are you doing?"

"You're making me feel guilty. If anything, I'm the one who should be worrying about your debauchery in my absence."

Ichiro paused a moment. "Come to think of it, you're right. It has gotten a bit lonely these nights . . . in this new single bedroom . . . all to myself. Hope you don't mind if I've invited a few . . . guests. Night-time guests."

"Thanks for the visual," Austin said. "Just don't lose your wallet on escort services."

A groan came through the line. "You have an uncanny way of turning punches into punch lines."

Austin scrapped the banter. "Itchy, remember the radio transmission I asked you to look at?"

"Hard to forget."

"Have you learned anything?"

"Let's see. I've checked just about every database I could find searching for historic maritime communications. I've looked at treaties. Broken down the language into numbers and then into binary. Searched for patterns. Run algorithms. Tried hexadecimal. Calculated frequency of each character and compared results with expected values from the English language. Read three chapters in a cryptology textbook, which—"

"But did you determine anything?"

He sighed. "Frankly, that project's been on hiatus for a while. I have a life, you know."

"As in, problem sets and midterms."

"Well, yeah."

"Ichiro, this is critical. Can you please make it top priority?"

"Doesn't that strike you as a tad unfair? You haven't told me why I'm doing the research. You haven't told me where you are. You've vanished."

"I'll fill you in soon enough, but for now, you'll have to trust me on this. Are you in front of a computer?"

"Yes."

"Would you mind running a few searches? Computer access is difficult at the moment."

"I've worked under a veil of obscurity this long. Why break precedent?"

"Start with this one. Look up the *Pearl Enchantress* and Pearl Voyages."

"Let's see. Give it a moment . . . and, there we go. I'm on their website. The *Pearl Enchantress* is the jewel of the Pearl Fleet, a magnificent luxury liner renowned for its lavish amenities. Enjoy sinful spas, spacious decks, gourmet cuisine, colorful casinos, spectacular nightly entertainment, full-service fitness centers, grand lounges, yadda yadda yadda. Looking for a private veranda? More than half the staterooms offer a view of the ocean from your own balcony. Getting into the lush life, are we?"

Austin ignored him. "Nothing useful will appear on their website. Do me a favor. Check any financial database for recent mergers or acquisitions."

"Here we go. Wow. I had no idea. Apparently, Sapphire Pacific bought them out in a transaction valued at four billion."

"When did this happen?"

"Four years ago."

"Run another search for me. Type in keywords 'Norwegian,' 'pirate,' 'insignia,' 'helmet,' 'attack.' "

"That's random. Whatever you say. Okay, I Googled it. Someone's MySpace comes up. Several encyclopedia entries on Vikings and Norsemen come up. A video game site . . ."

"Try substituting 'Ragnar Stahl' for 'attack.' "

"You'll have to spell that one for me." Austin did. "Okay, now we're talkin'. A Wikipedia article comes up entitled *Black Marauders.*"

"Click and read."

"Oops, apparently the article was recently modified, and not very well. Article lacks citations, links to other sources, and specificity. It's awfully vague, just one line about pirating in general with a mention of that guy's name. No worthwhile links, although I could try this one. Hmmm. Still nothing. Okay, I'll try Googling 'Black Marauders.' " Austin could hear Ichiro's fingers through the line. "Jackpot."

"You found something?"

"Several somethings . . ." There was a short interval while Ichiro digested what he'd found. He grunted. "Lots of news articles here. Whoa, these guys are hard-core."

"I'm putting you on speaker. Victoria will want to hear this, too. What did you find?"

"Why, hello, Ms. Clare. Pleased to officially meet you. I've seen you in differential geometry class."

"You, too," Victoria said. "Thanks for your help with this, Ichiro."

"I do my best. About the article . . . apparently the Black Marauders—*Svarte Sjørøverne,* in Norwegian—were a seafaring criminal legion based in Norway during the nineties. Pirates, smugglers. With their small flotilla of fast, maneuverable corsairs, they would routinely—and quite savagely—scourge the North Atlantic attacking defenseless merchant ships. Stolen cargo made its way into a black market. The Marauders had ties to the Middle East and often put themselves up for hire, transporting weapons from the Gulf of Aden to Central America, facilitating and brokering deals between a number of insurgent groups and Honduran drug cartels. They hold an almost mythical status among Somali pirate rings operating in the Red Sea."

"Fine role models," Austin said.

Ichiro continued paraphrasing the article. "Besieged vessels usually ended in wreckage, their crew murdered. Apparently these guys didn't want their faces remembered. Throughout their career, they were responsible for the ruthless slaughter of over four hundred innocent sailors." He skipped ahead. "The principal of the organization was a man named Ragnar Stahl. Survivors of Marauder raids have described him as a bony-faced giant. Fortunately for the civilized, he's no longer a threat. He grew careless in his later days, crossed the wrong people. He was turned in by a Russian crime syndicate after an arms transport deal went sour. Flotilla the Hun has been hacking lumber in a Siberian internment colony ever since."

"Wouldn't that be great," Austin said, his irony lost on Ichiro.

"Norway is such a peaceful country," said Victoria. "I wonder how these criminals got their start."

"Evidently from a gang of inmates," Ichiro explained. "They'd formed inside a maximum security prison in Oslo. This was in the seventies. After their release, they were responsible for dozens of armed robberies during a slow movement north through the country. Their brotherhood was constantly growing and shrinking as members were recruited, or arrested, or killed. They were first known as the *Åtseletere,* or 'Scavengers.' In 1975 they raided a manor in Narvik, killing the occupants. That's where . . . interesting," Ichiro said.

"What?"

"According to testimonies of captured members, that's where they found eighteen-year-old Ragnar Stahl, otherwise homeless, living in the manor's detached wine cellar. The boy was surviving on petty crime and stolen food. And he wasn't Norwegian. He was Swedish, and claimed to have run away from home. They took Ragnar with them on their way to Tromsø. By virtue of his youth and dependability, Ragnar became their cohesive linchpin. In subsequent years, he brought organization, hierarchy, leadership, and a sense of loyalty to their group. They built ships and established hideouts on several islands in Norway's three northernmost counties of Nordland, Troms, and Finnmark. To concretize loyalty to their brotherhood, Ragnar established the tradition of the Marauders' emblem: an ax and helmet, worn on a bicep. Sounds like a shout-out to their pillaging ancestors."

"We need more on Ragnar," Austin said. "Any survivor account transcripts?"

"There's one, with mostly physical descriptions, stuff we already know . . . plus it says there's a second tattoo on Ragnar's arm. A cursive spelling of the word *Firecat*."

Victoria looked confused and startled.

"*Firecat?*" she said.

"Does that mean something to you, Victoria?" Austin said.

"Yes, but it's probably coincidence. Five years after my dad was honored by the Royal Aeronautical Society, he was invited to an airshow in Stockholm to showcase his newest aerobatic biplane. It was a thing of beauty. I was thirteen, and still remember how those burgundy wings made red streaks in the sky. Dad's opening speech was supposed to end with a breathtaking finale. A Swedish Air Force pilot was to dive from the clouds and dazzle the audience with an aerobatic display."

"Supposed to?" Ichiro said.

"The day ended in tragedy. When Dad finished his speech, the pilot emerged from the clouds in a downward spiral. But he never pulled out of his nosedive. I remember the explosion like it was yesterday. That biplane . . . it was called the *Firecat*." She could hear Ichiro's fingers typing on the other end, running a new search. "The Swedish military's investigation proved the plane airworthy. There had been no faults in my dad's design."

"Pilot error?" Ichiro asked.

"The pilot had been one of their best, no drugs or alcohol found in his system. The cause of the accident remains unknown. Most thought suicide."

"Let me ask you something," Ichiro said after a brief pause. "Victoria, do you remember the pilot's name?"

"No. This was ten years ago."

"Then you better prepare yourself."

"Why?"

"He was a lieutenant colonel. An illustrious gent by the name of Benedikt," Ichiro said. "Benedikt Stahl."

Austin flipped the phone shut and handed it back to Victoria.
"We've got work to do," he said. "Tomorrow, you'll have to send this information to Jake. Can you go back to that Internet café?"

"Sure. New leads are good news. But we still have to figure out the passkey and snag the briefcase from Vasya. With him guarding it so carefully, I just don't see how that will ever happen."

"I've been thinking of a way to get the briefcase," Austin said.

"Care to explain?"

She noted something new in his expression, and it disconcerted her at first; he looked as if he were celebrating some morbid victory.

"We create a trap."

He stopped, pensive for a moment, wearing the look of a philosopher contemplating a Confucian proverb. Then the intensity reappeared. Victoria realized she was beginning to find the promise of his diabolic pleasure most enticing.

"What kind of trap?" she asked.

He didn't seem to hear her. Watching him gather a notepad and pencil, she realized the key to dislodging the lead in his ears was letting him capture his design on paper. He tore off three sheets from the hotel's notepad and connected them on the ground. Moving simultaneously with his thoughts, his right hand traced the shape of a town square and added a female stick figure to the center of the bird's-eye view. A dotted line linked the stick figure with the apex of a bell tower. He sketched in a roofline and a series of X's.

Three intersecting lines later, he held up his diagram to the light and pointed to the stick figure at the center. "This is where you'll go," he said, "and I know you're brave enough."

"What kind of trap?" she asked again, this time with his attention.

"More like two traps. One involves a Trojan horse. The other . . . sabotage."

PART IV

THE ACE AND THE AMATEUR

Hang tight, Doc," Rove said. "I'll come back for you. Right now I'm headed to the bridge for some star charts, with a brief stop in my room."

"If you can, bring back water and food," said Clare, clutching the bars of his cell. "Good luck, Jake."

Rove left the brig. He exited the hallway and passed the two bound watchmen, who had begun to regain consciousness and were now choking on their gags. On their belts, two radio transmitters buzzed with static. Voices crackled through the line, asking for a response. Rove unclipped the devices and smashed one of the receivers. He turned off the other and clipped it to his belt. First checking to see that no one aboard the *Pearl Enchantress* was watching from the upper levels, he ventured out onto the corsair's weather deck. He gathered his scuba equipment and formed a pile hidden from view. He left the tank and BC there, but brought along his mask, knife, and spare cylinder. Lifting the lid of a wooden cargo box, he loaded a Kalashnikov and swung it over his shoulder. Then, still wearing his wetsuit, he climbed a rope ladder dangling from one of the grappling hooks.

When he reached the top, he flipped over the rail and crouched behind a lounge chair, scanning the environment for hostiles through a slit in the backrest. The deck would have been pitch black had the Marauders not placed flares by the corners of the pool. Four sticks smoldered, lighting the way for Rove. Experience had taught him the problem of flickering light. Discerning real movement from the dancing shadows was an art and a virtue of survival that required he spend a few moments hiding, listening for sounds to be certain the way was clear.

He heard nothing but the flares, saw nothing but the shadows. There was no one on guard here. His mind was certain of this, but seeing movement everywhere, his eyes could never be. He clung to his logic, moving on despite the contradiction with his senses.

Still, he wasn't taking any chances. Avoiding the flares' glow, he kept the AK-47 ready and took eight steps toward a staircase that descended behind a swinging door.

The door came down, shattering under four rounds from behind. Rove whirled around and dove for cover, then fired two shots at a Marauder on patrol, puncturing the man's lungs. The man teetered and fell. Rove collected the corpse and flung it overboard. He jogged to the stairs and quietly descended to deck fifteen. Navigating the halls would be a greater test of skill. They were long and narrow, with few openings between either of the ends. Hijackers would be on watch. Should they enter the passageway and see him, they'd fire fast, and he'd have zero cover; his only line of escape would be a straight path, easily blocked. Worst case, they'd cover both ends and seal off all exits, trapping him in the center. He realized it would be like a less predictable version of Pac-Man, with no screen to show him where the flashing ghosts waited. If they sandwiched him in the middle of a corridor, it was game over. To make matters worse, his weapon would act like a magnet for guards. They'd swarm to the sound of gunfire. Any encounter had to be swift and silent. The dive knife was his main asset, the rifle a last resort.

Light from the patrollers' flashlights came infrequently and irregularly in the halls. Rove held his position long enough to deduce the sources of the beams. He formed a mental Cartesian coordinate system, placing dots on the map that represented the hijackers, each with a calculated radius of uncertainty. He moved along his y-axis, then edged toward the starboard side, which equated to a positive change along the x-axis.

Poking his head into the corridor, he looked both ways. A Marauder paced the floor to his left. Rove waited for the beam to sweep in a favorable direction. Making no noise, he crept up behind the man, placed a hand around his jaw, and snapped his neck. He dragged the body out of the hall and into the elevator foyer, then heard two more men coming from the other side.

The moment the guards discovered their dead colleague, they'd call for reinforcements. He could either hide the body or hide himself and assault them. The approaching voices told him he had time only for the latter.

The two Marauders rounded a corner, jolted by the sight of their fallen comrade. They had no time to react. Rove leapt out from behind a small trash can and landed the side of a flattened palm squarely on the first man's larynx. While the other aimed to shoot, Rove used the first man's flashlight to strike the second's cervical vertebrae with the heavy handle. The bone fractured, pinching his spinal cord and causing instant respiratory paralysis. The first man, one hand clenching his throat, attempted to retaliate. From a person of such size, a punch could have knocked Rove cold. But his inability to breathe had caused him to panic, and the path of his punch was predictable. Rove ducked and responded with a slash of his knife, slitting open the man's throat. He hid their guns and smashed their radios.

Rove returned to the hallway. The way was clear now, at least for a brief while, but he couldn't risk a snare without one last check. He unclipped the working radio from his belt, turned it on, and tossed it into the corridor. Perhaps the static would attract the attention he wanted. Not ten seconds passed before another Marauder entered the hall from the right and noticed the fallen device. Rove braced himself around the corner, waiting. The Marauder moved closer and bent over to pick it up, and Rove descended upon him, his knife carving into the man's trachea. The attack was soundless. Startled and panicked, the injured man spun around to face Rove and fumbled for a finger hold on his trigger. It was an act of desperation in the face of certain death. Rove countered with a foot to the man's wrist, sending his assault rifle soaring in an arc. A second kick leveled the man, and Rove caught the rifle before it struck ground. The man writhed under the force of Rove's foot, hands clasping his throat, until Rove reached down and finished him. With the bodies now a pile, Rove carried each one up the flight of stairs and tossed them overboard. It was a slow, painstaking process, but a necessary precaution to hide his work. A few bloodstains smeared the floor, noticeable against burgundy carpeting only to the keen eye. Confident he'd cleared the way for at least another two minutes, he sprinted down the hall and entered his room.

He never thought he'd miss the penthouse this much. He changed out of his wetsuit into the crewman's uniform and proceeded to tap a new message against the wall of his cabin.

Lachlan, you there?

Sixty seconds passed. Rove considered banging louder, but decided not to gamble with noise. Fawkes was probably asleep. He coded the message again with the same force. A reply came.

Here, hungry, cold, hate canned food, hate dark. Where you been?
Around. Learned ship was rigged with over a dozen explosives.
How do you know?
I know.
What to do?
Help me take down hijackers so we can access lifeboats and free passengers.
Old man against these big ogres?
Yes. First I need help reaching the bridge for star charts.
The bridge is probably full of hijackers.
I know. Must get them out.
Tell me what to do.
As steward you have access to cleaning chemicals?
Plenty.
What kinds?
Everything. Kept in special closet near laundry room.
Key required?
No. Go down hall, turn right, right again.
Stay ready. Will come to your door.

Rove checked the peephole for moving beams, then slipped out of his cabin and jogged over to the laundry room. He found the closet Fawkes had described, and used a Marauder's flashlight to illuminate everything he needed—chemicals, dyes, bleaches, cleaning agents, buckets, Ziploc bags, mops. He grabbed a bucket and filled it with the necessary ingredients before returning to Fawkes's room. He knocked, and the steward let him in.

"Jacob," Fawkes said in a low hiss. "You've been gone too long. Don't scare me like that."

"I've kept safe. Now, can you be brave?"

"What do you need me to do?"

"Inside this bucket are bottles of ammonia and bleach, along with a handful of sealed plastic bags. Help me empty chemicals into the bags without mixing them. We want to stuff this bucket full of concentrated ammonia and bleach."

"Why?"

"Together they produce noxious fumes—chloramine and chlorine, among others. We're improvising a chlorine bomb."

"Chlorine bomb?"

"Yes. Germans used the gas during World War One by releasing cylinders in trenches."

"We're mixing poisonous fumes in my room?"

"For later use."

"I didn't think this was what you had in mind," Fawkes muttered, "when you told your steward you wanted to develop a friendly chemistry."

R ed blemishes in the sky signaled the arrival of morning. A Marauder on patrol shut off his flashlight. He no longer wore the tuxedo, but the diamond ring remained on his middle finger.

Numb with boredom, he rounded a corner and entered the deck fifteen foyer, wondering whether it was necessary to police every hallway while passengers stayed in their cabins. Couldn't they have wired weapons to motion detectors or surveillance cameras? No, he finally decided: There were too many decks, too many corridors. Patrolling was the only way to ensure every passenger's eventual death.

The tedium was broken by an opening door. The patroller crouched low and aimed the AK-47 at a stateroom entrance ten yards down the hall.

"Don't move!" he bellowed.

"Please, no shooting," came a weak voice, choked by sobs. Her accent was Dutch. "We need food and water."

"You got your daily ration, lady. Get back in your cabin."

"Please, please, I have a baby," said the woman. "She's crying. She needs soft foods."

"You've had enough."

He could hear the infant's crying in the background.

"You . . . I recognize you," said the mother. "You're supposed to be a waiter. You're one of the pirates?"

"Get back inside. Close the door."

"You don't understand," she begged. "Can't you please bring us just a bit more food and water? Some custard or applesauce? We've gotten so little."

He mounted the rifle on his shoulder and took aim, astonished when the mother didn't move or even flinch. "No, lady. Shut up."

"Sir, I'm begging. Please. It's not for me. It's for my child. I'm pleading for my child."

"I don't want to hear anything, lady."

"If you can't provide food, then a blanket? With the heat gone, she's—"

"Get inside and close the door!"

She didn't move.

He fired a shot and deliberately missed. A piece of her door blew off. Her scream, following the explosion, became trapped in a series of suffocated sobs. The infant shrieked. The patroller kicked the wall at waist level and let out a whooping laugh from the bottom of his throat. He hadn't lost control of himself, nor did he find the situation amusing; he merely wanted to frighten her.

"Shut yourself and your baby up!" he said, approaching the closing door. He lowered his voice, certain she could still hear. "I'm not supposed to tell you this, lady. But you complained, so I will. It won't be long before this whole ship is sitting at the icy bottom, three kilometers below the surface. Sinking the ship is faster than shooting three thousand passengers. We need you alive for now, at least while the man in charge negotiates. Then, we need you dead. The food, the water . . . it's just a courtesy. This cabin will soon fill with water, lady."

He kicked the wall again and fired a shot through the hole he'd made in the door, blasting out their stateroom's window and inviting in a harsh wind.

"That will make it easier," he said, "if your baby's crying starts to wear you down. In the long run, it won't make a difference what you do."

His rifle stood vertical, parallel to the line of his body as he strode back to the elevator foyer. He reached for his radio device to report the incident.

"Come in, Lido Deck."

No response.

"Lido, come in."

Still nothing.

It was only one flight up. He climbed the stairs and shouted for his fellow patrolmen. There was no reply. Noting the scarcity of his colleagues, he returned to deck fifteen and leaned his head into the adjacent corridor. At least one patrolman should have been there.

His boot pivoted on the carpet, squeaking. He bent to the floor and touched it, then touched the wall. The carpet was moist, his fingers stained. He looked at a wall that should have been a spotless white. The vermilion streaks were faint.

Fawkes removed his spectacles and folded them on a box of aluminum foil. Carefully he unscrewed the lid of a bleach bottle and poured the liquid into a plastic Ziploc. With steady fingers he sealed the bag and placed it in the bucket. He did the same with four more bags.

There were sheets of crumpled foil on Fawkes's nightstand, as if he had done some heavy wrapping. Rove wondered if the man had been hoarding food rations.

"Be *very* careful," Rove advised. "Don't let them mix prematurely."

"How exactly are you going to release the ammonia into the bleach, mate?"

"I'd considered creating a divider using tape and your aluminum foil, then pulling out the divider at the right moment. But that's too risky. Foil is weak. If the divider broke too early, we'd have a problem. Plastic bags are better. They puncture easily. If one breaks, it's okay. If two break, we're still safe half the time. The bucket is more controlled this way, and when I want to release the fumes, all I have to do is slash my knife around a few times, then get out."

"Makes sense," Fawkes said, pouring bleach into another bag.

"Try not to get any of this on your fingers, either. With no running water to wash it off . . ."

Rove stopped. One of the bags he'd set aside had begun to inflate. He reached for it, but before he could throw it over the balcony, the plastic burst and the chemicals soaked into the carpet. A painful smell wafted, causing Rove and Fawkes to clamp their nostrils.

"Damn."

"What happened?"

"My mistake," Rove said. "I was opening a new bottle and accidentally mixed the two. We'd better get out of here. Grab your things and come over to my room. We'll finish the gas bomb on the other side of the wall."

"Can't we just open the sliding glass doors for a breeze? It wasn't much."

"Enough to cause lung damage. Grab your essentials and move."

C ome in, Captain," crackled a voice through Ragnar's radio, speaking Norwegian.

He held the device to his mouth. "I hear you, Gunnar."

"I believe someone is working against us. Possibly a renegade Marauder, but more likely a passenger with combat training."

"Why do you say that?"

"One soldier on the lido deck and four on deck fifteen have gone missing."

"How do you know?"

"They don't answer my radio calls, and I found bloodstains on the walls. I've alerted the others. They will notify me if they find any missing bodies. That's not the most telling sign, either, Captain. Someone found Jorgen and Sigurd tied up in the flagship with no sign of Oskar. Oskar was our only diver."

Ragnar grumbled, "Make an announcement to all soldiers. Tell them to keep a lookout for defectors or defiant passengers. If you find him and he's one of ours, bring him to me. If it's a passenger, shoot him."

"And if we don't track this person?"

"We'll have to search room to room, knocking on doors—knocking *down* doors. We question passengers and offer them sanctuary in return for information. If we find empty cabins, we comb through drawers and closets, looking for personal effects that might tip us."

A t least I can enjoy a nicer room now," Fawkes said halfheartedly. "Though the amenities are moot without electricity."

"Doesn't matter," Rove said. "You'll keep busy here."

"More work?"

"Letter writing. We're going to teach Mr. Stahl a game of reverse hostage."

"What exactly will I write?"

"Use the stationery by the nightstand to write the following message: 'Every hour, if the hijackers have not lowered and filled an entire lifeboat with passengers, you will find five more of your men dead.'"

"What if he turns that plan on its head? For every one of his men you kill, he could threaten to kill even more passengers. There are more of us than there are guards."

"He has no way of communicating a threat to me. He doesn't know who I am or which cabin I stay in. I, on the other hand, can write to him anonymously. With the public announcement system down, he can't respond. It's time to turn up the heat on him."

"How will I deliver the note?"

"I'll be back to pick it up soon. Start writing."

Rove left through the front door, carrying the rifle in one hand and dragging the bucket of chemicals with the other. With his scuba mask, spare cylinder, and knife at his belt, he proceeded to the forward elevators. He paused in the foyer to check the ship map. Then he turned a corner and entered a corridor leading to the bridge. At the sound of footsteps he withdrew into an alcove, opened a closet door, and hid. Two Marauders approached from his rear, snickering about some kind of payoff. They stopped near the closet. Rove peeked through a crack for a better look. They were listening to a new announcement sputtering through their portable radios: *All soldiers continue patrol, scout for possible defector or rebel passenger . . .*

The announcement finished, and the guards walked on. When they'd passed, Rove opened the closet and proceeded toward the bridge entrance. He came to the door, crouched low, and listened.

"We take over a vessel while the Viking relaxes," he heard someone say. "Captain, he carries no gun. He talks. We deserve a larger share."

"Be patient, Sverre." The voice belonged to Ragnar. As he listened, Rove removed his knife, punctured the plastic bags, and allowed the ammonia to mix with the bleach. He opened the bridge door and slid the bucket inside, already choreographing his next moves. "I agree with you," Ragnar went on. "But we can't speak of this till we sail home. Our legion has many ears."

"They will listen favorably."

"All it takes is one to ruin everything."

"You know your crew is loyal to you. And this isn't about treachery," another responded. "It's about merit. We've earned more than the Viking's pledge. If any extorter were to understand, it would be him—that turnabout's fair play."

Ragnar' reply was short and dutiful. "The Marauders will be rewarded."

"We know you feel a certain allegiance to the man who helped you avenge Benedikt," Sverre said. "Don't let that soften you."

"Spare me your griping," Ragnar said. "As soon as we sail, we'll find the Viking defenseless. That will be our . . . chance to . . ." He trailed off, sniffing. "What is that stench? My nostrils ache."

"I smell it, too," said another. "Pungent."

"A gas leak?" Sverre suggested.

The portal slammed open with a loud crack. Rove stood in the doorway, eyes protected by his dive mask. His finger clamped the trigger. A steady stream of bullets discharged, shattering the glass panels. Splinters from the wood of the walls flew off with the exposed wind. Ragnar dove for cover, as did Sverre. The other men rushed for their guns, but they were too late, caught in Rove's broadside. Five hijackers fell in a tableau of carnage.

A yellow-green fog seeped into every corner of the room. Rove inhaled through his handheld cylinder and tried to avoid the rolling creep of the fumes. The others coughed, choking as asphyxiation took effect. He knew what it must have been like for them; little razors were slicing at their throats as they breathed.

"Grab the bucket!" Ragnar roared. "Stop the gas!"

Sverre ran out from behind the center island of computers, his submachine gun firing. The monitors smashed into pieces as a row of bullets chased him. Before he could reach the source of the fumes, three rounds impaled his ribs. Pain exploded throughout his upper body, coupled with a sudden, crippling weakness, and he lost his balance. He landed hard, and Rove finished him with a round through the skull.

"It's just me and you in here, Ragnar," Rove shouted. "I'm protected from the fumes. You'd better get moving."

Gas continued to leach out.

Squatting behind an overturned table in the port-side wing, Rove heard: "My men will kill you."

"They have yet to put up a fight."

Ragnar emptied one of his rifles into the ceiling over Rove. A cloud of dust and debris fell around him, the bullets causing infinitely more damage to the ship than to Rove.

Ragnar asked, "Who are you?"

"I could ask the same question, but I'd prefer to start with why you're here. Whatever you say, do it fast. Unless you start running, you don't have much time to live."

The arms of the haze had begun to reach for Ragnar. He sputtered, resisting the chemical's strangle on him. He grabbed another rifle and fired at the table through obscured vision, kicking up a few more splinters. When his salvo failed, Ragnar reached for his radio and barked into it, "He's in the bridge. Send reinforcements. Beware the chlorine gas." His message in Norwegian was hacked by coughs.

Rove unleashed another volley. Ragnar yelled in agony when a bullet ricocheted and struck his elbow, splitting bone. Sensing an opportunity, Rove held his breath, ran for the bucket, and lobbed the full pail of cleaning chemicals. The liquids splashed over the island of computers and doused Ragnar, who wailed louder when the fluid spilled into his open gash. The wound festered, ammonium hydroxide mixing with his blood.

"We'll find you," he shouted to Rove. "Then you'll know pain."

Ragnar emerged from the haze, his jasper hair an unsightly clash with the greenish cloud surrounding him. He grabbed a rifle from the deceased and ran, showering Rove's table with one final bombardment, coughing uncontrollably. He flew through the newly opened window and fell into the crew's private area below, landing on a lounge pad and breaking his descent with a tumble.

Rove leaned over the edge and searched for his target, but the man had fled too far. He checked his watch and figured he had thirty seconds before a horde of Marauders poured in. He took another hit from his tank and rummaged for the celestial maps. There was a nautical almanac on the shelf, which he rolled into a tube. Then he readied himself for a leap out the window.

"Wait!" someone said.

Rove turned around to face the heap of bodies he'd toppled, but the voice came from another place. There was someone else sprawled on the floor, someone he hadn't noticed.

"Major . . ."

He spotted the man on the other side of the room.

"Kent!" he said, running to the man's side. "Did I—?"

The first officer lay with his hands wrapped around a bleeding torso. He looked seconds from death. The sweat on his skin had almost frozen, and yet he was no longer shivering.

"They shot me. You didn't."

"Who are they? What did they do to you?" Rove asked, bracing the officer. "Do you know what they want?"

"I've been here so long. They didn't finish me. Wish I'd died after the first shot."

"I know it hurts. Hang with me. What have you heard?"

Rove noticed a new wound in Trevor Kent's chest. A bullet from the recent fire had lodged itself in his rib cage. He didn't have long, and he'd begun to choke on the fumes. Rove tore off a piece of a Marauder's shirt and fashioned a bandage.

"There's . . . there's nothing we can do," Kent stammered. "They're going to leave soon. They're going to . . . destroy the ship. The radar malfunctioned, possible tampering. Broken radar. . . . I can't stay awake . . ."

"Stay with me, Kent!"

"Nothing we can do . . . the ship, too many charges . . . Don't let them find you. . . . They're—they're soon going cabin to cabin, looking for you. . . ."

"What did you say? What about the radar and tampering?"

The officer's head lolled.

"It hurts. I just want to go away . . ."

"Focus!"

"Selvaggio . . ." Kent said. "Selvaggio . . ."

His life came to an end. Voices filled the halls beyond; the Marauders were near. Rove took a running leap and vaulted out through the window, landing one deck down.

He sprinted down the corridor, opened his door, and found Fawkes finishing the letter.

"Here you go," Fawkes said. "Want to read it first?"

Rove scanned the message, then folded it into an envelope beside the nightstand and wrote Ragnar's name across it.

"Looks good. Stay here. The gas worked. This part of the ship's lousy with guards."

"Where are you going this time?"

"Stargazing with Malcolm Clare."

"With *whom*?" Shock leapt into Fawkes's face, now a pastel shade of pink.

"You heard right."

"*The* Malcolm Clare?"

"One and only."

"I'm flummoxed. Is he on the ship?"

"He's on a ship, not the *Pearl Enchantress*. One of the corsairs took him in."

"Quiet an expensive captive."

"That's not all I've learned," Rove said. "Some of the hijackers are breaking rank. I overheard them talking to Mr. Stahl on the bridge. Apparently the Viking's not paying them as much as they want. Sounds like Stahl plans some opposition."

"So there's mutiny on the *Bounty*," Fawkes said.

"It's a good sign. Proves the Viking has less control than he thinks."

"I don't know who to root for."

"Root for both. Let them duke it out."

He moved for the door.

"Jake, what are they going to do if they discover this is your cabin?"

"Won't happen." Clapping a hand over Fawkes's shoulder, he felt no bounce and took this as a sign of fear. "I'm headed to the corsair after a pit stop at the galley. Doc Clare's hungry."

THIRTY-ONE

While the receptionist was distracted by a phone call, Victoria unplugged the router from the hotel's lobby. If Vasya was conducting a negotiation, he would need email access. She figured he would soon have to find an Internet café.

She waited in an electronics store across the street, where she purchased a key-logger, a thumb-sized device that plugged inconspicuously into a computer port and tracked every keystroke—even asterisk-protected passwords. She also had the option of purchasing virtually undetectable computer monitoring software that could track all Internet activity, record periodic screenshots, or play back real-time video captures. The downside was, it took a few minutes to install. She needed a tool that was easy to insert and easy to remove.

Three hours passed before Vasya left the Boterhuis. She followed him from a distance, watching as he stopped for waffles at a market stall and continued to the café. He logged onto a computer and began typing. Victoria scanned the street for idle vendors or peddlers. There was a shoe shiner, a gangly fellow in a baggy shirt, leaning over a suited man's feet and rubbing polish into leather. When he finished his job, she approached him.

"Looking for customers?"

"Would you like a shoe shine?" he asked, already stooping.

"No, thank you, but I could use another service. There's a man inside that Internet café." She pointed. "He's my uncle, and I'm visiting him. He hasn't seen me in years, and I'd like it to be a surprise, so don't tell him you saw me. I'm hoping you could trick him into coming out and meeting me in the square."

"Trick him?"

"Just a harmless prank. But you *can't* say it was me. Tell him a large Arab man sent you and asked that he go immediately to the Tavern Brugeoise."

"Why would I tell him it was a large Arab man?"

"It's a little joke we used to have," Victoria said. "He probably won't remember, but I want to know if he can guess it's me. Just tell him it's urgent, that he should come now."

She handed him coins. He took them, walked into the café, and tapped Vasya's shoulder. Vasya looked annoyed by the interruption, and tried to shoo him off, but the shoe shiner insisted. She watched as Vasya eventually bought the man's story. He was trying to ask questions, but the shiner shrugged and walked out the door. Curiosity must have got the best of him. He set the computer on lock and left the café, briefcase in hand, for the tavern.

Victoria entered the café and sat down at Vasya's computer.

"That one's taken," said the clerk, a young female with pink highlights and a nose piercing. She was leaning back in her chair and sipping coffee. "The guy said he'd be right back."

"Sorry," Victoria said. She sat across from the console and improvised a new plan. She used her feet to unplug a few cords, then went to the counter. "This computer doesn't seem to be working. Would you mind taking a look?"

The clerk asked, "What's the problem?"

"I don't know," Victoria said. She was counting the seconds until Vasya returned. "I'm not good with computers."

"Is the monitor turned on?"

"Monitor? I'm not really sure what that is. Maybe you could look for me."

The clerk trashed her coffee cup and made an exaggerated show of rising to her feet. She stretched and ambled over to the computer.

"Let's see what's wrong," she said, and began sorting through a mess of cords.

Victoria stepped behind the clerk, crouching under the desk and searching for the keyboard's cable. Her fingers pushed through a tangle of wires. With some difficulty she found the plug and removed it. She then inserted the key-logger where there had been a direct connection. Leaning out the window, she saw Vasya marching back from the tavern, looking furious.

"You know, it's not all that important," Victoria told the clerk. "I can come back later."

"I'm almost done," said the clerk.

"Take your time. It's not a problem. Really."

"Whatever."

Victoria flipped on her sunglasses and slipped out the door as a host of tourists passed. In the reflection of a car window she watched as Vasya entered the café, unlocked his computer, and began typing.

A ustin walked into a leather shop.
    "I'll be with you in a moment," said the salesman, helping customers. "Don't go away."

"That's fine," Austin said.

The store window displayed handbags, satchels, jackets, suitcases. He was sure he'd find what he needed. After a few minutes, the salesman returned.

"Sorry about the wait. How may I help you?"

"I'm looking for leather briefcases."

"You've come to the right place, my friend." The salesman led him to a far corner of the shop, where the shelves were filled with cases of various sizes. "Anything in particular you're looking for?"

Austin scoped out the selection before gravitating to a particular design. If his memory served him correctly, it was a close match. "This one's nice," he said, running a finger along the leather. "But the wrong color. Can you darken it?"

"It's a beautiful case. Moroccan leather. Why dye it?"

"I'm picky."

"It's not easy to do once the briefcase has been made."

"Just a few shades?"

The salesman surrendered a sigh. "It's going to cost extra." He brought out a collection of fabrics that formed a color gradient. "Which one would you like to match?"

Austin pointed. "Right there. Nearly black, with a touch of russet."

W hen Vasya finished his emails, he logged off the computer, paid the clerk, and left the café. Trained on his every action, Victoria adjusted her turtleneck and seated a red knit cap on her head as she waited for him to reach a safe distance.

Inside, her first move was to send an email to Jake summarizing the information Ichiro had uncovered. She then accessed the keylogger and began sorting through a string of characters. Using the email address, password, and decryption keys she learned, she logged onto Vasya's account and snooped through his inbox and sent messages. Deeb's name surfaced. She opened the oldest message, sent days ago, to learn the former oil minister had flown into the Brussels airport by Gulfstream and hired a limousine to drive him to Bruges. So the man had a flair for the ostentatious.

Most messages were about logistics and meeting places. She perused a few more exchanges, identifying relationships and connecting the nodes in Vasya's network. There was a document in his inbox naming several dozen terrorist operatives. Detailing illicit ties and contact information for each criminal, the spreadsheet struck her as a who's who on the United States wanted list. She printed the file and emailed it to herself for safekeeping. She thought about the fun she'd have faxing this to the CIA, and writing the cover letter—*This may help*. She continued reading. In older emails she came across Dan Chatham's name. The explanation clicked as she learned how he played into the auction. So the story she'd pieced together with Austin was true. The Viking had pitted Glitnir Defense against a moneyed al-Nar confederate and countless other terrorist leaders in a bidding war.

She reminded herself that investigation wasn't her main purpose right now. Coordination was. She'd come to write three emails from two accounts.

Still logged into Vasya's e-mail, she composed a message to Farzad Deeb, doing her best to mimic the Russian's writing style and work within the context of previous messages.

Farzad,

Chatham has made his final offer. Let us meet tomorrow at noon at the top of the bell tower. There I will make a last call to the Viking. We can then proceed to a celebratory lunch. Please bring your computer so we may wire your money. I would prefer we met alone.

VAK

She clicked *send*, then erased the message from Vasya's outbox. She opened Yahoo and created a new account under her own name to send the following message:

Mr. Kaslov,

I tried to meet you in the town square earlier today. Thought you'd only come if you believed Deeb had called for you, hence

*the shoe shiner's story. But I was scared away when I thought
you had a gun.*

*My purpose in writing is to propose an arrangement to get
my father's laptop back. I am sure we can settle this peacefully.
Please meet me in the middle of the main square at noon tomorrow. I will come alone.*

Sincerely,
Victoria Clare

For a believable time lapse between messages, she waited till evening
to send the third:

Hello, Mr. Deeb,

*I'm the daughter of the man whose technology you want to
purchase. Your business with Vasya Kaslov, Glitnir, and my father doesn't concern me. One matter alone concerns me, and that
is my father's safety.*

*Ensure that Malcolm Clare lives, and I'm prepared to give
you the satellite's passkey. All you must then do is get the briefcase from Kaslov.*

*I assume you know Kaslov intends to double-cross and kill
you as soon as you wire funds to the Viking's account. No doubt
you're aware of his interest in acquiring Baldr for the SVR military technology procurement network he has worked for since
1991. He's dangerous. You should never meet him alone.*

*Tomorrow at noon I'll be standing in the center of the mar-
ketplace. Please meet me there so we can talk.*

Sincerely,
Victoria Clare

There's only one thing worse than hitting a roadblock going forward, Ichiro thought, and that's hitting a roadblock going backward. Elbows outstretched, he clenched his fingers around his hair and wrenched at the roots with a deepening sense of frustration. He stared at the paper and once again read the transmission aloud.

"'The way is off my ship. I am altering course to port. Man overboard. Keep clear of me. I am maneuvering with difficulty. I am now altering course to starboard. My ship is on fire, and I have dangerous cargo onboard—a naval mine shipment. Keep well clear. I have a diver down to assess propeller damage. Keep well clear at low speed. . . . Negative! I am altering my course to starboard. I already tried altering course to port. I repeat, the way is off my ship. You may feel your way past me. Man overboard.'"

He shook his head, his mind in a trench. "You're not the only one who's gone overboard," he muttered to himself, shading his words with self-pity. "What else does he want me to do? Austin, you jerk. I love you, but you're a jerk. I'll never slave for you again."

He wasn't fooling himself. He sighed, knowing full well the only thing angering him was his own failure.

Feeling useless, he uncapped his pen one final time and began shuffling letters in search of anagrams. Nothing worked. Hours of fiddling had turned his brain to mush.

He tapped in a number on his phone.

"Rachel, I'm bamboozled," he said. "Burnt, befuddled, and blatantly buffaloed."

"How terrible coming from a soon-to-be math Ph.D.," Rachel gibed. "Don't tell me someone asked you to solve a crossword puzzle or . . . *gasp* . . . interpret a poem?"

"I'm beginning to think this is worse."

"Shocking. Add rhymes, and you were starting to sound like Dr. Seuss."

"Believe me, any more dead ends, and you'll hear me spouting Seussisms till I turn gray."

"Okay, what is it?"

"It's this thing Austin gave me before he left. It's on the cutting edge of weird."

"The radio transmission you told me about?"

"Yep. I've reached an impasse. Austin told me it's urgent, but I'm hopeless. Would you be kind enough to stop by the oh-so-hopping Club 102 so I can plumb the depths of your knowledge?"

"Sure, I can swing by Escondido Village."

"Thanks, Rach."

"See you in a few."

She arrived wearing a short, drape-sleeve Juicy Couture mini dress, but Ichiro hardly turned his head to greet her. She found him hunched over a Scrabble board, playing with combinations of phonemes, more interested in the blocks than her strawberry print.

"I think I'm on to something," he said, divulging more skepticism than he cared to admit.

"Oh?"

"So I started looking for historical context, right? It made sense to search for books that might have a full transcript of the message. It might also help to know what ship sent the message, and to whom. Then I realized, maybe it's a code. So I've studied the text, run algorithms, consulted cryptology books, looking for embedded language or ciphers. Then I thought, maybe that's too complicated. Now I'm looking for anagrams. And look what I found."

Rachel read through his self-doubt and braced herself for the sub-enlightening.

"What did you find?"

"If you take the first letter of every complete clause, you get the words *tiki* and *miki* mixed in. There may be some sort of Polynesian code. *Tiki* refers to large wood or stone carvings made by Pacific island cultures."

"And the relevance . . ."

"Working on it. What do you think?"

"I'd say that train of thought has derailed."

"Pretty craptastic, I know. At least the prospect raised my spirits from a one to a two."

Rachel read the transmission to herself. "Mind if I use your computer, Itchy?"

"As long as you never call me that again."

"Don't count on it."

"Why not?"

"Because it's cute that you hate it." She turned to the computer. "Let me try a little research before reading any deeper. As they say, proper prior preparation prevents piss-poor performance."

"Never heard that one."

"Add it to your alliteration repertoire."

She typed something on his keyboard and stared into the monitor. Not sixty seconds passed before she felt an irresistible urge to flash him a mocking grin.

"You're awfully dense for a brainiac," she said, jotting something on paper.

He gave her a deadpan look. "You got it? Seriously, that fast?"

"Seriously, that fast."

She handed him the paper. He took it, glancing between the computer screen and her markings.

"Oh, my God . . ."

"Didn't you ever read *The Purloined Letter*?"

"Some time ago."

"The simple answer eludes you only because you have forgotten to do the obvious. When you first looked at the transmission, you saw a puzzle in the letters and words, but not in the sentences—obviously not the best way to *flag* it."

She winked, her golden curls now framing a smile Ichiro found so delicious he pulled her in and landed a wet smooch half on her lips, half on her cheek.

"Itchy, you've got to work on your aim."

THIRTY-THREE

It's no longer gourmet, but at least it will fill you up," Rove said as he handed over the bag of food he'd collected in the galley. "There's even some butter for the rye."

Clare inhaled the bread and water before moving to fruits. "Can't thank you enough, Jake. Just be glad the bars aren't wide enough to squeeze out this chamber pot, or I'd ask you to empty it and spare me the stench."

"Don't let it ruin your appetite. Eat up."

"What's that in your pocket?"

"Celestial diagrams in a Bowditch almanac. To help determine our location."

"That's nice. I don't have a clue where we are."

"Nor I. A vague idea, but then we don't need total precision for someone to find us. Using the trail of dots on Stahl's map, I should be able to pinpoint us to within a couple miles."

"When you send the coordinates to my daughter, have her forward them to Glitnir."

"I will."

"Thanks for the food," Clare said. "Until next time."

"Stay warm," Rove said as he left the brig.

He stepped into Ragnar's quarters and traced the corsairs' dotted course on his world map, moving his finger south from the Norwegian fjords across the Arctic Circle. He extended the path, then unfurled his own map of the cruise ship. The rear of the map charted their itinerary via smooth, curved lines connecting the continents. Using a ruler to match scale, he superimposed the intended circuit onto Ragnar's extrapolated plot and marked the intersection. Then he stepped onto the weather deck to compare the sky with the almanac's diagrams. Using tools on Ragnar's desk, he measured the declination of three stars, accounting for the month and hemisphere, and used the angles as a basis for an ellipse he sketched on the map. Its perimeter contained an area of uncertainty, while the major and minor axes intersected at a magic point. Crosschecking his two data points, he took their average and updated his estimations with a mark 350 nautical miles southwest of Iceland.

Rove heard a sound like someone rummaging through a toolbox. He tightened his grip on the AK-47. His apprehension didn't last. It was probably the ship's creaking, combined with days of repressed paranoia.

He turned on Ragnar's smartphone and checked the inbox. He read Victoria's email and absorbed the new information. So the hijackers had a name: the Black Marauders. He continued to scroll down, honing in on the meaning of both tattoos. He glanced back in Malcolm Clare's direction, thinking about the professor sitting in that miserable cell, and he started to piece together the relevance of *Firecat*.

Rove closed the email and composed a new one to Victoria. He sent his estimation of their coordinates along with her father's request that they be forwarded to Glitnir. Then he placed the phone back in his pocket, making sure it was on silence. He was almost smiling. It felt good to have made contact with someone on land. He began to ponder over how he would track down the chief Marauder. Outside, he took a moment to pan the constellations, hoping the twinkling lights would lead to an epiphany. None came soon enough. Blunt pain blasted down the back of his neck and spread throughout his skull. He spun around, spotting the glimmer of a wrench before his head landed on the gunwale. A new, starless sky dominated his vision.

* * *

The Viking's message was unequivocal, politely stated. "Your turn."
"Shut up and let me think!" Chatham said.
"Your competitor would be glad to know he's caused you to stall."
"Fine. Raise him another increment."
The line went dead.
Kate Dirgo looked at him sideways, as she would a man with no backbone.
"Have you totally lost it?" she asked. "Have you gone completely insane?"
"Getting there fast."
"We're up to three *billion* dollars."
"Would you prefer riding a bike to work and lighting your house with candles?" he retorted. "Not to mention a national meltdown?

I'm buying us time, entertaining this shyster while you find Baldr. Unless you can do my part better."

Why did he always have to go there? Since she'd become operations director, he'd been constantly paranoid she would hijack the Glitnir presidency.

"Working on it," she said.

"Progress?"

"Our electrical engineers and physicists think Baldr's deviation took it into a circumpolar orbit. They believe it passed over the North Pole yesterday. But it's just an unconfirmed guess. It could be drifting over Kansas City for all we know."

"Not specific enough, Kate."

"That's all I can say."

"Any update on Malcolm?"

"Good news on that end. This morning your secretary found an email from his daughter. Victoria said she has a source onboard the cruise ship who has verified their location with pretty good accuracy and informed her that Malcolm is on the vessel."

"He's alive?"

"Alive and onboard the *Pearl Enchantress* of Pearl Voyages."

"Where's the ship?"

"A couple hundred miles from Iceland."

"We need him. Have someone ready a jet to Reykjavik. From there we'll go by helicopter."

"Are you sure you wouldn't like me to forward the coordinates to the Pentagon for a naval dispatch?"

"No can do." She sensed the hesitation of a man looking for a justification. "He threatened to blow the ship apart, remember? He may be bluffing, but I sure as hell won't be the one to call him out on it. Just have a plane ready to take us over. And grab me some Cafergot for this migraine."

She left Chatham scratching his head and returned to her office, shutting the blinds as she always did. This time she also locked the door.

She ran a search online and clicked through a website to find the right page and telephone number. She dialed, and as the phone rang, she realized she wasn't sure if she'd have the breath to speak when someone picked up. Few things made her as nervous as this did.

"You've reached the Securities and Exchange Commission, Division of Trading and Markets," a middle-aged woman answered.

Dirgo threw a glance at the blinds even though she'd just closed them. She clicked her pen on her desk several times and began twirling it in her fingers.

"Yes, this is Kathryn Dirgo calling with a special request. I'm hoping you can direct me to the right person. An expert on trading violations."

THIRTY-FOUR

It was five to noon, and Austin hurried down a mobbed street to his rendezvous. He was passing under a medieval pennant when he felt Victoria's phone vibrate at his hip.

"Hey, Itchy," he said, remaining vigilant as he stepped through the crowd.

Austin knew his roommate inside out—every virtue, every defect. He expected cockiness, and he got it.

"Once upon a time, I was recited an ancient, mystical Hardyism," said Ichiro. "That he who explains radio transmission shall feast on rib-eye."

"Sounds vaguely familiar," Austin said, playing along. "Why, do you have something to explain?"

"Perhaps."

"You solved our riddle, huh?"

"Piece of cake."

"That easy?"

"That's what I said."

"Nothing ever gets by that stunning cerebrum of yours."

"I can just taste it melting in my mouth," Ichiro said. "The finest steak dinner I'll ever have."

"And who's going to treat you?"

"You, of course."

"Dream on," Austin said.

Ichiro bristled. "Sounds like this sacred word was delivered by a false prophet."

"Merely an omniscient one, who chooses his words carefully."

"What's that supposed to mean?"

"The rule was, 'He who *first* explains radio transmission shall feast on rib-eye.' You weren't the first."

"But—"

"You may be smart, kiddo, but you'll have to work a little harder to make Mensa. Rachel, on the other hand, is probably preparing for her induction into their hall of fame."

"How did you . . ."

"We spoke this morning," Austin said with deliberate nonchalance.

"But she's a vegetarian."

"Then it's a bust."

"You mean a waste!"

"Thanks for trying," Austin said. "By the way, Rachel says you're cute when you're frustrated."

He ended the call. With two minutes until the clock struck twelve, he now had to pay close attention. He panned the marketplace. In these dense crowds, it would be easy to make a mistake.

Victoria hardly blinked behind her aviators. She wasn't hard to miss, and this time she wanted it that way. As promised, she stood alone and vulnerable at the center of the main square, near a pair of statues. She checked her watch repeatedly. Timing was essential. All she could do was hope the proper parties had received her messages.

The fair buzzed with activity, the streets a conflagration of color. Farmers stacked cages of ducks and pigs and hens, keeping far from the berry stands so as to prevent feathers from drifting near edibles. Plants and flowers dangled from wrought-iron posts and lanterns. Aged by centuries, human visages carved into brick buildings were overlooking candy stalls, meat and cheese stores, butcher shops, fruit vendors, flower booths. She looked from head to head, scanning the crowds for her mark, and paced. Delicate threads wove this tapestry, any one of which could easily break. A feeling of helplessness threatened to overtake her. Somewhere in the crowd, at least three men were watching her, probably more. It made her feel like she was standing naked behind a one-way mirror. She saw no one she recognized, nor was she certain she could expect to.

She had despised the idea of entrusting her life to an enemy, but felt positive there was no other way. It had been difficult casting aside doubts, and now they were starting to creep back in. She began to wonder whether desperation had played any part in shaping their little gambit, and if so, whether she would be the one to pay for their haste. Instinct screamed for her to flee. She stood rooted, reminding herself never to act as flesh-and-blood bait again.

Chambered for a cartridge dating back to 1891, the Dragunov probed for its target. A practiced eye peered through the scope, sweeping through the crowd and centering on the face of a tanned female. There she was, clear as diamond in his tunneled view—an exquisite creature, he thought somewhat ruefully. The rifle's barrel extension rotated about a fixed point on a bipod. Flapping street flags helped Vasya gauge wind speed. It would make little difference at close proximity, yet he erred on the side of caution.

She seemed to be alone as promised, but he guessed her partner was out there. Having seen the emotional havoc he'd wreaked with his bluff, Vasya doubted Austin would leave the young woman unaccompanied again. They were planning something; Austin would be waiting at a calculated distance. At least Vasya hoped so. He had ambitions for two bullets, not one. He adjusted the focus on his telescope to search for her partner.

A skilled marksman, he had long studied techniques to engage moving targets at a distance, accounting for wind, weather conditions, elevation, and for exceptionally long shots, even the Coriolis effect. He used his left hand to support the butt of the rifle, screwing in the suppressor to reduce flash and noise, and assuming his firing position. Years ago, he had kept a mental checklist. Now a veteran's sense guided him, one that supplemented a natural ability to realize first-round hits.

Today he would not be using his backup adjustable iron sights, sliding tangent rear lenses, or quick-detachable optics. They weren't needed for this simple a target. He required no advanced elevation adjustment, no illuminated rangefinder grid, no night-vision reticle or infrared charging screen—only patience and a sunshade. His right hand gripped the small of the stock. Three fingers exerted a slight pull to secure the butt against his shoulder pad, which buffered the effects of breathing and pulse beat. He aligned the rifle with his objective, magnifying the selection eight times. His muscles relaxed. Unnecessary tension could compromise the procedure by generating twitches and tremors.

After scouring the scene for several minutes, he felt confident it was time. Despite her partner's apparent absence, he'd take the shot.

And if the young man was hiding somewhere, perhaps her death would lure him out. He tweaked focus one final time, framing her left temple in the scope's wire crosshairs.

The din of the marketplace was becoming less distinct. The white noise helped Victoria organize the tidal wave of thoughts raging through her mind's darkest tunnels. She had never felt as powerless and exposed as she did in the middle of the square.

She skimmed the rooftops. They sloped steeply, too steeply to allow a decent foothold for climbing. This had factored into their equation. No sniper could have assumed a safe position on the roofs. But in this market square, a sniper needed no roof when there was the bell tower.

Something had to happen, things would soon change, and she could only hope for the right change. With so much beyond her control, any slew of mistakes could dampen her chances of survival. A dozen pieces had to come together for Austin's plan to work.

With a furtive glance toward the belfry, she feared checkmate. There was no black protrusion from the tower's lancet windows, no glint of anything, but that didn't mean he wasn't there; she knew a sniper would rather shoot from the middle of a room than expose his barrel.

It was 12:02 p.m. Her spirits were sinking toward zero.

Does she know I'm here? Vasya wondered as he ogled her.

No. Any rational, self-preserving human would run. But she'd looked right at him.

His index finger clamped over the trigger and began to apply pressure.

A deafening racket shattered his concentration. His muscles tensed, and he let go of the trigger, slapping a hand over his ear as twenty-seven and a half tons of metal began vibrating to the tune of Beethoven's Ninth Symphony. He cursed the bells and checked his watch. It was past noontime.

Grating his teeth, he realized the midday chimes often lasted till quarter past. He would be compelled to take his shot in spite of the disruption. He reassumed position, forcing himself again to relax and take advantage of the precious instants between heartbeats.

———

The bells had bought her a few seconds. Victoria willed her legs to pace faster, imagining her own profile as viewed through a sniper scope.

She strode toward the bronze statues nearby. As they had defended fellow citizens from foes in the fourteenth century, two of Bruges's patriotic heroes, Jan Breydel and Pieter de Coninck, would temporarily protect her. She took refuge behind the pedestal supporting the Belgian nationalists. Then it occurred to her, maybe hiding was a mistake. What if it suggested to Vasya that she knew he was watching? If he suspected he'd been set up, he might bail. She continued to walk, using the pedestal as a shield only seconds at a time, still giving him at least a few opportunities to take the shot.

A hand clasped her waist. Two thumbs reached under her shirt and dug into her skin, one to still her and one, she suspected, to oblige a lustful desire. She tried to wriggle free but conceded when she felt cold metal burrowing into her back. She didn't turn around, nor did she care to.

"Don't squeal." The voice was deeper than a mineshaft. "Start walking."

Vasya looked askance. Who was that trailing behind her? Had the girl told someone else she'd be waiting there?

Through the lens he studied the new man's features. He was facing the other direction, but Vasya could tell he was hirsute and dark-complexioned. He remembered seeing the man before, sitting at another table in the Tavern Brugeoise. A bodyguard. How had Deeb's men learned of Victoria's rendezvous?

There was more to this than he knew, but it didn't matter. He'd kill them both.

He caressed the trigger again.

"Don't move."

It was Deeb.

Vasya felt an uncomfortable prickling on the nape of his neck as his hairs stood on end. Was another coincidence really destined to foil his shot?

"One moment, Farzad," he said, peering through the scope.

A thin veneer of civility dwindling, Deeb's answer was frosty. "I don't think so."

It was then Vasya realized the minister and his three bodyguards each had pistols, and they were all pointed at him. Standing at the outlet by the spiraling staircase, they had blocked his only exit. Their expressions seemed twisted, animalistic. They'd found him alone in the tower, cornered him.

"Put your guns away," Vasya dismissed. "There's no time."

"Four handguns against one unwieldy rifle. You figure the odds."

"Just holster your weapons. Let me take this shot."

"We want the girl alive."

"Why?"

"She knows the password." Vasya's composure flickered as he recognized his folly. He'd been tricked. What could he possibly say to Deeb now? "That means we have no more use for you, Vasya. Hand over the briefcase, and we'll make this painless."

He had no choice but to clutch at straws. He picked up the briefcase from the floor and used it as a shield in front of his chest.

"Don't shoot, or I'll hurl it over the edge," he threatened. "The laptop will shatter. You'll have no chance of claiming Baldr."

"You wouldn't jeopardize that kind of profit."

"I would with my life on the line."

Deeb snickered. "Maybe so. Maybe I shouldn't take my chances."

He fired two shots. Vasya roared in pain and began bleeding from both feet. Blood stained his shoes from the inside and began to pool on the floor. He slouched against the wall and dropped the briefcase.

"Farzad, you idiot! I'm trying to help you! I want you to have the satellite!"

"A moment ago you were ready to break it." Deeb took several steps forward and drove the heel of his boot into Vasya's fresh wounds. The Russian's face contorted. "You traitor."

"What?"

"As soon as I wire the money, you'll disappear and bring Baldr to the Russian Foreign Intelligence Service. I'm aware of your efforts to procure technology for the SVR."

"Farzad, you have it all wrong."

"Does it matter if I do? The laptop is mine now, and I will soon have Baldr's password."

"You don't know what you're talking about."

"I think I do."

"It was the girl, wasn't it? What did she tell you? She's trying to set you up, like she did me."

"If *she* set *you* up," Deeb said acidly, "how is it you were about to blow her brains out?"

"She's playing you," Vasya said.

"I think it's you who's been playing us—including the Viking."

Vasya shook his head, desperate to go on despite the splitting pain. "No, you're wrong . . . you have it all wrong . . ."

"I will be sure to tell him of your deceit."

"You don't understand. You don't know anything about this operation!"

"You're pathetic. The Viking would hunt you down and make you suffer if he learned of your treachery. It would be far worse than my way of dealing with you."

"Farzad, you moron, tell your men to put their weapons down!" Vasya shouted. "I *am* the Viking!"

THIRTY-FIVE

Rove would rather have remained comatose than wake with his hands and feet bound to a chair on the weather deck of the Black Marauders' flagship. Gradually his vision began to clear. A crowd of at least a half dozen soldiers had formed a circle around him. He'd lost his sense of time and bearing. The acute pain in the back of his neck had lessened to a dull throb. He distinguished little and heard nothing beyond the pulsations in his ears.

His head sagged as if someone had stuffed it full of lead. His mouth hung open, dry as a sandpit. Dehydration had begun to crack fissures in his lips. A memory of his previous torture room scorched through his mind. Scouts had captured him, and he'd been carried from the Colombian jungles into an underground cocaine factory. This time, he had no SEAL Team Four to bail him out. He was alone, and apparently he'd taken a few too many steps on enemy turf. He blinked, trying to remember what had happened and what he'd been doing. It was an odd feeling, blinking, like trying to move fingers on a hand without blood circulation. His eyelids responded slowly, out of sync with his mental commands. Through the fog he discerned the shape of a man standing in front of him.

"Hello, Jake," said the man, the blaze of red hair coming into focus. "I was ready to scrap you to the seafloor while you were unconscious. Seeing that you've killed several of my brothers and left me with something to remember you by, I reconsidered."

Ragnar held up his elbow. The discolored, chemical-eaten flesh had grown inflamed. Rove tried to speak, but his tongue stuck to his palette, and he felt too weak to remove it.

Ragnar unfolded a paper and waved it in the air.

"We found this in your pocket," he said. "Good idea, demanding I release passengers on lifeboats. I've never heard of a hostage turning his anonymity against the captors."

"Go on and finish this," Rove said, discovering a shred of utility in his vocal chords.

Ragnar grabbed Rove by a cheek and leaned in close. "I made a promise to you back on the bridge. I intend to keep it."

"Apathy is your best weapon," Rove said. "It's obvious I've affected you. If you intend to slake some kind of thirst for vengeance, do it behind closed doors. Don't let your soldiers see weakness in their leader."

"Since when is the desire for vengeance a sign of weakness?"

"Sometimes it isn't. You're clearly driven to exact revenge on more accounts than my own. I wouldn't blame all the hard feelings, especially after that *Firecat* incident." Ragnar flared up, never averting his gaze. "But for a flesh wound, it makes you look fragile."

"I don't yet know how many of my men you've killed." Ragnar was approaching a slow boil. "But you'll suffer for each of them."

His fist struck Rove's left cheekbone. After a second blow, Rove's nose started to bleed.

"I know what you're feeling," Rove said. "Now that you've started it, you can't go back. You're too ego-involved to finish this quickly. All your men are watching, listening. You can't look weak in front of them. A bullet to the head, a toss overboard . . . This far into the game, those wouldn't do. Why don't you give them fair sport? These men would love to see a knife fight. Unstrap me."

"No one will unbind you from that chair," Ragnar said. "You're not going to stand again."

"Just trying to help you save face. Not that there's much worth saving."

Ragnar smirked, then turned his back on Rove and began climbing back to the *Pearl Enchantress* by rope ladder. He spoke to the Marauders encircling the captive. "Don't hurry. Slow and deliberate. Remember our brothers he murdered. Tomorrow we set sail. The Viking will detonate the explosives, and this man will die knowing he succeeded at nothing to prevent the deaths of three thousand passengers."

THIRTY-SIX

K eep walking. No sudden movements. I'll shoot."
         The dark-skinned man led her to the outskirts of Bruges. Though she had multiple opportunities near policemen, she did nothing to draw attention to herself. She didn't scream, run, or cry for help.

They entered an empty alley, walked to the end, and crossed a bridge. They'd left the main town far behind. At the far side of the bridge a black limousine awaited their arrival. The driver came out and opened the door for them. Before letting her in, the man with the handgun patted her down, his fingers lingering on her waist and legs longer than necessary. She didn't protest. After a thorough search, they climbed into the car.

"Take a walk," she told the driver. "Come back in half an hour."

"No," said Deeb's bodyguard. He seemed confused by her order.

"You have the gun," she reminded him. "What do you care if it makes me more comfortable to be alone with one strange man instead of two?"

He nodded to the driver, still apparently circumspect.

As Victoria stared down the pistol's barrel, she couldn't help but appreciate an irony. She was confined in this stranger's automobile, held at gunpoint—yet thinking, everything's going swimmingly.

D eeb searched the Russian cannily, weighing honesty against treachery. As he studied the Russian's shifting face, his scale tipped toward the latter.

"You, Vasily Kaslov, the Viking?"

"I masterminded the ploy to pit the Americans against their enemies. I stole Baldr from Malcolm Clare and Glitnir Defense. I created the auction. I didn't merely facilitate the bidding war; I devised it, initiated it, carried it through on both ends. From the beginning, it was me."

Deeb looked dubious. "Why should I believe you?"

"You seem to be aware I was a KGB spy. My alias was Christian Lefevre—a Canadian international security consultant who moved to the U.S., where I was hired by Glitnir Defense in 1994. How else do you think I could have commandeered a top-secret satellite from a U.S. defense agency? It was only after years building internal connections that I managed to steal the most formidable piece of weaponry created by the world's leading military technologist."

Not a reason, Deeb observed. "You may well have planned the heist. But your intentions are unclear. When you commandeered the satellite, did you mean to sell it . . . or use it?"

"I no longer work for the Russian government," he said. "I only want to sell it. Why else would I go through the effort of organizing an auction?"

"To take my money and run," Deeb ventured. "Back to Russia, to your little wing in the SVR where I *do* think you're working. To restore Soviet clout with your new nuclear satellite in orbit. And to live off my oil revenues, like a prince."

"All speculation," Vasya said, "and no evidence. Put down your weapons. I'm losing blood."

"Tell me, Vasya. What was to keep you from disappearing after our transaction was over?"

"These accusations are ludicrous. I have no reason to cross you."

"My source has informed otherwise."

"The Clare girl!"

"She has a compelling reason to help me. You kidnapped her father."

Vasya shuddered, still slouched against the stone wall. "She's manipulating you."

"Right now she's sitting in my limousine with a gun to her face."

"Farzad, stop this pointless discourse. Tell your men to put away your guns and help me tend to the wounds you so needlessly inflicted."

Deeb's men held fast, their pistols unwavering. The tolling bells finished their routine and stilled. Deeb had the feeling Vasya was beginning to comprehend the extent of his debacle.

"You dug your own grave."

"How's that?"

"By confirming your Soviet history. No one has a better use for Baldr than yourself."

"Enough with theories. They're useless."

"Perhaps you are the Viking, and perhaps you did procure the satellite. Perhaps your intentions are good, my conjectures are false, and you are a reliable broker after an honest contract. It could be true." Deeb watched the grim understanding in Vasya as it blossomed into panic. Vasya had no appeal. "But like I said, it doesn't matter anymore."

A gunshot resonated through the carillon.

"Let's go," Deeb told his bodyguards. "Take the briefcase. The girl's waiting."

Victoria sat on the limousine's leather seats, her smile of respect concealing disgust for her captor's deficient hygiene, which had become apparent in the confined space. To make matters worse the guard's stare had come to rest on the usual places. Aware that a display of contempt might only feed him, she let him gawp at her form, and after a few minutes she decided a little conversation might help divert his attention.

"Not to sound impatient," she said, going for demure, "but how much longer till your boss arrives?"

The guard said nothing, and instead turned away and looked out the window.

Victoria prodded him.

"I look forward to meeting your boss."

With this she wheedled out a grunt. A little more cajoling, she thought, and she might actually extract real words.

"I'm grateful Mr. Deeb accepted my offer to meet," she said. "Forgive me, but I'm not familiar with your customs. Is there anything I should know before seeing him face-to-face?" If her goal was to elicit a response, she had failed again. The man felt his beard self-consciously, his vacant look mostly unchanged. "You know, it was I who suggested this meeting. You know I'm unarmed and unlikely to run, so you can put your gun away."

"Shut up," he said, revealing a set of golden-brown teeth upon which years of neglect had wreaked decay. "No talking."

Charming. She wondered why she couldn't have taken a seat by the driver.

The guard's phone rang. He took the call and murmured something in Arabic. What little she gleaned of the conversation, judging from the guard's general tenor, pleased her. Then he snapped the phone closed and gaped at her, his expression every bit as lascivious as before. He never lowered his handgun.

"He's coming," the bodyguard said.

THIRTY-SEVEN

Rove had managed to shake his stupor. The spells of vertigo subsided until the dizziness became indistinguishable from the ship's rocking. Feet scuffled on deck. Six Marauders in two lines moved in and flanked him, closing their formation around his chair like pincers.

"I'm flattered," Rove said, recharging. "Six armed men against one bound to a chair? Ragnar must have me pegged as a real troublemaker."

"You got the announcement like everyone else," one of the hijackers said. "The Viking said all agitators will be shot."

"Doesn't look like that's on your agenda."

"Not our immediate one. You heard Captain Stahl. He said, *slow and deliberate.*" His next words came off like an ostentatious display of rank. "My name is Gunnar Brun. I'm one of the five captains. My ship is the *Baduhenna.*"

Rove recognized the flat mouth, the blue eyes cut by a swath of aggression. He sensed a sadistic streak so warped it probably made his fellow outlaws uneasy. Certainly they feared him, but did they respect this man? If not, maybe Rove could reduce him in their view.

"Nice to finally know your name, Gunnar. Tell me, if you're not going to shoot me right off the bat, can I have another one of those delicious canapés?"

Using the back of his wrist, Brun cuffed Rove over the head, then adjusted the diamond ring on his finger.

"I must not have tipped you," Rove said. "How was it, posing as a waiter till the big boys arrived?"

Brun cracked a gummy smile and continued to play with the ring. "There was no dearth of good food."

"If you'd like my advice, you could work on your tableside manner. People don't like to be snarled at."

Brun was leering, as if he'd realized it would take more than a few punches to break this prisoner. It seemed to excite him. "You've been a prisoner before."

"How did you know?"

"Most would have soiled themselves by now."

"You've hardly touched me."

"But you know what's coming. To some, the agony is the anticipation." Brun struck him in the jaw. Rove had prepared for the blow by seating his tongue away from his teeth to prevent more bleeding. "You've got a tattoo, like we do. Who drew this pretty little bird?"

He ran a finger over the smiling toucan on Rove's deltoid.

"The last man to torture me. So I'd have a pet in hell."

Brun laughed. "Looks like good company."

"I should warn you, the artist didn't fare well."

"Judging from the burn scars on your chest and legs, neither did you."

"I'm still here, and frankly, getting bored."

"Let me entertain you then."

"Thanks, but I prefer the shipboard talent."

"Ever played a drinking game, Jake?"

"It's been a while."

"The more you play, the more you tend to break the rules. The more you break the rules, the more you drink. The more you drink, the harder it gets to obey the rules." He removed the ring from his hand and flipped it across the backs of his fingers as an experienced gambler would manipulate a poker chip. "This game works a similar way. I place the ring into a hand. After a flourish and possible sleight, I ask you where it is. If you're correct, we play again. If not, each of us bashes your skull. The ring becomes harder to follow. Understand?"

"Doesn't sound too hard."

Brun went on. "Prestidigitation has become a recent hobby of mine." He pinched the ring with the fingers of his right hand, then dropped the glittering piece into a palm as his left hand swept sideways. He closed both fists and held them out before Rove. "So . . . which?"

"Left," Rove said.

Brun unfolded his fingers one by one to reveal the diamond. "Good, Jake."

Rove paid little attention to what Brun was saying. He was straining his wrists behind his back, fingering the knots that bound him to learn how they were tied. Given hours of time, focus, and isolation, he knew he could escape, but at the moment he had none of these. He figured it was only a matter of minutes before they fully laid into him. What was more, they had him surrounded and could foil any attempt to break loose. And even if he did free his hands, he'd still have to work on his ankles.

"Try again?"

"I don't have much choice."

Rove watched as Brun repeated the motion, beginning by pinching the ring between three fingers. His left hand brushed through the open space of his palm and enveloped the ring. There was a flash of light that disappeared as Brun's left fingers clamped down. He exaggerated the motions, selling the performance.

"Did you catch it?" he asked.

"Left hand again."

With a sharp intake of breath, Brun tilted his head to the side. "Are you sure?"

"Yes."

Brun's fingers formed a cup, and he revealed the diamond. "You're either very quick or very lucky. Should I make this more difficult? Watch closely."

He prepared the third swoop, positioning the ring as before and drawing his left hand closer. Rove stared through the spaces between the fingers of Brun's right hand and observed as he dropped the ring into his palm before the left hand could grasp it. The five digits closed around air and continued sweeping forward, mimicking a transfer. But gaps between those fleshy fingers had provided three windows, three thin slivers of backlight. It was enough for a glimpse behind the stage that was Brun's right hand, and Rove felt certain he'd penetrated the ruse.

The fists closed tightly. Rove stared at one of them with confidence.

"Right hand."

Engrossed by his own theatrics, Brun extended his little finger and worked his way to the thumb of his right hand. He blew a puff of air and flaunted an open, empty palm.

"No bluff," he said.

Brun made a curt gesture to his men, whose patience had worn thin. They swarmed over Rove, leaving no appendage untouched. He felt something in his nose snap. An elbow bore into his temple, and another wallop drove his chin halfway to his neck. His ears rang like sirens, and the skin around his eye sockets began to swell, pinching off the upper and lower bounds of his vision.

"That's enough," Brun said. "His turn."

The men backed away.

Brun unscrewed a flask of brandy and took a swig. "Now you see how the game works."

Rove hocked up blood and spittle, his attention returning to the work of his own hands. He'd managed to relax a snug knot by a few cinches. Maybe it would be easier to break loose than he'd first guessed. If he could free a little more slack, he figured he could liberate one arm. The rope was coarse and chafed against his skin. Its clutch was still too tight on his wrist bone, but only by hairs.

He knew he had to seize every opportunity and slacken his bindings while the effort would go unnoticed. That meant waiting for the next beating before attempting to wriggle free. He tried to provoke them.

"Your men slap like schoolgirls in a catfight," Rove said.

Brun looked dimly amused. "Again, then?"

He placed the ring in his right hand, over a crease. The padding at the base of his thumb pressed the ring into his palm while muscle tension held it in place. For three seconds, nothing happened. Then with a shimmer and an imperceptible twitch of his thumb's flexor, the ring leapt as if animate, shooting skyward. It didn't merely levitate in idle suspension, but rather appeared to fall upward as if on strike against a fundamental rule of physics. Rove had the impression the ring would have continued indefinitely had Brun's other hand not caught it midflight.

His fingers twirled the ring and tossed it in the air. Rove watched the diamond come to a full stop about a yard over his own head. It descended, and when the ring reached eye level, the hands sped inward to clasp it. The steal happened in a blur, and at this point Rove had no idea which hand had snatched the ring. He eyed them both, looking for any sign of a bulge or space between fingers. It was all for naught anyway. Even if he chose correctly, the game would continue till he could no longer utter a selection.

"Left hand," he guessed.

Brun revealed the jewelry piece in his right. He shook his head. "My friend."

Rove felt like a statue at the mercy of an overzealous sculptor, one who had opted to use a sledgehammer instead of a chisel. He'd kept relatively dry through the first battering. Now it was as if they'd dug into a well. Blood spattered his cheeks and neck. His head felt like a blend of paste and pulp. The smiling toucan began to burn his shoulder as memories of his last tormentor were called from suppression. He was seeing those dark chambers again, where his legs had been fractured and his flesh melted with a blowtorch. His lips ballooned and broke in places where teeth carved painful trenches. He couldn't guess how many more poundings he could take. A voice screamed inside him, telling him these attackers were the ones who'd turned on the blender, and he'd be damned if he didn't find a way to throw a rock in it and rough up the blades.

He could hardly breathe under the onslaught of six men. He wobbled the chair, throwing his weight to knock it over and all the while loosening his bindings. The chair teetered, but the men caught him before he fell over. He used the ploy to buy a few extra seconds and begin working on the binds of his left wrist. As for his right, he'd wriggled it free.

THIRTY-EIGHT

The spiraling stairway of the Bruges bell tower favored the agile-footed and punished the clumsy. The cavity's narrow walls had little tolerance for a man of Deeb's girth. Even less forgiving was the low ceiling, which forced them all to stoop. A rope wrapping around the central stone shaft served as a handhold as they descended the 366 stairs. The twisting chamber fed into a courtyard. Deeb and his men exited under an archway and lengthened their strides as they crossed the civic center and entered a crowded vein. The minister tossed a glance at the tower, seeing in the looming belfry a monument to his latest kill.

He was holding the briefcase and enjoying the solid weight of it, his contentment bringing him to a meditative state. Deeb had always believed the ability to introspect, to look inside one's own mind and identify the roots of the emotions at play, was a mark of intelligence. Today he'd discovered a new possibility: regret without remorse. For killing Vasya, he felt no remorse, but a tinge of regret. Pulling the trigger had been an act of impulsive trust in the girl. Victoria had assured him she knew the code. If she had been lying, he had murdered his only source of the truth, and his only link to the password.

The sound of hooves plodding on cobblestone gave him pause. A horse-drawn carriage approached. He moved to the side of the street. He and his men were supposed to turn into an alley beyond the carriage, an alley that would lead to the limousine. A policeman stood outside a nearby coffee shop. The sight of the uniform struck fear into Deeb, a feeling that burgeoned when the officer looked directly at him. Or had he? Deeb clutched his firearm and made sure it was hidden from view under his coat. He'd just committed murder. He felt confident no authorities had yet discovered Vasya's body in the tower, but close as he was to leaving the city with what he'd come for, even mild threats were unsettling.

He noticed a congregation of officers ahead and wondered whether it was unusual for them to gather in one spot; had someone reported discovering the corpse? He assured himself this was paranoia, as hardly fifteen minutes had passed since he'd pulled the trigger. He relaxed when the lone policeman's gaze came to rest elsewhere, and he heard guffaws from the others in uniform.

"Ouch!" Deeb exclaimed.

The carriage driver spouted apologies to the people in his charge. The horse had accelerated from a leisurely trot to a brisk canter. Without warning the animal plowed head-on into Deeb, who jumped aside to avoid getting trampled. To spare his toes from the weight of the wheels, he shifted his balance and lost his foothold, twisting an ankle. He fell backward and nearly toppled a vendor's fruit stand.

"Watch where you're going!" he hollered, frightened momentarily as he realized the leather carrier had vanished from sight. Had the horse crushed it? Ignoring the pain, he scrambled to his feet. His bodyguards formed a triangle around him. "Out of the way!" he said, elbowing them. "Find the—" He let out a sharp wisp of air. "Never mind," he then said quietly. "It's here."

The briefcase was standing upright on the ground beside him, its leather having acquired a few scuffs, but nothing to suggest the contents were anything but safe.

The driver had returned. Victoria muttered relief when the limousine door opened and let in a refreshing cross-breeze. Deeb and his three guards arrived and slid into the car. He took a seat beside Victoria and instructed the driver, "Take us to Brussels Airport." He then looked at the man who'd been guarding Victoria. "Put the gun away, Jasim. She's with us now." The driver fired the ignition, and the limo pulled away from the curb.

Tempering her revulsion, she regarded Deeb with apparent disinterest. She concentrated on the hook of his nose, then moved to a blemish or scar—she wasn't sure which—on his cheekbone. He wore the look of a shrewd negotiator. She hadn't studied him in such proximity before.

"Thank you for seeing me, Mr. Deeb," she said.

He didn't answer for a full minute. He faced the windshield and watched the movement of the road. When his mouth did open, the iciness he projected began to thaw—or at least she perceived a change, detecting in his inflection a hint of genuine esteem for her. So he had a mercurial nature, she thought, and wondered how long he would remain cordial.

"I am honored," he said. "You are the daughter of a genius."

She, too, waited before responding, letting linger an interlude of silence. It wasn't until a few seconds' reflection that she heard the edge of hostility in his words. He had spoken bluntly, though it wasn't his candor she questioned; she was searching for the source of something else in his tone. There was an enmity, and a trace of apprehension, behind the flattery.

"I hope for your sake you haven't acted rashly," he added.

She attempted to ease his misgivings with a dispassionate smile. "I understand your reservations and would be equally skeptical in your position. Just know that I'm doing this for my dad. With his life on the line, I wouldn't do anything remotely stupid. Obviously he wouldn't approve of your owning Baldr, but sometimes a daughter's love calls for an overriding decision. I intend to keep my promise, if you keep yours."

They merged onto the A10 en route to Brussels. Deeb didn't bother to look at her. He was admiring the countryside. "For your sake, I hope what you say is true."

She wanted to add, *and for yours*. She bit her tongue, then said, "Don't mean to sound rude, but I am, after all, a passenger in this vehicle. Would you mind explaining why you're taking us to the airport?"

"I'm done here," he said with a baleful look. "My 'business partner' is dead."

She put on a mask of disbelief. Pitting Deeb against Vasya had worked, and her horse had come in first. "But why are you taking me with you?"

"To ensure you keep your promise."

"What about your end of the deal? How can I be assured of my dad's safety?"

"That's not within my power."

She had known this from the get-go, but couldn't let on. She jerked to the side, responding as she would to a dose of hornet venom.

"You lied to me!"

"There were no lies. You proposed a deal. I seized the opportunity."

"But my daddy . . ." She began to choke.

"He's already dead."

"Murderer!"

"I had nothing to do with it."

"But I thought—"

"Sit back and shut up."

Her tears streamed, though she was careful not to oversell the grief. She buried her nose in cupped hands and whimpered.

"Can . . . can you at least tell me where we're going?" she asked.

"To my mansion."

"Where?"

"The outskirts of Tripoli."

An hour passed, and she buffered her bouts of weeping with periods of silent consternation. She'd gag and stifle sobs every now and then, playing between intensities on the sentimental spectrum. By the time they reached the airport, she had dropped the act altogether, substituting a cold simmering for her misery. She dabbed her smudged mascara now and then, eyes tearless but still glassy and bloodshot.

The limousine bypassed the main terminal access. They swerved onto a narrow lane that wound its way around the back of the airport, then turned onto a gravelly road leading to an enclosure behind a chain-link fence topped with barbed wire. Police guarded the entrance with canines. The limo slowed to a halt. Deeb passed a card to the driver, who rolled down his window and handed it to the officer at the inspection booth.

The policeman barely glimpsed the card before handing it back. "Your plane is here," he said.

The security gate opened, and the limo rolled through, driving out onto the tarmac. The driver helped unload baggage onto the plane while Deeb dragged Victoria by the collar.

"Board the plane," he said.

She stopped at the foot of the stairs and turned back as if to run, but the Arab held her firmly.

"I can't!" she whispered, pleading. "I only said I'd do it for my father's safety!"

"Too late for that. Start climbing."

"You've—you've taken advantage of me."

"Move."

She started bawling again as she entered the jet's main cabin. Deeb's pilots filed into the cockpit and donned the headgear linking them with air traffic control. One of the other bodyguards shut the hatch and signaled to the pilot they were ready for taxi. Deeb thrust Victoria into a seat and instructed her to fasten her belt. She cinched it tight with little fuss.

The Gulfstream entered a lineup on the taxiway. After idling for fifteen minutes, the aircraft began to move, veering in a broad arc, and aligned itself with the runway. A brief interval of silence ensued before takeoff, and then the gas turbine engines started to roar as the pilots finished running through their checklists. The noise escalated, and the seats started to vibrate.

I'm being kidnapped, Victoria told herself—play the victim. Live the role.

Jet fluids discharged, and the cabin filled with sounds of internal combustion as the pilots powered thrust. A creep turned to a crawl until finally the Gulfstream was hurtling down the runway. The front wheels lost contact with concrete. The back wheels followed, and the aircraft nosed into the air.

*   *   *

Congratulations, Chatham. You win the auction."

Chatham wavered in a moment of reprieve. "It's over?"

"I can no longer reach your main competitor. He's dropped out of contact."

"And the other players?"

"They have conceded. As promised, I've run a fair auction."

Chatham held the phone on speaker up to everyone in the office. "Baldr's back!" he exclaimed. "Did you all hear that?"

The others didn't appear to share his jubilation, particularly Dirgo, who looked capable of strangling a gorilla as she leaned against the wall, her arms crossed.

"Not quite," said the Viking.

"What do you mean? We gave the highest bid. You just said that."

"Change of rules."

Chatham stood in disbelief, a thumb jutting awkwardly from a belt loop under his barrel chest. "What kind of change?"

"Since I've lost communication with my overseas negotiator, I must take extra precautions to enforce agreements."

"What do you mean?"

"It is only prudent to make sure no party deviates from plan."

"What rule are you changing?"

"The payment timeline. You need to pay *now*."

"That wasn't. . . . How can I be assured you'll deliver Baldr?"

"I haven't crossed you, nor do I plan to. You have twenty-four hours to wire the money to my account. If at this same hour tomorrow you've failed to do so, you will have ensured that the passengers aboard the *Pearl Enchantress* never see shore."

The line went dead.

Dirgo watched from the sidelines as Chatham flung the phone against the wall, his sanity braced by a fragile scaffold.

"There's nothing we can do about the ship," she said. "We've got to speak to Malcolm and recover Baldr."

"Once we've wired the Viking's money, he'll have no reason to squander the lives of those passengers. We'll call for a naval response, which should provoke little conflict since the ship's technically adrift in international waters. A rescue operation will be in order. None of this happens until we've consulted Malcolm. Is the plane ready?"

"Ready and waiting."

"Get your stuff together. No more time wasted. Let's head to the airport." He clapped his hands together. "Everyone get that? If you haven't heard from us in twenty-three hours and fifty-five minutes, transfer the money. Then send the cruise ship's coordinates to the Pentagon. If he calls beforehand, pass along my cell number. *Don't* disclose my location. We're headed to Reykjavik. From there we're taking a chopper to the vessel. If anyone can save the company, it's Malcolm Clare."

THIRTY-NINE

C hin up. Game's not over."

Brun's men appeared disconnected from the situation as he toyed with the ring. He placed the diamond in his left palm and closed his fingers around it, then showed his right hand empty and copied the same motion.

"You look tired, Jake," Brun said. "We'll make this one easy. Where's the ring?"

Rove batted a sluggish black eye. "Left hand."

"Still some wits about you, then. Now, eyes peeled . . ."

Fists still clenched, Brun gesticulated like a performer on stage, waving his arms. They came to rest before his spectator.

"Same hand," Rove said.

Brun shrugged. He threw open his hands. Rove waited expectantly to hear the ring clank on wood. No sound came.

"No more ring," Brun said with a cavalier shrug. "Where did it go?" Rove dropped his head, preparing for the worst. "I don't think you'll be making any more correct guesses. Boys, have at him."

Before they could move in, Brun's look of conceit melted. He sprang for shelter behind the ship's helm as the timber portals to the below-deck quarters burst open and disintegrated, raining fragments. Framed in the doorway was Malcolm Clare, who stood bracing an assault rifle against his shoulder, heralding the inevitability of gunfire.

"Better have a look at your brig locks, gentlemen." He held the rifle steady. "They've weakened with age."

"How did you break them?" Brun fumed.

"I'm afraid your old tumblers had corroded. A simple butter knife did the trick."

"Where did you find . . ."

Clare asked on a different subject, "Which one of you just tossed me a diamond ring? I'd like to deliver proper thanks."

The underlings turned to Brun, who crouched somewhere at the ship's bow. "Put the weapon down, old man," he said. "Someone might get killed."

"Someone was already getting killed before I arrived."

"Don't play with things you don't know how to use."

"If you doubt my skill with the rifle, then come out from hiding. I'm no threat to you."

Brun gave no ground.

"Listen closely, everyone," Clare continued, sounding like a lawman. "You all have ten seconds to jump overboard before I open fire. That means every one of your men. Ten . . . nine . . ."

He'd hardly pronounced "eight" by the time Brun and the other six had abandoned ship. They splashed into the water and swam. Clare began untying the ropes to finish the job Rove had begun.

"Thanks," Rove said.

"Good thing you remembered the butter knife."

"Didn't occur to me when I brought you the food that I'd also given you a decent lock pick."

"You don't miss a detail."

"Apparently not. I'm wondering, though, why didn't you just fire at them?"

"You don't know?" The professor started to laugh. "The magazine was empty," he said, stretching his smile.

Rove had a look of retroactive terror. "You're not serious."

"Apparently, it was the same AK-47 you'd already used. I fired the last of the bullets when blazing through the doors."

Rove eased up and joined him in his laughter. "Didn't realize I'd practically emptied it."

"No matter. It worked." Clare dropped the weapon onto the floor and brushed a hand through his white hair. "Serves him right for acting like some sort of Houdini. I, on the other hand, happen to be a real magician, and master of escape." He rolled up his sleeves.

"You saved my six. I wouldn't have lasted much longer."

"Glad it didn't backfire and get us both killed. Anyway, on to more important matters. We've a ship to save, and you're in awful shape."

"I'll live."

"You could use a few icepacks, to start."

"I doubt that'll happen."

"At least let me bandage you."

"There isn't time."

"They just beat the living daylights out of you."

"I may not look my prettiest, but we need to transport passengers onto lifeboats. They've run out of food and water. Soon people will have no choice but to leave their cabins. When they do, the hijackers will shoot them unless we bring them to safety. Which gives us reason to bring down as many Marauders as we can. Time to raise hell for Ragnar. Distract him. Take his mind off things. With me?"

"You're preaching to the choir," Clare said. "We magicians practice a fundamental called misdirection."

PART V

SABOTEUR

At ten thousand feet and climbing, the southbound Gulfstream V entered a dense, gray mantle, one that had looked like a pearly white pinnacle from afar. The cold cabin fell dark, soaring over lands that soon would feel the lash of rain and the pound of ice pellets. Isolated with unwelcoming company, Victoria stayed in her seat with the safety belt fastened, a kernel of uneasiness mushrooming within her as they breached the cumulus cloud. To the best of her knowledge, everything had worked without a hitch. But if that were the case, why were they still flying toward Libya at near sonic speeds?

Deeb unbuckled himself and moved to sit beside her.

"Hungry?" he asked.

He gave her a famished look, eating, drinking, and devouring her with his eyes as they roved from her pinched knees to the wealth of dark hair spilling onto her breasts.

"No."

She regarded him as she would a rabid dog, wondering how long her feminine authority would act as his muzzle.

"You haven't had dinner."

"I'm not hungry."

Deeb snapped his fingers at his bodyguards, now his flight attendants. "Prepare some soup," he said. "She'll come around." He set the leather briefcase on his lap and rubbed his hands over the surface to wipe away the dust. He ran a finger over the latch but didn't open it. "You know what's in here, don't you?"

Victoria remained snow cold. "It belongs to my father."

"Belonged. I'm sure you're aware it has exchanged hands multiple times."

"It won't be yours for long. Two people will come after you—my father, and the Viking."

"Both dead," Deeb said, noting an incongruity. She had reacted tearfully when he'd informed her of her father's demise. Was she not willing to accept his death?

Victoria shook her head. "Wrong on both accounts."

"Your father died in a plane crash in the North Atlantic. The Viking perished atop the Bruges bell tower by my own pistol."

"Vasya Kaslov wasn't the Viking. Either that, or you believe in flying carpets."

"He admitted his alias before I shot him. It wasn't until you tipped me off that I realized his intentions."

"Which were?"

"Restore Soviet power. Incite a new arms race. Steal Baldr and use nuclear EMP satellite technology against its creator."

"You make a great conspiracy theorist. Maybe so, but he wasn't the Viking."

"How do you know?"

"Think you might tell a lie at gunpoint? Unfortunately for him, it didn't deter you." She sighed. "I know he's not the Viking because I hacked Vasya's email account and saw messages between him and the mystery man. They were communicating. Unless he's an odd case of Jekyll and Hyde, Kaslov was not what he claimed to be in the tower."

"You could be lying."

"Sure. But I also read some meaty exchanges between you and Vasya. Arrival times, travel plans, meeting places, transportation logistics, rides, even confirmations of your bidding history. Slogged through it all." Comprehension began to strain his face. "And if I could hack the account of an ex-KGB agent, you can bet the daughter of Baldr's inventor knows its password."

Deeb flushed, his hands becoming talons. He lunged for her neck. "Tell me the password now, or—"

"Hands off."

The voice belonged to a still, slender silhouette—one that seconds before had unfurled from the coat closet near the cockpit. Austin Hardy stretched his muscles after leaving the cramped space, though his firearm didn't once peel from its target. He took several steps forward and stood still and serene as a Grecian statue over the minister, who stared down the tunnel of a silenced Mak.

The bodyguards reached for their pistols. Austin held up a warning hand.

"I'd rather not play quick-draw at these altitudes," he said. "Haven't you seen *Goldfinger*?" Withering, Deeb fluttered his eyelids. "Tell your men to toss their guns on the floor with the magazines removed."

"Do as he says," Deeb instructed. They obeyed.

"Now, raise your arms and rest your hands behind your head. Allow Victoria to take your pistol."

She unbuckled herself and confiscated Deeb's gun. Assuming a new position beside Austin, she disengaged the safety.

"Strap in tight," he said. "Or do you require a seatbelt extension?"

Deeb's fists trembled. "Has either of you ever fired a gun before?"

"We're dying to try," Victoria said. "Tell your men to sit down and buckle their seatbelts like you."

"What do you hope to accomplish by this?"

"A change of course."

Deeb's open mouth suggested he was still doubting the reality of this mess. Nonetheless he waved to his men, and they fastened their belts.

"How did this man get here?" he shouted at them.

"I've been your shadow since you left the bell tower in Bruges," Austin said. "Hid in the treasury rafters while you and Vasya stood off. When you walked down the stairs, I went up to find Vasya. Took his pistol. Let's see how well it works."

While Victoria kept her aim pinned on the minister, Austin lowered his gun and fired a shot. The bullet pierced straight through the briefcase, discharging from the Mak with a muffled noise. The round tore a clean hole in the leather.

"Idiot!" Deeb exclaimed. Austin showed no concern. "You just destroyed a tool worth hundreds of millions!"

"Open the briefcase."

Deeb flickered in shock when he opened the lid. The case was empty but for three paperweights taped to the sides.

"Where . . . ."

"Right here," Austin said, reaching back into the coat closet and pulling out an identical case. "Custom-dyed Moroccan leather. Yours is a replica. This briefcase belongs to Dr. Clare. I caught up with you in the marketplace and paid a carriage driver handsomely for a little diversion. The stallion nearly trampling you was no accident."

The realization visibly struck him, his resentment curdling as he searched for a buried bluff. He found nothing but sincerity.

"That's when you made the switch. When I stumbled."

"Naturally I had to swap the cases early. Couldn't risk letting you get ahead of yourself with Baldr. Who knew when you'd start grilling

Victoria for the password? What if I lost track of you in the crowds, and you ran off with the real thing? If anyone's to blame for not catching on, it's you. You'd have noticed sooner if you paid more attention to the people working in your circle. If only you'd tipped the limo driver."

Deeb stammered bewilderment.

"That was *you?*"

"All the way from Bruges to Brussels, through the private gate, and onto the tarmac."

"Another switch?"

"I admit I had to pity the real chauffeur. Holding an innocent hire at gunpoint was no fun for me. Poor soul was terrified. But he handed over the keys. Bet you'd have never guessed you were riding a stolen vehicle that whole time. From the tarmac I started loading your baggage onto the plane. Found my hiding spot in the coat closet, and voilà. Here I am. Amazing how easily some people forget the people who do these nice little things for them."

Deeb turned to Victoria. "You said you pried into Vasya's email account. And it was you who told me to meet in the bell tower. The whole thing was a setup!"

"Don't feel too bad," Austin said. "The same trick worked on Mr. Secret Police."

"That's why Vasya was poised with the sniper rifle. You tried to lure him to the same place. The only viable vantage point for a shot . . . was in the bell tower."

"Now you have it."

Deeb stuck his finger through the bullet hole in the empty briefcase and began fidgeting. It was a nervous gesture, reminding Victoria of a cornered animal. She kept alert while Austin continued.

"Even if I had shot the real laptop," he said, "no damage would have been done. After the switch, I opened the Baldr program, entered the password, and cancelled the override. Glitnir Defense has regained control of the satellite. There's nothing you can do about it."

"What was the password anyway?" Victoria asked.

"You mean you didn't actually know?" Deeb said.

Austin thought for a moment. "I hadn't told her yet, and I suppose there's no harm in sharing now. The night Baldr was stolen, I was there in Dr. Clare's office. Inside one of his cabinets was the transcript of a strange distress call sent by radio from an unknown ship. The distress call was never sent; the mysterious vessel never existed. The transmission was a simple code Professor Clare would use to jog his memory should he forget Baldr's key."

"Ichiro figured it out?" Victoria said.

"Actually, my friend Rachel solved it. But to give due credit, she said Ichiro offered exceptional moral support."

"How did the code work?"

"Ever heard of INTERCO?"

"My dad's mentioned it. International Code of Signals?"

"That's right. Merchant and naval vessels need a way to communicate with each other despite language barriers. Blinker lights, Morse code, semaphore, and radio calls all fall under INTERCO. Sir Home Riggs Popham, a British admiral during the French Revolution and Napoleonic Wars, developed a signaling flag system to encode numeric messages for the Royal Navy, which famously used his cipher during the Battle of Trafalgar. After generations of use, the code has undergone extensive modification. Presently the International Maritime Organization, manager of INTERCO, admits a single set of universal flags and ascribes to each a special meaning. Each of the phrases in the radio transmission corresponds to a specific, internationally recognized maritime pennant."

"So the distress call references nautical flags," Victoria said. "What do they mean?"

"Each flag conveys not only a message, but a letter. The phrase 'the way is off my ship' corresponds to a flag depicting a red square with a yellow cross—and also the letter *R*. A yellow flag with a black dot in the center means, 'I am altering my course to port,' while also indicating the letter *I*. Strung together, the flags in your dad's radio transmission spell the password: *Rio de Janeiro.*"

"The place he met my mother," Victoria said.

Austin focused his attention on the minister, who had taken on a jaundiced hue. "As for you, Mr. Deeb, it's time for you to inform your pilots of a change in flight plan. You won't be seeing your al-Nar buddies for a while."

"I am not al-Nar."

"But you're a benefactor, and that puts you under the 'terrorist' category in my book. Funny, you don't seem to like having your own plane hijacked."

"It's going to be a long ride home for you, Mr. Deeb," Victoria said.

"I'd prepare your statements. Defense authorities will have plenty of questions to ask you about your murderous associates."

"They won't hear anything from me."

"You must have a penchant for prison food."

Deeb grimaced. "Your father mated a pit viper," he blurted. "A camel spider."

"Tell your pilots to bear northwest toward Iceland," she said dismissively, "our layover destination before returning to the States." She called up a text message on her phone. "My dad is alive and well, and onboard the *Pearl Enchantress,* along with thousands of other passengers who've been sitting ducks for days. The coordinates are 37°25'40.48" North, 122°10'11.66" West."

"We'll find a seaplane in Keflavik," Austin said.

Begrudgingly Deeb walked to the cockpit and spoke with his pilots. The wings began to slope, and before leveling, the Gulfstream banked into a turnabout.

FORTY-ONE

Without the drawl of working turbines, the engine room was eerily lifeless. Clare struck a match from a packet he'd found in Ragnar's desk. A glow illuminated his path inside and revealed a plaque on the wall that read, *Safety First.*

A network of interweaving ducts and conduits reminded him of his old desktop screensaver, in which multicolored pipelines zoomed across the screen in three dimensions. Whereas the diameter of the screensaver's pipes remained fairly uniform, these in the engine room varied in size. Some were large enough for him to swim through. Others could hardly accommodate a tennis ball. Pressure gauges and round handles, some requiring multiple sturdy arms to rotate, surrounded shoulder-height vats and yellow cylinders cased in steel. A white metal staircase reached to the bottom floor of the two-story room.

"Safety first," he muttered to himself, clutching a new Uzi he'd claimed from a cargo box aboard the corsair. He'd made sure this one had ammo. Rove had covered him as they'd boarded the *Pearl Enchantress* and descended to the lower decks. They'd parted ways on deck four and agreed to reconvene. Clare relished the feeling of walking on two legs again. Amid outliving his own airplane, drifting in a raft for days, and sitting in a cramped cell with scant space for four limbs, he'd nearly forgotten what it was like to tread on firm ground.

After exploring the upper perimeter of the engine room, he descended the staircase to the first level, where he found several generators. Where the devil did they keep their oil? He doubted he'd find stray barrels here.

The match flame reached his finger and nicked him. Startled, he dropped the match, leaving himself in darkness. He stepped backward and caught his heel on a protruding bolt, losing his footing and falling on his rear. He bounced down a few steps, causing a clatter. When he reached the bottom, he stood upright and brushed himself off, too distracted to hear the foreign footsteps.

The bottom level was no less sterile than the top. It reminded him of the underground in the sci-fi classic *Metropolis,* the chamber stripped of luxury, packed full of machines sustaining the privileged elite above. There were no plush carpets in the engine room, only hard floors. There were no chandeliers, only utility lights. No wall sconces, only boiler temperature dials. The lower decks of the ship were a different realm, a realm few passengers would ever see or comprehend—a realm Clare found much more fascinating than the lavish upper decks. Though austere, this was the engineers' world. It provided function, and therefore it was a modern Cave of Wonders.

He lit another match.

Sparks showered over him, accompanied by the rattling of an automatic weapon. Clare dove for cover. The match continued to burn on the floor.

The rifle fired through a thirty-round banana clip. Metal clanked on metal when the clip dropped. Clare heard the solid click of a reload.

He clung spread-eagle to the side of a cylindrical piece of machinery, finding it impossible to see the intruder or distinguish human movement from flickering shadow. He heard the footsteps now and tried to pinpoint the source. They were slow and purposeful, probably a patrolman's. The intruder's boots landed on a thin, steel grate. He wondered if he could shoot up through the grate. If he were going to take a chance, now wasn't the time. He'd have to wait until the footsteps came closer.

The flame died. He could smell the smoke. He dared not light another.

The intruder expended another third of his clip. The barrage had no particular direction, but in an environment like this one, with plenty of metallic surfaces for ricochet, aim didn't matter much. Fired in volleys, the rounds had a good chance of striking a target.

He'd missed the professor, but the intruder seemed unfazed and continued his walkabout at a leisurely pace, scouring the perimeter of level two in pitch black.

"Hello, Dr. Clare," said the intruder. "Recognize my voice?"

Rove's torturer, Clare realized.

The footsteps were almost directly above him. Clare didn't make a sound. The other man's unhurried strides suggested that he enjoyed a little sport.

"It's me, Gunnar Brun," the man continued. "After jumping ship, I swam to another corsair and boarded the *Pearl Enchantress.* When you and Jake came aboard, I followed you here. This time, I brought a weapon."

He punctuated his last sentence with two quick shots into the black void that was the engine room. The rounds clinked onto the floor. A pipeline broke. From the fissure trickled a small course of water. A few wisps of hot steam escaped, built up over days of unreleased pressure.

"You know what I like about you, Dr. Clare? You're crafty. Foxes make for interesting hunts."

Clare paid no attention to the words themselves—only to where they were coming from. In pin-drop silence he crawled to the wall on his hands and knees. He found an open utility closet, reached inside, and felt a small paint can, which he lobbed to the other side of the room. It clanged against a boiler. Brun zeroed in on the noise and fired another burst. He'd emptied two clips now. How many magazines did the man carry? Clare tossed a few more objects across the room: a spray-paint lid, a mallet, a duster. His hand reached into the darkness and clasped something new, a heavier can. While Brun fired, he unscrewed the lid and whiffed the contents. He recognized the smell of paint thinner.

He tiptoed to the foot of the metal stairs and spilled most of the liquid. The remainder he poured in a thin trail leading back to his hiding spot. All he needed was bait. He took aim with his own Uzi and blazed the steel grate above him. When he stopped, Brun spoke.

"And here I thought you were skulking around the north end of the room."

Clare fired a few more rounds, each one a grasp at faith, as he truly had no idea what he was shooting at.

"Are you going to keep taking cheap shots from up there?" Clare said. "Or are you going to come down to my level and end this the right way?"

He played a dangerous game with his next move, unleashing a hailstorm of submachine-gun fire, bullets pinging off the steel-encased machinery until no ammunition remained. The notorious click at the end of his salvo rang out. He had no spare clips. More than anything, he wanted Brun to hear the sound of his empty chamber.

It worked. Brun quickened his step and began descending the staircase.

"Okay, Professor. I'll play."

Clare waited. He'd have to time this well. The treads came closer. Brun had nearly reached the bottom. This man had an irritating flair for the dramatic, Clare thought. Why couldn't he get the hell down there before the vapors spread?

Clare counted the steps. It was almost time.

Finally Brun emerged from the stairway. Fingers trembling, Clare struck his match and dropped it at the head of his liquid fuse. A trail of light erupted from the darkness, whizzing toward its target like an arrow and summoning a ball-shaped inferno upon reaching its mark. Engulfed in the explosion, Brun shrieked, his screams echoing with the initial blast. He tried to bolt, but slipped and fell, soaking his clothes in more solvent. His flailing goaded the fire. Funneling spires leapt around him, searing his flesh, the flames blinding against a plain black backdrop. Clare watched from a safe distance as the conflagration died.

When the flames had subsided, he retrieved Brun's rifle and fired one merciful shot through his temple. The quivering body stilled.

No oil barrels here, Clare thought, but paint thinner would work.

He returned to the closet and gathered as many cans as he could carry.

"Deck fifteen is clear," Rove told Fawkes back in his suite. "Plenty of Marauders are still roaming the lower decks, but we can start here. Help me round up as many passengers as you can. Go door to door. Convince them the way is safe. Lead them back to my penthouse. Have them wait inside. When the time's right, we'll shepherd them into lifeboats."

The bespectacled steward looked hesitant. "If we don't have power, neither will the lifeboats, mate. Besides that, if they discover you're leading an evacuation, they'll shoot every passenger and probably do worse to you."

"I'm confident this will work, Lachlan."

Fawkes chewed over the likelihood. His face toughened, his words turning brittle. "Why the constant hankering to create a disturbance? Don't you realize the hazard? You're gambling with lives."

"Murder is the only safe bet, and that's if we do nothing. These passengers have had almost no water, no nourishment. People will soon start leaving their staterooms by necessity. They'll wander and be shot."

"What do you expect to accomplish by putting them on lifeboats?"

"At least they'll have emergency supplies. They have a right to try to reach land, however slim the chances. Some may opt not to go."

"But without electricity—"

"They'll have oars."

"We could be hundreds of miles from land."

"We are. Along the way, maybe they'll find us a rescue boat and send help."

Fawkes softened. "It's a last resort, and you may only manage to save dozens among thousands. But if that's the best you can do, I suppose it's still worth the risk."

"Those dozens may capture the attention of a merchant vessel, who might in turn alert the closest frigates. I'll give our passengers guns. They'll be equipped to defend themselves if a corsair follows them. They'll also have food and water."

"From where?"

"I'll transfer provisions from Ragnar's flagship, which has a special reserve for his own crew." He looked sternly at Fawkes. "Even if they do reach land but we never hear from them . . ."

Fawkes no longer appeared skeptical. "Jake, you have an unnatural ability to persuade, however foolhardy your little schemes. I could always stay here like a drongo and drink with flies"—his favorite dictum—"but not today. Count me in."

Fawkes spent the next hour knocking on doors, marshaling passengers into the suite. "Walk lightly," he told them all. "Remember, this is entirely elective. No obligations. I'm sure you're all aware of the risks involved. You're in good hands. The man was a military hero, for heaven's sake." Apparently mistrustful at first, many of the passengers stayed behind, but as more and more migrated to Rove's cabin, it seemed even the uncertain felt emboldened.

Rove reentered the penthouse about an hour later. He stood on a couch to address the mustered passengers, seeing strength and fear and resilience, and prayed Clare had thus far met similar success with his side of the plan.

"Listen," he said. He lowered his tone for emphasis. Against the hush of the shell-shocked group, his voice carried the power of a snare drum in crescendo. "We're going to move to deck seven and use the portside lifeboats. It's a long way down. You're going to have to stay absolutely silent as we go." His audience watched him. "Every one of you should realize: If you come with me, you may die. I can't guarantee anything." He felt reassured of the passengers' trust when no one questioned or interrupted. He had their attention. "I'll do everything I can to protect you. You'll have to be brave. There's a buddy of mine out there. A clever buddy. He's going to keep the bad guys distracted."

D r. Clare threw the sealed cans onto a corsair moored along the starboard side of the *Pearl Enchantress*. He grabbed a rope and swung from an overhang on deck six, nearly smashing an ear against the corsair's foremast, and landed against the cushion of the staysail. The grappling hook jangled against the cruise ship's gunwales, but held strong till he found solid footing aboard the neighboring vessel's quarterdeck. He uncapped the lids on the cans and began pouring systematically, scattering paint thinner across the weather deck, the helm, and inside the halyard locks so the hoisted sails would fall when their supporting ropes singed through. Clinging to the overhaul for balance, he doused both the jib and the mainsheet. From bow to stern he drenched the planks with gallons of liquid. When his work was finished, he stood on the stanchion and dropped a match. There was no sudden blast, no angry explosion; the liquid layer had spread and shallowed, causing instead a wall of flames to sprint across deck and sneak into the crannies he'd smothered. The sails caught, injecting pillars of smoke into the night air.

Clare dove headfirst into the Atlantic, the impact driving the breath from his lungs. The cold jarred his body into a state of shock that left him disoriented and gasping for breath. He thrashed, his muscles increasingly unresponsive. Bergs floated in these waters. Foolishly he wondered why he'd cast himself out of the blaze, which suddenly seemed so attractive. He collected his wits and headed for the nearest craft. Still weak from days of confinement and hunger, he managed to negotiate the swells using a breaststroke. Eventually he discovered a handhold on the hull of the nearest corsair. He turned backward, pleased with his work as with each passing moment the vessel more closely resembled a torch.

P anic sputtered through Ragnar's radio.
    "Captain, come in! We have an emergency! Come in!"
The beleaguered sailor raised the device to his lips. "What?"

"Both prisoners have escaped. Malcolm Clare is no longer in the brig. He helped rescue the other American."

Ragnar's hands might have snapped the rails. "Don't bother looking."

"Why not?"

"It seems no one can finish his assigned duty. I'll do it myself."

"Sir, that's not all. Our soldiers have a new task at hand: to salvage one of our corsairs. The *Baduhenna* is on fire!"

"I know," said Ragnar. "I'm standing on the sundeck of the Pearl ship, watching the flames."

Fifty passengers made the trek in a triple-file line, women and children taking the center while men flanked. Rove directed them, careful to safeguard the passengers at each pivot point as they descended the flights. His trigger finger was ready to joggle.

His following reached deck seven, where they proceeded around the top portside perimeter of the atrium. This racked nerves, particularly Rove's, as Ragnar's gunmen could have used any number of furniture pieces to conceal themselves. But the carpet beneath their feet muted their footsteps. If they were swift, they would attract little attention.

The three-story grand hall was dark, its chandelier a mere shadow. It was the passengers' first occasion to comprehend the entirety of the ship's blackout, and to experience the full effect of the ship's steep canting without stabilization by the gyroscopically controlled fins. Passengers had felt the sways of the swells, but never had these people tried to walk in a straight line for any distance with the rocking. The instability came as a surprise.

Rove held up a hand and mouthed the word "Stop."

He peered over the rail down through the open space of the atrium, teetering on the horns of a dilemma. Two floors down on deck five, a Marauder patrolled the floor, oblivious to the evacuation taking place above him. Rove had two options: shoot to kill and risk the noise, or try to evade detection. He had a clear shot. It would be easy—but loud.

The guard looked tired and bored, but Rove knew he'd be foolish to dismiss any danger. The guard might have welcomed conflict if for no other reason than to break his tedium. Rove made the decision. With a finger to his lips, he motioned for everyone to crouch. They dropped to an uncomfortable squat.

The guard halted and turned on his heels. Rove held his breath. Little stopped him when it was his own life at stake. Now that he'd appointed himself leader of a civilian cohort, the stakes had changed. After a few moments of inactivity the guard began to move again. When he reached the other end of the floor, he did an about-face. Rove studied the man's pattern of walking.

The people looked to him for a report. He held up a cautionary finger and whispered, "Wait."

After two more cycles, while the guard was facing away, Rove signaled for everyone to get up and move. The group inched their way across the carpet. Thirty seconds later, they crouched again, repeating the sequence until reaching safe harbor at the opposite end of the grand atrium.

Rove opened the door and checked the exterior walkway, a promenade that spanned several hundred yards. The portside was clear. He shepherded them outside.

"I need a pair of strong arms to help me lower the lifeboat," he said. Two athletic men raised their hands and stepped forward. One was in his late thirties and carried a toddler. The other, wearing a flannel sweater, was a sandy-haired jock with a hockey build. "What're your names?"

"Howard." He passed the child to her mother.

"Jordy."

"Thanks for stepping up. On the other side of this ship is a burning vessel belonging to our hijackers. Once they get the fire under control—or after their vessel sinks—they'll scatter, and they'll be furious. Can't say you'll be a dot in the horizon by then, but hopefully you'll disappear in the fog." Rove led them outside and began instructing them on how to untie the knots and use the rig of pulleys to manage the weight of the boat as they lowered it. "I've loaded your boat with guns. If they pursue, protect yourself."

"Never fired a gun before," Howard said.

"Hopefully you won't have to. If you do—ready, aim, fire."

Jordy, too, looked doubtful. "You sure?"

He gave them a quick demonstration without actually firing.

"Just don't forget to remove the safety. In the boat you'll find emergency supplies, first aid, water, food, the works. The supply is limited, especially for so many people. Ration it out. You won't have a working motor. You'll have to row. The others can help with that. Bear northeast to find land. The nearest country is Iceland. Along the way, if a ship picks you up, radio for military assistance. You will drift quite a bit, so write down these coordinates. Got a pen?"

"I do," Howard said. He used a dollar bill as paper and copied the numbers Rove dictated.

"That's an estimate of our current location," Rove explained. He continued to unfasten rope. "Don't lose that bill."

"I won't."

Rove grunted as he made one final tweak to the gear, then rested a hand on the fiberglass hull. "Okay. She's ready for lowering. Let's get those passengers onboard."

"What about you? Why aren't you going with us?"

"More lifeboats to fill. They need my help."

"You can only create so many diversions."

"I'll do my best."

Clare collapsed in the library aboard the *Pearl Enchantress*. The climb up the rope ladder had proved arduous and slippery. Rather than ascend all the way to the lido deck, he'd alighted on deck eight and navigated the darkened corridors to an unpatrolled, windowed area without being discovered. With fresh mental stamina he gazed through the panels at the deep blue, finding hope amid a turbulent seascape.

The departure of a single lifeboat had triggered his optimism. He watched in admiration of Rove's work as the boat made contact with water, and passengers rowed away. There was also a somber note to his musings. Courageous as they were, these passengers had to know the possibility of rescue was slim. He shook aside his doubts. He trusted Rove. He trusted his daughter. After a while he succumbed to physical exhaustion. He began to float, no longer able to wage the battle against sleep.

Undaunted by wind or tempest, the lifeboat crept north.

FORTY-TWO

I promise, we're noble thieves," Victoria told the bearded Icelandic native as he surrendered his seaplane. His please-don't-shoot-me expression twisted into one of fresh mystification as she added, "If we return this in anything less than mint condition, I'll buy you a new one."

It was still dark out, an hour before dawn. The air was biting, their newly bought parkas scuffing each other as the duo exited the flight shop and sprinted down a jetty. At the end floated their aircraft, its checkered nose, red propeller, and black circles on the wings all reminiscent of an RAF Supermarine Spitfire. It was called the *King Otter*. They were not deceived; this seaplane was no dogfighting machine or high-performance interceptor, but a pacific amphibian used for touristic joyrides. It would do. They clambered into the two-passenger cockpit, and Victoria took the helm.

"At this rate, we'll soon have earned an international reputation," Austin said. "This makes the second piece of expensive equipment we've 'borrowed' at gunpoint in two days."

"Three, if you count the limo from Bruges."

She began navigating the waterway.

"How'd you learn to fly?" Austin asked.

The floatplane droned as it traced a semicircle and taxied toward an open channel, the garbled whirr unbecoming of an aircraft dressed as a WWII fighter.

"Dad taught me." She angled the plane out to sea. "It's been a while, though, and I've never actually flown a seaplane."

"Uh-huh." Spotting her devil-may-care grin, Austin purged his mind of worry. "I'm not falling for it. You look fully competent."

His last words were shaved off by the roar of the radial engines as she reached overhead, toggled a switch, and drew the yoke into her breast. She jammed the twin throttles full forward, throwing Austin back in his seat. For a period of sixty long seconds he believed the ocean might actually prevail. Transfixed by the zooming whitecaps, he wondered how the body would ever break its connection with the sea. The underbelly dragged, hardly breaking a rock-throwing velocity. Yet soon the craft was slicing through the water, attaining speeds worthy of a WaveRunner, the pontoons lifting, and the previously sputtering amphibian rose out of its own salty spray. A jarring *thump-thump-thump* rattled the cabin as their skis slapped the wave tops. Austin realized this had to be the transition from floating to gliding. The bumps lasted only a few seconds before they climbed into a smooth sail.

The propellers continued to murmur as Victoria let the aircraft yaw at will. Abruptly, Austin clutched the pilot by her shoulder.

"Look out!" he cried.

Victoria pitched left, their wing nearly scraping a swell as she reacted to avoid colliding with a flock of pink-footed geese. The waterfowls had veered in a crosswind, and she nearly lost control before catching a draft and sailing over the birds.

"Sorry about that." She was calm. "Avian traffic."

"Reckless flyers," said Austin. "Don't they know right-of-way?"

"A goose wouldn't," she quipped, "but perhaps a more intelligent bird would know to wait its . . . *arctic tern.*"

The engine groaned as she circled toward a coastal cliff. The *King Otter* banked southwest and stalled. Victoria cut power and they went into a gentle dive, and for a moment Austin thought they might pancake into the choppy seas. Then she gunned it, and the seaplane leveled out.

"You're having too much fun," Austin said.

They'd long since departed the southern Icelandic shores, and the sun cast its rays on a small archipelago ahead. The Westman Isles, they were called, or Vestmannaeyjar in the native tongue. The fishermen who had discovered the cays in 1963 upon noticing smoke rising in the horizon could never have conceived a more explosive history for the islands, which had known blood feud, slavery, abduction, retribution, and volcanic eruptions. Soon after Ingólfur Arnarson, first permanent settler of Iceland, sailed from Norway and created his homestead in Reykjavik, he learned that a host of Irish slaves had murdered his kinsman, Hjörleifur. Enraged, Ingólfur tracked the slaves to the isles. The archipelago was later named after the Irish slaves who died there. In later centuries the Westman Isles would see kidnapping, raids, and other acts of barbarism from Turkish pirates.

"Check those out," Austin said, pointing to two craggy, cone-shaped landmasses rising from an island.

"Volcanoes," Victoria said. "Helgafell and Eldfell, the latter of which means 'mountain of fire' in Icelandic. An eruption in 1973 nearly caused a complete evacuation of the island. Ash destroyed a great many homes, and a river of lava nearly closed off the harbor. Since fishing's their main source of income, you might say the inhabitants were worried by the crisis."

"What happened?"

The seaplane's wings tipped toward the mountain rims.

"Emergency responders pumped enough seawater onto the molten rock to stop its advance from sealing the harbor. Resourceful islanders later generated electricity and hot water using the cooling lava. They were even able to extend their airport's runway using volcanic fallout."

"How do you know all this?"

"Worldliness and erudition."

"Or a tourist guidebook you picked up back at the flight shop."

She shrugged, not the least bit defensive. "You decide."

They glided over the harbor and continued southwest to circumnavigate the remainder of the archipelago. They admired its topography, the sheer-faced monoliths jutting from the ocean's surface like fingers reaching up to wave at the sky.

"You don't think Deeb or his men will escape the jet, do you?" she asked.

"Victoria, I've never seen that much duct tape used for ducts, let alone people. Besides, he's sheltered in a private hangar. No one's going to find them. They're not going anywhere."

"I guess you're right. As long as nobody—hey, did you see that?"

"If you're talking about the pyrotechnics show, then yes."

A bright red light streaked into the air leagues ahead of them, a dense, smoky trail in its wake.

"Someone shot a flare," she said.

"Could be just the distress signal we're after."

"Let's have a look-see."

She angled the plane seaward. They glided for a while and flattened off at an altitude of two hundred feet. Victoria reached into a glove compartment and handed her wingman a pair of binoculars.

"See anything?" she asked.

"Looks like a dinghy," he said, adjusting the focus. "Wait . . . there's writing on the side. It's a lifeboat!"

"We must be close to the *Pearl Enchantress*. The ship must be hiding in that fog up ahead."

Austin studied the tender. "Can't tell if they're pirates or fugitives. One thing I do know for sure is, they've got guns." They continued their approach, the boat no more than a mile away.

"You think they're dangerous?"

"At second glance, no. I see women and children aboard. They don't look like hostages. Take us down."

She spiraled downward in wide circles. "Brace yourself. If you thought takeoff was rough, you're in for a surprise. Landing never was my expertise."

FORTY-THREE

All hands to the lido deck," Ragnar said through his radio. Within the hour over a hundred Marauders were crowding the topmost level of the cruise ship. He pinched a bar stool between his legs and stood on the crossbeam for elevation. "The Viking has completed his negotiations. He now plans to detonate the explosives. We have one hour to load all ammunitions and set sail."

"What about the *Baduhenna*?" a soldier asked.

"Unsalvageable. We've lost one corsair. With several of our crew dead, we should manage to fit everyone aboard the four remaining. Now start loading."

"One moment, sir," said another. "What do we do with *him*?" The soldier broke rank holding a weathered man by the collar. Malcolm Clare's hands were tied behind his back. "Despite your instructions, we conducted a search anyway."

The first soldier spoke. "We found the prisoner sleeping in the library lounge beside the ship's movie theater."

Ragnar did not appear disturbed by his subordinates' failure to observe orders. "The jailbird flies home to roost. Welcome back, Dr. Clare." The chief grabbed the professor by the arm and flung him into the Seahorse Lagoon. Clare struggled with only two limbs for control. For a good minute he floundered without breaking the surface of the pool, until Ragnar stepped down from the stool and yanked him out. Clare emptied a mouthful of water on the tiled edge.

Ragnar lifted a fist, but the sound of gunfire ruined his moment. His men scattered under a rain of shelling. Leaving Clare bound by the poolside, Ragnar dashed toward the nearest enclosure.

"Where's it coming from?" he shouted.

An underling answered. "Overhead!"

It was Rove, perched atop the cruise ship's smoke tower. He had full cover and an extensive view of the deck. He began picking the Marauders from their hiding places one by one, like a man in a crow's nest with a slingshot.

"The tower has back access," Ragnar cried out. Only a few dozen heard. "Surround him."

Rove's ambush wasn't the only thing that challenged his calm. Ragnar cupped his ears and listened. A faint buzzing noise, stemming from somewhere close, was growing louder. He concentrated, trying to determine what it was over the shelling. He peeked out of his alcove and surveyed his surroundings, careful not to enter the line of gunfire. He saw nothing but fog. A cloud had descended upon the *Pearl Enchantress* and obscured all view. Something was approaching. He was sure of it . . .

Four rounds hammered the wall shielding him. He ducked, still listening.

A winged body materialized. His attention leapt to the sky in the northeast, and he gawked at the sight of a black-circled pattern he at once recognized as belonging to a Spitfire. A specter in the fog, the plane banked in a sharp loop over the deck. What was a British WWII fighter doing in the high seas off the Icelandic coast?

I'm ditching the canopy," Austin said.

The clear shell broke away. Air whooshed against them, wickedly cold even at low altitude, the nips and prickles lasting until the gale's icy needles had administered their anesthetic. Austin could have sworn his face was lodged in a mold of ice. Victoria didn't slow.

"Sounds like gunfire on deck," she said. "Hear it?"

"I don't just hear it. I see it. Right now I'm trying to sort the good guys from the bad. Bring her down closer, but not too close. I don't know how much shelling the *King Otter* can tolerate."

"What do you see?"

"They all seem to be shooting at the smokestack. . . . That's why. There's someone there, outnumbered but holding his own." Austin leaned over the side for a better look. "Not for long, though. Several men are advancing from behind, climbing rope ladders. Soon they'll have him surrounded."

"I'm circling back. How much ammo did the lifeboat passengers give you?"

"An automatic rifle for each of us and five spare clips. Should be plenty."

"Ever fired a gun before?"

"There's a first for everything."

"I'll do a flyby while you strafe the stern. Make it count."

The plane veered over an iceberg for another run. When it leveled, Ragnar realized the aircraft was no Supermarine, but a rickety floatplane with a professional paint job. He spoke into his radio. "All soldiers: Fire at the aircraft. Shoot it out of the sky."

His fingers trembled as he tried to refasten the device to his belt. He dropped it, and it fell to the ground, crossing the line of fire. A bullet smashed the transceiver. Angrily, he snatched it up and tried speaking. Nothing came through, not even static. He deep-sixed the radio and noticed Clare crawling for cover. He couldn't let that happen. He needed his hostage. Clutching his rifle, he sprinted toward the professor. A bullet grazed his calf but failed to impede his momentum.

From the tower, Rove watched as the red-haired juggernaut caught Clare between chambers. He reloaded quickly.

Ragnar lunged at Clare and got him in a headlock. Ragnar's other hand jabbed Clare's side with the tip of his AK-47. Rove wondered why the man even bothered with his weapon. He could snap the professor's neck in an instant.

"Cease fire, Jake!" Ragnar bellowed.

The Marauders had nearly reached deck sixteen. Any higher, and they'd have a direct shot at Rove.

"You ready?" Victoria asked.

"Aye, Captain," came his reply. "Just don't try any loops, rolls, or corkscrews."

She forced the yoke toward her knees. They entered a nosedive and gained speed. Austin centered his aim on the moving targets. When they eased into a horizontal, he opened fire on the advancing front. Two Marauders dropped free of the rope ladder. Their own craft suffered minimal damage in the face of a skyward volley.

"Nice work," Victoria said.

"Loop back. Let's do it again."

"Controlling this baby is so awkward. If it weren't for the weight of the pontoons, I could maneuver better."

"You're doing fine."

She tried a new tack. Rather than fly parallel with the plane of the ocean, she came up at an angle. From nearly skimming the swells she climbed aloft and gave Austin a head-on view. It was a straight course to the ship.

"Not a good idea, Victoria," he said tentatively. "You won't be able to turn away in time. We'd best stay astern. Don't give them an easy shot from the main deck."

"I can pull away in time."

"Maybe with a real dogfighter. Not this poker."

"Then duck!"

They came within range, and Austin could already see there was no turning back. He fired over Victoria's head and knocked another three into the water. Practice had helped. A few others had reached the gunwales. *One more good strafe . . .*

Victoria remained hunched after Austin had finished firing. They'd entered dangerous territory.

"Pull away," he said. "Do it now."

She uncurled herself and manned the yoke. They came within yards of actually striking the mast. She tilted toward the ship's starboard side and swooped low over the lido deck.

Bullets hailed them from all angles, and they heard sounds like sleet flogging a tin shack. A small, rectangular piece of their wing flew off and splashed into the ocean. Another stream of bullets ripped seven holes in the rear fuselage.

"We're hit," Austin said. "Pull away, now!"

The volley didn't cease. The drone of their arthritic engine became a violent, percussive rattle. The craft sputtered and stalled.

"We're pouring smoke," she said, dipping below the apex of the ship. They finally left the fire zone. "We have to land."

"Not yet. If we don't go back, they'll close in on him. One more flyby."

"They've ruptured the fuel tank. If they hit the fuel system in the engine compartment, the whole thing could blow."

"Victoria . . ."

He spoke no more. From a near dive she pulled up and rammed the twin throttles to full. She positioned herself as she had for the first strike, lining up for a sidelong strafe. When she reached an altitude of two hundred feet, the engine died.

The *King Otter* glided serenely alongside the neighboring cruise ship, her smoky tail contrasting sharply with the gray of the fog. Austin loaded another clip, poked his upper torso out of the open cabin, and held down the trigger. The automatic quivered against his shoulder until the magazine had emptied. His final target collapsed, half dangling over the gunwale. A belt of wind whipped down from the brewing clouds and flung the corpse over the edge.

Fire had ceased on deck. Ragnar's headlock tightened around Malcolm Clare.

"Drop it!" he shouted. "You have three seconds!"

Rove had no choice. He stood erect at the top of the tower in plain view and threw his rifle on the ground.

"Come down here," Ragnar ordered. "Take the port stairs. Try anything clever, and I'll kill him. It will be easy."

Approximately one hundred automatics were pinned to Rove. He descended the stairs with his hands raised. They were too many. His hour of bravado was over.

"You shouldn't have, Jake," Clare reprimanded. "Now they'll kill us both."

Ragnar's lips puckered. "Come closer," he said.

After a glimpse at his watch, Rove obeyed, turning each second into three with his unhurried pace. He wondered how long his delay tactics would work before Ragnar grew dangerously impatient. Five minutes. He figured that was all he needed before the nameless aviators would show. But even if they did, he thought, what chance would they stand against scores of armed men?

"Come closer," the chief repeated.

Rove looked at Clare, who showed no appreciation; he was pleading for Rove to stop, to do something to save his own life. Rove's smile read, *I couldn't take the chance.*

"Stop there," Ragnar said. "On the ground."

Rove dropped to his knees and bowed his head only slightly. Could he buy any more time? Where were the aviators? *Who* were they? Judging by their flybys behind the smokestacks, he knew one thing: They were on his side.

"All the way down," Ragnar demanded. "Cheek to the tile."

Rove said nothing. He folded his arms behind his back and lay flat.

Ragnar beckoned three of his men, who surrounded him with readied guns.

His carotid artery pinched, Clare was beginning to lose circulation. Relishing complete control, Ragnar let the silence last. There was only the gentle creaking and an occasional whistle as winds blustered across the deck.

The *King Otter* steepened its angle of descent and plowed toward a drifting iceberg. Deprived of power, the amphibian barreled into a plunge. Closing the remaining fifty feet to impact, Austin and Victoria curled their arms around their knees.

A shaft of water ejected from the ocean and became a lunging white cloud of a splash. The tail whiplashed when a front pontoon struck water. Before any part of the hull could strike the wall of ice, the seaplane spun out and nearly inverted when the elevator caught in a swell. The yoke jumped out at Victoria in a painful jab that knocked the wind from her stomach. Smells of smoke and avgas filled the cabin. If it weren't for their firm wedges in their seats, the first collision might have catapulted them forward. Drenched in sweat and seawater, they held strong.

A stolen glance out the window, and Austin saw the white cloud of water—but to him it was filled with the sparks of his emergency landing in the Azores. He was ten years old, hearing the frantic announcement over the plane's PA system—*explosive decompression . . . hydraulic systems failure . . . emergency landing on Terceira.* His hands covered the back of his neck to protect against flying shrapnel. Perceptions converged, the sights with the sounds, and from all the noises filling his ears he discerned a single wavelength, harsh, inescapable, pulsating, causing his head to throb. It was a communion of the senses—senses in their most heightened form, working together, channeling more information than he could process, forcing his brain to race, awakening a primal life-preserving instinct that shut out despair but ushered in unfiltered memories of the belly landing on Terceira.

He saw lights, multiple lights, not glowing like auroras, not radiant like haloes, but sharp and defined, hissing and spitting like electric sparks, each one searing the insides of his eyelids. They were bright, dazzlingly bright. He wanted to close his eyes and force out the lights.

He tried to close them . . . but they wouldn't close. Why wouldn't they close? He realized: They were already closed. He squeezed the lids more tightly, and the lights intensified. They were smoldering hot. He wasn't sure if his retinas were burning, or if his head were exploding. It was the impact, he told himself. It was just the impact. He was spinning. It would all be over soon. His fingers were still interlaced around the nape of his neck. A thousand forces tried to pull them apart as the spin persisted. The sparks began to blur. Slowly they dissipated, fading like brake lights in a fog. He could only believe he was experiencing the spinout in slow motion.

He looked around and saw no hills, no vegetation as there had been on Terceira—only water and icebergs.

It was over.

The floatplane skimmed to a stop and tipped on its side, the odors of fuel replaced by salty mist.

They both let go, and their bodies rolled out of the cabin, landing in the water by the bow of the cruise ship. Emerging from a daze, Victoria found her arms wrapped around Austin's waist like a flotation ring. When she realized what she had clasped, she peeled her arms away and began treading water on her own, her face blue.

"You okay?" he asked, shaking out his hair, held buoyant by a scissor kick.

Her indigo eyes pooled with embarrassment. "All but for the cold," she said. "Sorry about the rough landing."

"That felt like a long crash."

"It was only three or four seconds."

"Seemed like minutes."

"Don't expect wonders from an unpracticed pilot."

"The gunners nearly ripped our hull to shreds. I'm only glad we're unhurt." He pointed to the aircraft's body. "Can't say the same for the *King Otter*. Water's already seeping into the seats."

She wasn't listening.

"What's wrong?"

"No more gunfire," she said. "We'd better find out what's happening up there."

"Don't shoot him," Ragnar said, too preoccupied to hear anyone climbing over the rails onto the ship. "He's killed too many of our men, and his accomplice torched one of our vessels. Tie his hands behind his back. Make the knots strong." Ragnar released Clare and dropped him on the ground. Three more Marauders moved in and stood guard around him.

Ragnar looked straight at Rove. "You are a man of the sea. Fitting you should die at the bottom." He gestured to his men. "Find a weight. Fix it to the ropes."

The professor yanked at his own bonds to no avail. He knew there was nothing he could do to save his friend.

"What's the matter?" he spat. "Is this going to make you feel better? Knowing he drowned?"

Ragnar kicked Clare in the thigh. There was no restraint in his kick. "If you want to join him, I'd be happy to oblige." He used his ankle to roll the man onto his back, then dug a heel into his abdomen so Clare couldn't breathe.

A soldier raised his rifle and shouted. "Captain!"

A wet foot connected with Ragnar's stomach, followed by a strike that would have collapsed his windpipe had his reflexes been a second slower. The thrust behind the foot was strong, but his abdomen was stronger, causing his assailant's foot to rebound. To block the attempt at his throat, he held up a fist and swept his hefty arm to the side. He was shocked to identify his attacker as a six-foot female. He couldn't see her face; there was a tangle of hair glued to her cheeks by seawater. She had sprung from behind the elevated Jacuzzi tub. Judging from her plan of assault, she was an amateur in physical combat but a rough, determined fighter, undeterred by his size or strength. She seemed to channel her adrenaline in ways that allowed her to remain disciplined even after taking the worst of blows. With a decade of experience and a hundred more pounds of muscle, she would have made a decent opponent.

He cuffed her and shoved her backward with sufficient force to level her. Her fall broke a lounge chair. He was impressed by the speed and agility of her recovery. She sprang back into play with no sign of damage and assumed a kickboxer's stance, then went straight for an uppercut. He blocked her jab and hooked her in the neck. She didn't yelp or squeal as she fell back again. The young woman landed against the jagged plastic edges of a broken lounge chair. A second time she bounced elastically to her feet and resumed her fighting posture.

Her imminent defeat was not for lack of willpower; strong and flexible as she was, even her most artful attacks had little effect against the mountain that he was, and he protected his vulnerabilities well. So far he had only cat-toyed with her. The moment he decided their match was over, he spun her around and grabbed her throat from behind. He gave it a squeeze.

Glass shattered, and a shard plunged through Ragnar's thick pelt. He dropped Victoria and spun to face his second opponent, this one taller than the first, his forehead matted in brown waves.

Austin delivered a punch using his left hand, which Ragnar took with practice by angling his head downward and rolling with the blow. The impact was nil. Austin steadied himself once more, then lunged with the broken wineglass. The swipe nicked Ragnar in the forearm. Austin felt like he was cutting through leather, but he had drawn blood and took this as a small victory.

Ragnar's hand shot out toward Austin's and clamped down around his wrist, causing him to lose control of his crude weapon. Defenseless, Austin took a knee in the stomach and tottered back. At the same time, Ragnar conveyed one last kick to Victoria, who had managed to pry free a crossbeam from the lounge chair and was attempting to use it as a bludgeon. She landed against the wall of the elevated Jacuzzi and stayed there, realizing that even between the two of them their chances were zero—and if they somehow defied the odds, a hundred or so rifles were still trained on them; the only reason none had discharged was that Ragnar stood in the line of fire.

"Stay down," said Ragnar. "Both of you, whoever you are, remain on your knees and crawl to the poolside."

They obeyed.

At her father's side, Victoria said, "Hi, Dad."

Clare looked at her, his disapproval unmistakable. "*Victoria?* I've been terrified for you through all of this. How could you be so *stupid* to come here yourself?" She caressed his cheeks and kissed him on the forehead. His admonishing glare turned to one of surprise at the sight of Austin Hardy. "I don't believe it!" he said. Austin felt powerless to do anything. Guns had turned to him. "Victoria! Austin! What are you doing here?"

"Long story, Professor," he said.

"You came with her?"

Victoria answered him. "We'll fill you in later," she said. "We recovered the satellite. Glitnir Defense has full control of Baldr. Unfortunately, your laptop was the only casualty. It just went down in flames. Crash landing." She started to untie him. "We're both okay, but you should have seen the *King Otter.*"

Her father sighed. Despite the pain in his wrists and the soreness in his body, he gave her a doting grin.

"Looked more like a Spitfire to me," he said.

When he saw she'd begun to undo his bonds, Ragnar ripped her away. "Hands off!" he said, bridling. "We have a schedule to meet. Soldiers, start loading the cargo. And dump the waste into the sea."

Three Marauders dragged Rove by the foot toward the railing. It was a long drop to the ocean, and even farther to its floor. For the first time since surrendering his weapon, he resisted. Though his hands were bound, they struggled to subdue him. It was a poetic moment for Rove. He'd spent his life at sea and knew nature's forces often worked in mysterious ways.

"That's the man who's helped us from the beginning," Clare said mournfully. "Jake Rove."

The hijackers finally stood him up, one at each leg and one holding him by the neck. They forced Rove against the railing. The weight dragged him down. He hardly winced as they swung him back for the final heave.

Rove panned the ocean one last time.

FORTY-FOUR

Jake, you old seadog!"

The words rang like an epitaph.

"Look at the trouble you've gotten yourself into. Why couldn't you just keep a low profile?"

It was Lachlan Fawkes. He wore no spectacles, no tuxedo, no prim attire but a rugged vest and jeans. He'd slung a travel sack over his shoulder. The mantle of fog thickened around him as he emerged from the doorway, his eyes shining with a macabre sparkle.

The Marauders whirled around to face the newcomer, who held up a cautionary hand. "Set him down, boys. I realize mercy is a matter of politeness for you. For me, it's a passion. He'll go with the rest." He looked at the professor. "Untie them both. Have your men board their ships, Ragnar. Prepare to sail."

The chief looked like he'd been asked to don a skirt.

"Do it, Ragnar," the wizened valet ordered.

Ragnar nodded to his men, who set free both Rove and Clare. Austin and Victoria huddled with the released captives.

"That was my steward during the cruise," Rove whispered to them.

Fawkes continued. "Looks like I've come to the party in full swing, albeit without an RSVP. Forgive the intrusion. I've a boat to catch. But before I leave, a toast." He strode behind the bar and mixed himself a White Russian. "To the day's heroes," he said, and took his first sip.

Victoria squeezed her father's shoulder while Austin and Rove exchanged glances. They'd just met, had hardly said a word to each other, yet their shared cause seemed to bond them like old friends.

Fawkes spit out the drink. "It's not the same without ice, but alas, refrigeration is hard to come by these days. Booze without the rocks, anyone? It's on me."

No one said anything. Ragnar simmered.

"Come on, folks! It's a time for celebration. The end of troubles." He reached into his pocket and pulled out a chrome-colored cylinder about the size of his thumb. "At least, it soon will be. Days ago, a diver lined the hull of the *Pearl Enchantress* with explosive charges. They're timed to blow in thirty minutes. That is, unless anyone acts stupidly and compels me to do it sooner. I can push this little red button ahead of schedule, and the *Enchantress,* with its three thousand passengers, will be reduced to wreckage."

The rhythm of rotor blades could be heard in the distance, the source hidden. Rove stepped forward. "You're quite a legend, Lachlan Fawkes, just not the one you project to the public. Or perhaps I should call you by your real name: Clifford Pearl."

The old man's face contorted with surprise. He mulled over the allegation, then let out a cold laugh. "Well done, Jake."

The professor, his daughter, and Austin watched in silent amazement.

"Gotta admit, you had me in the beginning with that disarming Australian yokel," Rove said. "Too bad there's not an ounce of Aussie blood in you. But then there's your second alias. That name suits you better."

"You're right. It is befitting," Pearl said. "Granted, I may not match the physical stereotype, but there's a gratifying likeness. The Vikings were explorers and longship sailors. And what is Pearl Voyages if not a fleet built for exploration? Of course, there's more to the pseudonym. Vikings hardly sailed for leisure. They were warriors, raiders, pirates, like my associates here."

Half distracted by the growing background noise, Rove said, "Give up, Clifford. We know what you're up to. We have all but a few missing pieces."

The whipping sound drowned out the end of his sentence. A gray, twin-engine Augusta corporate helicopter descended from above, closing in at fifty yards, its airstream flattening hair and apparently gaining strength until power was cut to the rotors. A shaky tail boom suggested the pilot was battling unruly winds. Rove watched as the dark body edged toward the stern, its skids kissing the ship's helipad. The blades slowed to an unhurried slice, then idled to a full stop.

Pearl looked more entertained than surprised as two strangers in jumpsuits and flight helmets appeared at the nearest stairwell. One was a stout man, his chest rounded like a cask, the other a petite woman with a decisive gait and an unflappable air of authority. They assessed the scene from a ledge before joining the others on lido deck level. Clare looked partially relieved to see them.

"Welcome, Mr. Chatham," Pearl said. "This is a happy surprise."

Chatham looked uncomfortable. "Who are you?"

"We've been speaking on the phone the past few days. Don't you recognize my voice?"

A look of unease turned to downright consternation on Chatham's face. He glanced at his companion. "I brought one of my colleagues, Kate Dirgo."

Dirgo left her boss's side and walked to Clare.

"You all right, Mal?"

"Doing okay, Kate. Thanks. Awfully shocked to see you."

She whispered in his ear. "We have Baldr back. Somehow . . . don't ask me how . . . we regained control. All we have to worry about is—"

"I know," Clare said with a gesture toward the detonator in Pearl's hands.

Chatham was studying Pearl from the toes up. "It was *you?*"

"It was me."

Lips quivering, Chatham searched the depths of his vocabulary for something to say. What finally erupted from his mouth sprang from its basest pits. It wasn't so much his language as it was his aggressive advance—he practically lunged—that caused the old mariner to brandish a vintage Luger and center it on Chatham's chest.

"Anyone who moves like that again dies. Your lot is outnumbered more than twenty to one. You'll go out like Butch Cassidy and the Sundance Kid."

"Why are you doing this?" Clare said. "Why damage your own company? The news will spread like wildfire. Your whole cruise line will burn in the flames."

"Did it occur to you," Pearl said, "that this might be what I'm after? Recall, the corporation is no longer officially mine. It belongs to Sapphire Pacific."

Rove realized his wounds and sleeplessness were catching up to him. Feeling faint, he crumpled his bruised face and constricted his abdominal muscles to force blood to his brain. Black spots threatened to encroach upon his peripherals and transform his vision into a narrow tunnel. He was beyond fatigued, having consciously to inject his voice with volume to compensate. He divided his energy among speaking, managing the pain in his head, and remaining conscious.

"Took me a while to figure out why he'd wreck the company he spent his life building," he said. "Then it dawned on me. Clifford

Pearl has been managing two, though not entirely independent, schemes." Pearl flashed the whites of his teeth, goading Rove to explain. "The first involved the theft of an armed satellite equipped with nuclear power. Dr. Clare here engineered the Baldr satellite not for its explosive faculty, but for its electromagnetic potential. Baldr would lend us the ability to cripple our enemies without killing innocents or suffering the political repercussions typically associated with nuclear detonations.

"The project had to remain classified. The consequences of divulging this top-secret development could be catastrophic. Enemies would try to destroy it, or worse, steal it. With the capacity to debilitate major terror cells in remote locations, foil international outlaws, and shut down entire rogue states and hostile territories, Baldr would become the number-one technological target shared by our enemies.

"Enter Clifford Pearl, a titan of the cruise industry—merged three major petrochemical shipping companies in the mid-sixties into what would become Pearl Voyages. By 1975 a rival cruise line, Sapphire Pacific, had captured substantial market share. Despite the interests of the company, you refused their persistent acquisition attempts, until your own board fired you for your stubbornness. They completed the transaction without you. Whatever it was you lost—pride, ownership, money—you needed a way to settle the score.

"You weren't entirely disheartened. There's opportunity in adversity. As you had expanded your fleet, you had developed a few less-than-reputable associations, perhaps some with access to intelligence circles."

"You'd be surprised how many foreign intelligence officials one meets as a front-runner in global shipping and transportation," Pearl said.

"Someone along the way must have informed you of Malcolm Clare's work establishing Glitnir Defense."

Austin and Victoria traded knowing glances.

"His name was Kaslov," Austin interjected. "Vasily."

Clare stiffened. "I know that name, Kaslov. He worked for me at the beginning, but it was under an alias—Christian Lefevre. He'd been a contracts manager before one of our employees discovered his attempts to hack our computer systems." He stopped cold, then said, "Kate, it was you, wasn't it?"

Dirgo nodded her head. "I remember deporting Lefevre."

"A generous sentence," Victoria said. "He nearly killed us more than once."

Austin directed a statement at Pearl as the piece fell into place. "So you had a partnership," he said. "Forged from greed." His look was outright savage. "When you learned of Glitnir Defense and how its technologies could make you richer, you hired Vasya as a private investigator of sorts. Rather than set foot in the Virginia office where he'd be recognized, he hooked up surveillance in two less conspicuous places: Professor Clare's Stanford office in the Gates building, and the apartment belonging to his nuclear consultant, Fyodor Avdeenko.

"By sifting through Vasya's audio feeds, you gleaned information about a monumental project underway. You also learned of the superseding program the professor had created—one that could uplink to the Baldr satellite and intervene should any political party attempt to harness the technology unethically. Dr. Clare gave himself complete, secure, and exclusive overriding control of Baldr from his own laptop. He and Avdeenko were the only two individuals in the world aware of the duplicate."

Clare scratched his head, estimating they had twenty-five minutes. He looked stunned to learn he had been meticulously studied and exploited via bugs within his own university office.

"So we thought," he said.

Austin resumed his account, glaring at Pearl. "So you now had information that would prove critical in staging the satellite's heist. Vasya would put you in touch with eager buyers. There were two things you needed to pit Glitnir Defense against its enemies: leverage and security. You needed insurance Glitnir would deposit the funds into your account if they won the auction. Meanwhile, one of your biggest customers, Farzad Deeb, wanted a demonstration of his toy. So you'd give him one, but Baldr wasn't enough for the job. The pulse would eliminate power, but you still needed to place bombs, and plenty of them. You also had to prevent passengers from escaping in lifeboats. You needed a team of capable hijackers to impede evacuation and plant explosives.

"You did your research. You learned of the Black Marauders and the captain of their pirate flotilla, Ragnar Stahl. He and his men could help you seize any vessel for the right price. You stood to net billions, so it made little difference how many you had to hire. You had only to meet Ragnar to discuss your plans and convince him of the possibility. Your pawn Vasya would later prove helpful, once again, by providing aerial support of Ragnar's escape from the penal colony. And he'd make sure governmental authorities would look the other way.

"Long before Ragnar's escape, Vasya learned of Dr. Clare's invitation to showcase his newest biplane—the *Firecat*—in Sweden. But the airshow ended tragically when the Swedish Air Force pilot—a man named Benedikt Stahl—failed to pull out of a nosedive. Swedish military authorities launched an investigation vindicating Stahl of drug abuse, and Clare of faulty design work. No one could explain the accident. This must have come as staggering news to Benedikt's brother, Ragnar."

Ragnar trembled, reliving the moment.

"Impeccable sleuthing," said Pearl. "I'm sure Ragnar would tell you that. He did love his brother very much. They shared a common enemy growing up. Their papa was a rather harsh disciplinarian." He spoke as if the man weren't there to hear him. "So Ragnar killed him and fled to Norway, living off petty crime. Over time, he discovered new vocations. Larceny. Grand theft. Extortion. Kidnapping. Trafficking. Money laundering. You name it. He recently added fraud to the list by hacking Malcolm's email account, contacting his teaching assistants so a capable grad student would assume responsibility for his class. It was Ragnar who ambushed and kidnapped Dr. Clare at Stanford, with every intention of murder.

"Anyway, when I learned of the Marauders, the 'accidental' destruction of the *Firecat,* and the death of Benedikt Stahl, I saw a fit with my own objectives. I could offer Ragnar not only riches, but vengeance upon the man who designed the plane that killed his brother."

Chatham began to sweat again. He dabbed himself and tried to avoid notice.

Clare took the comment like a stab to the eye. "The accident was tragic, but as the Swedish military investigation revealed, there was nothing wrong with the *Firecat*. With all due respect to your brother— and he was a fine pilot—he tried to execute the impossible. He didn't pull out of his dive in time. Dan, who was there, can tell you."

Ragnar slammed a fist onto the railing. "You're running away from your mistake with a lie. My brother wasn't careless. He didn't make stupid errors. It was the biplane."

"Which had flown successfully before the accident, many times," Clare said. "Have you considered, maybe he was committing suicide?"

"You didn't know the man whose dignity you insult."

"And you don't know me," said Clare. "At least now I understand the message you wrote in my blood. 'Remember the *Firecat*.' In your mind, you were staging a death comparable to your brother's." Clare looked at Pearl. "You sick old man. You let him believe Benedikt's death was a result of my negligence?"

Pearl shook his head. "I'm afraid you've *both* been misled," he said. "Ragnar, my apologies . . . but the misinformation was a powerful motivator."

"What's behind this?" Clare said. "Tell us, so we—Dan, you all right?"

Chatham's heavy breathing was beginning to approach hyperventilation. He unzipped his jumpsuit and let the wind cool his body.

"Yeah, I'm okay," he said. "I'm okay." He was dripping.

"Actually," said Pearl, "the *Firecat* disaster was no accident."

"You're a liar," Ragnar said, staring at Clare. "You killed Benedikt. I'll kill you."

"Before doing that," Pearl advised, "I would talk to Mr. Chatham over here, as the professor suggested. Surely he can shed light."

Chatham appeared to have entered an almost hallucinatory delirium. "I . . . what?"

"I said surely you can describe what happened—the biplane crash?"

Glitnir's president held a hand around his overhanging belly as if to steady its contents. He looked to Dirgo in the hopes she would shield him from the question.

"Care to enlighten us?" was all she said.

"What is this, an inquisition?" he muttered. "It was . . . a long time ago."

"Poor fellow has amnesia," Pearl said.

"You heard Malcolm," Chatham answered. "He just told you what happened. I agree with his story."

"Perhaps I can jog your memory," Pearl said. "When Vasya was still conducting reconnaissance, he followed you and Clare to Stockholm. And on the eve of the air show, he saw you leave your hotel for the *Firecat*'s hangar." Pearl sharpened his tone. "Why did you tamper with the controls, Mr. Chatham?"

Clare looked at his colleague, scandalized. "*What?*"

It appeared the wind blowing across Chatham's neck and arms did little to reduce his temperature. "That's a . . . random claim without proof."

"Oh, we have a few dozen pictures," Pearl said. "What did you do? Cause the yoke to jam when he entered a dive?"

"It's not true," Chatham said. "Don't believe him, Malcolm. It's a colossal . . . a misconstruction."

"I'm still trying to figure out the motive," Pearl said. "You and Dr. Clare were roommates at MIT, weren't you? Studied the same subjects? And one of you was always *better* at it, wasn't he? Was there a grain of enmity that burned deep into your psyche, Mr. Chatham? Malcolm went on to achieve great things, didn't he? Earned all sorts of prizes and awards from aeronautical societies, if I'm not mistaken. He became the famous inventor, not you. He had the glory, the celebrity, the recognition . . . the *ideas*. Not to mention a beautiful wife and daughter. How viciously unfair that his brain work should become your grunt work. The air show seemed a perfect opportunity to tarnish the ungrateful bastard's name. Send the *Firecat* into a blaze while thousands looked on!"

Chatham shook visibly. "That's a lie!"

"No—a theory," said Pearl, "for why you'd tried to pin the blame on one of your closest friends. But it didn't work. Investigations cleared his name. Was it worth murder?"

"You've killed before!" Chatham exclaimed. "You've done it! That's what this whole thing is about!"

Clare showed no pity as he was jarred into the realization that friendship had usurped the place of disgust for this fraud for almost fifty years. Still, his contempt apparently paled alongside Ragnar's. The man had hated learning his reprisal efforts had been misdirected.

"You filth," Ragnar vented. "You killed my brother!"

"Stay back, Ragnar," Pearl cautioned. "He'll be yours in minutes. We must first unmask the extent of Mr. Chatham's treachery. You see, a person so enslaved by his own falsity—whether he admits it or not—*wants* to be found out. Truth cuts the ball from his chain.

"Before beginning the auction, I called Chatham. We struck a deal. If he cooperated by bidding, I promised not to demystify the *Firecat* scandal that would strap him with murder. If he raised the bid high enough, I offered two percent, straight to his personal account. So you see, all those negotiations at Glitnir, the screaming fits, the tantrums, the protests—it was one grand charade. Chatham wanted the auction to continue. If he stopped bidding, he knew I'd release the pictures of his tampering, and if he pushed the bids higher . . . well, two percent of three billion was worth a little playacting."

"He blackmailed me," Chatham yelled. "Can't everyone see that?"

Dirgo looked ready to rip a hole in his chest. "So you were behind the auction all along. There were times I seriously considered you might be on the Viking's team. I should have trusted my gut."

"Of course he was with me," Pearl said. "Unfortunately for us, that little gambit failed. You recovered the Baldr satellite. I won't see a dime from the auction."

"Like I said," Rove piped in, "your plan had a part two."

"Care to share?" Pearl said.

"Soon after the acquisition of Pearl Voyages, you planned to destroy Sapphire Pacific. Not only that, but with one pulse you could temporarily deflate the cruise industry. You knew the hijacking of the *Pearl Enchantress* would send shockwaves through international media. Imagine what vacationers would do after learning terrorists had devastated a ship with three thousand passengers. Millions would cancel itineraries. Every cruise line would take a hit. Hotels and restaurants would feel the burn. An attack of this magnitude would wreak havoc in the travel industry."

"Go on," Pearl said. "Where's the opportunity?"

"By seizing the *Pearl Enchantress,* you were killing three birds with one stone. One, you had leverage against Glitnir in the auction. Two, you gave Deeb his demonstration. And three . . . you stood to gain by short selling Sapphire Pacific stock."

Pearl nodded. "Not only Sapphire Pacific, but a number of hotel chains. As you pointed out, this single act of destruction will have astoundingly far-reaching effects. The only two people who posed any threat to my plans were Clare and Avdeenko. I thought perhaps one of them could find a way to recover the satellite. Vasya was ordered to assassinate Avdeenko, and Ragnar would think he was avenging his brother's death by killing Clare."

Chatham began to shout. "It's a pack of lies. I had nothing to do with any of this! It was all Clifford Pearl."

Dirgo looked as if she were about to slap him. Instead, she curled a fist and walloped him so hard in the cheekbone it might have fractured had he not withdrawn from the blow. "You're a good actor, Dan, but you didn't quite pass the smell test," she said. "Why don't you face up to the truth? Back in the office, you announced to everyone that Baldr was hovering a little south of the Arctic Circle when all I'd previously said was, 'Somewhere over the North Atlantic.' How were you able to offer that precision?"

"That doesn't prove anything," he said.

"No, it doesn't. But it does conveniently corroborate the hunch I explored on my own. I called the SEC to report my suspicions and ask for assistance." She yanked some papers from her jumpsuit pocket. "Nice investment portfolio, Mr. Chatham. Seems you don't have much confidence in the tourism industry, either. You sold short in Sapphire Pacific soon before the auction started. If that doesn't prove you were in cahoots, I don't know what does."

"You had me fooled, Dan," Clare said with sadness. "Never gave me any reason to mistrust you."

Dirgo added, "When Clifford Pearl called at one point, he said integrity had taken a vacation within our premises. The reference to you is now clear."

Chatham glanced around, seeing the rails. A feeling of desolation swept over him. He looked out over the wave crests, the undulating swells, the frothy whitecaps blowing over a plane of icebergs. It was the sea's warning that no trespasser would go unpunished.

"You knew from the get-go Pearl intended to sink his own ship," said Dirgo. She had the opportunity to kick him where it would count, but had every intention of letting Ragnar do his worst. "You knew three thousand people would die."

Chatham looked at Pearl's detonator, his voice still quavering. "So what?" he said. "What was I supposed to do?"

"Good point," Dirgo answered. "You're already a murderer. Why stop now?"

"I can't take this anymore," Chatham said. "I can't!"

Ragnar's strides toward the man were slow, controlled. He closed a hand around Chatham's throat. "I saw you eyeing the rails," Ragnar whispered so no one else could hear, his voice lacquered with venom. No one was standing in his way now—not even Pearl. "You can't wait to die."

Chatham threw a fist at Ragnar, who caught the blow with his free hand, held the fist at arm's length, and squeezed with a force that snapped two metacarpals. His hand shattered, and Chatham shrieked, squirming, exhausted of the will to fight as Ragnar crushed his knuckles and proceeded to break three phalanges.

"Bind his wrists behind his back," Ragnar told his soldiers. "Have you heard of a strappado, Mr. Chatham?" Three Marauders approached, having hoisted up one of the ropes dangling from a grappling hook.

Before they could control him, Chatham bolted toward the stern of the ship. A host of automatics turned to follow his sprint, waiting only for their commander's nod to open fire. At first Ragnar assumed the getaway attempt was a product of mania, the dash nothing but an ill-planned, short-term escape strategy. Then he realized where Chatham was headed.

"Don't shoot!" he shouted to his legion.

Bounding up the stairs to the helipad, Chatham had made a beeline for the Augusta. Soon after he disappeared inside the craft, the rotor blades began to revolve, accelerating, lifting the giant piece of machinery skyward.

"Not yet . . ." Ragnar said.

The chopper hung suspended before banking north, the rhythm of the blades growing louder as it passed over them toward Iceland. Ragnar held up a hand, waiting for the helicopter to fly out of range of his corsairs. Then he signaled.

"Now!"

The chopper lurched. Even Dirgo withdrew at the sound of a hundred streams of bullets blasting the airborne chassis. Its twin engines aflame, the helicopter ascended thirty yards but remained well within reach. The tail boom quivered, its smaller rotor showering sparks. The canopy smashed inward, and the rear vertical fin twisted beyond recovery. The Augusta slowed its climb into the fog. The sound of tortured metal shrieked above all else, until the volley bombarded the swash plate that stabilized the rotors. The Augusta spiraled nose-first into the water.

The legion ceased fire, and the last they could see of the chopper was the tail boom disappearing beneath the surface.

"Your work is done," Pearl said. His extended arm swiveled to face Ragnar, the Luger trained on the bulk of the man's torso. "Today, no guilty party goes scot-free. Let this be a lesson to your men. I have been informed that some of you, unsatisfied with your share of profits, are staging a little mutiny. I feel I've been generous. For entertaining the demands of these insubordinates, your leader will join Mr. Chatham in these waters." He waggled the Swiss pistol. "Over the rails, Ragnar."

Ragnar sprinted toward Pearl like a bull, banking on his ability to survive a raft of haphazard bullets.

Pearl fired one shot.

FORTY-FIVE

T he bullet ripped through Ragnar's lower leg, shattering his tibia. His knees buckled, and the man's upper body slammed down on the deck. He groaned, clasping his wound, and stood again, balancing on one foot and using the rail for stability.

"Into the water," Pearl said, "while you still have one good shin."

Ragnar knew he'd lost his only chance to tackle Pearl. The pain was excruciating.

"Don't be a coward like Chatham." Pearl sneered. "Do this for your crew. You've avenged your blood brother. Now redeem your sea brothers."

Limping, he swung his intact leg over the railing.

If the sea was his shrine, he was kneeling at the altar. He balanced there, staring into the roiling waters, and realized it wasn't the churning he dreaded, but the cold. Even with a wound to hinder his ability to tread water, he knew it was the hypothermia that would kill him. The Marauders hailed him as he made his most difficult decision. He shut his eyes and flung his other, bleeding leg over the rail, hanging there for a moment, the few glories of his life flashing through his mind. His nostrils flared, allowing a salty scent to pervade.

The tension in his body released. He let go of the rail.

D id you see that?" Pearl shouted. "No one else crosses me."

One of the Marauders spoke to him. "Cargo's loaded, sir. We're ready to sail."

"Have everyone board your ships. I'm almost done here. Only fifteen minutes to the firework show, one I'd prefer watching from a distance."

"Step onto one of those corsairs," Rove said, "and you'll sail straight to hell."

Pearl faced Rove and folded his arms. "I'm curious, Jake. How'd you know it was me?"

"A few reasons," he said. "For starters, you were sloppy about your horn-rims. During poker games in the card lounge, you wore the glasses to study your hands and squinted without them. I figured you were far-sighted. Then it struck me. After dinner with Selvaggio, second day of the cruise, the waiter had brought out a dessert menu. You didn't have your glasses with you, yet you had no trouble reading the fine, cursive print. Baffled by this, I borrowed your glasses once, only to discover they made no difference. They're fakes, part of your disguise. Your vision is fine. At this point I knew there was something you weren't sharing."

Pearl chuckled. "Impressive."

"On the night of the pulse, I'd been sipping a drink on the balcony. As soon as we lost power, I heard shattering glass and watched someone fall from one of the bridge wings. Someone had been murdered. Less than an hour later, I knocked on your door. When you answered, your trousers were dusted with flakes of glass. I later pieced together that you'd been on the bridge. It was you who shot Selvaggio and forced him out the window."

Pearl looked riveted. Rove keep talking, seeing Victoria's growing worry as they idled in conversation under a clock ticking toward demolition. Trying not to aggravate her concern, he hoped she wouldn't act on impatience.

"I noticed a few strange things during the blackout. Cameras and other small electronics didn't work anymore. When I determined it was a pulse, not a generator failure that had taken out the ship's power, I thought back to Selvaggio's public broadcast. He had warned of a ship-wide power outage. But how could he know about the pulse before it happened? There were only two explanations. Either he had inside knowledge, or someone had invaded the bridge and held him at gunpoint during his announcement. He was all nerves that night, so I guessed the latter.

"Later I returned to the bridge myself, and found Trevor Kent near death. In his last breaths he uttered Selvaggio's name. This raised my suspicion again. I thought maybe I was wrong, that he was the one who'd planned the seizure of his own ship. But Selvaggio never turned up again. He'd disappeared. His body had broken through that window and fallen overboard. After you forced him to make the announcement, which you'd written to prevent mass hysteria from getting in the way of yours plans, you shot him. Big picture: If anyone knew how to handle an emergency, it was the captain. Your hijackers wanted him dead.

"It goes deeper. When I came to your room to make the chlorine bomb, I noticed the sheets of crumpled aluminum foil on your nightstand. What had you been wrapping so heavily? Maybe you'd been protecting something from the pulse. Maybe you'd created a Faraday cage. All you'd need was a shell of conducting material to block out harmful electromagnetic radiation. A few layers of aluminum foil would do the trick. The question remaining was, what had you needed to shield?

"While we were bagging the cleaning chemicals, I intentionally spilled some ammonia in with the bleach. That was no mistake. As toxic gases began to fume, I told you to gather your things and move to my room. I watched what you chose to bring with you. When you thought I wasn't looking, you reached into a drawer and took out a satellite phone. This verified my Faraday cage theory. Why would you bring a phone if it had been destroyed by the pulse? Of course, it hadn't been; you'd come prepared. From your own stateroom, you'd been communicating with people on land. Chatham, apparently. The foil had protected the circuitry from the pulse, making your phone one of the only pieces of working electronics aboard the *Pearl Enchantress*. You must have brought plenty of spare batteries.

"I began to think back on other events. Two stood out. On the day we met, you practically invited yourself to be my guest for the bridge tour and dinner. It seemed strange a veteran steward would find the idea of a bridge tour so enthralling. Would a flight attendant on a commercial jet ask for a chance to see the cockpit? Then I understood. You needed an excuse to get inside the bridge so you could alter the radar system. Kent had suspected tampering. During the tour, you stepped aside to install a virus that would later mask the corsairs from the radar screen. Five unidentified vessels bound for the *Pearl Enchantress* would cause alarm. You concealed them."

"All accurate so far," Pearl said. "You said there was a second event?"

"My night dive. You saw me enter the water by climbing down the fire hose. Our cabins are practically connected. You watched my descent from your window. When I resurfaced, the hose was untied.

Someone had tossed it into the water. At the time I'd assumed it was the work of a hijacker, but later I realized you had done it. You knew I threatened your scheme, so you tried to kill me by removing my only means of returning aboard. You figured one of Ragnar's men would finish me. Which explains your surprise when I next came knocking at your stateroom. It became clear when, soon after I brought food to Dr. Clare, your men captured me. I'd told you right where I was going to be."

"Right again," said Pearl. "But if you suspected me, why would you trust me to help you shepherd those fifty passengers onto a lifeboat?"

"I watched you carefully, made sure you were always in a position to go down with the others if they heard us. Besides, fifty out of three thousand is a drop in the bucket to you. From your perspective, a few fugitives could even be a good thing. These eyewitnesses could testify to the horrors they observed aboard the hijacked vessel. Reports from a few survivors would help tank Sapphire Pacific, which you wanted to happen."

"And how did you eventually connect Lachlan Fawkes with Clifford Pearl?"

"It wasn't easy. Your Aussie accent and vernacular were convincing, at least to an ignorant guy like me. But there's a portrait of you in my stateroom. You were younger and wearing your uniform. I began seeing traces of resemblance, even though you had a beard and a bald head in the painting. It hadn't occurred to me you'd actually shaved yourself smooth for the portrait. When I realized it was you, I laughed at myself for not picking up on the clues you'd dropped. 'Cliffy and I go way back,' you'd told me. Then there was the Viking's letter ending with, 'The *Pearl Enchantress* is mine.' How literal."

"Clever," Pearl said. "I've enjoyed getting to know you over the course of our strange misadventure, Jake. I really am sorry for it to end like this. I should have known better than to find someone I genuinely admired, knowing how it would go."

"It doesn't have to end like this," Rove said.

"I'd have preferred to let you live." He threw his hands open. "I'd have preferred to let you all live. But you understand—at least, the professor does—that reputation is everything. I've a name to protect."

"And a retirement to look forward to," Rove said. He saw Victoria eyeing a rifle on the ground, only yards away. He tried to catch her attention to warn her against it, but she wasn't looking.

"Nice chatting with you all," Pearl continued. "Our conversation must be over now. The ships are loaded. I'll be the last aboard, but the first to sail away from this cold place."

Victoria began to move for the rifle. Rove cleared his throat loudly. She didn't hear him.

"Victoria," he said quietly.

She seemed intent.

Austin and Malcolm Clare didn't seem to notice what she was up to. Dirgo stared furiously at Pearl, holding her arms in her favorite position—akimbo.

"Where do you plan to go?" Clare asked. "You can't get away with this."

"I plan to go ashore and continue my life as normal," he said, "supposing it should begin with a good shave of the head. Somewhere out there, if investigators are thorough, they'll learn of a suspicious Wall Street trader with a strange prescience for disaster. They'll trace the transactions to an Australian steward whose identity exists on paper only."

"Someone will turn you in."

"Who? Everyone who knows the truth is dead, or soon will be."

Victoria began tiptoeing toward the rifle. Rove got her attention with a soft clap of his hands. His expression read: *Don't do it. Let him go.*

She stared back in defiance—*Are you crazy?*

The old mariner sauntered to a rope ladder connecting the cruise ship with a corsair. "If anyone thinks of cutting the ropes as I climb down, I'll detonate the charges. And if you find a gun and shoot me, my finger will almost certainly spasm over the button."

"What does it matter to us?" Victoria said. "You said you're going to blow the ship anyway, as soon as you reach a safe distance."

"Stop challenging him," Rove murmured, so Pearl wouldn't hear.

"Wait, and you'll at least have time to try to fill another lifeboat with passengers," Pearl said. "Won't you?" The old man tossed his Luger overboard and began descending the rope ladder.

"We can't let him do this!" Victoria cried. She made for the gun. "Stop him! He'll kill thousands!"

Rove grabbed her by the waist. She resisted. He cupped a hand around her mouth.

"Shhh," he said. His voice had reduced to a whisper. "Let him go."

Confused, Austin said, "She's right, though. If we do nothing, we're all going to die. We have at least five minutes to help passengers onto lifeboats."

Clare shook his head. "It wouldn't be enough time. Not even for one."

"It's already over," Rove said.

His expression was serene, untouched by pain, dread, or remorse.

Victoria wrenched Rove's hands away and peered over the edge in desperation. "How can you give up like this?"

Below, Clifford Pearl landed safely aboard the corsair. Several dozen hands awaited his command. "Cast off," he said. "Let's go."

The sails billowed with a violence that threatened to fray their canvas. Mooring lines disengaged from the cruise ship's cleats. Four corsairs pushed off from the hull of the *Pearl Enchantress* and began to grope their way through the fog.

The old man stood on the bow of the flagship *Jarnsaxa,* leaning into a wind that whisked over a berg.

The *Pearl Enchantress* had faded to a silhouette. The corsairs would soon leave range.

The metallic cylinder felt cool in his hands as his thumb hovered over the button. He waited until the outline of the ship's dolphin-nosed bow had fully faded, and pushed it seconds before the charges were set to detonate. It would feel more like an act of will that way.

Pillars of seawater soared skyward like geysers. Flames erupted from beneath the surface, clinging to flotsam and debris.

Hearing the roar, the wrinkled mariner laughed.

Over the hum of the engine, Austin heard the words through his headset: "Grab the yoke. She's all yours."

He looked through the windshield at Stanford's campus. Hoover Tower shot up ahead. The Farm lay nestled in foothills rising up toward higher mountains. Evening was near. They soared toward the Coast Range into a deeply flushing sunset fire.

The biplane stalled, and her nose dropped a few degrees before Austin led her into a plunge. More words came through his leather hearing device. "Careful now." The words faded to static.

The aircraft lost altitude fast. Austin let several seconds pass without altering course, feeling the pressure his waist exerted against the safety belt. He loved the sensation of weightlessness and the funny tingles that accompanied free fall.

They gained speed. Sensing an updraft, he eased up the yoke and channeled the plane's momentum into a vertical climb. Rapture crackled through his headset in the form of a high-pitched laugh. His copilot howled with thrill.

"How's it look?" Austin said.

"Keep a firm grip!" Clare replied. "Pull the yoke into your chest."

The straps around Austin's groin tightened, imparting a little reassuring pain. He sustained his heavy clutch. The draft aided him. Their angle steepened until finally the biplane turned back on itself. For a moment Austin could no longer feel his own inertia, and he swore he saw tiny particles of dirt and debris suspended in space. Blood rushed to his head, causing his ears to prickle. He leveled the craft.

His patent exhilaration told his copilot he wasn't finished.

"Ready for more?" Austin said.

Clare returned a fiendish gaze. "Who's stopping you?"

Austin rotated the plane's belly toward the sky and executed an inverted half-Cuban eight, followed by a tail slide and ending in a series of barrel rolls. The professor helped him.

"Welcome to Glitnir Defense," Clare said. "If you'll forgive the pun, I'd say you've passed your first lesson with flying colors."

"That one's hard to forgive," Austin said. "But I'm glad I took the job."

"With Chatham gone, I'm appointing Kate Dirgo president of Glitnir. You'll begin as projects engineer. Your first assignment will arrive sooner than you might imagine. Until then, I want you to focus on your studies and keep out of trouble."

"Roger."

"You'll begin training soon."

"How soon?"

"Sooner than you may feel comfortable with. I work in ways that are certain to capture your attention."

"You're really selling this hard, Professor. What kind of training?"

"Let's first discuss the purpose. I established Glitnir Defense to protect the rights of the ultimate minority."

"Which group?"

"I'm not talking about a group."

A sun ray caused the wings to glitter. "I understand."

"By pioneering new frontiers in military technology and empowering our armed forces—even joining the front line if necessary—Glitnir protects the rights of the individual. Our tools of retaliatory and *defensive* force are designed to oppose the *initiation* of force. Self-defense demands we be able to discern friends from enemies. Some enemies are easy to identify; they hold a knife to your throat or a gun to your head. Others, well, not everyone can see them."

"Who are you talking about?"

"Enemies of the mind, of reason, of life. These enemies don't always carry the guns themselves. But they are still enemies." Austin continued to look pensively at a glittering wing of the plane. "Some live overseas, many not as dangerous as those here at home. You'll learn to identify them, to understand how they think and operate. If you reject their vision for your life—and your death—as I think you will, you'll choose to fight them."

"Sounds like you're proposing a philosophical education."

"To supplement your aerospace studies, yes. My goal is to equip you with a kind of X-ray vision that sees straight to the heart of issues, issues that might now seem hazy or unsolvable. I'll present you with a set of principles for living, intellectual ammunition to help you appreciate the nature of the battle rational men face. But you must be the one to integrate the concepts and abstractions, evaluate the system of thought, and judge the correctness of what I teach." Clare was looking directly at Austin. "I think you'll leave these lessons with a renewed and refined sense of purpose. And you'll look back on your life so far, on what you've done—and feel prouder than ever. This isn't to say your training will be purely philosophical. There will be other facets."

"Such as?"

"Oh . . . some things that are just plain *fun*."

"I'm listening."

"You'll learn to dive, sail, fly a helicopter, among other things. All important skills for what you'll eventually be doing."

"You mean as an engineer?"

"Beyond that. You'll go through rigorous physical training. And you'll surely enjoy the spy games."

"Dare I ask what those are?"

"Wouldn't want to spoil any surprises. You'll meet your instructors at the Glitnir Academy in Mojave. I've recruited many special operations retirees over the years. Green Berets, Night Stalkers, Rangers, SEALs, Delta Force, among others. They lead physical, tactical, environmental, and weapons training. You'll get acquainted with all kinds of technologies used in strategic planning, unconventional warfare, and counter-terrorism. You'll be in expert hands. Consider your recent adventure a mere overture."

"Hard to imagine keeping up with those aerospace studies at the same time."

"You'll stay at Stanford, keep after the degree. At first you'll work summers. No need to go full-time yet. You're not going into combat, remember. Training's meant to help you understand strategy and warfare."

"I'll look forward to June, then."

"You can be introduced sooner, if you want. Any plans for winter break?"

"Nothing pressing. I'll be going home to visit my mom and dad."

"Maybe you'll visit our Mojave headquarters."

"I'd like that."

"You should know something else. Until now, my daughter has been relatively unaware of the goings-on at Glitnir. She knows of our existence and purpose, has low-level access to some classified files.

But she knows little of our special projects. This isn't for lack of trust, but for lack of reason to disseminate secrets."

"I'll be mindful of that."

"You needn't be. I'm going to try to hire her, too."

"When did you decide that?"

"I've thought about it for years. She's come far in her mathematical studies. I'm confident her expertise will prove valuable alongside yours. The two of you may collaborate on future assignments. I've also taken the liberty of consulting with your friend Ichiro's professors. They say his computational skills are remarkable. I'd like to invite him to Glitnir."

"I should introduce you to Rachel Mason," Austin said. "She and Itchy are thick as thieves, and wonderful as a team."

"Please do. This is an exciting time for Glitnir. We're expanding operations, can hardly keep up with hiring needs. I like to handpick the talent myself. I've even thought about asking Jake Rove to instruct at the academy."

"Can't imagine a finer choice, if you manage to convince him. He's set on returning to his beach house in Mexico."

"I'll do my best. One final thing." Clare reached behind his seat and produced a square box. "Open up. Careful the wind doesn't claim the contents." He set the container on Austin's lap. Austin felt the edges of the container before lifting the lid. "Victoria thought this would make a good gift for you. I happen to agree. For reclaiming the satellite."

Austin opened the box and beamed. Its velvet liner cradled a pure-white, wide-brimmed Stetson. He lifted the hat from the fabric and nestled the roof of his head in its crown.

"Fits perfectly," he said. "Great feel."

"It's one hundred percent beaver fur. Looks sharp."

"I'm married to it already. Thanks, Professor."

"Thank Victoria," Clare answered. "Anyway, the sun's setting. We'd better head back to the landing strip. Can you find it, tucked away in the mountains? Head toward the satellite dish and bear northeast."

"We'll set her down soon. Before we do, might I petition air traffic control for a flyby of Hoover Tower?"

"No one knows about our landing strip in the hills," Clare said. "And as far as I know, this airspace falls under no control tower's jurisdiction."

Ichiro quickened his pace along Serra Mall as he dialed a number on his mobile. There was no answer. Hearing the voicemail prompt for the third time, he snapped his phone shut and lengthened his stride toward the lawn.

Where was his roommate? So focused on the question was he that he failed to notice a faint buzzing noise growing louder.

They were supposed to meet for dinner at the Oval—all of them. A small group congregated in front of the quad up ahead. Rachel was there, wearing a satin, crochet-trimmed batwing top and looking fashionably elegant alongside Victoria in her cashmere cardigan. She had removed her aviators in the twilight hour. A man stood with them, one Ichiro didn't recognize by face, but he knew who it was.

Rachel spotted his approach and lit up.

She shouted. "Ichiro Yamada, you're late!"

His gait accelerated to a jog. "*I'm* late?" he said, huffing. "What about Austin and Professor Clare?"

"Them, too. That's okay. I can extend the reservation. Gives me time to make an important introduction." He caught a sideways wink from Rachel, who motioned to the man and said, "This is the gentleman you've heard so much about."

He looked grave and scarred, his countenance weathered. Most would have found his appearance forbidding, even malevolent. Ichiro could see he was acquainted with damage.

"Ichiro," Rachel said, "meet Jacob Rove."

The two clasped hands in what was, at least for Ichiro, a moment for reflection.

"I'm honored to meet you, Mr. Rove," he said. "You've saved the life of a close friend of mine. Not to mention Victoria and her father, whom I will surely come to know and hold dear."

Rove bowed his head only slightly. "If it weren't for Austin and Victoria's detective work, along with Rachel and you cracking the coded radio transmission, the Baldr satellite might have fallen into enemy hands. Our whole continent might have lost power."

"Speaking of which," Rachel said, "I'm still trying to get this story straight. What happened to Deeb in Iceland?"

Victoria spoke up. "After the explosion, Mr. Rove alerted the Navy of the need for rescue ships to transport three thousand thirsty, starving passengers ashore, along with a small group of people who had escaped on a lifeboat. He also told them a certain former Algerian oil minister, bound and gagged in a private jet, would require an escort to detainment facilities for questioning."

"He sang like a canary," Rove said.

"Where's the man now?"

Rove darkened. "Set free."

"Impossible!" Rachel said.

"By disclosing the names and whereabouts of over two dozen high-level al-Nar associates, he complied with his interrogators, thereby meeting the terms of his release."

"There's good news, though," Victoria said. "Back in Bruges, I printed a document identifying agents from other terror groups. Vasya Kaslov had stored the list in his email account. All the participants in the bidding war, including leaders of eight extremist groups, were on the list. I faxed it to the Pentagon this morning. Did that ever feel good. Deeb's name was on the list, so at least we have a general idea of his whereabouts should the CIA—or perhaps a private defense corporation—go after him."

The news brought Rachel a measure of ease. "You sly thing." She placed a hand on Rove's shoulder. "Well, Mr. Rove, how'd you enjoy your vacation?"

"At least I squeezed in some recreational diving."

"Not to mention one very important night dive," Victoria said.

"You should call that banker," Rachel suggested. "Tell him the cruise was . . . subpar. He'd send you on another."

"As appealing as that sounds, my catamaran in Mexico is getting lonesome. You kids are always welcome down for a sail."

Victoria smiled at him. "I'll never forget my confusion on the lido deck of the *Pearl Enchantress,*" she admitted. "When you told me not to leap for the gun, I didn't understand. All I could think of was the detonator twirling in Clifford Pearl's hands and what would happen when he pushed the red button."

"What detonator?" Rachel asked.

"Clifford Pearl ordered Ragnar Stahl and his legion to line the ship's hull with explosive charges. On the last day, Pearl sailed off with the Marauders on one of their corsairs. He had every intention of sinking his own cruise liner." The hard edge to her tone began to melt. "What Pearl didn't realize was, several nights before he sailed away, Jake had scoured the hull and switched the charges. He'd removed them from the cruise ship and fixed them onto the corsairs."

Rachel said, "So when Pearl set off the charges . . ."

"He blew the ship he was sailing on, and all the other corsairs, to smithereens." She imagined the burial site in those waters south of Iceland, where Ragnar and Dan Chatham also lay entombed in the sea's lower lockers. The thought gave her peace.

"I'm still wondering how one has a dogfight with a cruise ship," Ichiro said.

"Sharpshootin' Hardy can tell you that one better than I," Victoria said. "By the way, where *is* Austin?"

It was then that Ichiro noticed the buzzing noise. He glanced up and pointed. "Look!"

A glossy biplane barreled toward them, revolving in tight corkscrews. The aircraft glinted in the waning sunlight, smooth and buffed like the handcrafted models in Clare's office. It plummeted toward them with no sign of pulling out of its dive, coming so close they could smell the exhaust fumes, then flattened its trajectory and ran parallel with Serra Mall. Any lower, and Ichiro felt he could have reached out and touched the fuselage.

The biplane nosed up and banked south for the mountains. Watching from below, Victoria could have sworn she'd noticed one of the pilots sporting a white Stetson.

Rachel squinted and gestured toward an unfamiliar object gliding toward them. The object appeared to have fallen from the plane's cockpit. "What's that?"

"A paper airplane," Rove said. He jogged to the street and caught it by the tail. "There's writing on the wing. It says, *To Victoria Clare.*"

The others looked curious as she unfolded the creased paper. When she finished reading the message within, she stuffed the paper into a pocket. She looked devilish.

"They're running late for dinner," she said. "They'll meet us at the restaurant. Let's go."

Later in the car, Victoria unfolded the paper and reread the message to herself.

You'd make a ravishing copilot. No uniform required.
                                                                —AH